Oric And The
Lockton Castle Mystery

Lesley Wilson

My special thanks go to Val Atkinson whose dedicated input has been invaluable, especially in the construction of a Cockentrice.

Love always to my husband, Mike, who acts as my roadie when I'm out selling my books, and who does everything I haven't got time to do.

My grateful thanks go to Linda Diggle of Book Boffin. Without her endless patience and expertise, this book might never have seen the light of day.

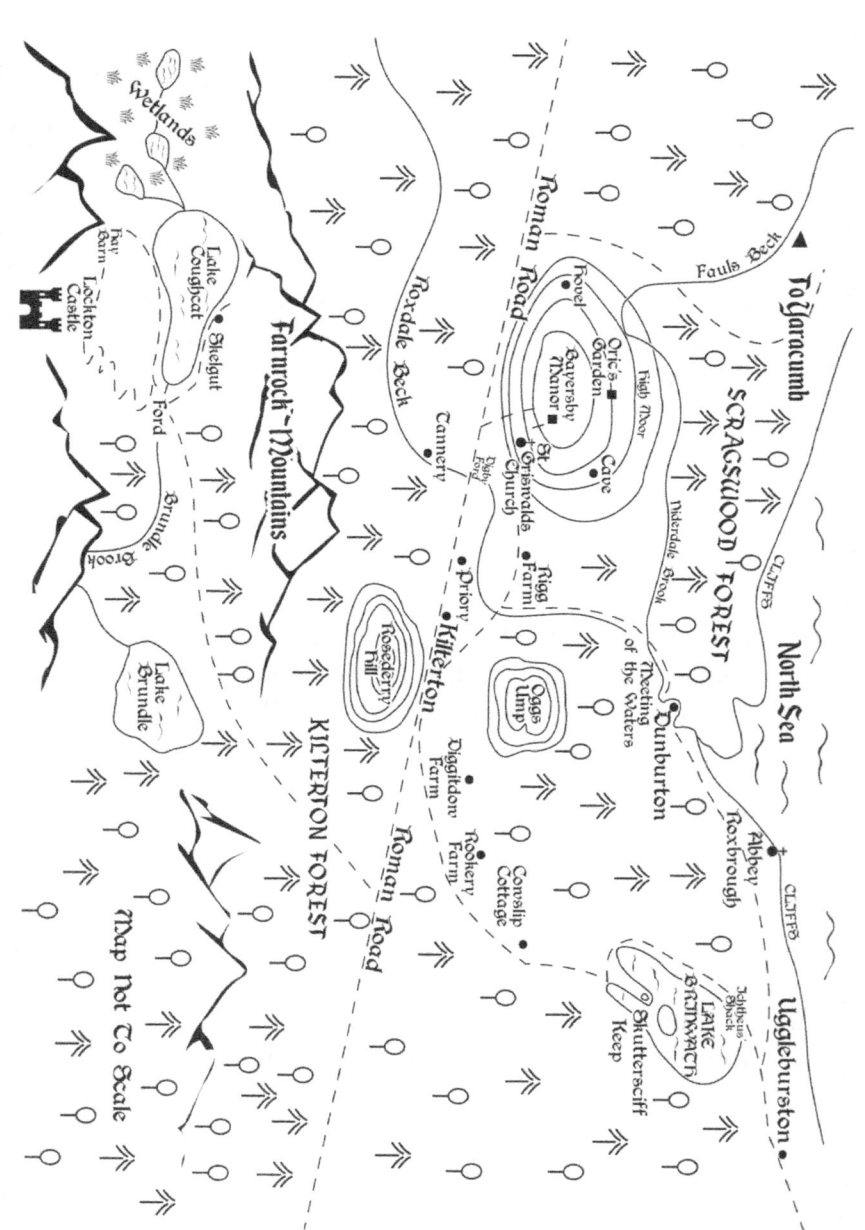

Prologue

Esica Figg, moneylender and villain, travels to the village of Dunburton to arrange a substantial loan for the incumbent lord of Dunburton manor. A good deal of silver changes hands, and Figg gleefully calculates the repayments he will demand. His acquisitive thoughts end abruptly upon the arrival of marauders who ransack the manor. Sated, after a night of carousing, Dunburton's inhabitants swiftly fall under the marauder's violent onslaught.

To escape death Figg hides behind a wall-hanging tapestry. He spies through a hole in the fabric as the robbers make off with everything they can carry. They built a pyre with the remaining furniture in the Great Hall and set light to it. The marauders depart and Figg creeps from his hiding place to survey the scene of destruction. He cares naught for the slain inhabitants of Dunburton but he does care about the money he has loaned, for it is unlikely that he will see any of his silver again.

The slam of a door sends Figg scuttling back to his hiding place behind the tapestry. Through the same peephole he watches a lone youth run into the Great Hall and drop to his knees beside the still form of Deveril, the Dunburton Alchemist. The old man passes a key to the boy and, hidden only feet away, Figg hears every word that passes between the two. He learns that the key will unlock the secret to great wealth; he also overhears that untold disasters might occur should the key fall into wrong hands. Upon those words Deveril breathes his last.

The pyre of furniture sends sparks into the rafters and sets the thatched roof ablaze. Figg determines to seize the mysterious key for himself but, in his haste to escape the burning building, he loses sight of the boy.

-oOo-

Devastated by the death of his beloved mentor and the loss of his home, Oric wanders through the forest, his mind in turmoil. The key has a double knot engraved upon its narrow shaft, an emblem Oric has never seen before. And what did Master Deveril mean about wealth and danger?

Open country replaces the forest and Oric kneels beside a stream to drink. Raising his head, he sees flickering lights in the distance. He makes his way toward them and comes upon Bayersby Manor, home of Sir Edred and Lady Myferny. The Bayersby apothecary, Ichtheus, opens the kitchen door to Oric's knock.

In a very short time Oric proves his worth, and the elderly apothecary sets him on as an apprentice. Orphaned at an early age, Oric soon learns to love Ichtheus as a son loves his father.

-oOo-

Returned to his money-lending business in Kilterton, Figg is intrigued to see the Bayersby apothecary enter the village accompanied by the boy from Dunburton. Figg's desire to get his hands upon the alchemist's key becomes all-consuming. An attempt to kill the apothecaries fails when a large wolfhound intervenes. Undaunted, Figg sends his henchmen to kidnap Oric, but once again the boy escapes.

No closer to getting his hands on the alchemist's key, Figg returns to Dunburton to seek clues to the meaning of the alchemist's final words. Inside the charred manor house he unearths a chest with a double knot carved upon the lid. He smashes the lock, prises open the lid and discovers gold coins, a few valuable trinkets and several pouches of black powder within. Since Deveril was an alchemist, Figg imagines the powder to be the makings of gold. His spirits are further lifted when he comes across a rolled parchment, perhaps the recipe for the production of gold. But the words are penned in Latin – a language Figg has failed to learn. Unwilling to relinquish his find into the hands of a translator, Figg experiments with a small amount of the evil-smelling powder. A fireball erupts, temporarily blinding him. When he regains his sight the parchment has disappeared, burned, Figg surmises, in the fire. Undaunted, he attaches the remaining pouches of powder to a belt. Uncomfortable and cumbersome as they are, he keeps them hidden under his tunic at all times.

To drive the Lord of Bayersby from his manor becomes Figg's obsession but, to achieve his aim, he needs to assemble another army. With the aid of several disreputable henchmen Figg robs, maims, and sometimes kills all rich folk that come his way. Though he accumulates much wealth the paltry wages he offers fail to attract experienced soldiers. His parsimony costs him the battle against Sir Edred, and Figg barely escapes with his life. Thanks to Oric and the Bayersby apothecary's interference, Figg also loses the plunder he has so painstakingly squirrelled away.

-oOo-

Oric saves the Lord of Bayersby's life during the battle with Esica Figg and, deeply grateful, Sir Edred rewards Oric with a small plot of land and a pouch of silver.

Ichtheus promotes his apprentice to the position of assistant apothecary, and Oric's reputation as an accomplished practitioner spreads across the district like wildfire. He grows herbs on his land, which he concocts into medicinal remedies to heal the sick. The residue of his potions he sells on the stall he shares with Master Ichtheus at the local market.

As a man of modest means Oric begins tentatively to pay court to Dian Cole, a pretty servant employed in the Bayersby household. The arrogant Bayersby heir, Guwain, also shows interest in the girl and often locks horns with Oric, making the young apothecary's life difficult.

The mystery of Deveril's key remains unsolved and the promise Oric made to his former mentor to safeguard the key preys upon his mind. Eventually he relinquishes his precious key into Master Ichtheus' safekeeping.

In the burned-out shell of Dunburton Manor Oric stumbles upon an iron box with a double knot engraved upon the lid. The symbol matches the smaller version of the knots on the shaft of Deveril's key. The smashed lock dangles from its hasp and the box is empty apart from a thin layer of black dust that coats the base. Oric lugs his find back to Bayersby Manor and tries Deveril's key in the broken lock. It fits, confirming Oric's suspicions that the chest must once have belonged to his former mentor. Since the old man was an alchemist, Oric also wonders if the black dust might be the makings of gold. He experiments with a few particles of the powdery substance and it ignites in a spectacular fashion. Unfortunately the exercise achieves nothing more than a singed tabletop. All that remains of the black powder now reposes in a leather pouch in Ichtheus' secret hiding place beside Deveril's key.

Oric continues to agonise over the strange situation, and he eventually shows his friends Dian, Egglebart, Etheldrida, Sir Oswold and Lady Malla the key. A few trustworthy souls on the lookout for the double knot symbol could do no harm and may even raise his chances of solving Deveril's mystery. However, Oric chooses not pass on the alchemist's words about wealth and disaster, nor does he mention the black powder.

Chapter One

Soothsayer's Warning

Kilterton's wide thoroughfare hummed with activity, and the rancid stench of human sweat and animal dung filled the air. Market traders vied for shady spots beneath the giant chestnut trees that lined the street and, frazzled by uncommonly intense summer heat, stall holders' fists began to fly.

To avoid being trampled by a farmer with a bull in tow Ichtheus, the district apothecary, sought safe haven behind the herbal medicament stall he shared with his young assistant, Oric.

"If folk carry on at this rate we shall be called upon to mend a few broken skulls before the day is done," growled the tall, thin apothecary.

"Good thing we brought an ample supply of Solomon's seal ointment to soothe their cuts and bruises," replied Oric, showing two rows of white teeth in a broad grin.

Glancing at his assistant brought a smile to Ichtheus' lined face. The lad's sun-bronzed skin glowed with health, and a generous crop of freckles dusted his nose. An unruly thatch of straw-coloured hair sprouted from his skull and his blue eyes danced with mischief. A tease and a scamp the young fellow might be, but he worked hard and was always keen to learn. Ichtheus supposed the lad to be around sixteen years old but, orphaned at an early age, Oric was unable to confirm the exact date of his birth.

A long queue formed in front of the apothecaries' stall and Oric dosed his customers with pills and potions. All the while, he darted nervous glances up and down the road.

"For goodness' sake, lad, stop hopping about like a cat on hot embers," snapped Ichtheus, tugging irritably at his long white beard. "You are making me uneasy."

"I cannot help but feel nervous," mumbled Oric. The recent battle between Sir Edred, Lord of Bayersby, and the villainous moneylender Esica Figg remained fresh in Oric's mind. "Mark my words, sir, Figg might still be creeping about amongst the crowd."

"Nay, lad!" Ichtheus exclaimed, his blue eyes flashing with irritation. "Yon rodent will be miles away by now, still running with his tail between his legs."

"You are overly complacent, Master Ichtheus! Figg lost face, not to mention a small fortune. Once he raises sufficient funds to employ another mercenary army, 'tis my belief he will attempt a second assault upon Sir Edred."

"Are you mad?" Ichtheus countered. "Yon rogue carries a price upon his head. He is unlikely to risk life and limb by returning to Kilterton."

"I sincerely hope you are right," replied Oric, recalling the blood, some of it his own, so recently spilled.

Trade slowed, and Ichtheus stood back to watch Oric examine an elderly peasant. The old fellow pulled back his sleeves to reveal crusty scabs on both arms. "Looks like leprosy to me, Master Oric. I am a goner for sure."

"Nay, Master Tweedle! Where would you have contracted leprosy? You never leave the district and, to my knowledge, there is none of the disease hereabouts." Oric rubbed his patient's scabs with a forefinger to prove his point. "Your rash is not infectious. I reckon 'tis naught but an allergy to your mangy cat." Selecting a small bottle of extract of celandine, Oric offered it to the old man. "Rub this juice upon the affected area twice daily and your affliction will soon disappear."

Master Tweedle dragged his sleeves down, and shook his head. "Thank you, Master Oric, you have put my mind at rest, but I lack the wherewithal to pay for your potion."

"You could always get rid of your cat," said Oric, his blue eyes twinkling with good humour.

"Get rid of my tomcat!" exclaimed the scrofulous old man. "He might be a bit mangy but he is the best ratter in the district. I could never part with him."

Oric nodded toward a wispy little woman with a basket of eggs on her arm. "I would gladly swap my medicament for two of your wife's nice brown eggs."

"There are more ways than one to skin a cat, Master Ichtheus," Oric tittered at his own joke as he carefully wrapped Mistress Tweedle's eggs in a piece of sacking.

Four and twenty moons had passed since Oric first arrived at Bayersby Manor. Already able to read and write, the homeless youth had swiftly learned the apothecary's trade and, with no family to call his own, Ichtheus had grown to love the quick-witted boy as a father loves his son. Impressed with Oric's ability to learn, Ichtheus had recently elevated him from apprentice to the position of fully-fledged assistant. Thus far Ichtheus had no reason to regret his decision.

The villagers eventually overcame their squabbles, folk settled down in their chosen spots, and noontime passed without further trouble. Money handed over in exchange for pills and potions flowed into the apothecaries' coffers, raising Ichtheus' spirits. But his euphoria was short-lived.

From her vantage point on the steps of the elevated village cross, an ancient soothsayer clanged a large handbell. "Hark all ye serfs and sinners!" she screeched. "On Summer Solstice Eve a plague of demons will rain down upon the earth. They will kill everyone that crosses their path."

A collective gasp rippled through the crowd, and trade around the market stalls ground to a halt. Despite her unsavoury appearance, most folk set great store by Mother Olive's words, for they believed her to be a wise woman.

"What can we do to protect ourselves from this dreadful onslaught?" yelled Aidie Kirtle from the depths of her well-stocked stall. Somewhat eccentric, the Kilterton haberdasher had tied up her frizzled grey hair with bright ribbons and swathed her body with so many different fabrics she looked like a brightly-coloured ball. Today no-one laughed at her bizarre appearance.

Taking advantage of the villagers' stunned silence, Mother Olive jabbed a bony finger at a bracken-clad hill that rose up in the near distance. "If you wish to save your lives every man, woman, and child must depart the village on Summer Solstice day. Climb Rosederry Hill and build beacons upon the summit. When the sun drops below the horizon you must set light to the piles of timber." Mother Olive let rip with a blood-chilling cackle and twirled around on her bandy legs. "Fire is the only element that will stay the wicked demons."

"What is yon silly old trollop on about?" bawled a cocky youth. He winked at his friends and pointed to the cloudless, sun-bleached sky. "We shall get no rain come Summer Solstice, let alone a downpour of demons!"

Mother Olive hawked and spat. "Stupid boy! Disregard my warning and you will die. The demons will kill any adult that crosses their path, and they will take children to use as slaves."

The young troublemaker paled at the thought but, rather than lose face, he made a defiant gesture and strutted after his cronies with as much bravado as he could muster.

Her job done, Mother Olive climbed down from the monument. She gathered her ragged clothes about her thin frame and ambled away. No-one attempted to stop her.

Business along the high street resumed but, thanks to the intense heat of the day and the soothsayer's worrisome prophecy, the villagers' tempers frayed once again.

"Lord knows what Mother Olive is on about this time!" Ichtheus pushed irritably at tendrils of silver hair that escaped the confines of his bonnet. "Yon old harpy causes trouble wherever she goes." Tutting loudly, he returned to do battle with bunches of herbs he had tied together too tightly.

Excused from her duties at Bayersby Manor, Dian Cole sought gewgaws for her mistress. Lady Myferny had also given Dian a copper or two to spend on herself and the little maid had bought a comb from Mistress Kirtle's stall, plus a length of red ribbon to tie back her abundant chestnut curls. Dian had enjoyed the first part of the morning, but Mother Olive's words frightened her. Clutching her purchases, she sidled up behind the apothecaries' stall, loath to move on. "That old crone did not speak the truth about a deluge of demons, did she, Master Ichtheus?" Dian's hazel eyes searched Ichtheus' blue ones for reassurance.

"Argh! Yon soothsayer's demons pose less threat than many a mortal," snapped Ichtheus, visualising Esica Figg's cadaverous features in his mind's eye. "Pay no attention to Mother Olive – she is naught but a nasty old troublemaker."

Oric jigged from foot to foot, poked out his tongue and crossed his eyes. "If any demons dare to threaten you, Dian, I shall scare them off."

Dimples indented Dian's rosy cheeks as she smiled. "Thank you, Oric, I feel a good deal safer now; nevertheless, may I travel back to Bayersby Manor with you and Master Ichtheus at the end of the day?"

"You are most welcome," replied Oric, his heart beating a little faster than normal. He had developed a soft spot for the pretty, hazel-eyed young maid and he could imagine nothing nicer than to journey home with her. "Meet us beside our stall later this afternoon and you can ride home upon our cart."

Comforted, Dian scurried away to visit her siblings and her parents, Eadbald and Frida Cole, who lived in a rundown cottage at the far end of the high street.

-oOo-

Aware that he might not live to see another sunrise should he be recognised, Esica Figg bent his back and shuffled along Kilterton's main thoroughfare like an old man. Disguised by a newly-grown beard and clad in ragged clothes he mingled, unnoticed, with the market-day crowds. He had long since given up any idea of securing the key belonging to the apothecary's assistant, and he was now preparing to recoup everything he had lost in his unsuccessful battle against Sir Edred of Bayersby by fair means, or foul.

Two wretched fellows, incarcerated in the stocks for minor misdemeanours, used their hands to ward off a barrage of rotten vegetables hurled at them by a group of noisy urchins. Miscreants could be shackled in the stocks for days if the lord of the manor forgot to order their release. Figg shuddered, not daring to think about his own fate should he be caught.

Head down, deep in thought, Figg blundered into a stall that protruded into the walkway and came almost nose to nose with Oric and Ichtheus. Afraid the apothecaries might recognise him, Figg hastily backed into a nearby alleyway and crouched behind a pile of refuse. When Oric stepped into the alley Figg's terror intensified, but the boy merely relieved himself against the wall and departed.

Bile rose into Figg's throat caused partly by the stink of refuse but mostly from anger. If the young apothecary and his poxy mentor had not meddled in his affairs, he would now be Master of Bayersby Manor instead of skulking like a vagrant behind a pile of flyblown rubbish.

A cat foraged for food, but no-one else entered the alley. Deeming it safe to move on, Figg kicked the mangy feline out of his way, and escaped the loathsome pile of debris.

Sprightly as a young pullet, Mother Olive trotted past the entrance to the alleyway. Figg thrust out his hand and grabbed a fistful of her lank hair.

"Lawks-a-mercy," she brayed. "What the…"

Figg dragged the soothsayer into the alley. "Be silent you stupid baggage, 'tis I, Figg." He let go of her greasy hair and tossed a copper coin at her feet. "Take your reward and clear off."

Mother Olive eyed the money but made no attempt to pick it up. She had stirred the village folk at Figg's behest, now she wanted the piece of silver he had promised.

"Pay me like you said," she demanded. "Else I shall cause more trouble than you will find flies on a corpse."

Figg's rank breath fanned the soothsayer's face. "If you stick your bony beak into my business I will see it chopped off," he snarled.

"You twisting, good-for-nothing skinflint," hissed Mother Olive. "You will get your comeuppance one of these days and I pray that I live long enough to see it happen." Swiping Figg's coin up from the pathway, she stormed back into the market square.

Unperturbed by the soothsayer's threat, Figg bent his back once more, left the alley, and tagged along behind a crowd of noisy villagers. At the end of the street he risked a hate-filled glance at the two apothecaries. The meddlesome duo looked like goose grease would not melt in their mouths. *Let them enjoy themselves,* Figg sneered. *The insufferable pair have no inkling that their days are numbered.*

Chapter Two

The Tournament

Sir Edred's annual tournament brought many folk to Bayersby Manor. Knights and their ladies rode in a multi-coloured cavalcade alongside fields of summer crops dotted with scarlet poppies and blue cornflowers. Nearby orchards burgeoned with rosy apples, pears and damsons and a herd of sleek cattle munched on grassy pastures. Beyond and behind the manor stretched acres of rugged heather, and bracken-covered moorland.

"Devil take this weather," grumbled a black-clad knight, dashing beads of sweat from his brow. "I swear I am hotter than a boar upon a spit." Reining his huge horse to a standstill, he shaded his gold-flecked eyes against the sun's searing glare. On the hillside not far ahead stood a stone-built manor. "Praise the Lord," he breathed. "I believe yonder dwelling is our destination."

Joffrey drew his chestnut pony to a halt alongside Sir Ragnald's bay stallion. Only age separated the two males, for the tall, rangy fifteen-year-old boy was the swarthy-skinned, tawny-eyed double of his sire. Eager to start on the final leg of the journey, Joffrey heeled his mount into a canter. "Let us make haste, father," he shouted. "We are wasting precious time!"

Sir Ragnald watched as Joffrey galloped his pony down the hillside and sighed deeply. He had shared his son's enthusiasm for life once upon a time, but the youthful fire had gone from his belly. At thirty-nine years of age white hairs were beginning to streak his raven locks; nevertheless, he kept himself physically fit. "Ride on," he bid his two squires, "we may as well follow the boy."

Noisy people filled the outer compound that surrounded Sir Edred's large manor house. A wine store buzzed with activity, a separate dairy and washhouse abutted the kitchen. Some distance from the house lay a workshop, chicken run, pigsty, and a bountiful vegetable garden. Sir Ragnald smiled with satisfaction; Bayersby Manor was a plum, ripe for the picking, and Sir Edred's tournament provided a perfect foil to reconnoitre the estate.

"Hey, serf," Sir Ragnald bawled above the din. "Attend to our horses!"

"Who? Me?" asked a tall, well-built youth, pointing an index finger at himself.

"Yes – you!" Sir Ragnald swung down from his saddle. "What is your name, boy?"

"Oric," the youth replied tartly.

Sir Ragnald removed his helmet and dropped it into his squire's waiting hands.

"Well, Master Oric, before you stable our horses I suggest you call that bag-of-old-bones and get him to lead us to our quarters."

The 'bag-of-old-bones' was Ichtheus, senior apothecary of Bayersby and Kilterton and Oric took the slight personally. "Now see here…" he began.

"Hush, lad," Ichtheus intervened. "In the absence of other available servants, we may as well oblige our visitors."

Perceiving Oric to be naught but a common serf, Joffrey also demanded assistance.

Oric scowled, his fair skin flushing red with anger. Another spoiled brat to join forces with Sir Edred's son, Gawain, would add to the servants' already overstretched workload.

Guests in brightly-coloured finery milled around the Great Hall. Below stairs in the manor kitchen serfs stirred pots of stewed leveret, and chopped mountains of vegetables to feed the influx of visitors. One of the serf's young sons, his pale skin mottled red from the fire, rotated a large boar impaled upon the spit. The beast dripped fat onto smouldering logs below and the delicious aroma of roast pork permeated the entire building.

Wearied by the racket, Ichtheus retreated to his domain at the far end of the kitchen. Sweet perfume wafted from bunched herbs that hung from the rafters to dry, and many jars of powdered roots, and seeds, and flagons of liquid lined the whitewashed walls. With Oric's assistance Ichtheus had scoured the summer countryside for supplies, and he believed he now had herbal remedies to deal with every known ailment. But, with Sir Edred's pending joust, Ichtheus worried he might have insufficient quantity.

"I can barely wait for the morrow," Oric stated as he joined his mentor in the kitchen. Grinning, he added, "I reckon we shall see some grand sport."

"Say what you like, I do not relish the task of mending broken bones and stitching up gouged flesh," Ichtheus grumbled, "but once the contest begins I fear we shall be given little choice."

Oric's grin faded. "Aye, Master, you are right. I forgot about the injuries."

Visitors' mutts snapped and snarled in a bid for supremacy and, for the sake of peace, Sir Edred's shaggy wolfhound relinquished his regular position beside the inglenook fireplace. A scrofulous bloodhound immediately jumped into the empty space. In an attempt to shift the whiskery usurper, Ichtheus received a nasty nip for his trouble. "Ye gods," the old man exclaimed, "I never imagined I would be the first patient in need of my own medicaments."

"Strange mutts should never be trusted," tutted Oric, scooping bruised root of comfrey from a large pot on the nearby table. "Best leave well alone, Master Ichtheus, especially when you are dealing with a strange animal. Please sit down whilst I spread ointment on your wound."

All of a tremble, Ichtheus did as he was told.

"According to my *Almanac*," said Oric, flipping to the correct page, "comfrey is so powerful it will bind together pieces of severed flesh." He rolled his eyes expressively. "No doubt we shall have the opportunity to put that theory to the test over the next few days – what say you, Master Ichtheus?"

"I would rather he said nothing at all," squawked the dishevelled Bayersby housekeeper, her rolls of fat all of a tremble as she shook a greasy ladle at Oric. "Your gut-churning descriptions make me want to puke."

Ignoring Mother Morghan's barb, Oric concentrated on his mentor's injury. The job done, he strolled over to a side table and helped himself to a selection of cold vegetables. Clutching his full platter, he squeezed into a space on a bench beside Dian.

The little maid looked tired, her usual rosy face pale and drawn. "How are you coping with all these extra people?" Oric asked, concerned for Dian's welfare.

"Well enough, I suppose, and the visitors certainly are interesting." Dian dipped her spoon into a wooden bowl of soup she held on her knee. "Lady Myferny has given me leave to attend the fair tomorrow evening." She smiled hopefully at Oric. "Are you going, too?"

Before Dian had chance to raise the spoon to her mouth Mother Morghan snatched away the bowl. Hot liquid spilled onto Dian's lap and she gasped with shock.

"A body would think you were the lady of the manor instead of a mere serving wench! Get yourself back to work afore I flay your hide." Mother Morghan turned on Oric. "As for you, Master Clever-Dick, do not think you can fill your belly; not whilst there are chores still to do! You will get your meal when the gentry have finished gorging themselves," the housekeeper sniggered nastily. "Always supposing Sir Edred's guests leave owt worth eating!"

Oric wanted to snatch the ladle from Mother Morghan's dirty hand and beat her with it, but he dare not. The wretched woman was the apple of Lady Myferny's eye, supposedly running herself ragged for her mistress. But Oric knew differently. Left to her own devices Mother Morghan lolled in her chair, dishing out orders to the other servants. Her pendulous belly and pasty face indented with sly, blackberry eyes sickened Oric. He had suffered many unpleasant altercations with the unsavoury woman in the past, and he was quite sure he would be on the receiving end of plenty more in the future. But, just for now, he planned to leave well alone.

Upstairs in the Great Hall knights and their ladies wolfed down food faster than their servants could keep up the supply. Globs of uneaten food rotted amongst the rushes on the floor along with dogs' droppings and vomit. Many candles guttered in wall-mounted sconces, thickening the already rancid atmosphere with smoke. Noise rose to a deafening crescendo and a small group of minstrels became inaudible because of the din. A gaggle of serfs added their voices to the overall cacophony, bickering over whose lord was the greater warrior and which of the knights' ladies was most beautiful.

Toward the end of the banquet, Sir Edred staggered up from his carved-oak chair. Six feet of solid muscle, the copper-haired, bright-eyed knight presented an awesome sight. "Gentlemen!" he bellowed, banging his dagger handle on the table for silence. "Be aware that the Bayersby knights are a force to be reckoned with. Last year we trounced the moneylender, Figg, and his raggedy-arsed army." He roared with laughter and delivered a hefty *thwack*! to the black-clad knight seated on his left. "If I were you, sir, I would be shaking in my boots." Fuddled with mead, Sir Edred crashed back onto his seat.

Sir Ragnald narrowed his tawny eyes and rubbed his shoulder, but he said nothing. In the fullness of time the loud-mouthed Lord of Bayersby would pay dearly for his insult.

-oOo-

Daylight filtered into the kitchen, striking shafts of pale, morning light through the smoky atmosphere. Benches supporting sleeping serfs stood against the rough stone walls, and the sound of gentle snores and farts rattled around the long room. Soon the peace would be shattered as everyone awakened to begin another day of noisy work.

Hoping to avoid a crush at the breakfast table, Ichtheus rolled off his truckle bed and donned a purple tunic. He ambled across to the other side of the inglenook fireplace where Oric sprawled, still fast asleep. "Wake up, lad!" he whispered, giving Oric a jab with his toe. "Time to start our day."

"But I only just got to bed," Oric wailed, squeezing his eyes tight shut. "I ain't ready to get up yet."

"Too bad," snapped Ichtheus. Twisting his thin white hair into a knot, he secured it under his bonnet. "I intend to be out of the kitchen before Mother Morghan embarks upon another of her tirades. You can catch up on lost sleep some other time." He knotted a leather thong around his waist and thrust his narrow feet into a pair of kid boots. "I will meet you down at the jousting arena."

Fortified with goat's cheese and a chunk of coarse bread, Oric quaffed the last dregs of his ale. He shrugged on a doublet, grabbed his cap and stepped outside.

A blood-red sun oozed over the horizon and treetops in the valley floated like abandoned ships in a sea of pink mist. Nothing stirred in the still, humid air. Summer Solstice was almost nigh and thoughts of Mother Olive's market-day prophecy disturbed Oric. He shivered despite the clammy heat and prayed that the old woman's demons were not about to put in an appearance.

Hot sunshine quickly dispersed the mist, and folk thronged to the paddock where the tournament was about to begin. Serfs and villeins jostled for the best positions in the stands and, in good voice, they boomed out popular chants to while away the time until the competition began.

Lady Myferny, Sir Edred's dainty, golden-haired wife, entered the lists accompanied by roars of approval from the crowd. Traditionally elected as Queen of Love and Beauty, she would present the victors with their prizes at the close of competition. It was not a task she enjoyed, for she abhorred violence of any kind. Resigned to her task she lifted her white gown clear of her feet, and climbed the wooden stairs that led to her place of honour in the galleries. Dreading the bloodshed that was likely to take place, Lady Myferny rested her head against the chair back and closed her violet eyes.

Frida Cole, sweaty and grubby, pushed her way to the front of the stands. "Just look at her hoity-toity ladyship," Frida tittered, jabbing her plump neighbour with a sharp elbow. "Given half a chance I would exchange every one of my seven brats for a single jewel from Lady Myferny's bonny skullcap. My Dian did well to gain a place in such a wealthy household, did she not?"

"Aye, she did that," replied Mistress Goodall. "I reckon Lady Myferny's silver and white kirtle cost a bonny penny an' all. Imagine the likes of us wearing summat like that; it would be blacker than the smithy's forge in the blink of an eye." Both women roared with laughter as they imagined themselves out of their well-worn peasant garb and decked in Lady Myferny's finery.

In a field below the jousting arena, armourer and farrier workshops clanged with activity. Squires poured with sweat as they dashed back and forth to make last minute inspections of their masters' weaponry. Nearby archery butts, quarterstaff and wrestling enclosures stood ready to entertain the masses.

"Make way," bellowed a muscular farmer, leading a mighty beast toward the bull-baiting ring. "This creature is dangerous."

Oric wondered what sort of miserable day the doe-eyed bull was about to endure, for the poor animal looked agreeably docile.

Discomfited by the press of people the donkey Oric led snickered and pranced. Panniers upon the animal's back shook and the contents clinked and rattled. Oric tightened his grasp on the halter. "Whoa, Braccus. I will never hear the end of it if we spill Master Ichtheus' potions."

A bleary-eyed spectator observed Oric's antics. "I like to

see plenty of blood spilled during jousting competitions," he burbled, quaffing liquor from a large, stone flagon. "I reckon you could be in for a few busy days. What say you, Master Apothecary?"

"If you continue to guzzle ale at that rate," Ichtheus scolded, arriving in time to hear the man's comment, "you will be insensible before the first joust begins." Thoroughly disgruntled he strode toward the pavilion set aside for medical emergencies.

Coaxing Braccus along at a steadier pace, Oric followed his mentor.

Ichtheus unlaced the pavilion set aside for the apothecaries, and entered into the dim confines of his tent. The odour of crushed grass and mouldy canvas pervaded the interior, and the atmosphere was airless and clammy. Removing his bonnet, Ichtheus rolled up his sleeves and prepared himself for a long, hot day. When Oric failed to make an appearance, Ichtheus stuck his head outside the tent flap to look for the boy. Oric was taking time negotiating the crowds to avoid upsetting the donkey. "For Heaven's sake, boy, unhitch those panniers before Braccus jiggles my medicaments to bits."

With their supplies unpacked and laid at the ready, Oric strolled outside to watch the competitors exchange challenges. He was relieved to see each knight strike his chosen opponent's shield with the blunt rather than the sharp end of his lance. A strike with the sharp end meant a challenge to the death. Though keen to hone his medical skills, Oric had no desire to see anyone die.

Sir Ragnald remained in his pavilion until only the puniest of entrants remained. After challenging the vapid young knight he rode his muscular charger up to the gallery and reined the animal to a stop before Lady Myferny.

Tipping his lance he bowed his dark head and begged for her favour.

Barely able to hide her distaste, Lady Myferny eyed the knight's insignia. Sir Ragnald's shield bore a black serpent on a red background; a matching serpent reared from the crest of his helmet. Lady Myferny disliked snakes. *Horrible slithery creatures.* Intuition warned her that Sir Ragnald was of similar substance. Nonetheless, she complied with the knight's request and draped a blue silk scarf over his proffered lance. "May God protect and keep you, gallant knight," she said through stiffened lips.

Sir Ragnald pressed the wisp of sweet-smelling fabric to his lips, wheeled his horse away and joined the cavalcade.

Feeling liverish Sir Edred chose not to take part in the joust but, duty-bound, he lead his column of mounted, armour-clad knights onto the field. His shield, emblazoned with a rampant green wolf on a silver background, felt heavier than usual. Hot sun beat down upon his helmet, his head pounded, and he longed to join his wife on the cool, shady stands.

Sunlight burnished the riders' breastplates, and their destriers, resplendent in bejewelled bridles, pranced and caracoled in the face of the noisy crowd. Competitors displayed their favours around muscular biceps, or tied them to their crested helmets.

Lady Myferny caught her breath at the sight of her blue, silk scarf fluttering from the serpent on top of Sir Ragnald's helmet.

His duty done, Sir Edred dismounted and took his place on the stands beside his wife but his familiar bulk failed to bring Lady Myferny any comfort. She slipped her small hand into her husband's mighty paw. "I do not like Sir Ragnald," she whispered. "I fear that arrogant knave will cause trouble."

"What?" Sir Edred roared with laughter as he squeezed his wife's fingers. "Yon fellow is naught but a cocky popinjay. If I could be bothered I would show him a thing or two in the lists. Never you fear my love – he will get his comeuppance in due course."

"Have you seen the poor little fellow he has challenged?" Lady Myferny wailed. "Sir Ragnald will fell such a puny opponent with a single blow."

Sir Edred's copper eyebrows bristled with amusement. "Do not be so sure, my dear. Yon 'puny' knight is deceiving, for he has the backbone of a true warrior and determination enough for three men. Let us bide our time…"

The first two combatants faced each other from opposite ends of the lists. They slammed their cheek-guards shut and lowered their lances.

"Let go," roared the Joust Constable, slashing down his truncheon.

Lances at the ready, pennants flying, the knights bore down upon each other from opposite ends of the lists. Clods of earth flew from their destriers' massive hooves and lance clashed against lance with a sickening crack. Neither contestant was unhorsed.

The crowd roared its approval.

In the third and final charge a lance snapped. No blood was shed, no bones were broken, and the two combatants left the arena with their dignity still intact.

Sir Ragnald, his swarthy face hidden by a mighty helmet with nose guard and cheek plates, faced the young man he had challenged earlier in the day. At the Joust Constable's shout he dug his heels into the sides of his black destrier and charged down the lists. He smashed his lance into his opponent's shoulder. The slender young knight rocked in his saddle but retained his seat. Shaken, Sir Ragnald prepared to make another charge. His opponent's looks were deceiving; the young fellow was clearly more wiry than puny.

In the second tilt the young knight delivered a power-packed blow that reduced Sir Ragnald's lance to splinters. Felled like a giant oak, the older knight crashed from his horse and landed heavily on top of his squire. Suffering nothing more than a bruised ego Sir Ragnald strode from the field.

Ichtheus and Oric attended to the squire's broken arm and dislocated shoulder. "I am glad to see Sir Ragnald bested," said Oric, bathing dirt from the squire's battered face. "But I am sorry you have suffered physical damage because of your master's inadequacies."

The boy shrugged, and wished he hadn't, as red-hot pain seared through his shoulder. "These kinds of misfortune go with the position," he whispered, smiling ruefully. "My bones will mend soon enough and I am thankful that my neck is not broken."

Throughout the hot June day competitors lunged and thrust at each other with lance, battle-axe, and broadsword. One knight lost a finger, sliced off by his opponent's sharp blade. The injured man ran to the apothecary's tent, carrying his detached finger, but Ichtheus could do little more than staunch the knight's flow of blood.

Temperatures soared and the stench of body odour, coupled with the smell of lathered horses and dung, became overpowering. Several females fainted and were carried away to recuperate under the shade of a nearby oak tree. Oric wafted a pungent mixture of pennyroyal and vinegar beneath the ladies' noses to help them recover.

A melee, where several Challengers fought a similar number of Adversaries, followed the joust. Sufficiently recovered from his malaise, Sir Edred donned his armour and joined in. Excelling in melees, he kept his two squires on the run with replacement weapons.

Throughout the long, hot day battered combatants filed into the apothecaries' tent. Ichtheus sewed up cuts and gashes with horsehair and bound broken bones with strips of wet leather. "The strapping shrinks as it dries," he explained to Oric. "Thus the limbs are held in position until the bones knit together."

Oric coped with lesser injuries. He massaged sprains with a mixture of bishop's weed and honey, pasted abrasions with salve of primrose, praised the winners and sympathised with the losers.

At last, a vivid sunset brought day one of Sir Edred's tournament to a close. The gentry returned to Bayersby Manor for a cold supper, leaving the common folk to wander into the meadow below the lists. Traders' stalls buzzed with activity as local vendors vied for business alongside peddlers from outside the district. A dusky stranger drew female customers like moths to a candle flame and the Kilterton haberdasher, unable to compete against the fellow's exotic beads and brooches, packed up her simple wares and trudged home in a sulk.

Released from her duties at Bayersby Manor, Dian changed her clothes and ran down to the fair to seek Oric. She found him watching a sword-swallowing act. "I cannot bear to look," she gasped, turning her face away.

Oric paid close attention as the man thrust a sharp blade down his gullet. "How does he do that without slicing his windpipe? I would not attempt that trick for all the silver in Christendom."

"Come away, do." Dian pulled at Oric's sleeve. "Let us seek less gruesome entertainment elsewhere."

Easily distracted, Oric stared at Dian. She looked

completely different from her workaday self. Her hair, freshly washed, was a riot of sun-streaked, chestnut-brown curls. A forest-green bodice laced tightly above a full, russet-coloured skirt showed off her slender waist. White linen frilled from the top of her bodice, preserving her modesty. Oric blushed. He needed to avert his eyes before she caught him ogling. Unable to help himself, he raised his eyes to her rosy lips and blushed more fiercely as he imagined kissing her.

"What are you staring at?" Dian's sharp words brought Oric out of his reverie. "Do I have a smut on my cheek?"

To cover his hot confusion, Oric nodded. "Aye, you do," he lied. "Stand still and I will rub it off." He held out a piece of clean rag for Dian to spit on before applying it to her unsullied face. "There," he said, stuffing the rag down the front of his tunic. "All done." He gulped and added, "You look as clean and rosy as a... as a boiled beetroot."

Hardly able to believe what she had heard, Dian tittered nervously. Judging by the colour of his face, Oric was the one that looked more like a beetroot.

Oric died a thousand deaths. *Ye gods! I just called her boiled beetroot! What in Heaven's name is the matter with me?*

Beside a stall filled with sweetmeats a monkey danced to the tune his master played on a flute. With every move the little animal made, his shiny black eyes remained fixed upon the nearby delicacies.

Glad of a distraction, Oric laughed and dropped a copper coin into a hat the little animal proffered. "Yon wizened fellow and his whiskery mate look so alike it is hard to pick which is which. Be sure to reward your furry friend with a sweetmeat or two," he urged the flute player.

Across the way a queue of impatient customers jostled to buy food. The plump, raven-haired stall holder's culinary abilities were second to none and she was besieged with customers.

"I had best give Etheldrida a helping hand," said Dian. "Looks like the poor woman is rushed off her feet."

Left to his own devices, Oric wandered into the paddock where Etheldrida's husband, Egglebart, drummed up business for quarterstaff and wrestling bouts.

"Roll up, roll up," chanted the old war dog. "Who will challenge me to a round or two?" One eye lost in a long-ago battle, Egglebart's remaining blue eye gleamed with ferocious enthusiasm. Bare chested, his hairy torso rippled with muscle and his mane of carrot-red hair and ginger beard glistened in the light of many flares. A friend of longstanding, Oric knew the man's looks belied his kindly nature; nevertheless, the normally gentle giant was capable of knocking the stuffing out of any yokel brave enough to take up his challenge. To avoid being inveigled into a contest he was sure to lose, Oric hastened back to Etheldrida's pie stall.

Trade continued briskly with Etheldrida's pigeon and rabbit pies as top favourites. Her cart, full of provisions at the beginning of the fair, was now almost empty.

"May I buy two pies," Oric asked a smiling Dian who was having trouble keeping up with folks' demands.

Etheldrida whacked Oric between his shoulder blades almost felling him to the ground. "Charge the lad for two, but give him three." She winked knowingly at Dian. "Young fellows have hollow legs what needs filling."

Oric accepted a free pie, for he knew argument with the plump woman would prove futile. He waited until Etheldrida was distracted by another customer, then surreptitiously handed the third pie back to Dian. "I meant you to have one anyway."

"Thank you, Oric, I am famished." Dian smiled and dimples indented her cheeks. "Mother Morghan kept me so busy before I left Bayersby Manor, I missed the midday repast."

Hidden behind another cart nearby, two ill-kempt youths salivated. Ned, the elder of the pair jerked dirty fingers through his matted hair. "By heck, Joe, I would kill to get my hands on one of them there pies."

Smaller than his friend, Joe looked pale and undernourished. "Aye, but we dare not try to pinch one as long as Oric hangs around." Joe's thin shoulders sagged. "If he catches sight of us, he will have us dragged back to Bayersby Manor as sure as eggs is eggs."

Working as pick-pouches in the employ of Esica Figg, the boys had been captured by Sir Edred's men during the moneylender's unsuccessful battle for Bayersby Manor. In view of the boys' tender years, Sir Edred had spared their lives and set them to work under Mother Morghan's jurisdiction. The boys, recently escaped from the woman's clutches, were happier living rough and fending for themselves.

"I shall never return to Sir Edred's manor as long as I have breath left in my body!" Ned stated. "I'd rather starve than submit to Mother Morghan's regime again."

"Ye gods!" Joe's brown eyes grew large with fright and he pressed back against the slab-sided cart. "You must have tempted fate, look who is forging toward us."

Mother Morghan, elbows stuck out like jug handles, forced her way through the crowd.

"Best we get out of here before yon eagle-eyed harridan spots us," Ned urged.

In her haste to grab one of Etheldrida's rapidly diminishing pies, Mother Morghan's heel came down upon a fellow's instep and he growled with pain.

"Saints preserve us," Mother Morghan exclaimed. "Is that you, Master Figg? I thought you were dead and buried long since."

Figg clamped his moist palm across Mother Morghan's mouth."For God's sake hold your tongue woman. Do you want to see me hanged, drawn and quartered?"

Mother Morghan cared little one way or the other. She pushed Figg's hand away from her face and wiped her mouth. "Where the devil have you been, man?"

"Never mind where I have been – 'tis where I am going that counts." Not one to miss an opportunity, Figg forced a sickly grin. "You once spied upon Sir Edred at my behest; would you care to do the same again?"

"I might," Mother Morghan sniffed. "On the other hand I might not. If I do decide to join forces with you again, I shall expect a more lucrative reward than I received last time I helped you out." She took in Figg's ragged appearance. "Right now you look like a vagrant without a copper to his name."

Figg glared at Mother Morghan, his grey eyes icy. "Make no mistake, madam, I shall soon be solvent again. Until then, I need somewhere to lie low. Can you suggest a suitable hiding place?"

"St Griswald's Church served you well enough in the past, and the building is within easy reach of Bayersby Manor and the village of Kilterton. No-one hereabouts dares to go near that place, especially after dark." Mother Morghan cackled. "Folks believe the place is haunted but we know different, do we not, Master Figg?"

Figg nodded, recalling how his cronies had scared folk away in the past. "In that case I shall return to St Griswald's. Keep me informed of all that is going on at Bayersby Manor and you shall be well rewarded."

Head down, Figg pushed through the fairground crush until a stealthy movement in the vicinity of his pouch stopped him dead. He grabbed the culprit's hand and was rewarded with a pain-filled gasp.

"Let go afore you break my fingers," howled the boy.

"Be thankful 'tis not your neck," Figg growled, immediately recognising the youngster's voice. "It seems your pouch-picking skills have deteriorated since last we parted company." Bending back Joe's wrist, Figg manoeuvred him across the paddock and away from the crowd. Rather than cause a commotion, Ned kept step behind his former employer and followed him into the nearby forest.

"You mangy turd," Joe cried. "We served you well, but you abandoned us after you lost your battle against Sir Edred. Ned and me have been living hand-to-mouth ever since."

Figg hoisted Joe up and snagged the back of his tunic onto a tree branch. "Shut your mouth or I will silence you for good!"

Joe's spiky black hair stood out from his scalp like a crown of thorns. Left dangling like a cloak on a peg, the neck of his tunic tightened around his windpipe and he began to choke.

"For pity's sake let the lad down before he strangles to death," begged Ned. "I am sorry we tried to rob you, Master Figg, only we never recognised you with that new-grown beard and a hood pulled over your head."

"I will free yon poxy weasel if you both pledge to work for me again," said Figg, seizing the opportunity to add another pair of thieves to his team.

"Aye, we will," Ned promised, prepared to say anything to save his friend's life.

Figg unhitched Joe and dropped him on the ground. "Remember St Griswald's? That is where I plan to set up my headquarters again."

"Aye, we remember the place all too well," retorted Ned.

"Join me in the crypt when Sir Edred's tournament is over," ordered Figg. "In the meantime hone your skills amongst the crowd. With all yonder wealthy folk to pick from, I expect you to amass a plentiful haul."

Ned watched the ex-moneylender melt into the dusk of evening. "Master Highfalutin' Figg ain't looking as well-heeled as he used to. What say you, little'un?"

"You could be right," Joe rasped, rubbing his aching throat. "But I reckon the evil sod will soon claw his way back to where he was, and Heaven help folk hereabouts when he does."

Chapter Three

The Cockentrice

Day one of Sir Edred's tournament produced no fatalities, but knights with broken bones and minor injuries kept both apothecaries busy. The final joust of the day clashed to a halt without incident, and Ichtheus laced up his pavilion.

Long shadows crept across the countryside, and a nightingale sang from the depths of a briar rose bush. The little bird's musical trills soothed Ichtheus' weary soul, but his peace was shattered the moment he entered Bayersby Manor's hot, steamy kitchen.

"What time do you call this?" Mother Morghan shrieked.

Ichtheus balked at sight of the lumpy, grey mess the housekeeper thrust into his hands. "Is this the best fare you have to offer a hungry apothecary?"

Mother Morghan shrugged. "Take it or leave it! Tripe is all I have left."

Almost too tired to eat, Ichtheus sat down on the hard bench beside Oric and Dian. "Did you enjoy the fair?" he asked.

"Aye, we di…" Oric's reply was cut short by the noisy arrival of the Bayersby heir.

Having recently completed his education with the monks at Roxbrough Abbey, Guwain was full of himself. Legs straddled, fists planted firmly on his hips, he confronted Ichtheus. "My father demands that you attend him in the Great Hall at once!"

Ichtheus popped a piece of tripe into his mouth, sure that Sir Edred would have requested, rather than demanded, his presence. "Did your father say what he requires of me?" he asked, chewing slowly upon the gristly mouthful.

"No, he did not," snapped Guwain indignantly. "But he wants to see you immediately so get yourself upstairs at once."

Too late, Dian shrank behind Oric.

Guwain reached over Oric's shoulder and tweaked one of Dian's lustrous curls. "Follow me, girlie. You can be my serving wench for the evening." He leered as he smoothed down the front of his scarlet tunic. "If you look after me nicely I shall reward you well."

"Send word if Master Guwain misbehaves himself," whispered Oric as Dian squeezed past. "There is little I can do openly, but I would drug his ale with a sleeping draught rather than see you ill-used." Snub-nosed, short and stocky with brown hair and pale blue eyes, Sir Edred's son reminded Oric of a pugnacious dog.

Guwain bounded back upstairs to the Great Hall and Dian reluctantly followed him. She wanted nothing from the high-handed Bayersby heir but she dared not disobey him. To make matters worse she had learned that he would remain at Bayersby Manor indefinitely, to learn first-hand the running of the family estate.

Tension between the two boys was palpable, and Ichtheus worried that trouble was brewing. Sir Edred held Oric in high esteem, for the young apothecary had saved his life during a battle with Esica Figg. But would the mighty lord take Oric's side against his own flesh and blood? Agonising over what disaster was about to unfold, Ichtheus abandoned his bowl of tripe and climbed the stairs to the Great Hall.

No matter how often Ichtheus entered the Great Hall, he always marvelled at the intricately-worked tapestries that lined the walls. A massive oak trestle with benches on each side seated many people, but the family and notable visitors dined at a separate table on a dais at the far end of the room. Steps abutted to the wall led up to a minstrels' gallery where musical instruments lay at the ready for evening entertainment. During winter months a huge log fire blazed on the central hearth, sending smoke and sparks flying high. Soot-encrusted rafters supported a straw roof and Ichtheus believed it was a miracle the tiny embers did not set the thatch alight.

Comfortably seated in his carved chair on the dais, Sir Edred beamed down upon his apothecary. "Ah, there you are, Master Ichtheus. I have an interesting challenge for you."

Ichtheus' heart sank. More often than not Sir Edred's challenges caused unnecessary work. "What is your command, my lord?"

"I want you to prepare a Cockentrice for tomorrow's feast." Keen to impress his visitors, Sir Edred believed that Ichtheus would do a better job than Mother Morghan and her indifferent cooks.

Ichtheus removed his bonnet and bowed low. "I will do my best, sir." Irritated beyond measure, he stomped back downstairs to the kitchen. "Oh, my giddy aunt," he cried, throwing up his hands in despair. "I am commanded to concoct a Cockentrice."

"A what?" Oric tittered. "I have never heard of such a beast."

"Neither have I," growled Ichtheus. "I am an apothecary, not a cook!" He rammed his bonnet back on his head and gazed at his rows of medicaments, as if seeking inspiration.

Enjoying the old man's discomfiture, Mother Morghan drew Ichtheus' attention to a wooden box in the corner of the kitchen. "Yonder container once belonged to a scribe who liked to cook, but his outlandish experimentations with food brought about an eruption of the master's bowels. Sir Edred became so ill he threatened to have the fellow hanged, drawn and quartered." Mother Morghan hung out her tongue and crisscrossed a finger across her ample belly. "The scribe took fright and departed in such a hurry he left his belongings behind." She smirked nastily, her blackberry eyes almost invisible beneath her heavy lids. "Who knows, you might find the recipe you seek among his abandoned possessions."

"When am I supposed to concoct this culinary delight?" Ichtheus expostulated, skewing his head around to glare at the housekeeper. "Before, during, or after administering to joust casualties?"

Mother Morghan shrugged. "I neither know nor care, Master Apothecary." Without uttering another word, she plopped onto her battered chair and promptly fell asleep.

"Fat lot of help she is," grumbled Oric, "but worry not Master Ichtheus, between us we will organise something." Undaunted he sifted through the would-be cook's box and, after a few moments, he brandished a crumpled sheet of parchment. "Here we are –

"*Cockentrice... An Easy Recipe for Beginners.*

Chop the cooked chicken's flesh, and mix together with herbs. Cut off the pig's backside and the front of the chicken. Stuff the chicken mixture inside each creature and sew the two together."

Oric's eyebrows disappeared under his sun-bleached fringe. "The recipe says the finished creation must resemble a mythical monster."

Ichtheus lit a lantern, and placed it on the table beside Oric. "Read on, lad, and we shall see."

Oric read aloud, running his finger down the list of ingredients. "We need a suckling pig, and a large chicken." He looked up, his brow furrowed in consternation. "The next instruction says we must kill and disembowel both creatures, keeping the pig's head intact, scald them both, and drain them until dry. Not so difficult, Master Ichtheus, would you agree?"

"Surely there is more to the recipe, else what spectacle would there be in that?"

"Aha! Now I see where it's headed!" exclaimed Oric as the ongoing words proclaimed how the spectacle was to be achieved. *First, make a stuffing mixture, using raw eggs, broken bread, some saffron, salt and pepper, and shredded fat. Using both hands, combine it well.*

"We must make a forcemeat," cried Oric, triumphantly, feeling that the job was all but done.

"Read on, lad. There must be more to it than that."

"Aye, I am afraid you are right," said Oric, allowing his eyes to rest on the following instructions. *Next, cut the pig in half, around the waist, then cut the chicken in half around the waist.* "This recipe is beginning to sound a little strange. We must cut both the animals in halves," he gasped, "then employ needle and thread to sew the back half of the chicken onto the front half of the pig."

"For pity's sake, Oric, stop fooling about!"

"I am not fooling, Master! It now says that the front half of the chicken must be sewn onto the back half of the pig! Then we must stuff them, and skewer them onto the spit. We are going to end up with two, very strange, mythical beasties!"

Ichtheus snorted with disgust. "What a waste of time! Why can we not enjoy a simple chicken stew, or a nice roast loin of pork?"

"We had best obey Sir Edred's orders." Oric replicated Mother Morgan's stomach-slitting gesture, his eyes twinkling with mischief. "We do not want you going down the same path as the other, unfortunate cook."

Ichtheus was sure that no such thing would happen; nevertheless, thoughts of the night ahead made his head throb. "The sooner we start the sooner we shall finish."

The corners of Oric's mouth drooped. "I doubt we shall get much sleep this night."

Ichtheus snatched the parchment from Oric's hands, reassuring himself that the boy had spoken the truth. "I suppose we must now raid the henhouse and slaughter the wretched bird."

"Not to mention a piglet," mumbled Oric, feeling more miserable by the heartbeat. He pulled a dagger from the cuff of his boot and stropped the blade on a piece of stiff leather. Killing animals was his least favourite pastime but, with the aid of a sharp knife, the poor creatures would die swiftly.

The unsuspecting chickens had already gone to roost, enabling Oric and Ichtheus to grab a large, heavy bird and secure it in a sack. Halfway across the yard to the slaughterhouse Oric tripped and sprawled, full length, on the ground. He lost his grip on the sack and, squawking fit to raise the devil, the chicken made his bid for freedom.

"Quick!" Ichtheus screamed. "Catch the little beggar before he gets away!"

Oric dashed about, and cornered the escapee right

where he had perched, with his feathers all fluffed out with indignation. Taking advantage of the bird's confusion, Oric nabbed him securely and shoved him back into the sack.

"You need to conserve your energy, lad, to capture and slaughter the piglet. Meanwhile, I shall neck the chicken and take him inside for Dian to pluck."

His unsavoury attack on the piglet over, Oric decided that butchery was an occupation he had no desire to pursue. Bathed in sweat and drenched with his victim's blood, he stepped outside the slaughterhouse to be confronted by Guwain and Joffrey.

Standing next to the two youths dressed in their evening finery, Oric felt like the lowliest of serfs.

Guwain flicked his fingers dismissively. "Hard to believe yon creature was recently promoted to the position of assistant apothecary, ain't it?"

"Aye, and judging by the fellow's gory state, some poor wretch has recently fallen foul of his ministrations," Joffrey sneered nastily slanting his tawny cat-like eyes at Oric. "Should I require medical attention in the future, I shall seek advice elsewhere."

Disinclined to explain himself, Oric made his way back to the kitchen. Guwain was naught but a braggart and a bully, but Joffrey's cold confidence was disturbing.

The preparation of Sir Edred's feast was time-consuming and painstaking. The pig/chicken combinations were dutifully sewn together, filled with forcemeat, and the remaining opening closed over with more thread.

The Cockentrice was impaled upon a spit above the fire, and the young boy seconded to wind the handle began the onerous chore.

"You had best get some sleep, lad," said Ichtheus. "I will call you when I am in need of a rest. I will spell the boy every hour or so." He placed more logs on the fire, settled back in his chair and prepared himself for an uncomfortable night.

Sticky with the residue of his night's work, Oric wandered outside and drew a bucket of cool water from the well. He removed his blood-spattered tunic, and sloshed it about in the bucket. Drawing more water, he washed himself. Too hot to sleep inside the inglenook, he spread his tunic out near the fire to dry, and sought a bench beside the open kitchen door. Curled up on his side, he soon nodded off to sleep.

Ichtheus glanced across the room at his assistant. Four and twenty moons had passed since the boy had first arrived at Bayersby Manor. Taught by the Dunburton alchemist, Oric was able read and write and, in need of an apprentice to help lighten his workload, Ichtheus had taken the boy in. Lessons in the application of medicinal herbs had followed over the ensuing months.

A new purpose in life, coupled with a wholesome diet, had swiftly turned Oric from a skinny waif into a well-muscled youth. The lad was possessed of a cheeky wit, but he was also honourable and brave. Oric's golden hair and fair complexion suggested that Saxon blood ran through his veins; whatever his lineage, Ichtheus loved him like a son.

Caedmon, Mistress Myferny's black-and-white tomcat, streaked across the kitchen and jumped onto the apothecary's table. Jars and pots rolled over and crashed onto the flagstones. Ichtheus hurled a boot, missing the cat by a whisker. Caedmon leaped onto an overhead rafter and fixed his aggressor with a malevolent yellow glare. For a delicious moment, Ichtheus toyed with the idea of serving 'Catentrice' alongside Sir Edred's Cockentrice.

The fire crackled, the lantern burned low, and Ichtheus dozed.

A shifting log sent out a shower of crimson sparks. Jerked awake, Ichtheus smacked at several bright embers that landed on his boots and leggings. *At this rate,* he thought, *my appearance will soon match that of Sir Edred's singed wolfhound.* But tonight, Parzifal had abandoned his usual spot by the fire for the cooler and quieter comfort of the stables. Thinking the dog had the right idea, Ichtheus gave Oric a gentle shake. "Stir yourself, lad, 'tis your turn to watch over Sir Edred's feast. I am going outside for a breath of air."

Many moons had passed since a band of marauders had ransacked his former home, but still Oric could not erase the mental picture of Dunburton Manor engulfed with fire. Nor could he forget the death of his former mentor, Master Deveril. The old man had produced a key with a double knot emblem on the shaft and had used his last breath to issue a warning: *"This key will unlock the secret to great wealth. You must promise to keep it safe. If it falls into wrong hands, untold disasters could occur."*

Oric had agonised over the meaning of Deveril's words ever since. He had almost lost the key on one or two occasions and, for safekeeping, he had hidden it away with Master Ichtheus' few precious belongings in a specially created cavity under Braccus' stall. *One day,* he thought, *I will solve the mystery of Deveril's key; I will make his killers pay for their crime – however long it takes.*

The Cockentrice pair was roasting nicely, and smelled delicious. The young boy had been spelled many times, and Oric thought it might be time for Dian to take her turn at watching over the meat. The little maid slept on the far side of the kitchen, one hand curled tightly under her cheek. Her chestnut-gold curls tumbled over the bench on which she lay, and Oric's heart swelled with love. *If only I could find the words to tell how I feel,* he thought. Rather than disturb her he decided to soldier on with the Cockentrice. Dian had enough work to cope with during the day, and she needed her sleep.

In between tending the Cockentrice, Oric dozed, and dreamed, until fingers of pink dawn slanted through the open kitchen door. He rubbed sleep from his eyes, checked the spit, yet again. The meat was done to a turn, and Oric sent the boy off to bed. Donning his dry tunic, he went in search of his mentor.

-oOo-

Day two of Sir Edred's tournament continued much the same as day one, and Ichtheus was glad when it drew to a clashing finale. He yawned, stretched, and doused his head with a pannikin of cool water. Refilling the dish from a trough of well water, he passed it over to Oric. "Freshen yourself up, lad. We must now find the energy to serve Sir Edred's Cockentrice."

Oric tied on an apron to protect his clothes from spillages, and he assisted Ichtheus to heft the spit with the odd pair onto the bench. They slid the meaty oddities from the spit and prepared to arrange their platter for presentation to Sir Edred.

Still referring to the ancient recipe, it read: *When cooked, gild the outside with egg yolks, ginger, saffron and parsley juice or mallow juice.*

"Please allow me to make the mixture," begged Dian; the excitement of the venture now becoming infectious for the three of them.

The ensuing result was spectacular. The creatures

gleamed with the glossy brew, side by side, on a silver platter, and looked as if they had always been thus. The head of the pig now held a rosy apple in its mouth, and the chicken was resplendent with an arrogant plume of black and white feathers emerging from its rear end.

Stepping back to view the finished article, Oric's eyes twinkled mischievously. "Sir Edred would take a fit if he knew where those quills came from," he chortled.

"And where would that be?" Dian asked, sloshing her sticky hands in a bowl of tepid water.

Oric plunged his hands into the same bowl and tickled Dian's fingers. "I will tell if you promise to keep it a secret?"

"I promise," she giggled.

"From the tails of Sir Edred's prize fighting cocks."

"Ooh!" Dian gasped. "If he ever finds out you will likely end up as filling for his next Cockentrice." She dried her hands and wiped up drips of gravy from the platter's rim with a corner of her apron. "Let Sir Edred enjoy his strange feast; I would rather eat a tasty vegetable stew any day."

"Aye, and stewed vegetables do not take all night to prepare," grumbled Ichtheus as he prepared to carry one end of the enormous platter upon which the Cockentrice rested. "Come, Oric, let us present this culinary creation to the folk upstairs."

Hundreds of flares shed light across the Great Hall. On the gallery above Sir Edred's dais a trio of minstrels came to the end of a lively tune. The Lord of Bayersby, a golden coronet upon his head, beamed down upon his guests. "I have ordered a culinary masterpiece," he boomed. "My apothecaries are bringing it up from the kitchen as I speak."

"How exciting, my lord," cried Lady Myferny, clapping her hands in anticipation. Dripping with jewels, and dressed in royal purple with a bejewelled cap set upon her pale locks, the lady of the manor looked like a queen. "I can barely wait to see what you have organised, my lord." She planted a kiss on her husband's bristly cheek. "You spoil us and we love you for it."

Slumped in a chair, Guwain feigned disinterest in his father's culinary delight. Banned from the tournament because he had disobeyed too many of his father's commands, Guwain was in a belligerent mood. To add to his misery the scarlet tunic and breeches he wore were uncomfortably tight, for he had gained weight since he had last worn them. "For Heaven's sake bring on the jester," he snarled. "I have had my fill of twanging harps and screeching fiddles."

Lady Myferny made eye contact with her son, trying to still his tongue with the merest shake of her head. The last thing she wanted was another unpleasant altercation between father and son.

Arrogantly ignoring his mother's warning, Guwain raised his voice. "How much longer must I endure this racket?"

"For as long as I deem it necessary," Sir Edred snapped. "And, for the benefit of our guests, try to look as if you are enjoying yourself."

A pre-arranged horn blast announced the arrival of the Cockentrice, and the two apothecaries lowered the platter onto the table before their lord and master. Dagger at the ready, Sir Edred congratulated Oric and Ichtheus on their culinary triumph.

Dian watched the proceedings from the top of the kitchen stairs. Proud of Oric's achievement, she clapped and cheered along with the rest of the hungry guests.

Twisted with jealousy, Guwain tore the apple from the pig's mouth and hurled it at Oric with all of his might.

The fruit cracked into the back of Oric's skull.

Momentarily stunned he stumbled to his knees. Sir Edred's guests guffawed and cheered at the unexpected entertainment.

"More! More! More!" they chorused.

Mustering his dignity, Oric retrieved the apple and returned it to the pig's mouth. He bowed low and said, "I pray the feast is to your taste, my lord."

Sir Edred inclined his head in appreciation, then he flashed a look of deep anger at his son. *The boy is insufferable,* he thought. *I must address the problem before the situation becomes unmanageable.*

Seated at the far end of the top table, Sir Ragnald observed the exchange between father and son. *Perhaps young Master Guwain's dissatisfaction can be exacerbated,* he thought. Internal disruption could be worthwhile if wisely deployed. Joffrey had already formed an association with the boy; he needed to expand upon the friendship.

Oric returned to the kitchen, wondering what punishment Guwain would receive for his bad manners. Whatever happened, the Bayersby heir's ill-feeling would be misdirected, and Oric determined to exercise great care around him in future.

-oOo-

The last day of Sir Edred's tournament dawned hotter than ever as competitors and spectators endured the most uncomfortable weather in living memory. Regardless of the enervating heat, Lady Myferny trailed into the lists one final time to hand out prizes to the winners. High ranking competitors received golden clasps, small jewels and a gerfalcon or two. Lesser folk were given chaplets of flowers and laurel wreaths.

Sir Ragnald's loss of face in the tilts was fully restored when he claimed his prize as melee champion. He accepted his award from Lady Myferny and clasped her hand, allowing his wet lips to linger a moment too long on her white skin.

Repulsed by the feel of Sir Ragnald's fleshy mouth and bristly whiskers, Lady Myferny jerked her arm away. Without thinking, she rubbed the back of her hand on her pale-blue underskirt.

Sir Ragnald looked deeply into Lady Myferny's violet eyes. *When I become Master of Bayersby*, he thought, *I will teach this beautiful woman to be more respectful.*

-oOo-

Instead of returning home immediately after Sir Edred's tournament, Sir Ragnald chose to reconnoitre the lands that lay south of Bayersby Manor. A one-day ride usually brought visitors from Kilterton to Dunburton, but Sir Ragnald and his party took time to explore every highway and byway. Not until late afternoon on day three did they reach the ancient settlement.

The novelty of sleeping under the stars had swiftly palled for Joffrey and he hoped Dunburton boasted an inn that would provide a decent meal and a comfortable bed. Entering the village, his hopes plummeted. The place was deserted and derelict cottages lined both sides of the road. A gaggle of scrawny chickens scratched amongst vegetable patches long since gone to seed, and a hot wind tossed rolls of dead grass along the dusty thoroughfare. The village had a sinister feel and Joffrey shivered despite the late afternoon heat.

Arnald, the wounded squire, had also hoped for a

comfortable billet. His broken bones, strapped with leather to aid the healing process, ached abominably. Long days in the saddle and nights spent upon hard ground had sorely tested his powers of endurance. He glowered belligerently at Sir Ragnald's broad back; even if they set off immediately they faced several more nights of sleeping rough before they would return home to Lockton Castle.

"The Lord of Bayersby can expect no assistance from this godforsaken hole," Sir Ragnald cried, his voice echoing back from the tumbledown buildings. "Seems to me Sir Edred's pick of soldiers must come from Kilterton and, as far as I can tell, folk there are naught but country yokels." Sir Ragnald guffawed. "When the time is right my superior force will eliminate Bayersby's pompous windbag and his paltry gaggle of supporters."

In troubled times thieves were commonplace, and Sir Ragnald dispatched Joffrey and Erik, the able-bodied squire, to make sure no-one lurked in any of the derelict buildings. Well versed in the art of hand-to-hand fighting, the two boys would make short shrift of anyone that crossed their path.

Only one cottage retained a complete roof and, after a cursory inspection, Sir Ragnald moved in with the injured squire. The owners of the cottage were clearly long gone, for nothing of value remained within. *So much for a period of rest and recuperation here,* thought Sir Ragnald. Keen to enjoy the pleasures of a larger town, he decided to move on to Roxbrough the following morning.

The boys made a preliminary search of the village but found little sign of recent, human habitation. Satisfied they had the place to themselves they found a barn, dragged out a few stooks of straw that had not gone mouldy and loaded them onto their horses. On the return journey they caught and necked two chickens. A clutch of eggs lay under a bush and Joffrey helped himself. In a happier frame of mind he lit a fire on the hearth inside the cottage. They had bedding, albeit on the prickly side, and food. Arnald found a battered cooking pot, filled it with water and scrunched it down amongst the fiery branches on the hearth. A few onions that had not gone to seed were added, along with the chickens. The birds were old and took a while to tenderise. Toward the end of the cooking process Joffrey dropped the eggs, still in their shells, into the hot stew. The meat remained tough but tasty and no-one went to bed hungry.

Another hot night coupled with the uncomfortable straw beds made for disturbed sleep and Joffrey arose early. Leaving his companions to slumber, he grabbed a couple of cold eggs and shelled them as he wandered outdoors into the milky light of dawn. His cursory inspection of Dunburton Manor the day before had left him wanting, and he returned to the house to make sure he had missed nothing of value.

The bitter smell of charred timber remained within the stone walls of the manor, and small pieces of blackened thatch crunched beneath Joffrey's boots. Glancing up he saw that the roof was gone, destroyed in what must have been a spectacular blaze. The dwelling was large but, even in its prime, the house could never match the faded splendour of his own home.

One night at Dunburton proved enough for Sir Ragnald and, in the mood for some good food, comfort and entertainment, he led his party on to Roxbrough-by-the-Sea.

Whilst Arnald nursed his broken bones in bed, raven-haired Joffrey and Erik, fair as a field of ripe corn, used their good looks to woo as many of the local young females as they could find. More often than not they were forced to run the gauntlet of furious fathers.

A gambling ring was operating at the Roxbrough Inn

and, with the aid of his loaded dice, Sir Ragnald swiftly won enough money to pay for the best of everything the town had to offer. The inn's patrons became suspicious, and their joviality changed to belligerence. The Lockton Castle inhabitants had enjoyed a wonderful time, but now it was time to leave before anything untoward happened.

Joffrey wished he was schooling his pony on the grassy plateau upon which Lockton Castle stood. Instead, he was gallivanting around the countryside with his father. He missed his turret room and the view over the valley, and Lake Coughcat where he swam and fished during the summer. The castle was enormous and, if he wanted to hide away, there were plenty of areas that remained deserted. Within the castellated walls a small chapel provided a place of worship, not that he prayed very often. Other stone buildings that had once housed workshops, a flourmill, and blacksmith's forge now stood empty. *At least the well continues to produce a plentiful supply of clean water,* Joffrey thought. He fondly visualised the mighty drawbridge over the moat, the only entrance to the castle, and the gatehouse containing the winding gear for the stout portcullis. Not so fondly he recalled the crabby drunkard, Rory, who operated the gate. He raked his eyes across the rolling hills around Dunburton, comparing them to the mountain range that rose up behind Lockton Castle. Unlike Dunburton, his home was impenetrable to most would-be marauders. Impenetrable to most people, maybe – but not his father all those years ago.

Joffrey tried to recall the women who had worked at the castle but, apart from one unpleasant housekeeper, he could think of none. No other woman had stayed at Lockton Castle long enough to temper the harsh masculine world in which he had matured; nevertheless, he remembered his upbringing with satisfaction. Along with his father's squires,

Erik and Arnald, he had learned self-sufficiency, how to ride, and how to wield a sword. They had enjoyed several years of indolence, but now Lockton's coffers were almost empty. The acquisition of Bayersby Manor and Sir Edred's wealth was paramount if Lockton Castle was to be saved from ruin.

Chapter Four

A Priest for St Griswald's

Re-established in St Griswald's crypt Esica Figg supplied food and shelter for anyone who volunteered to join his band of ruffians, but he paid no wages. To keep his bully boys loyal to the cause, Figg promised riches beyond their wildest dreams when he became the next Lord of Bayersby. Promises he had no intention of keeping.

Hersica Horzefell, a stick-thin old crone known to Figg from old, returned to the fold as cook and skivvy. She snared rabbits, stole produce from Sir Edred's fields and cooked meals for the inhabitants of St Griswald's crypt. Hersica believed overmuch use of soap and water sapped her strength, and her appalling body odour permeated the cramped quarters below the church. Sick to death of the men's verbal abuse, she gathered up her meagre possessions and moved into the manse on the opposite side of the graveyard.

Built of rough stone with a thatched roof, the manse had once provided comfortable, single-room accommodation for the incumbent minister. Long since deserted, a patch of ground, set aside for growing vegetables, had fallen prey to a fine crop of dandelions and other weeds. The overgrown area would stay that way, for Hersica had no intention of doing anything with it other than to pull a few dandelion leaves to add to her greasy stews.

Mother Morghan visited Hersica regularly and, seeing the Bayersby housekeeper clomping along the pathway one sultry afternoon, Figg braved the appalling stink inside the manse to accost her. The woman repulsed him. Her thin strands of mousy hair were drawn back into a tight bun at the back of her head, and her skin was brown and warty. She reminded Figg of a toad.

"Why have you not reported back to me?" Figg demanded. "When we met at Sir Edred's tournament, you agreed to spy on my account."

"Oh, I did, did I?" Mother Morghan lay back in a broken-down chair and laced her stubby fingers over her pendulous belly. "Correct me if I am wrong, Master Figg, but did you not fail to claim Bayersby Manor when you challenged Sir Edred?" She fixed cold, dark eyes upon Figg's face. "No thanks to you, I barely escaped that ghastly fiasco with my life. Why on earth should I oblige you a second time around?"

"Because things will be different," Figg retorted pompously. "This time I shall oust Sir Edred and become the most powerful man in the county."

Mother Morghan sat bolt upright in the chair. "If I risk my neck for you a second time, you will need to offer me a far greater incentive."

"Rest assured, madam, any person that assists me will share generously in the wealth I seize." Figg twisted a coil of lank hair around his index finger, and narrowed his slate-coloured eyes until they were barely more than slits. "On the other hand, folk that cross me can look forward to a miserable future."

Since Mother Morghan could think of no other way of getting rich, she reluctantly agreed to keep Figg posted on the comings and goings of wealthy visitors to Bayersby Manor.

A routine of sorts was established within St Griswald's crypt, and Figg's men returned with their plunder to the church each evening. They ate the unpalatable food that Hersica provided and discussed which victims to target the next day.

The first disastrous battle against Sir Edred had taught Figg a valuable lesson. No more cheapskate fly-by-night renegades to form his mercenary army; once he accumulated the wherewithal he planned to employ the best soldiers money would buy. Before tallying up the day's takings and squirrelling away the plunder, Figg waited for his henchmen to fall asleep. They were a raggedy-arsed bunch of ne'er-do-wells and he suspected they kept a few coppers from each robbery for themselves. However, as long as his wealth continued to accumulate, Figg planned to turn a blind eye to the men's petty thievery – for the time being.

-oOo-

Much rubbish had accumulated during Sir Edred's three-day tournament and, feeling less than enthusiastic about the day ahead, Oric and Ichtheus arose early to help with the clean-up.

Floor rushes thick with food scraps, vomit, spittle, and dogs' droppings were barrowed away from the Great Hall. Dian sprinkled sweet-smelling herbs over the residue of filth packed too hard to shift, and serfs dropped clean straw and rushes over the top. Mother Morghan issued orders left and right, but did little of the work. Any underling that failed to follow her instructions was soundly beaten with a large soup ladle.

Oric set light to combustible material dumped in the compound and, with no breeze to disturb the atmosphere, a choking pall of smoke gathered around the manor. The sun climbed higher and temperatures soared.

"Why are we bothering with all this cleaning?" grumbled one reluctant worker, his grimy face running with sweat. "If Mother Olive's market-day prophecies come true we could all be dead within the next few days!" The man jerked his head at Mother Morghan. "Though I doubt yon harpy needs to worry. One glimpse of her ugly visage and the soothsayer's demons will adopt her as one of their own."

On his way back from the stables, Sir Edred overheard the remark and cuffed the serf's ear. "Can you not find something useful to do instead of filling folks' heads with stories of doom and gloom? Seek out Master Ichtheus and ask him to attend me in the Great Hall."

Upon receipt of his master's summons Ichtheus trudged upstairs from the kitchen.

Sir Edred, seated at the breakfast table with a piece of clean linen tied around his neck, waved his greasy dagger toward a group of surly attendants. "Yon servants' rattle over Mother Olive's prophecy is wearing me down. I instructed the young priest recently come to Kilterton's new priory to put a stop to all this ridiculous rumour-mongering but, as far as I can fathom, he holds no sway over his congregation. Tell me, Master Apothecary, how long has it been since we had a preacher at St Griswald's?"

"I believe the church has been deserted for several moons, my lord. Folk hereabouts refuse to go near the place because they believe it is haunted."

"Haunted? Utter rubbish!" Sir Edred pinched his bottom lip thoughtfully. "What we need is a fire and brimstone preacher who will nip all talk of demons, not to mention ghosts, in the bud." He skewered a chunk of meat with the point of his dagger and popped it into his mouth. "My son informs me that a priest by the name of Father Chrispian terrified the students at Roxbrough Abbey with threats of hellfire and damnation. Such a preacher would surely be the ideal man to discipline our unruly serfs and villeins." He swivelled his dagger around and pointed the blade at Ichtheus. "You, Master Apothecary, must fetch this priest from the abbey and install him in St Griswald's Church."

Ichtheus wondered why he had been singled out for such a menial task. "You require me to leave now, my lord?"

"Yes, now." Sir Edred spat a chunk of gristle onto the floor, and Parzifal immediately gobbled it up. "The sooner some God-fearing sense is instilled into folk hereabouts, the happier we all shall be."

Ichtheus stroked his beard thoughtfully. "St Griswald's Church and the manse looked all but derelict last time I was there. If we are to engage another priest the buildings will require substantial refurbishment to make them habitable."

"I shall send carpenters to assess what is required," said Sir Edred. "In the meantime fetch Father Chrispian and see that he is made comfortable."

Ichtheus was about to leave, but Sir Edred was not finished.

"A messenger came recently with word that Lady Myferny's sister, Elfine, is not well. Since she is domiciled at Roxbrough, I would be obliged if you would take a look at her whilst you are there."

Ah, thought Ichtheus, *now we have the true crux of the matter.*

Deeming his problem solved Sir Edred scraped the remains of his breakfast onto the floor for Parzifal to finish off, and hastened away to inspect a new foal born overnight.

Irritated beyond measure Ichtheus stomped downstairs. He had planned to replenish his medicaments over the next few days, for the tournament had left his stock perilously low. Blessed with better than average intelligence Parzifal followed hot on Ichtheus' heels, hoping to find more food scraps in the kitchen.

"I believe the servants' discontent over Mother Olive's prophecy has blossomed way too far to be nipped in the bud, as Sir Edred so eruditely puts it," growled Ichtheus. "To cap it all, I am now faced with a long journey to Roxbrough-by-the Sea and a new priest to cosset. It seems I must also pay a visit to Lady Myferny's sister whilst I am there. "

"Please may I come with you, Master Ichtheus?" Oric begged. "The friars at Roxbrough Abbey are renowned for their medical skills and I would dearly like to see what they have to offer." He grinned sheepishly. "Besides I have never been to the seaside."

At Ichtheus' nod Oric picked out a spare set of rough clothes and threw in two bed rolls for sleeping along the way. Clutching his bundle he raced outside to harness Braccus to the cart.

A little while later Dian appeared in the yard with a large hamper of food. "I wish I could come too," she said wistfully, thrusting the basket into Oric's hands. "But Mother Morghan says there is too much work to be done here."

-oOo-

Dunburton, Oric's former home, lay between Bayersby Manor and Roxbrough-by-the-Sea. The small village and manor house, laid to waste after an attack by marauders many moons past, remained uninhabited. Rather than risk an unfriendly encounter with itinerants that passed through the village from time to time, Ichtheus directed Oric to take a roundabout route across High Moor.

Fierce sun beat down upon Oric and Ichtheus as they descended into the valley of Nidderdale. Grassland soon replaced rough, purple heather and, arriving at the edge of Nidderdale Brook, Oric jumped down from the driver's seat. He grasped the donkey's bridle and led Braccus across the watercourse made shallow by drought.

Not far into Scraggswood Forest huge trees blotted out the sunlight. An all-pervading smell of wild garlic made Oric's eyes water, and he imagined the gloomy atmosphere to be an ideal place for robbers to lie in wait for lonely travellers. They did not venture far before Oric's worst fears were realised. An empty, overturned cart with a broken wheel blocked the pathway.

"Oh, my giddy aunt, someone has had an accident," cried Ichtheus. "Perhaps the driver lies injured hereabouts." He climbed down from his seat to search amongst the long grass around the abandoned conveyance.

Oric hastened to help with the search but, finding no-one, he tugged nervously at Ichtheus' sleeve. "Let us clear the track and be on our way. There is naught else we can do here."

"Aye, since I see no horse the fellow has probably ridden away to seek a new wheel," replied Ichtheus. "We need to put our best foot forward, for we still have a goodly distance to travel. You drive for a while, I feel like a snooze." He hitched up his long, dark-green tunic and climbed into the back of the cart. Making himself comfortable amongst the bedrolls his snores soon rivalled the birdsong.

Sleep would have been the last thing on Ichtheus' mind had he known the owner of the overturned cart, a recent victim of Figg's bullyboys, lay dead in a shallow grave not twenty paces away.

Long rays of evening sun slanted through the trees and Oric called a halt beside a chattering brook. He unhitched Braccus and tied the donkey to a tree beside a patch of juicy grass. Ichtheus unpacked food from the hamper that Dian had packed, and Oric gathered fallen twigs and branches to light a fire. They dined on chicken and boiled onions and washed their food down with a hot drink brewed from stream water and shredded mint leaves. Before retiring for the night, Oric stoked up the fire to keep wolves at bay.

Fully refreshed after an uninterrupted sleep, the two apothecaries ate a hearty breakfast of leftover chicken and resumed their journey at dawn. Late afternoon found them trouble-free on the edge of Roxbrough-by-the-Sea.

Perched on a cliff top, Roxbrough Abbey's sandstone walls glowed in golden shafts of sunlight. Below the abbey closely-packed dwellings tumbled down the hillside, the final row of wattle and daub cottages stopping short at the edge of a wide, natural harbour. Flocks of gulls wheeled starkly white against the indigo bay, their haunting cries echoing eerily back from a steep cliff face. Entranced, Oric watched small waves slap and shush onto the pebble-strewn beach. Water beyond the harbour entrance stretched as far as he could see and he imagined the ocean to be never-ending.

The tide ebbed to reveal Roxbrough's muddy harbour bottom and a multitude of sea-birds arrived to peck grubs out of the glutinous slime. A pair of black cormorants landed on the barnacle-encrusted spine of a sunken boat and hung out their wings to dry. "I heard the ocean was vast," Oric shouted above the gulls' raucous cries. "But I never imagined it to be like this."

Ichtheus breathed in the pungent smell of seaweed and grinned at Oric's delight.

A stall on the roadside promised a gift for Dian. The woman in charge offered Oric dried-herb posies, ribbons or combs but some corn dollies took his fancy. "I would like one of those," he said, pointing to three pieces of plaited corn shaped into a heart and gathered together with a red ribbon.

The woman handed the dolly over to Oric with a knowing smile. "For your sweetheart, is it?"

"Aye, mistress, it is." Oric blushed hotly, for it was the first time he had admitted out loud that he would like Dian to become more than just a good friend.

The stall holder winked boldly. "You will know that your feelings are reciprocated if the young lady pins your dolly over her heart."

Oric also purchased a blue ribbon and handed over a few coppers. If his courage failed a hair ribbon might make a less meaningful substitute for the corn dolly.

Tucking his purchases inside his pouch, Oric returned to gaze at the ocean. "I believe I could view this wondrous sight all evening, Master Ichtheus."

"Be that as it may," replied Ichtheus. "We need to find a place to lay our weary bones before nightfall."

"Can we not stay with Lady Myferny's sister?" Oric asked. "Surely she would be glad to put us up for the night."

Ichtheus rolled his eyes at the very idea. "It would take a braver man than I to stay with Mistress Elfine and her family. She has a brood of unruly children who swarm over me like a rash. I am too old to cope with such an unrelenting onslaught. Well-meaning they may be, but I prefer to stay at the inn. We shall pay Mistress Elfine a visit in the morning, before we drive up to the abbey."

Roxbrough's only inn offered reasonable accommodation and, after stabling Braccus, Oric joined his mentor inside the establishment for supper. Gutted herrings hung over an open fire and the sharp smell of smoked fish filled the room. Two fishermen, each with a pot of ale in his hand, leaned against a sturdy table. Word of a forthcoming plague of demons had spread far and wide and the fishermen eyed the two strangers suspiciously. Ichtheus nodded politely but he made no attempt to engage the men in conversation; he was far more interested in the smoked herrings the landlady served for his supper.

A ladder led Oric and Ichtheus up to the inn's loft where several pallets of straw lay in readiness for sleepy guests. Oric and Ichtheus were fast asleep when the two fishermen stumbled up the ladder and fell onto another pair of pallets at the far end of the loft.

Oric slept well and, eager to explore the seaside, he crept from his bed before anyone else awakened. Outside the inn a thick sea-fret obscured the cliffs and foreshore. Invisible in the mist the gulls' cries took on a haunting quality and, unable to see a hand in front of his face, Oric returned to the inn.

"Weather taken a turn for the worse, has it?" Ichtheus asked, observing Oric's moisture-spiked hair and damp cape.

"Conditions outdoors are fit for neither man nor beast," exclaimed the landlady. "First we endure unbearable heat and now this soggy mist descends." Removing a hot skillet from the fire she slid fillets of cod onto two wooden platters. "I would not be the least surprised if this sudden change of weather has summat to do with the Kilterton soothsayer. God knows what kind of mayhem we face if the woman is right about those demons."

"Mother Olive talks naught but nonsense." Exasperated by the landlady's ignorance, Ichtheus attacked his breakfast. "I assure you, mistress, there will be no demons." Well-fed and packed ready to go, Ichtheus paid the landlady and followed Oric outside. "Dear Lord," he exclaimed. "I can barely see past the end of my nose. 'Tis a good thing I know where Lady Myferny's sister resides, for I shall need to feel my way there."

Mistress Elfine had not married as well as her sister; nevertheless, her husband owned a fleet of fishing boats and he was wealthy in his own right. The family lived in a grand house on the hillside overlooking the bay.

Ichtheus rapped on the door. The sound was swiftly followed by a cacophony of shouting children and barking dogs. A harassed servant opened the door with one hand, whilst trying to restrain numerous children and dogs with the other. She lost her battle, and Oric and Ichtheus were immediately overwhelmed. Children vied to greet the visitors, and dogs swarmed around their feet. A puppy seized hold of Ichtheus' voluminous cloak and began to pull at it playfully. The material became entangled around the old man's feet and he tripped over.

"Oh, my giddy aunt," Ichtheus exclaimed, extending his hand to Oric for help. "Would you kindly stop that horrid little animal ravaging my clothing?"

Barely able to contain his mirth, Oric helped his mentor up, and prised the pup's sharp teeth from the hem of Ichtheus' cloak.

Ichtheus stated the reason for his visit and, followed by a gaggle of children and dogs, the maidservant led the apothecary to Mistress Elfine's chamber.

The lady of the house lay in bed, propped up by many cushions, her face as green as grass. "Good day to you, Master

Ichtheus," Elfine smiled wanly. "I suppose my husband sent word that I am unwell, and you have come to look me over."

"It seems he did," replied Ichtheus, unwinding the sticky arms of a small child from around his lower limbs.

"My husband worries overmuch, and I am afraid he has caused you an unnecessary journey." Elfine dragged her smallest offspring onto the bed, and gave Ichtheus an old-fashioned look. "I have not yet told the silly man that I am with child again. Once the sickness that goes with early pregnancy wears off, I shall be as right as rain."

Ichtheus nodded sympathetically, whilst surreptitiously counting children that hung off the bed posts, crawled about the floor, and played tug-o'-war with the dogs. Reaching number eleven, he gave up. "The best idea would be for you to contact a good midwife, my dear," he advised. "Meanwhile I shall give you something to ease the nausea."

Before Ichtheus could stop her, Elfine instructed the maidservant to make up a pair of extra beds. "You and your assistant must stay overnight, Ichtheus. We can catch up on news of my sister over dinner."

"Thank you, mistress," replied Ichtheus hastily, "but... we have not come just to see you, we are also here to visit Roxbrough Abbey."

Suddenly overcome by another wave of nausea, Elfine nodded her understanding. "Perhaps next time..." Reaching for a bowl, she vomited into it.

"There, there, dear lady," soothed Ichtheus. "Fetch a decoction of lady's mantle from the cart please, Oric. Take regular sips of the medicament, Mistress Elfine, and it will help to ease your condition."

Mist continued to swirl up from the foreshore and Ichtheus and Oric peered from left to right, wondering which way they should travel to reach the abbey. High above the town a bell began to toll and, glad of some audible guidance, the apothecaries led their donkey and cart up a steep, rutted track toward the mournful sound.

A plait of horsehair dangled beside the abbey door and Oric gave it a sharp tug. Somewhere deep within the abbey a shrill bell clanged. Moments later the massive iron-studded oak door squeaked open to reveal a monk swathed in a voluminous black habit.

"Good morning, brother," said Ichtheus, bowing as low as his aching back would allow. "I am Ichtheus the apothecary and I am here to represent Sir Edred of Bayersby. My master wishes me to discuss a matter of business with the abbot."

"I hesitate to bid you good morning, Master Ichtheus, for it is anything but," Brother Martin smiled sympathetically and ushered his damp guests into the cavernous entrance hall. "If you would care to follow me I shall guide you to our Holy Father."

"This young fellow is my assistant," said Ichtheus, responding to the gentle pressure of Oric's elbow applied to his ribs. "He is keen to learn new medicinal remedies and he would like to talk with the abbey herbalist."

"That is easily arranged," smiled Brother Martin, stopping a hosteller monk on his way to the refectory. "Please take this young man and introduce him to Brother John." Grinning from ear to ear in anticipation of an interesting morning, Oric followed the tonsured monk down a long corridor.

Brother Martin, his leather sandals slapping on the stone floor, ushered Ichtheus across damp cloisters and into the abbot's modest dwelling. A stained-glass window in the entrance hall faced what might have been a wonderful view of Roxbrough had the mist not been so thick.

The abbot, a wizened old man of indeterminate age, listened to Ichtheus' request, then shook a small bell that he lifted from a carved table by his elbow. As if he had been waiting outside the door, Brother Martin reappeared instantly. "Kindly convey a message to Father Chrispian," said the abbot, beaming happily. "I care not what he is doing – instruct him to report to my quarters immediately."

Somewhat taken aback by the abbot's enthusiasm, Ichtheus awaited the priest's arrival.

Father Chrispian came at a gallop. He had reduced the pupils under his care to a dithering state of terror, and he imagined the abbot was about to offer his congratulations.

Tall, thin and obsequious, the cleric's bald head shone like a bauble of newly-blown glass. A few whiskers that had escaped the razor's blade sprouted like black bee stings from his chin. Surprised to see a stranger in the room, he said, "You sent for me, Reverend Abbot?"

Ichtheus was not impressed with the priest; nevertheless, he inclined his head politely and explained the reason for his visit.

Upon hearing Sir Edred's generous terms Father Chrispian begged the abbot's permission to accept the offer of employment.

The abbot swiftly granted his permission. He waved Father Chrispian a cheerful goodbye and Ichtheus gained the impression that the old gentleman was pleased to see the back of his unattractive priest.

Father Chrispian disappeared to collect his belongings, and Brother Martin went in search of Oric. He returned with two friars, several boxes of samples, and Oric looking very pleased with himself.

All signs of obsequiousness left the priest the moment he set foot outside the abbey.

"You surely do not expect a person of my rank to ride upon that contraption, do you?" he protested, glaring at

Ichtheus' donkey-drawn cart.

Ichtheus shrugged indifferently. "Please yourself."

Father Chrispian cast his pale-blue eyes around for another form of transport. "What, pray, is the alternative?"

"To walk beside it," replied Ichtheus.

Having an aversion to any kind of physical activity, Father Chrispian climbed onto the cart. Looking as though he had sucked a quince, he eased his narrow backside onto the hard bench beside Ichtheus.

Oric chuckled as he hefted the priest's luggage onto the cart alongside boxes of seeds and plants. Master Ichtheus was on his high horse and there would surely be some entertaining cut-and-thrust encounters before the day was done.

Halfway across a single-track bridge that spanned the river, the cart lurched upon a deep rut. Ichtheus secured a firm grip upon his seat but Father Chrispian catapulted from his perch and, vestments flapping, he sailed over the bridge's guard rail. The incoming tide provided insufficient depth of water for swimming and he hit the riverbed's foul-smelling mud with a resounding *thwack!*

Convulsed with mirth Oric looked down upon the hapless priest. "Do you suppose we ought to help him out of his predicament, Master Ichtheus?"

"I am sorely tempted to let him float up with the incoming tide," Ichtheus muttered. "But we had best fish the fellow out before he drowns."

With the aid of a stout rope, Oric dragged the priest back onto dry ground. Saturated and covered in mud Father Chrispian dripped and ranted.

Without comment Ichtheus waited.

Eventually, the unwelcome passenger climbed back onto the cart and Ichtheus drove on.

The sun's fierce rays soon melted through the sea fret,

and Father Chrispian's muddy clothes steamed, and stank. He dabbed at his nose with a soggy square of linen. "When I meet my new employer," he bleated, "I shall inform him of your gross incompetence."

Ichtheus remained impervious.

At the end of a very long day, Oric and Ichtheus spread out their remaining food. Father Chrispian ate more than his share, then helped himself to both bed rolls. His complaints continued long after Oric and Ichtheus lay down on the bare ground to sleep.

Father Chrispian continued in much the same vein the next morning and Ichtheus was relieved when St Griswald's bell tower came into view. He drew the cart to a halt in front of the manse and turned to face the priest. "Here we are, Father," he said. "This is your new home."

Red blotches spread across Father Chrispian's pale cheeks. "First I am confronted with your wretched conveyance, then I am obliged to spend a night outdoors with little more than a moth-eaten blanket on which to sleep. Now you have the audacity to suggest that I take up residence in this ghastly hovel. Oh, no! I think not!"

To avoid further upset, Ichtheus drove the priest to Bayersby Manor and handed him over to Sir Edred. Having no desire to share the same roof as Father Chrispian for a moment longer than necessary, Ichtheus determined that the manse would be refurbished as soon as possible – even if he had to tackle the job himself.

Chapter Five

Father Chrispian

Oric stumbled out of bed and joined Ichtheus at the breakfast table. "All thanks to my meeting with the Roxbrough friars I barely slept a wink," he said, rubbing his eyes. "My head is in danger of bursting with information."

Ichtheus hid his smile behind the parchment he was reading. "Would you care to share your newfound knowledge with me? After all we do not want to put your poor head at risk, do we?"

Oblivious to his mentor's teasing tone, Oric chattered enthusiastically. "Stinking Gladwin is a plant I have always avoided because of its loathsome odour, but the good friars have assured me the plant has excellent qualities." He got off the bench and began pacing up and down. "For example – juice pressed from the leaves will diminish lesions." Oric pulled up his right sleeve to reveal a scar of puckered, silver-grey skin on his forearm. "I plan to experiment on myself and, if the potion proves successful, I will use the treatment to help other similarly disfigured folk."

Ichtheus touched the damaged area on Oric's arm. The

boy had warded off a blow intended for Sir Edred during the battle with Esica Figg's mercenary soldiers, and Ichtheus silently thanked God for his assistant's deliverance. "You were exceedingly brave, Oric. 'Tis thanks to you that our lord and master is still with us."

"Think nothing of it, Master Ichtheus," replied Oric brushing off the compliment. "I am sure you would have done the same had you been in my place."

Dian banged a bowl of gruel on the table. "There you go, belittling yourself again! We are proud of you and I believe you richly deserve the piece of silver and the small plot of land Sir Edred awarded you." She smacked her apron straight and stormed off.

Embarrassed by the attention, Oric returned to his seat. His courage rarely failed him, so why did the corn dolly he had purchased for Dian at Roxbrough-by-the-Sea still remain in his pouch? He had given her the less meaningful blue ribbon, which she was now using to tie back her curls.

To cover his confusion Oric attacked his breakfast. "Dyer's weed is another botanical specimen I plan to establish in my garden," he mumbled, his mouth full of hot gruel. "The friars told me that the plant protects against plague and pestilence, and they gave me some cuttings to plant."

A fever epidemic had carried off Oric's parents when he was a small boy and he was keen to develop a remedy that might save lives in the future. He pushed his empty bowl to one side and wiped his mouth with the back of his hand. "And I learned something that might interest the Bayersby dairymen."

Ichtheus gave up trying to read his parchment. "What might that be?"

"No doubt you will know the plant as medick fetch, Master Ichtheus, but it is also known as cocks head or red fitching. 'Tis said it improves milk yield if added to cattle fodder. I am hoping that Sir Edred will allow me to raise an experimental crop on his land."

"Sir Edred is always keen to boost his dairy yield. I am sure he will be interested in what you have to say." Ichtheus arose from the table. "But right now 'tis time we started work. We have a lot of medicaments to concoct."

"Please could you spare me until noon?" Oric begged. "My new plants must be dug into the ground or they will not survive."

"Yes, yes, of course! I had forgotten you still had a cart full of greenery to deal with." Ichtheus flapped his hands. "Run along! I can manage without you this morning."

On his way out Oric helped Dian carry dirty breakfast bowls to the well for washing. "Would you care to see how my plot is faring?" he asked as he wound up a bucket of icy water from the depths. "I would like you to see what I have achieved so far."

"Indeed I would," replied Dian. "But I doubt I can get away from the manor so early in the day. If Lady Myferny does not need me, Mother Morghan always finds extra chores for me in the kitchen." She smiled wistfully. "But I will do my best to escape later."

Oric's quarter-acre plot lay on the edge of High Moor. Scrubby and hard, the ground had required much work and barrow-loads of rotted humus to improve the soil. In the beginning Sir Edred's flock of sheep had eaten many of the new plants and, to keep the animals at bay, Oric had surrounded the garden with a wall of stones gathered from the moor. In the near future he planned to construct a small hut, for he needed a peaceful place to experiment with new medicaments. A pile of timber lay stacked in readiness inside the garden wall. All Oric needed was time to build.

Arriving at the garden gate with a hand cart full of plants, Oric's heart missed a beat.

Several rows of established herbs lay roots up on top of the soil. He dropped the bundle of stakes and roll of sack-cloth he carried and vaulted over the wall to investigate the damage. Sheep were certainly not to blame; nor could he point a finger at moles, for there were no tell-tale piles of earth. Closer inspection indicated that a two-legged vandal had caused the damage, for there were footprints all over the newly-turned soil.

The morning wore on and the sun blazed down. Lathered in sweat, Oric stripped off his wet tunic and continued to dig. By mid-morning his uprooted plants were back in the ground along with the new herbs supplied by Roxbrough's friars. Pleased with his efforts, Oric lay down his tools and rested his sun-burned back against the rough garden wall.

Blue-black swallows swooped low, catching insects on the wing. Bees buzzed about, sipping nectar from dainty blossoms of pink ling and, in the distance, bell-heather drifted hazy purple colours across the moor.

In a soporific mood Oric's thoughts strayed to the key that remained hidden alongside Master Ichtheus' valuables in a box under Braccus' stall. Oric deemed his promise to Deveril to keep the key safe was fulfilled but, thus far, he had failed to unravel the mystery that surrounded it. Thanks to his former mentor, Oric had learned to read and write and, as a result, he had landed his position with Master Ichtheus. Fond though he was of his new mentor, he still missed Deveril and the desire to revenge his death weighed heavily on Oric's mind.

Shaking off his melancholy, Oric returned to work. He erected a framework with the stakes he had brought and tacked on sackcloth to shade his seedlings from the searing midday sun. A nearby spring provided water and Oric lugged bucketfuls to soak each plant. The job finished he took a long draught to quench his thirst, then he tipped all that was left of the cold water over his head.

Dian's rosy face appeared above the warm stones atop the wall. "Where are you, Oric?"

"Over here," Oric called, hastily donning his soggy tunic. "You managed to get away, then?"

"Not exactly." Dian's dimples appeared in a comical grimace. "Father Chrispian sent me to fetch you. He is madder than a cat in a sack."

"Why should the priest be mad at me?" Oric spluttered. "I have done naught to ruffle his fur!"

"Oh, 'tis not you that has caused the upset, 'tis Mother Morghan." Dian smothered a fit of giggles behind a corner of her apron. "The priest called her a lazy, good-for-nothing slattern, and threatened to report her to Sir Edred if she fails to mend her ways." Dian's giggles turned into guffaws of laughter. "Mother Morghan made such peculiar choking noises I thought she was about to take a fit."

Oric did not immediately see the funny side "So? What does the priest want with me?"

"He wants you to collect up tools, hasten to St Griswald's manse and make it habitable right away." Dian wiped her streaming eyes. "He says his actions may well become a hanging offence if he spends many more moons beneath the same roof as Mother Morghan."

At last Oric saw the joke and he burst into laughter. He grabbed Dian around the waist and twirled her around his garden until her homespun skirt billowed out around her ankles. She missed her footing, stumbled, and fell against his chest. Oric longed to hold her close; instead he made an inane remark about Mother Morghan's likely demise at the hands of the priest and the moment of intimacy was lost.

They returned to Bayersby in relative silence, neither one knowing how to broach the uncomfortable situation.

-oOo-

Ichtheus peered at Oric and Dian over the pile of household goods that blocked access into the Bayersby kitchen. "Thank God you are back, I can never find a spare serf when I need one. For goodness' sake help me to shift this lot, for I can neither come nor go."

"Where do you want it putting?" Oric asked, scratching his head in perplexity.

"In the cart!" Ichtheus harrumphed furiously. "I doubt Lady Myferny imagined the priest would be so needy when she suggested he take from the manor whatever he desired to make St Griswald's manse habitable."

Oric eyed the mountain of furniture, tapestries and books. "Does anything of worth remain inside the Great Hall?"

Muttering about the priest's selfish attitude, Ichtheus squeezed through the gap that Oric made. "You had best harness both donkeys, for we shall need two carts to carry all these goods – not to mention the tools we require to effect repairs upon the manse."

Oric groaned. Two carts meant he would have to use the little donkey he had acquired from a rich merchant in exchange for medications. He had tried and failed to hitch Otty to a cart several times and bore bruises as testimony. "Can we not make do with just one cart and a couple of panniers?" Oric wheedled.

"No we cannot!" Ichtheus disappeared into a nearby shed whereupon bangs and crashes issued from within. After

a few moments he reappeared with his arms full of tools. "If we are to deliver Father Chrispian's home comforts this side of Yuletide a second conveyance is essential."

Resigned to his task Oric changed into a rough, belted tunic and pulled on clean leggings. With no time to clean his filthy boots, he rammed his feet into a pair of wooden clogs. He rounded up the two donkeys and backed Braccus between the shafts of the first cart. He loaded up with the tools Master Ichtheus had dropped on the ground and added a few of Father Chrispian's household effects on top.

Nodding his approval, Ichtheus fastened his cloak tightly under his chin, and climbed upon the driver's seat. At the click of his driver's tongue, Braccus set off at a smart trot. "Make haste, boy," Ichtheus shouted over his shoulder as he hurtled through the compound gates. "I shall expect to see you at St Griswald's shortly."

Having seen Braccus harnessed to the first cart, Oric hoped Otty might be less skittish. He grasped her halter firmly and, issuing gentle commands, he guided her backwards. Nearing the loaded cart, Otty shied away from what she perceived to be some kind of monster.

In the nearby kitchen garden Dian picked vegetables. She waved a bunch of freshly-harvested carrots and shouted, "Hey, Oric – try distracting the little beast with some of these."

Whilst Otty munched on her juicy treat, Oric carefully pushed the cart toward her rear end. *All well and good,* he thought, securing Otty's harness to the shafts. *All I need to do now is to persuade the wretched animal to move forward.*

Dian placed more carrots in a loosely-woven basket and secured it to the end of a long pole. She carried the contraption to where Oric stood beside the donkey. "Climb up on the driver's bench," she urged.

Oric climbed aboard, trying not to spook the donkey by rocking the cart.

Dian handed the pole with the carrots up to Oric. "Dangle the basket in front of the donkey's nose. She will see them and walk forward to try and seize a mouthful. Thus she will pull the cart along without realising what she is doing."

"I am not so sure about this," said Oric, securing one end of the pole to his driver's seat. Safely fastened, he manoeuvred the basket of carrots between Otty's ears as if he were after a fish.

Otty spotted the carrots immediately and, greedy for more, she lunged forward.

The unexpected jolt threw Oric backwards from his seat. His legs shot in the air and both wooden clogs fell from his feet and crashed down on top of his head. The donkey, her neck stretched to its full extent, careered through the compound gates in pursuit of the carrots. Oric scrambled to gain a handhold on the cart and clung on for dear life.

"Oh dear Lord!" Dian cried. Afraid that Oric may be injured she picked up her skirts and hastened after the runaway donkey.

The braying donkey fled past a herd of cattle, scattering them in all directions. "You stupid dolt," yelled an attendant dairyman. "I shall report you to Sir Edred for reckless driving."

Scarlet with effort and embarrassment, Oric clawed his way back to the driver's seat just as the basket of carrots broke free from the pole and fell to the ground.

Otty stopped dead.

Oric flew through the air and landed in a heap beside the fallen basket.

Stepping over Oric, Otty gobbled up the spilled carrots.

"Are you alright?" Dian cried, puffing hard after her sprint.

Oric remained supine whilst he checked for broken bones. Satisfied that he was still intact he replied, "Aye, I think I might live."

The only damage done was to Oric's dignity and when Dian saw that he was unhurt she fell about laughing. "I never dreamed my ruse would have such an instant effect on your donkey."

Oric battled to still his trembling legs. "Remarkably, I am still in one piece – though I doubt my nerves will stand a repeat performance." He unhitched Otty from the cart and handed the reins to Dian. "Kindly lead the donkey back to the manor while I drag the cartload of supplies."

Mother Morghan watched the maid, the donkey, and the apothecary's assistant with the cart in tow cross the compound. "What mischief have you pair been about?" she yelled from the kitchen doorway. The housekeeper was more agitated than usual, for she had been unable to warn Figg of the priest's imminent move into St Griswald's manse. "And what are you doing with all that stuff?"

"Father Chrispian wants it transporting to St Griswald's manse," said Oric, abandoning his loaded cart against the manor wall. "The donkey bolted. I must now fetch Braccus back from St Griswald's to shift the rest of the priest's furniture."

Mother Morgan paled at Oric's words. Father Chrispian clearly intended to move to the manse sooner than she anticipated. Playing for time, she screeched, "If yon stiff-necked preacher thinks he can claim all those items for his new abode he had best think again." Without further ado she marched into the kitchen and reappeared moments later with a couple of burly serfs. "Take all this stuff back to the Great Hall at once." Arms folded across her heaving bosom, Mother Morghan glowered at Oric. "And if yon poxy priest dares to object, refer him to me!" For all her bravado

Mother Morghan quaked as she imagined the upset if the current occupants of St Griswald's crypt returned to find Father Chrispian in residence. She fervently hoped that a manse with precious little furniture would delay Father Chrispian's occupation, and gain her some much-needed time to warn Figg.

Oric strapped a pair of panniers to Otty's back, loaded them with the few small items that had escaped Mother Morghan's notice, and added his own clogs. Father Chrispian would be vexed over his pruned home comforts, but Oric was past caring what the priest thought. He swung into the saddle and, freed from the troublesome cart, the little donkey moved forward without a qualm.

Oric and Otty entered St Griswald's Churchyard in time to see Ichtheus unload the last few items from the first cart. "Where have you been?" he demanded crossly. "I thought you must have lost your way." His gaze fell upon the paniers. "What happened to the second cart?"

"Suffice to say that Otty is no use between the shafts." Oric put on his clogs and tethered the jenny to a tree. "Just be thankful that I am here at all."

"Foolish boy," replied Ichtheus waspishly. "Now you must take Braccus and the cart back to the manor to collect Father Chrispian's furniture."

Oric's blue eyes sparkled with ill-concealed merriment. "There is naught there to collect, for Mother Morghan had two serfs return almost everything to the Great Hall. If Father Chrispian attempts to claw anything back, I doubt he will see the light of another day."

Ichtheus chortled. "For once I am in agreement with Mother Morghan – but right now we had best get started on some repair work else we shall be here for the duration."

Inside the manse Oric was taken aback to see evidence

of a recent fire on the central hearth. Remnants of food littered a worm-eaten table, and a ragged cloak lay draped over the only chair. He gagged at the smell, and hairs on the back of his neck stood on end as he recalled the rumour of a witch burned in St Griswald's Churchyard. Perhaps the old woman had returned to haunt the manse. Oric darted outside and voiced his fears to Master Ichtheus.

"Passing itinerants are the most likely culprits," Ichtheus returned a little too hastily. He had also witnessed ghostly apparitions in St Griswald's Churchyard in the not too distant past and, having no desire to delay Father Chrispian's departure from Bayersby Manor, he had not mentioned his unpleasant experience to the priest.

Mollified by Ichtheus' explanation, Oric cleared the manse of debris. He dragged the shabby chair and table outside, topped them with a ragged bundle of clothing, and set the pile alight; meanwhile, Ichtheus banged nails into the broken manse door and declared it fixed. Together they carried the pieces of furniture Ichtheus had brought from Bayersby Manor and placed them inside the manse. With so few home comforts Ichtheus worried that the priest might refuse to move in.

Twilight shadowed the churchyard, and Ichtheus downed his tools. "That will suffice for today, Oric. If we continue at our current pace we should accomplish the repairs sooner than we anticipated." The dank manse gave Ichtheus the creeps and he was keen to return to Bayersby's cosy kitchen before nightfall.

"I doubt we shall finish ahead of time unless Sir Edred sends a carpenter and stonemason to help us," Oric added dolefully.

"I am sure he will." Ichtheus sounded more confident than he felt. Sir Edred was notoriously absent-minded, especially when horses were not involved.

A sudden breeze rattled the dry branches of a copper-beech tree and Ichtheus shivered despite the warm evening. "Let us be on our way, lad. 'Tis almost supper time and my belly is banging on my backbone."

-oOo-

Hersica spent the afternoon foraging for wild mushrooms, stealing turnips from Sir Edred's fields and checking her snares. A brace of hares, along with the vegetables she had collected, would make a fine supper for Figg and his men. Nearing St Griswald's Church Hersica caught a whiff of acrid smoke. She approached with caution and peeped over the churchyard wall. A bonfire burned in front of the manse. Hersica waited and watched, but no-one came to tend the fire. Upon closer inspection, she saw that her meagre possessions had been set alight. In a panic she fetched water from the churchyard well to douse the flames, but she was too late to save a single item.

Another day of thieving drew to a close and Figg, accompanied by his henchmen, returned to St Griswald's. He left his men to feed and water their horses whilst he transported the day's haul into the crypt.

Hersica Horzefell galloped down the crypt stairs. "Master Figg! Master Figg! Something terrible has happened."

"Ye gods," cried Figg. "What ails you, Mistress Horzefell?"

"Me few sticks of furniture, me cloak and me spare kirtle is smouldering on the pathway outside the manse door."

Figg smiled thinly. "Really?" He could think of no better end for the woman's unsavoury possessions.

"Not only that – all kinds of tools and household goods are lying within the house." Hersica's sallow face wrinkled in consternation. "I reckon someone intends to move in."

Taken aback, Figg paced around Hersica. "Are you sure?"

"Of course I am sure!" Hersica grabbed at Figg's sleeve. "For Heaven's sake, cease prowling round me, man, you are making me dizzy. I ain't stopping in the manse no more; from now on I shall be sharing quarters with you lot."

Bertram, one of Figg's bullyboys, entered the crypt in time to hear Hersica's threat. "Gawd help us," he snarled. "For the love of all that's holy, woman, can you not sleep outside amongst the graves? You smell like a rotting corpse and will cause them no offence."

Hersica kicked at the man's shins. "Hold yer whisht – you lot ain't perfumed like no bunch of violets, neither." She raised her knee and made swinging motions back and forth with her foot. "If anybody else makes nasty remarks about me he will get my boot up his arse."

Returned to the crypt, the other robbers tittered nervously. Many of them had been on the receiving end of Hersica's ill humour and they were pleased to see someone else getting the rough side of her tongue for a change.

"Be silent, woman!" Figg roared, his mind in turmoil. "Why has Mother Morghan not reported this new development?"

"She ain't been here lately," said Hersica. "Perhaps she knows nowt about it."

A nervous tic twitched at the corner of Figg's eye. "Who in God's name would want to move into that filthy old manse? Besides, folk hereabouts believe the place is haunted – they are afraid to come anywhere near." He steepled his fingers thoughtfully, and then cracked each knuckle separately. "Nevertheless, methinks it might be wise to seek quarters elsewhere."

Unable to face another dollop of yesterday's rancid stew, Ned bit into a raw onion. Juice sprayed into his eyes and tears streamed down his cheeks. "Why can we not remain here, Master Figg?"

"Because, you imbecile, our hiding place is in danger of being discovered," Figg thundered.

"Not if we shift into the other half of the crypt," suggested Ned, wiping his drippy nose down the length of his sleeve.

Figg boxed the boy's ears. "What are you babbling about?"

The blow sent Ned reeling, and he crashed into his friend, Joe. Both boys sprawled on the floor in a heap. As they struggled to their feet, a crumpled sheet of parchment slid from beneath Ned's tunic.

"You thieving little turd," screamed Figg, snatching up the parchment. "This belongs to me!" He hauled Ned to his feet by the scruff of his neck. "Where did you find it?"

Ned tittered nervously. "You dropped it, Master Figg. I have been looking after it for you – I just kept forgetting to give it back."

"Damn your eyes, I thought the document lost." Blinded by fury, Figg grabbed a branch of firewood from the hearth, and began to thrash the boy.

Joe leapt upon Figg's back, beating him about the head and shoulders with his small fists. "Leave Ned be or I will kill you."

Everyone joined in. Dust flew and blood spurted as the inhabitants of the crypt punched and kicked, releasing days of pent-up aggression and anxiety.

"Stop it! Stop it at once!" shrieked Hersica. "Do you want to fetch the entire district here to investigate the ruckus?" She grabbed two of the assailants by their hair and dragged them apart. "We stand little chance of defeating Sir Edred if we squabble amongst ourselves."

"The woman is right," agreed Figg, his reason returning. "If we are to achieve our aim we must all pull together." He threw down the branch, and kicked Ned's backside. "If you wish to save your miserable skin, boy, I suggest you show me the 'other half' of the crypt immediately."

Ned pushed through a tangle of discarded religious paraphernalia, and beckoned Figg to follow.

"If this is a ruse to avoid punishment I shall cut off your ears and feed them to the crows," threatened Figg.

"Why would I lie to you, Master Figg?" Ned yanked aside a tapestry to reveal a narrow door in the wall. Beyond lay another, smaller space. "I never mentioned the secret place 'cos you never asked."

Figg took a turn around the room. The area was small, but it would suffice for the time being. A steep flight of steps led up to a door in the far wall. "What lies beyond yonder entrance?"

"Only an overgrown section of graveyard at the rear of the church," said Joe. "I reckon the door is there to provide an escape for any priest needing to clear off in a hurry." Keen to ingratiate himself, he babbled on. "And there is an underground passage that me and Ned found under the inglenook fireplace in the Bayersby Manor kitchen."

Ned gesticulated for Joe to shut his mouth, but he was too late to silence his friend. In an effort to gain something from Joe's careless confession, he sidled up to Figg with his hand outstretched. "More information should be worth a copper or two. What say you, Master Figg?"

"I think not!" Figg had more than a passing interest in the tunnel, but he had no intention of allowing the boys to know how keen he felt. He curled his fingers over and inspected his nails nonchalantly. "Do you know where this tunnel ends?"

"Aye, it leads into a cave on the hillside below Bayersby Manor." Believing his chance of gaining a reward was gone, Ned curried favour. "The entrance is hidden by thick vines and I doubt anyone knows of its existence."

Figg struggled to remain expressionless. A secret passage that afforded access to Bayersby Manor was nothing short of a godsend.

Left to his own devices, Figg smoothed out the parchment. He thought it, and the black powder he carried in pouches around his waist, had once belonged to Deveril, the Dunburton alchemist. He now believed he held the recipe and the substance for making gold. Unable to find a trustworthy Latin-speaking translator, he had experimented with a small amount of the substance. A spectacular and fiery eruption had occurred. Once recovered from the shock, Figg began to devise ways of making better use of his find. The parchment was clearly not the recipe he hoped for – but what was it? One day he would find a trustworthy scholar to look at it, but his need for a translation was no longer quite so urgent.

Everyone settled into the second half of the crypt, the small space made tighter by the addition of Figg's locked, plunder-filled boxes. To ensure his employees' continued loyalty, Figg reiterated his promise to distribute generous rewards and positions of rank, once Sir Edred was dead. Life returned to normal and Figg's men continued to rob unsuspecting travellers.

Hersica sloped off into the woods and, left on his own in the crypt, Figg filled a bucket with drinking-water. A small iron grill in the stone wall afforded him a clear view of the graveyard and he perched on a stool in front of it. No longer willing to rely on Mother Morghan for information, he intended to stay put until he discovered who was about to move into St Griswald's manse.

-oOo-

Sir Edred promised to send a carpenter and stonemason to address the structural damage to St Griswald's Church and manse, but neither tradesman materialised.

Keen to get the job done and Father Chrispian out of their domain, Oric and Ichtheus continued to tackle repairs to the manse as best they could. Later in the morning Father Chrispian joined them. He perched on a gravestone like a gaunt bird of prey and read aloud from his Bible in a reedy voice. At noon he helped himself to Oric and Ichtheus' lunch. Replete, the priest returned to his stone perch, and continued to read from his Bible until Oric felt inclined to throttle him.

Around mid-afternoon, the distant sound of hoof beats caused Father Chrispian to change tack. He leaped down from the gravestone, picked up a handful of earth and smeared his face and clothes with dirt. Grubby from head to foot, he snatched up a spade and began to dig as if the devil were on his tail.

"Has yon fellow taken leave of his senses?" Oric mouthed.

Ichtheus shrugged. "I care not what he is about – just so long as he remains silent, though I know not why he is digging."

A few heartbeats later Guwain and Sir Edred rode into the churchyard.

Father Chrispian stretched, clutched his back and emitted a melodramatic groan.

Delighted with the repairs to the exterior of his property, Sir Edred sang the priest's praises. "The manse is a credit to you, Father, it seems I have two workers rolled into one: a priest and a handyman. And well done to you Master Ichtheus and Oric for aiding Father Chrispian so willingly. No doubt the church is next on your list of jobs to do."

Guwain smirked. "I am pleased to see our cleric is keeping you busy, Oric."

Father Chrispian preened and simpered. "Yes indeed, my assistants are bowing to my superior knowledge." He waved his spade in an off-hand manner. "However, when one is engaged in holy endeavour, the pursuit of honest toil is no hardship."

"Well said!" Guwain's saddle creaked as he eased himself into a more comfortable position. He looked every inch the gentleman in his kid boots and fancy riding gear. Directing another smirk at Oric he added, "Servants need to be busy at all times; honest toil is the best way to keep underlings out of mischief."

Oric coloured up but he held his tongue. This was not the time nor the place to cross swords with the Bayersby heir.

Father Chrispian graciously accepted an invitation to join Sir Edred for dinner. He threw down the spade, brushed himself off and clambered onto Braccus' back. Without a backward glance he followed after Guwain and Sir Edred.

"That crafty preacher must have known Sir Edred planned to pay us a visit this afternoon," Oric grumbled. "And, since he has seen fit to commandeer one of our donkeys, I must now walk home."

Ichtheus patted his assistant on the back. "Take heart, lad. A moderate amount of work will see the job finished despite the lack of a carpenter and stonemason. We shall be rid of Father Chrispian very soon."

-oOo-

From his hidey-hole, Figg watched the apothecaries depart and stretched his cramped limbs. Relieved to escape the stuffy crypt, he wandered across the churchyard to perch on the gravestone that Father Chrispian had recently vacated. Figg did not see the priest as a great threat; nevertheless, the man had to go.

Chapter Six

Mother Morghan Takes Fright

Sir Edred and Lady Myferny entered the Great Hall, to see Father Chrispian and a gaggle of other diners already seated at the breakfast table. Hoping to avoid another lecture on her servants' inadequacies, Lady Myferny chose a place as far away from the priest as possible. Though her stomach rumbled with hunger, etiquette decreed that she wait for the priest to be served first.

Father Chrispian blessed the platter of bread and honey that Dian placed before him, and then set about the food with indecent haste.

"When are you proposing to leave us, Father?" Lady Myferny's practised smile blunted the sharpness of her words.

Father Chrispian scooped a drizzle of honey from his chin, and eyed the flaxen-haired woman with distaste. "I shall depart immediately after breakfast, my lady." He did not hold with the finery well-to-do women draped upon themselves, and this lady was no exception. Father Chrispian believed that wearing jewels and embroidered kirtles was ungodly, especially at breakfast time. All women would be dressed in sack cloth if Father Chrispian had his way. As for the Bayersby household – it could not be further from his taste. He could barely wait to get away from the noise and smelly humanity that lived therein. The huge wolfhound that skulked around, gobbling up every morsel of food that fell to the floor, should be chained to a post outdoors. Father Chrispian never missed an opportunity to kick the unsavoury creature whenever Sir Edred's back was turned. Parzifal suffered the painful assaults, but his patience was wearing thin.

Dian placed a bowl of apples on the table beside her mistress, and Lady Myferny caught hold of the maid's arm. "Please accompany Father Chrispian when he leaves for the manse," she murmured. "Make sure that all is well. If his new quarters are clean and comfortable he will be less likely to return to the manor."

"Just as well he is about to leave, my lady," chuckled Dian. "If Father Chrispian stays here much longer I reckon Parzifal will take a chunk out of him."

Dian skipped downstairs to the kitchen. "He is going, he is going!" she cried, jumping up and down with delight.

Ichtheus put down the pannikin of elderflowers, nightshade and boiled coltsfoot he was mixing. "Who is going where, child?"

"Yon horrid priest," Dian trilled, "is leaving for St Griswald's as soon as he finishes his breakfast."

A tidal wave of relief engulfed Ichtheus. "Praise the Lord! Oriiiiic – where are you?"

The contents of the basket Oric carried rattled as he put his load down on the flagstones. Water dripped from the front of his grey workaday tunic. "I have been washing these flagons as you asked, Master Ichtheus. What would you like me to do next?"

"Saddle Braccus as quickly as you can. Father Chrispian plans to leave the manor immediately after breakfast." Ichtheus rolled his eyes. "I doubt our unsavoury guest will want to walk to St Griswald's and we certainly do not want to delay his departure."

"But we have not yet finished the repairs to the priest's dwelling," wailed Oric.

"You are capable of completing the few chores that remain around the manse." Ichtheus put on an innocent face. "Besides – Dian tells me that she is to help with the final clean-up of the priest's quarters. When you are done, you can both bring back the donkey with the cart and our tools."

The chance to spend time alone with Dian was a great incentive and Oric ran outside to do as Ichtheus asked.

An old saddle hung on the stable wall and, in the spur of the moment, Oric lifted it down. He wiped away a tangle of cobwebs, strapped the worn saddle onto Braccus' back and hid the good saddle behind a bundle of straw.

Father Chrispian sauntered out of the manor with a pile of books balanced under his chin, and a rolled-up tapestry under one arm. He dropped the books into one of Braccus' panniers and thrust the tapestry at Oric. "Let us be on our way, boy." Mounting Braccus, Father Chrispian wriggled around, his bony knees almost reaching his chin. "I do not recall being this uncomfortable when last I rode this beast," he snapped. "Is this wretched saddle not adjustable?"

Lies tripped easily from Oric's tongue. "The usual saddle is away being repaired and the stirrups on this replacement are as low as they will go." Oric hid a smirk behind the rolled tapestry. "Look upon the discomfort as a penance to strengthen your immortal soul, Father."

Tittering over Father Chrispian's plight, Oric and Dian dawdled on foot behind the donkey and his reluctant rider. No longer able to hear the priest's tirade, they enjoyed each other's company. Oric debated whether or not to take hold of Dian's hand and eventually used the excuse of helping her over a section of poor track. Once past the corrugations Dian showed no inclination to let go of Oric's fingers. Sir Edred's pastures soon gave way to pine-scented woodlands, and they were both disappointed when St Griswald's grim bell tower came into view.

Inside the manse Dian swept the floor, and polished the few pieces of furniture Father Chrispian had managed to commandeer from Bayersby Manor. Oric hung the priest's tapestry on the wall, and used his hammer to knock wooden pegs into the last few timber planks that had broken free from the interior framework of the building. He had already filled outdoor cracks between the rocks with wattle and daub, and the manse was now relatively draught free and waterproof. Golden sunshine warmed the grey stone walls, and white daisies had popped up amongst the newly-scythed grass. One or two of the burial mounds sprouted blue forget-me-nots, making the headstones appear less sinister. And St Griswald's ivy-clad bell tower did not look quite so grim in broad daylight.

Dian folded up her pile of grubby cloths and collected the broom. When she emerged from the manse Oric was waiting for her.

"Well timed," he said. "The cart is hitched, the tools are aboard and Braccus is ready to go. Throw your things in the back and let us be gone before Father Chrispian finds more jobs for us to do."

"I hope we never set eyes on yon pasty-faced cleric again," Dian grunted as she hauled herself up onto the cart's bench. "He is a truly horrible man. Let us forget him and talk of other things." She slid across the driver's seat, closer to Oric. "Have you any new projects now your work at St Griswald's is done?"

"Aye," replied Oric, smacking the reins on Braccus' back. "If Master Ichtheus can spare me from the manor from time to time, I plan to build a hut on my plot of land." He glanced longingly at Dian. He did not want to discuss mundane things, he wanted to share his true feelings. *But what if Dian does not feel the same?* he thought. *She may have her sights set higher than a mere apothecary. The lass is bonny enough to attract any fellow she sets her heart upon.* Unable to bear the idea of rejection Oric decided to play things safe, and promote a strong friendship rather than court romance – for the time being.

-oOo-

The evening meal over, Ichtheus attended Sir Edred for his daily chat in the Great Hall. Logs smouldered on the open hearth, making the atmosphere uncomfortably smoky. *The sooner an inglenook fireplace with a proper chimney is installed in the Great Hall, the better,* thought Ichtheus. But he could not envisage such renovations happening any time soon. Sir Edred was inclined toward parsimony – unless the expenditure involved his horses.

Only two items were on the lord's agenda: Father Chrispian's ability to persuade folk that Mother Olive's demons were not going to appear and annihilate the entire population of Kilterton and Bayersby; to get the villagers to attend the priest's services without exercising brute force.

"It will prove no easy task," Ichtheus admitted, preparing himself for a lengthy tirade from the lord. "Father Chrispian has not endeared himself to local folk and I doubt they will listen to anything he has to say."

Sir Edred glowered at his apothecary. "Why so? The man appears to be approachable, not to mention kind and understanding; yet you say he is unpopular."

That Sir Edred had failed to notice Father Chrispian's peculiarities did not surprise Ichtheus, for the wily priest had not put a foot wrong in the lord's presence. Battling a smoke-induced coughing fit, Ichtheus said nothing. Had he realised the effect the priest was about to have on nobility, villeins and serfs alike, he would have been at his wit's end.

Meanwhile the Bayersby servants went about their own business and the kitchen became unusually quiet. The inglenook fire blazed at the end of the room despite the summer heat, and the cook would soon reappear to begin preparations for the main meal of the day. Oric seized the rare moment of solitude to take another look at the substance he had scraped from the bottom of Deveril's iron box. He removed the pouch that contained the black powder from his medicine chest and trickled a small fistful into a wooden dish. Wondering if his *Apothecaries' Almanac* might contain information on the subject, Oric ran his finger down the index, looking for anything that pertained to black powder. Intent upon his task, he failed to hear Guwain sneak up from behind.

"What a boring book worm you are," sneered Guwain, clattering a pair of boots onto the table. "Since you appear to have nothing better to do, you can clean my footwear."

Oric almost jumped out of his skin.

"Got a guilty conscience, have we?" Guwain challenged, looking to pick a fight.

"You startled me, Master Guwain." In a hurry to return the powder to its pouch, Oric spilled a little on the tabletop.

Dian entered the kitchen with a basketful of mending, and Guwain swiftly lost interest in Oric. "Methinks I shall take a walk by the river. Come with me, wench," he demanded. He had developed a keen fancy for the girl and he wanted to get her to himself.

Dian bobbed a hasty curtsey. "Alas, sir, I cannot spare the time at present, for I am busy with tasks for your mother."

Much as he would like to dally with the maid, Guwain had no wish to incur his mother's ire. Leaving Dian to her work, he bounded back to the Great Hall. A game of dice with his father's squires would probably cause a good deal less trouble.

Frustrated by his inability to spare Dian from Guwain's unwanted advances, Oric vented his fury by hurling the heir's boots under the table. He would clean them later.

The log fire, kept alight day and night to cook food for the dining room, made temperatures in the kitchen almost unbearable. Beads of sweat glistened on Oric's face, and he prayed that the bothersome weather conditions were nothing to do with Mother Olive's market-day prophecy. Tired with the worry of it all, he found a cooler spot near the kitchen door and returned to his *Apothecaries' Almanac*.

His meeting with Sir Edred over, Ichtheus returned to the kitchen and was gratified to see his assistant engrossed in a book. He was not so pleased to see Mother Morghan enter through the outside door.

The housekeeper gave Oric a spiteful jab as she sidled past him. "You lazy, good-for-nothing boy. Can you not find something more useful to do than bury your nose in a book?" Her unsteady gait indicated that she had imbibed a drop too much liquor. She had sought out Esica Figg with news of Father Chrispian's move into the manse and, late with the information, Figg had abused her up hill and down dale. To drown her sorrows Mother Morghan had supped a drop too much of Hersica's home made blackberry wine.

"Yon housekeeper looks rougher than a badger's backside," said Oric, snapping shut his *Almanac* in disgust. "I am off before the woman causes trouble."

"Aye, very wise, lad." Ichtheus changed out of his daytime clothes and shrugged into a voluminous nightshirt. "Methinks I shall retire to my bed."

Not yet ready for sleep, Oric beckoned for Dian to join him at the far end of the gloomy kitchen. Often too busy to talk to each other during the day, they had taken to chatting for a while before they retired to their respective sleeping places.

Twilight faded into a moonless night and Mother Morghan set up several beeswax candles. The taper she used to light them singed her fingers and she dropped the spill, still aflame, onto the table. A streak of fire crackled and spat across the tabletop.

"Lord preserve us," Mother Morgan howled, leaping back in alarm. "What kind of sorcery is this?" In her haste to escape the flames she tripped over her own feet and tumbled backwards onto the flagstones.

Oric hastily smothered the fire with an empty sack, his heart hammering against his ribcage as he tried to assimilate the spectacle he had just observed.

Barefoot, and dressed in his nightshirt, Ichtheus hastened to where the housekeeper bawled and thrashed on the floor. "For pity's sake hold your tongue woman. Do you want to fetch the entire household down here to investigate your racket?"

"Get out of my way, you foolish old coot," screamed Mother Morghan. "Evil forces are at work within this very manor, I must warn Sir Edred and Lady Myferny before it is too late."

Ichtheus grabbed a handful of Mother Morghan's kirtle, bringing her to her knees before she made for the stairs. "Quick, keep tight hold of her, Oric, whilst I prepare a draught to calm her."

Disturbed by the uproar, serfs gathered around Oric and the housekeeper. "What ails the woman?" quavered the cook.

Ichtheus brandished a bottle and a spoon. "Return to bed everyone, there is naught to see here. The housekeeper has simply imbibed a drop too much liquor. I shall give her a sleeping draught and all will be well."

"I ain't taking none of your poisonous filth," screeched Mother Morghan, clamping her mouth tight shut. She thrashed her head from side to side until her bun came undone, causing wisps of grey hair to stick to her damp warty face.

Dian leaned on the housekeeper's chest and pinched her nose shut. Unable to breathe, Mother Morghan unclenched her teeth.

Ichtheus snatched his chance and spooned the sedative mixture down the housekeeper's throat.

"There, there." Dian patted the woman's greasy head. "You will be as right as rain by morning."

Oric hoped Dian was right, for he did not want Mother Morghan spreading rumours that he might be a sorcerer; more often than not sorcerers met with an unfortunate end.

The sleeping draught swiftly took effect, and Mother Morghan's raucous snores rattled around the kitchen.

"Ye gods, Master Ichtheus! What did you administer to make her sleep so soundly?" Oric asked, gladly releasing his hold on the mountainous woman.

"A small dose of poppy syrup is all, but coupled with the liquor she has drunk the mixture has knocked her out.

Leave her be, a night on the floor might teach her a lesson," Ichtheus cackled. "She will have the mother and father of all headaches when she wakes in the morning."

"Please God Mother Morghan remembers nothing of the incident, for I suspect something evil is afoot," mumbled Oric.

Ichtheus confronted his assistant. "Incident! What incident? And what do you mean by something evil?

Oric looked troubled. "Remember the iron chest I found at Dunburton Manor? I was experimenting with a small amount of the black powder I found inside. Some of it must have spilled on the table. Mother Morghan was lighting candles and I reckon she dropped a lighted taper onto the tabletop... I ain't never seen anything like it."

"For Heaven's sake boy – anything like what?" Keen to return to his bed, Ichtheus' patience was growing perilously thin.

His eyes large with fear, Oric described the flames that had materialised as if out of nowhere.

"How much more of the substance do you have?" Ichtheus asked, his imagination filling him with dread.

"Less than a fistful," Oric admitted. "But what if the person that broke into Deveril's chest unearthed a good deal more of the powder? Perhaps the episode with Mother Morghan has something to do with the disaster Master Deveril warned me about?"

Ichtheus was already way ahead. "Did any of the other servants witness what happened?"

"Apart from Mother Morghan, only Dian and me, I think," replied Oric.

"I sincerely hope you are correct," said Ichtheus. "Clear every sign of the fire from the table and let us keep this occurrence between ourselves."

More afraid than they cared to admit, Oric and Dian scrubbed away every trace of soot from the tabletop. Oric pushed the small pouch of black powder to the bottom of his apothecary's chest and locked the lid.

The following morning Mother Morghan arose from her uncomfortable sleeping place on the kitchen floor. Head throbbing, she crawled along to the apothecary's table and used it to haul herself upright. "Lawks – I 'ad a terrible dream! This 'ere piece of furniture burst into flames before my very eyes." She sniffed the table, then tapped the clean planks suspiciously. "As far as I can tell nowt seems to be amiss. P'raps summat I ate caused me a nightmare."

Another crisis averted, thought Ichtheus. *But for how long?*

Chapter Seven

Trouble at St Griswald's

Gaining Sir Edred's permission, Oric felled trees and carted the timber to his garden on the edge of the moor. Many hours stolen from his duties as assistant apothecary, not to mention a great deal of hard work, saw a cosy, one-roomed hut ready for habitation. Delighted with the finished result, Oric invited Dian to inspect his new project.

"What a fine place you have built, Oric." Dian moved across the room and described an area with her toe. "A straw mattress would fit in here, perhaps a table and bench over there." She imagined how homely the place could look with a jug or two of wild flowers and a tapestry on the wall.

Oric beamed with pride. "Aye, 'tis not a bad job for an apothecary with only basic carpentry skills and two left thumbs," he grinned. "I plan to construct a bed frame and a table with two chairs soon. The brazier in yonder corner will keep the place snug in winter."

"You had best begin your woodwork sooner rather than later," she laughed, thrusting a package into Oric's hands. "You will need somewhere to put this."

The package contained a bedcover Dian had sewn together from scraps of brightly-coloured fabric. Overwhelmed, Oric blushed and stammered his thanks. Deeming the moment right he opened his pouch and removed the slightly crumpled corn dolly that he had brought back from Roxbrough-by-the-Sea. "I – er, bought this little gift for you a while ago but I was not sure if you would like it."

Dian's hazel eyes sparkled with pleasure. "Thank you, Oric, I like it very much." Removing a small square of linen from inside her bodice, she carefully wrapped up the corn dolly. "I shall treasure it," she smiled, her cheeks glowing rosy pink.

-oOo-

Word of Oric's new herbal remedies spread across the Bayersby and Kilterton districts and sales from his market stall quadrupled. Even with Ichtheus' input, Oric doubted that his plants in the moorland garden could keep up with the demand. Fierce sunshine parched the land and he was obliged to lug water from a nearby moorland spring to keep the plants alive. He installed a water butt in which to catch rain but the sky remained blue and cloud free. His hope of a bountiful crop was further dashed when someone continued to uproot his precious plants. Searching the countryside for replacement stock was time-consuming and, at his wit's end, Oric agonised over what to do next.

Bone-weary Oric locked up his hut and then secured the garden gate with a piece of twine. Not that these precautions ever stopped the mystery marauder. As he walked back toward Bayersby Manor a solution popped into his mind.

What I need is a live-in gardener, a caretaker.

Dinner was on the table in the manor kitchen and, fiercely hungry, Oric swiftly demolished a platter of stewed leveret, carrots and cabbage. Thus fortified he sought out Master Ichtheus to discuss his new idea.

"You had best get Sir Edred's permission first," Ichtheus advised. "He is usually amenable if propositions are feasible and, as far as I can see, your suggestion seems to be a sound one. Do you have anyone in mind for the job?"

"I thought Dian's brother, Josh, might fit the bill – if he is willing." Bolstering his courage, Oric left the kitchen and climbed the stairs that led up to the Great Hall.

Lady Myferny's younger sister, Demzel, and her daughters, Rose and Madeleine, were spending a short holiday at Bayersby Manor. The visitors were grouped together at the far end of the room with Myferny and the scribe's wife, Anna. The harp, often played by one or another of the Bayersby ladies, remained untouched in its corner and, instead of singing, the ladies were engaged in noisy discussion.

Demzel fanned herself with a piece of parchment snatched up from a low table. "You have no idea how uncomfortable the city can be in this heat." Married to a rich merchant, Demzel's family quarters, though sumptuous, were situated above her husband's place of business within the walled city of Yaracumb. An epidemic of sweating sickness had lain many of the common folk low and Demzel dare not open the shutters for fear ill humours may drift into their quarters.

"My husband insisted I bring our girls here to avoid infection." Demzel's violet eyes, one shade darker than her sister's, clouded with worry. "Now I am concerned for my poor Rodrick. What if he becomes ill when I am not at home to take care of him?"

Twisting raw wool into thread with her distal and spindle, Myferny recalled the city's privations with distaste. "Rodrick would be far more worried if you remained at home. How you cope with the stench of butchers' offal thrown into the streets, not to mention the legions of rats that feed upon it, is beyond me." Myferny shuddered at the thought. "No doubt the privies built along the edge of the city moat are still disgorging their stinking contents into the water, too. And I dare not contemplate the thieves and cut-throats that abound after dark. Why do you not build a house in one of the villages outside the borough?"

"Because my husband will not leave his business, and I will not live without my husband," Demzel stated. "So there is an end to it!"

"What about your daughters' welfare?" asked Myferny. "Should you not take that into account?"

"We do not allow the girls to venture outside the front door during the fetid summer months," Demzel retorted waspishly. "And, before you tell me they need regular doses of sunshine to thrive, they are happy to walk in the walled garden behind our building."

Nora, Lady Myferny's newly-installed companion, lugged a basket of raw wool into the Great Hall, and dumped it down in front of Demzel. "In this instance, mistress, you might well have jumped from the cooking pot into the fire."

"Whatever do you mean?" Demzel retorted, startled by the woman's abrupt manner.

"Surely you have heard about the plague of fire-breathing demons that is expected to arrive in the district on Summer Solstice Eve?" Nora shook her head vigorously, sending loose hairpins sliding down the back of her outrageously pink gown. "The Kilterton soothsayer told us to seek higher ground and that is exactly what I plan to do."

Childless and recently widowed, Nora had gladly accepted Lady Myferny's invitation to move to Bayersby Manor and act as companion. But she was not prepared to look after Demzel's needs, too. The woman was spoiled and heartless and the sooner she returned from whence she came, the happier Nora would be. Picking up her own distaff and spindle, she began to work a hank of waxy wool.

Sir Edred lolled on the back legs of his chair with his feet crossed on the tabletop. "Is there no peace to be had anywhere in this beleaguered establishment?" he roared. "Why do those foolish women cling to every piece of bad news that comes their way – never mind what I say?"

Seated beside his father, Guwain wore an expression of petulant boredom. "I could not care less about mother's worries, nor those of her ladies. All I seek is fun and entertainment, which, thanks to the soothsayer's prophecy, is sadly lacking hereabouts."

Sir Edred ignored his son. "One wonders what I am paying Father Chrispian for," he grumbled. "Seems to me the wretched fellow has totally failed to quash Mother Olive's ridiculous prophesy. Far from calming the local populace, the priest seems to be adding fuel to their fires."

"Do not be so sure, father," smirked Guwain. "I hear tell that the priest threatens his parishioners with hellfire and damnation if they refuse to do exactly as he tells them. Many do not know which is worse – Father Chrispian's hellfire or Mother Olive's demons. Frankly, I see naught but trouble ahead."

Sir Edred dropped his feet from the tabletop to the floor with a crash. "More upset is precisely what we do *not* need. I am paying Father Chrispian to drive away people's fear with some God-fearing sermons, not to terrify them into a greater state of panic."

Oric entered the Great Hall in time to hear the tail end of the angry exchange between father and son and, thinking it wise to delay his request to employ a gardener/caretaker, he tried to retrace his steps.

"Hey! What are you after, boy?" Guwain shouted, his scowl deepening.

Unable to escape, Oric fronted up to the dais and bowed before Sir Edred. "I have a request, sir."

Guwain wobbled his head from side to side. "I have a request, sir," he mimicked.

Ignoring his son's childish behaviour, Sir Edred turned his attention to Oric. "Yes Master Apothecary, what is it that you require?"

Oric came swiftly to the point. "Every time my back is turned someone vandalises the plants in my herb garden, sir. I need help to…"

Sir Edred cut Oric short. He was not interested in gardens and he was in no mood to discuss the subject. "Can you not enlist Master Ichtheus to help you?"

"Master Ichtheus and I cannot spare the time to watch over the garden continuously, sir, but I believe a caretaker may go part way to solving my dilemma."

"Ah, I see. Do you have anyone in mind for the job?" Sir Edred's face took on a greenish tinge and he rubbed his belly. He had eaten too much and he needed to visit the latrine.

"Yes I have, sir. 'Tis Josh Cole. His sister is already employed here as a maid. I am willing to pay their father, Eadbald, to release Josh into my employ. Furthermore, sir, I am prepared to pay the lad a small wage with money I make from my market stall."

Sir Edred downed a pot of mead, hoping it might settle his stomach. "I can think of no reason to gainsay your suggestion, but offer low for young Josh. His father is a wastrel and a drunkard and he will likely let his son go for the price of a flagon of ale." Sir Edred leaned across the table and fixed Oric with shrewd, blue eyes. "Mark my words – if I hear one whisper of trouble regarding the Cole boy, out he goes. Do you understand?"

"Indeed I do, sir," Oric nodded vigorously. "And thank you for your advice." He bowed again and beat a hasty retreat before Sir Edred could change his mind.

-oOo-

The shepherd at Rigg Farm had sent word that his children were unwell. Oric left his bed early, packed his satchel with a few medical supplies, and informed a sleepy Ichtheus that he was going to look them over.

"Since Rigg Farm is halfway to Kilterton, you might as well continue on after you administer to the shepherd's boys," said Ichtheus. Saddened by the regular ruination of Oric's plants, he was keen to see someone installed as caretaker of the herb garden as quickly as possible. "If you make haste you might find Master Eadbald still at home. He rarely arises before the inn opens for business and it would be a good idea to talk to him whilst he is still in command of his wits. I have heard that he becomes exceeding belligerent after a few pots of ale."

Recent robberies in the district made Oric nervous and he whistled for Sir Edred's wolfhound. Ferocious if his loved ones were threatened, Parzifal's whiskery bulk gave Oric a feeling of comfortable security.

The summer morning was alive with the sound of buzzing insects and trilling birds. The sun just recently risen was not yet uncomfortably hot. Oric enjoyed the walk until, nearing St Griswald's Church, a terrible racket stopped him dead in his tracks. He grasped Parzifal's collar and crept through the graveyard toward the noise. Inside the church Father Chrispian shrieked from a pulpit that towered above the nave. His congregation cowered in terror below.

"Master Guwain is right about the hellfire and damnation," Oric whispered to the dog. "The priest is almost insensible. No wonder everyone is afraid."

Thoroughly enjoying the consternation he was causing, Father Chrispian leaned out from his pulpit one last time and wagged a forefinger at the spittle-bespattered villagers below. "Ignore Mother Olive's foolish prophecy and go about your everyday business as usual. Anyone who fails to obey my orders will roast in Hell's eternal fire." About to return to the room behind the pulpit to change out of his robes, Father Chrispian was halted by angry shouts.

"I am hanged if I know which is worse," howled a work-worn farmer from the body of the church. "Yon priest's eternal hellfire or Mother Olive's demons. Either way we ain't got much to look forward to, have we?

"Do not dare to gainsay me, farmer!" Father Chrispian bellowed in return. The largely unsupervised post at St Griswald's offered a perfect outlet to accumulate wealth for himself, and he was not about to let a few recalcitrant country-folk spoil his plans for a comfortable future. He pounded his Bible with renewed vigour and shouted louder. "Bring offerings for the Lord to every service I conduct; the more you give the more comfortable your places in the afterlife will be. Let us pray for your immortal souls."

Unable to contain himself, Parzifal wormed and squirmed until he freed himself from Oric's grasp. Toenails rattling on the stone floor, he hurtled toward the object of his hatred. The congregation screamed, thinking the grey streak to be one of Mother Olive's demons.

At the bottom of the pulpit steps Parzifal skidded to a halt. A deep growl erupted from his chest and he drew back his lips in a ferocious snarl.

Trapped in his pulpit, Father Chrispian tentatively extended his hand. "Nice doggy! Good doggy!" But he had kicked the wolfhound once too often.

Eyes glazed with a single-minded desire to savage the man's bony fingers, Parzifal lunged forward. Father Chrispian snatched his hand back in the nick of time. Undeterred, the dog snapped his teeth shut upon the priest's booted foot.

A tapestry, hanging from a wooden pole above the pulpit, offered Father Chrispian his only escape. He grasped the fabric and began a frantic ascent.

Parzifal clung to his victim's boot until all four legs swung free of the ground. Gaining the safety of the pole, Father Chrispian clung on like a monkey up a stick.

The congregation guffawed, their fear of Mother Olive's demons and Father Chrispian's hellfire temporarily forgotten.

Oric clambered onto the pulpit and prised open Parzifal's jaws.

Father Chrispian's kid boot hung in tatters and his savaged toes oozed blood. "You misbegotten spawn of the devil!" he shrieked. "I shall see that insane beast destroyed and you, boy, thrashed until there is no skin left upon your back."

Oric doubted Sir Edred would allow any harm to befall his precious dog, but would the mighty Lord of Bayersby be as forgiving toward his young apothecary?

Chapter Eight

Hellfire and Damnation

The shepherd's youngsters at Rigg Farm suffered only minor chills. Greatly relieved that the boys' malady was nothing more serious, Oric offered licorice juice to ease their symptoms, and accepted an invitation to join the family for their midday meal in exchange for his services. He spent longer at the farm than he intended and did not arrive in Kilterton until well past noon.

Leading Parzifal along the dusty thoroughfare, Oric was concerned to see that members of St Griswald's congregation from earlier in the day were gathered together in the village square. Mistress Goodall, the village gossip, was in full voice.

"I did what Sir Edred ordered and attended the service at St Griswald's," she cried, her ample bosom heaving in agitation. "Now I wish I had not bothered, for I no longer know what to believe."

"Father Chrispian's hellfire or Mother Olive's demons – take your pick," Frida Cole yelled. "We are doomed whichever course we choose!"

Oric observed the skinny woman, perplexed that such

a female could have given birth to a beautiful girl like Dian. The pair were as different as chalk from cheese. The mother unkempt and raucous, the daughter clean and gentle.

Noise from the crowd penetrated Kilterton Priory where Father Franciscus was at his devotions. The newly-installed young priest leaped to his feet and hastened to the door.

Father Franciscus knew Chrispian from old and he believed the man to be a dangerous charlatan. Determined to pour oil on troubled waters, he clapped his hands for silence. "Good folk of Kilterton," he cried. "Come into the priory and we shall sing a few rousing hymns to dispel your fears."

"Dispel our fears?" Frida Cole challenged. "I doubt it!" She flapped a grubby hand at the villagers. "You lot do as you please! I ain't going to no more prayer meetings here or at St Griswald's. And I will tell you something else for nowt. I ain't dragging my brood up Rosederry Hill come Summer Solstice Eve – it is too far and too hot." Without further ado she stomped into her shabby cottage and slammed the door.

"Yon stupid woman's laziness may well cause the death of her entire family," squawked Mistress Goodall. Her face looked red and sweaty, and her cap sat askew on top of her tangle of black hair. "Who would you rather believe?" she cried. "Tried and true Mother Olive or some fly-by-night cleric that we barely know?" She jerked her thumb at Father Chrispian. "As for you, young feller – I know you mean well but you ain't been in the business of preaching long enough to be any match against demons. Summer Solstice Eve will find me and mine on top of Rosederry Hill and that's that!"

"Why not put your trust in the Lord?" Father Franciscus ventured gently.

"Oooh – I am all for that!" Mistress Goodall replied vigorously. "But I plan to do it from the top of yonder hill."

Most villagers liked Mistress Goodall's logic and,

believing they would be closer to God the higher they climbed, everyone decided to forsake their homes for Mother Olive's promised safety of Rosederry Hill. Hedging their bets, everyone agreed to return to St Griswald's for evensong in case Father Chrispian had anything new to add. Bearing gifts for the Lord, as the priest had suggested, might just tip the balance in their favour.

A cacophony of hammering drew Oric's attention away from the Priory and, glad to escape from the disgruntled crowd of villagers, he wandered down the street to investigate the noise.

Uther Tidwall teetered on top of a ladder in front of his cobbler shop, hammering nails into strips of timber.

"Good day to you, Uther. What on earth are you doing?"

Uther descended his ladder and spat a mouthful of nails into his palm. Tannin from the leather he tooled had yellowed his hands and years of cobbling had bent his back. "A very good day to you, too, Master Oric," he replied, squinting up at the young apothecary. "To answer your question," he continued, "I am securing my premises so no villain can steal my property whilst I am away."

"But where are you going?" Oric asked, surprised that Uther planned to abandon his shop.

"I am heading to higher ground with everyone else. And, if you want my opinion, you should do the same."

"I would go," Oric admitted hesitantly, "but Master Ichtheus refuses to leave Bayersby Manor. I am beggared if I know what to do for the best."

Uther poked Oric's shoulder with the stock of his hammer. "I am not saying all the nonsense that folk are bandying about is true, but trouble of some sort is brewing. Come Summer Solstice Eve chaos will reign one way or another and I propose to be as far away from Kilterton as possible."

"Cooee, Master Apothecary," Frida Cole's neighbour beckoned from her cottage door. "Can you spare a moment to look at my bairns?"

Oric tied Parzifal to a tree and followed the young woman into her cottage. Several youngsters sprawled on the dirt floor, vomiting where they lay.

"How long have they been in this condition?" Oric asked, dropping to his knees to examine the infants. Their ashen faces and clammy skin indicated that something was seriously wrong.

"They been like this ever since they came home from the woods last night," cried the anguished young woman. "I had nothing to feed them on at home and the foolish little beggars mistook toadstools for mushrooms." Tears made tracks in the dirt on the young mother's cheeks. "The bairns were hungry and filled their bellies. They have done nowt but puke ever since."

Engulfed with sadness, Oric reached for his satchel. Toadstools were deadly more often than not and there was little he could do save ease the children's cramps. He handed the mother a flask of barberry juice. "Give your little ones a few spoonfuls of this, but I fear you must prepare for the worst."

The woman's howls of anguish rang in Oric's ears as he walked away from the cottage. Infuriated by his inadequacies and the lack of effective medicine, he strengthened his vow to spend more time experimenting with new remedies.

At Oric's knock Josh Cole opened his parents' cottage door. "How do, Oric. You will need to turn a deaf ear if you come inside. Ma is better in health than temper today."

Oric's eyes had barely adjusted to the gloom inside the fetid dwelling when Frida Cole launched into another of her diatribes.

"How am I supposed to go trekking up Rosederry Hill when I hardly dare set foot outside my own front door?"

"What prevents you from venturing outside, Mistress Cole?" Oric queried.

"Because folk are robbed at every turn – is why!" Frida bawled. "I go in fear of my life every time I step outdoors." She clapped a fly that buzzed past her face. "Remember the loathsome vagabonds that robbed us before Sir Edred's battle with Esica Figg? Say what you like, I believe the same mob is at it again. Either that or a band of new thieves has taken over where t'others left off." She scraped the squashed fly from her palm with a thumbnail and flicked its carcass onto the floor. "If you ask me, Sir Edred should send his men into the village to protect us. Moreover, he needs to get rid of that Father Crispital, or Crunchian, or whatever his stupid name is. We have more than enough to cope with, without some horrible cleric frightening us all witless! I reckon the fellow is insane."

Josh squirmed with embarrassment. There was no stopping his ma once she got going.

"And I never get no help from that wastrel husband of mine." Frida threw her hands in the air. "What bit of money he earns doin' odd jobs is swallowed up at the inn. Stupid addle-pate reckons if the world is coming to an end, he plans to die with his belly full of ale."

Looking around the hovel that Frida Cole called home, Oric was not surprised that Eadbald spent most of his time at the inn. Even so, the man had no right to drink away his wages whilst his family went hungry. "Actually, 'tis your husband I wish to speak to," he ventured.

Frida sidled closer to Oric. "Is that right?" she said, eyeing him suspiciously. "As I said, Master Cole is at the inn and, if I were you, I would not be disturbing him unless you seek a bloody nose."

Rather than confront the drunken Eadbald, Oric put his offer of employment for Josh to Mistress Cole. "What do you think? Would you allow your son to work for me?"

"I might." Frida's aggressive expression changed to one of avarice. "But only if you make it worth my while." She haggled but not for long. Oric's offer of money in exchange for Josh was tempting and the lad's departure would mean one less mouth to feed, one less body to clothe and house.

Elated by his new chance in life, Josh gathered up his meagre possessions. He bent to kiss his mother farewell and Frida grabbed his arm. "Mind you send your wages home. 'Tis time you stumped up summat after all the years we have looked out for you." She jiggled the coins Oric had given to her, and pushed Josh out of the cottage door.

-oOo-

A group of urchins surrounded Parzifal in the street. They threw small stones into the air and cheered loudly when he caught them in his mouth. Oric quickly unhitched the wolfhound from the tree. "We had best get going. I shall answer to Sir Edred if I return his precious dog with a mouthful of broken teeth."

As the boys hastened away from the village, Oric discussed the dilemma of his wrecked plants with Josh. "My duties at Bayersby Manor keep me busy a good deal of the time and I am unable to tend my plot of land as often as I would like. Apart from weeding, watering and disposing of caterpillars, I need you to keep watch over my herbs." Oric lengthened his stride, for daylight was waning. "Whenever I am away from the garden someone or something wrecks my plants."

Josh flexed his biceps enthusiastically. "Leave it to me, Oric. I shall catch the culprit and thrash him soundly. I doubt he will dare to return when I have finished with him."

"Nay, Josh! There is no need to play the hero." Though the lad was sturdy and probably able to take care of himself, Oric did not want to put him at risk. "Simply keep watch and report back to me. Sir Edred will dole out whatever punishment he deems appropriate – if we can identify the wretched fellow."

Oric described the hut he had built on his plot. "You will have a safe place to sleep and a brazier to keep you warm when winter comes." Dashing beads of sweat from his brow he added, "If we ever see cold weather again!"

As they walked Oric stole an occasional glance at Josh. The boy had the same hazel eyes as his sister and an abundance of chestnut hair – though not nearly as clean as Dian's curly locks. Josh may not have been as fastidious as his sister but he clearly had a feisty nature.

Approaching St Griswald's Church, Oric related the strange service he had witnessed that morning, and of Parzifal's rooted dislike of Father Chrispian.

Visualising the dog's antics, Josh laughed so hard he stopped to clutch his stomach. "I would dearly like to hear one of the priest's rants," he spluttered, once he recovered his breath. "Ma has spoken of little else since she first heard Father Chrispian preach. If you want my opinion, I reckon the fellow is stark staring mad."

"I suspect Master Ichtheus will want to witness the priest's antics, too." replied Oric. "Perhaps we should all return to the church and observe his next service."

-oOo-

At sight of her brother, Dian tore across the Bayersby compound. "It is so good to see you, Josh." She hugged him and then held him at arm's length. "How are our younger brothers and sisters faring without me?"

"Surviving despite our parents." Josh dropped his small bundle of belongings onto the ground and returned Dian's hug. "Mother does nowt but complain and father spends most of his time at the inn. Truth to tell, I am glad to escape."

Oric left Josh and Dian to catch up on family gossip and went in search of his mentor. At the kitchen door Parzifal became entangled between Oric's feet and the pair crashed onto the kitchen floor.

Ichtheus dropped his pestle and rushed to help Oric up. "Oh, my giddy aunt! Are you injured? You have not been set upon by rogues, have you?"

"Nay, nay, Master Ichtheus, I tripped over the dog." Oric pushed Parzifal out of the way. "There is naught wrong with me, though I wish the same could be said for Father Chrispian."

"What ails the priest now?" Ichtheus hoped he had seen the back of Father Chrispian and he was irritated that the man remained the main topic of conversation.

"I ain't never seen anything like it." Oric blew out his cheeks. "Yon fellow has surely taken leave of his senses."

Ichtheus smashed his pestle into the mixture of chopped roots in his mortar. "What are you on about, boy?"

"As you know, I was on my way to Rigg Farm, which took me past St Griswald's…"

"Yes, yes, I know where you went! For pity's sake tell me what has happened."

Ichtheus became increasingly concerned as Oric's story unfolded. "There will be the devil to pay if Sir Edred hears of this! We must get over to St Griswald's at first light and put a stop to the priest's dangerous nonsense before he causes a riot."

Before retiring to bed, Oric went in search of Josh to make sure he had a comfortable sleeping place for the night. "You seem to have had a dramatic arrival one way and another," he said, grinning ruefully, "and I suspect the drama is going to continue. Master Ichtheus is keen to observe Father Chrispian's antics and I suspect the priest is about to receive the drubbing of his life." Oric's grin widened, exposing his neat, white teeth. "Master Ichtheus and I are off to St Griswald's first thing tomorrow morning, perhaps you might like to come along and watch? I believe the outcome will surely be worth the walk."

Josh nodded enthusiastically. "That I would! Yon priest has caused much upset amongst the villagers of Kilterton and I would dearly like to see him put in his place."

-oOo-

The following day dawned hotter than ever and vicious gusts of wind whipped Ichtheus' silver hair and beard into his eyes. He hung onto his whiskers with one hand, and hauled himself astride Braccus. "Hurry up," he urged Oric and Josh, applying his heels to the donkey's flanks. "If we make haste we might catch yon cleric in full rant."

The first people Ichtheus saw inside St Griswald's Church were his friends Egglebart and Etheldrida. "Why are you paying attention to this charlatan?" he demanded. "I had higher hopes of you both."

Egglebart chuckled, his one eye twinkling with good humour. "We are not taken in by Mother Olive's prophecy. As for Father Chrispian's hellfire and damnation, I have never heard such hogwash. No, dear friend, we are here for the entertainment." He tapped his nose with a finger. "Besides,

Etheldrida wants to know exactly what is going on before she begins baking." Egglebart winked. "Whatever the outcome on Solstice Eve, my wife is convinced that folk will starve without an ample supply of her tasty pies."

Lady Malla, a midwife recently come to the district to assist expectant mothers, had married the Lord of Bayersby's old friend, Sir Oswold. The newlyweds lived in a modest cottage not far from Egglebart and Etheldrida's smallholding. An astute judge of character, Lady Malla believed Father Chrispian to be a dangerous charlatan. At the first suitable opportunity, she determined to tell the congregation to disregard everything the man had uttered.

Candles dripped tallow from sconces attached to the church walls, adding the stink of fatty mutton to the odour of human sweat. Every seat was taken and latecomers leaned against the church walls. Bronze and silver ornaments, small pieces of jewellery and flagons of wine lay stacked against the altar alongside poor folks' handmade clay pots and vegetables.

"Look at those valuables," exclaimed Oric. "Father Chrispian's demands to bring offerings have clearly not fallen on deaf ears."

Ichtheus' normally pale cheeks flushed pink with anger. "It seems members of the gentry as well as poor villagers have been sucked in by the priest's abominable diatribes. This is not at all what Sir Edred expected from his new preacher."

The vestry door creaked open to reveal Father Chrispian. Rays of early morning sun struck through an east-facing window and surrounded the black-robed priest with an aura of crimson light.

"Saints preserve us, 'tis Lucifer himself," wailed an elderly woman.

Thoroughly rattled, Ichtheus strode up to the priest. "What in God's name are you hoping to achieve, frightening these simple folk? Sir Edred clearly has no idea what a troublemaker he has employed."

Father Chrispian pushed Ichtheus roughly to one side, causing him to stumble to his knees. "Get out of my way you foolish old man! You know not what you are talking about."

Chrispian was born the only son into a family of girls. Plain and thin with a nasty disposition, he was teased and taunted throughout his childhood. As payback for his sisters' ill treatment he stole their dolls, placed them on miniature pyres, and set them alight. His father caught Chrispian dancing around one such pyre and beat his son soundly. Chrispian ran away from home. He wandered from place to place until he met a crazy priest. Thus Chrispian's fate was sealed. Man and boy travelled from town to town, causing mayhem wherever they went. Any poor woman with a black cat or a strange birthmark became a target for the unstable pair. When the old priest died Chrispian was left to fend for himself. He joined a closed order and took his vows. Unable to stomach the quiet lifestyle of the monastery, he sought out a new position and became tutor priest at Roxbrough Abbey. For many years he terrified his students with tales of fire and brimstone, death and destruction.

Father Chrispian climbed the steps to his pulpit and stretched his arms wide. Horribly fascinated, Oric listened as the priest's voice rose to screaming pitch.

"Anyone who fails to obey my teachings will be pitchforked onto the devil's pyre. Your flesh will melt and drip like so much tallow into the jaws of Hell." For good measure he added that Mother Olive was naught but an old witch and she deserved to burn at the stake.

No-one cared what happened to Mother Olive, for she had caused all the trouble in the first place. Eager to escape the confines of the church, the parishioners bolted every which way. They disappeared into the lurid glow of sunrise, each person determined to put as much distance between themselves and the priest as quickly as possible. They would deal with Father Chrispian's threats of hellfire and damnation – if they survived Mother Olive's demons.

"That went down well," Ichtheus growled, standing outside with his friends. "Thanks to yon meddling priest, we now appear to have a riot on our hands."

"I cannot believe that people are so gullible," muttered Sir Oswold.

"The man is a charlatan," added Egglebart, "and I reckon all those offerings around the altar will disappear into the priest's coffers as sure as night follows day."

The congregation dispersed but Ichtheus and his friends lingered to talk over what should be done. Coming to no sensible conclusion, they eventually bid each other farewell and went their separate ways.

Father Chrispian thought the apothecary and his friends were never going home. Keen to barrow the parishioners' offerings from the church to the manse, he ran back and forth like a scared rabbit. All manner of peculiar occurrences made the churchyard a terrifying place once the sun went down, and he had no desire to remain outside after dark.

Chapter Nine

Haunting St Griswald's

Father Chrispian selected two oatcakes, a chunk of cheese, and an apple from the stash of offerings brought by his parishioners. He washed his supper down with a slug of holy wine, and snuffed out all but one candle. Lying down, he had barely closed his eyes when bestial howls jerked him wide awake. In his haste to get out of bed he knocked over the single candle, plunging the room into inky blackness. Any idea that such noises could be made by humans fled from his mind and, overtaken by terror, Father Chrispian fumbled along the wall until his fingers made contact with a timber crucifix. Lifting down the heavy cross, he held it in front of his chest like a shield and wrenched open the manse door.

"Whoever you are," he quavered, "I am a God-fearing Christian. If you are seeking a convert for the devil you have chosen the wrong person."

More ghastly howls accompanied by hollow rattles reverberated around the gravestones.

Father Chrispian leaped back into the manse, slammed the door and slid the bolts home. Suffocated by the darkness inside, he crept to a narrow window in search of air. An illuminated, hollow-cheeked visage glared back at him through the aperture. Lightheaded with fear, Father Chrispian hugged the crucifix to his chest and crawled under his bed. There he stayed for the remainder of the night.

-oOo-

In the hidden side of St Griswald's crypt, Hersica Horzefell chomped down a breakfast of partridge eggs. "When I peeped through the window with that lantern held under my chin, I swear yon cleric soiled his breeches." She wheezed with laughter, exposing toothless gums slimy with yolk. "You did a grand job lads, waving your lanterns around the churchyard. If Father Chrispian don't fly the coop soon, I shall eat my boots – muck an' all."

Ned held an ancient ribcage aloft and rattled the bones. "Surely the priest will run away after our performance last night."

"Do not count your chickens too swiftly!" growled Figg. "I doubt we have seen the back of the Holy Father yet. He has much to lose if he leaves too soon."

"Any normal person would be scared out of his wits after the tricks we played," Hersica whined. "Why can we not kill him and be done with it?"

"Because Father Chrispian's sudden demise might arouse Sir Edred's suspicions," snarled Figg. "Try harder to frighten the priest away; otherwise I may well get rid of you."

-oOo-

Lady Malla had attended only one service at St Griswald's and, disgusted with what she had seen and heard, she shared her feelings with anyone that was prepared to listen. "Unless Father Chrispian ceases his scaremongering forthwith, I shall report him to Sir Edred," she stated angrily. "Furthermore, I urge folk to cease donations of food and household goods to the church, and to keep well away from the priest. In my opinion the man is deranged."

Word of the midwife's meddlesome interference filtered back to Father Chrispian and he curled back his lips in a snarl of disgust. As a result of the woman's carping, barely anyone had visited the church lately. His food supplies were dwindling and he could think of no new way to entice his parishioners back. Lady Malla claimed to be a herbalist, but Father Chrispian knew different. He had seen her black cat familiar, and the midwife also had a crescent-shaped mole on her neck.

In his saner moments Father Chrispian wondered if the Bayersby apothecaries had a hand in the nocturnal manifestations around St Griswald's Churchyard. With this in mind, he planned to confront Oric and Ichtheus as soon as he finished breakfast. Yellow grease dripped down his chin as he bit into a slab of fat bacon and he cackled, reminded of juices that had spurted from the body of his last victim. Tied to a stake on top of a pyre he had built for the purpose, the witch had rendered down nicely.

-oOo-

Escaped from her duties at the manor, Mother Morghan jogged along the path to St Griswald's as fast as her bulk would allow. Snorting like an overworked carthorse, she opened the secret doorway at the rear of the church and clattered down the stairs into the crypt.

"Be more careful, woman," Figg snapped. "If the priest sees you here between services he will wonder what you are doing here. You could draw his attention to our secret hideaway – then we may be forced to kill him."

"No need to concern yourself," Mother Morghan sneered, picking at a spot on her chin. "Father Chrispian is at Bayersby Manor giving the apothecary a piece of his mind." She laughed and her belly wobbled like a tub of coltsfoot jelly. "His High and Mightiness claims that Master Ichtheus paid someone to haunt the manse."

Figg regarded the Bayersby housekeeper with distaste. "Is that the only information you have?"

"Give me chance to draw breath, man." Mother Morghan plopped down on a bench and fanned her moist face with her grubby apron. "Folk are in such a state I reckon the district will be deserted come Solstice Eve."

Figg drummed his nails upon the table. "What about Sir Edred? Will he abandon Bayersby Manor along with everyone else?"

"I reckon he will, but he is mighty angry. He reckons Father Chrispian has made matters worse with his threats of hellfire and damnation, and that is not what the priest is being paid for. Lady Myferny is insisting that the entire household leaves the manor for higher ground." Mother Morghan smirked knowingly. "Sir Edred ain't convinced, but his lady usually gets her way." She held her plump palm out to Figg. "I have done everything you asked of me, ain't it time you parted with some money? Stump up else you can forget any further help from me."

Figg ignored Mother Morghan's outstretched hand. "Be patient for a little longer; I have an army to pay before you get your share. Rest assured your life will change soon enough."

-oOo-

Father Chrispian strode up and down the manor kitchen, berating Ichtheus at the top of his voice. "I have your measure, Master Apothecary. Indeed I do! No doubt you and your assistant are responsible for bribing a bunch of urchins to fool around my churchyard after dark." He pounded his fist on the table. "And I demand that you put a stop to these ridiculous capers at once!"

Ichtheus resisted the urge to throw his pestle at the priest. "I am not responsible for anything that happens at St Griswald's Church, neither is Oric. I suspect your 'so-called' visions are brought about by overmuch rich food and holy wine before you retire." Ichtheus dare not admit that he had once seen visions in St Griswald's Churchyard similar to the ones Father Chrispian described. And, on the night in question, he had also imbibed a drop too much wine. To this day he was not sure what had caused the apparitions and he had no intention of making a fool of himself.

Father Chrispian's protuberant Adam's apple bobbed up and down his neck as he swallowed repeatedly. "How dare you speak to me thus? I know exactly what you are about – you want rid of me, do you not? Well let me tell you, if I suffer one more disturbed night I shall report you to Sir Edred."

"Do as you please," Ichtheus replied tiredly. "But, for the sake of your own safety, I urge you remain indoors after dark."

Returned to the manse, Father Chrispian felt as though his complaints had fallen upon deaf ears. *The apothecaries need not think they have me fooled,* he thought. *They are to blame for the nocturnal disturbances – for sure.*

The nightly visitations continued and lack of sleep kept Father Chrispian abed until noon most days. After another bad night, he staggered into the afternoon light and gazed blearily around the graveyard. Everything seemed unnervingly normal in the bright sunlight. A family of field mice scurried along the pathway and birds in the trees fluffed out their feathers. Father Chrispian hopped along the pathway, vigorously flapping his elbows. *Soon I shall be able to fly like the birds. When I soar above these stupid locals they will take notice of what I say.*

Chapter Ten

Scraggswood Forest

St Griswald's Church steamed in another sticky, airless night. Unable to sleep, Figg kicked life into each of the men who sprawled and snored on the crypt floor. "Stir your stumps," he growled. "Time you were out on the road again."

Bertram, Figg's head man, rolled off his straw pallet, letting rip with a noisy fart as he got to his feet. "Where are you sending us this time?"

Disgusted, Figg nipped his nose between his thumb and forefinger. "Ye gods, man, you stink!" Bertram reminded Figg of Hersica Horzefell's deceased son Zebediah. He was hulk-like and similarly hirsute, but Bertram was more intelligent. Had Zebediah been brighter he might still be alive today.

Figg longed to be rid of Bertram and the motley crew of rogues, but his coffers were not yet full and he needed to work the men for a while longer. "Mother Morghan tells me that wealthy merchants are coming to Kilterton for the horse fair." The woman did not come up with useful information often and Figg planned to milk it for all he was worth. "Ride to the outskirts of the village and rob as many travellers as you can lay hands on. If they offer any resistance, kill them. Whatever you do, make sure not to leave any clues that might lead anyone back here."

The men shambled to their feet, every one of them believing Figg would provide them with a generous share of the spoils when he became master of Bayersby Manor.

"Do we have to go an' all?" wailed Ned. "Me and Joe have other things planned for today."

"Everybody goes – including you," snapped Figg. Determined to remove his accumulated plunder from the crypt to a safer hiding place, he wanted St Griswald's to himself. Carelessness had already cost him one fortune; he was not about to risk losing another.

Hersica Horzefell banged pots of ale and a loaf of bread onto the stained tabletop. "Say what you like, Master Figg, I ain't going on no jaunt. My poor old legs are too tired to walk all the way to Kilterton and back inside a day." The old woman tore off lumps of bread green with mould. "Besides, I have plenty to keep me occupied in the woods hereabouts."

Bertram sniffed at a chunk of bread, then hurled it to the ground. "Have you nowt better to offer than this fetid crust, woman? A man needs something decent to fill his belly afore he goes to work."

"No, I ain't!" Hersica snarled. "Lack of food is the reason I plan to visit the woods. My time will be better spent setting snares to catch rabbits."

Figg did not care what the woman did, just as long as she was out of his way.

Finished their sketchy breakfast, the men departed and were soon swallowed up in the predawn gloom. Afraid to openly disobey their master, Ned and Joe pretended to follow the robbers. Hersica dawdled and Figg hassled her to get a move on. A few heart beats later she left for the woods with a bundle of snares in her hand.

Suspicious over Figg's indecent haste to dispatch everyone, Hersica returned to hide behind the churchyard wall. The ex-moneylender was an untrustworthy mongrel, and she meant to find out what he was up to.

Father Chrispian had taken to sleeping late and Figg deemed him unlikely to cause problems. With that thought in mind, he pushed his first barrow-load of valuables across the churchyard to his pre-selected hiding place.

Ivy grew across a row of ancient graves behind the church, and Figg pulled back thick tendrils of woody greenstuff to expose the earth beneath. He dug holes in three burial plots and dropped in his bags of plunder. More barrow-loads of items followed. With everything safely stowed away, Figg shovelled earth back into place and rearranged strands of ivy over the new hiding places.

-oOo-

Keen to see how his plot of land fared, Oric begged leave to visit the site. In view of Oric's hard work during the refurbishment of St Griswald's manse, Ichtheus gladly gave his assistant permission. Whistling a merry tune, Oric loaded the cart with horse manure, harnessed Braccus to the shafts and set off for the moor.

Bathed in pink rays of early daylight, his garden looked well-tended but, on closer inspection, Oric was disappointed to see spaces like missing teeth amongst the neat rows of herbs.

The hut door opened and Josh stepped out, hoe in hand. Wearing a hessian sack over his rough tunic, he looked every bit the country boy.

"Good morning," Oric called, looking around appreciatively. "You have certainly smartened the place up. Are you enjoying your new occupation?"

"Aye, I like it well enough," replied Josh. "But something very peculiar is going on. I try to keep awake at night but sometimes I cannot help but nod off. When I do, more plants disappear. I tell you, Oric, the culprit is proving more slippery to catch than an eel."

"Good Heavens, Josh, I do not expect you to sit up all night! Whoever is causing the damage will surely make a mistake and reveal himself eventually. All I ask is that you ascertain who the culprit is and report back to me. In the meantime give me a hand to spread this cartload of horse muck." Oric tittered. "The pong will surely deter our vandal."

Upon his return to Bayersby Manor, Oric broached the subject of another foraging excursion with his mentor. "Josh has dug my plot over ready for more plants and I would like to find new supplies to fill the empty spaces."

Having had yet another unpleasant altercation with Mother Morghan, Ichtheus readily agreed to Oric's suggestion. "I could certainly do with a little time away from the manor and yon horrible housekeeper." He wagged a weary finger. "If you want to accompany me, be ready to leave for Scraggswood Forest early tomorrow morning. With Summer Solstice almost upon us, we must return to Bayersby within the day."

At first light Oric donned his work tunic and an old pair of breeches. He dashed off to fetch digging implements and to harness Braccus to the cart. Dian prepared a hamper of food to keep the apothecaries going for the day and handed it over, a worried frown creasing her brow. "Please take care," she urged. "There are many vagabonds and cut-throats abroad these days."

"You have no need to worry," replied Ichtheus, striding into the compound. Over his shoulder he carried a satchel in which he had placed his favourite trowel and one or two simple medicaments in case of minor injury. "Robbers prefer thoroughfares that merchants tread rather than the area of forest we plan to visit. Plants we seek grow well away from the beaten track." He sighed as Parzifal bounded out of the kitchen. The dog had been left at home once too often of late and he was not about to miss another outing. "I doubt we shall be allowed to escape without our trusty guard dog."

Hedgerows of hazel and dogwood lined the narrow path, and tall clumps of purple foxgloves thrust up from sandy patches of ground. Oric took careful note of the location, intending to collect one or two specimens on the return journey. The plant had many medicinal properties including the treatment of scabby head, a condition that was currently rife amongst the youngsters of Kilterton.

Due to the lack of rain Nidderdale Brook had dwindled to a miserable trickle, and Oric jumped down from the cart to lead Braccus across the stony riverbed. Parzifal did his usual water dance and caused a few small fish trapped in shallow pools to swim around madly. Tired of his game, the dog sniffed amongst trees that jostled for position on the opposite bank.

The forest crowded in more closely, barely leaving enough space for the donkey and cart to squeeze through. Oric began to worry. "Are you sure you will be able to find our way home, Master Ichtheus?"

"Of course I will!" Ichtheus puffed out his chest. "I am blessed with an infallible sense of direction."

Golden-brown whorls of fungi erupted from a fallen tree trunk and Oric cut some free with his dagger. A few paces further along the pathway, a plant with feathery purplish-green leaves drew his attention.

"Is that hound's tongue, Master Ichtheus?"

"Aye, lad, and an excellent plant it is. The roots, ground and taken as a decoction, stay hair from falling. 'Tis said the same remedy heals a mad dog's bite." Ichtheus passed a trowel to Oric. "Dig some up but beware – the leaves and roots exude a putrid smell."

Nutlets with prickly hooks hung from the plant and stuck to Oric's clothes as he brushed past. He tried to pull them off, but they clung to the rough fabric of his breeches.

Ichtheus grimaced. "I forgot to warn you about the seeds. They make mighty prickly bedfellows, be sure to rid yourself of them all."

Entering a clearing, Ichtheus looked for the sun. "The day is well past noon, methinks 'tis time we stopped for a bite to eat."

Propped against a giant oak, they devoured the food that Dian had prepared and afterwards fell into a doze. Parzifal lay down, dropped his great head onto his paws, and began to snore.

Nearing his dinner time, Parzifal awoke and licked Oric's face. Oric woke with a start, wondering what the time might be. Shafts of crimson light slanted through the trees and he gave his mentor a shake. "The sun is almost set. We must get going if we are to return to Bayersby Manor before dark. Which way do we go?"

Feeling less than confident, Ichtheus set off in what he hoped to be the right direction. They proceeded until twilight darkened the woods and the birds went to roost. An owl swooped overhead, his hoot making Oric and Ichtheus jump.

They came upon a stream and Oric hauled Braccus to a stop. "I do not wish to cast doubt upon your abilities, Master Ichtheus, but this does not look like Nidderdale Brook."

"Ye of little faith," admonished Ichtheus. "If we follow the watercourse it will lead us to the edge of the forest."

The stream, fed by a substantial spring, was a tributary that ran into Nidderdale Brook, but Ichtheus followed it in the wrong direction.

Way past his feeding time, Braccus dug in his heels and brayed dolefully. He poked at a bulbous lump on a tree trunk with his nose. An ominous buzzing sound erupted from within.

"Oh, my giddy aunt," Ichtheus cried. "The donkey has disturbed a wild bee's nest and the insects are forming a swarm."

Braccus shook the angry bees from his thick coat without a qualm. Oric, Ichtheus and the dog were not so lucky. The furious little insects descended, stinging wherever they found a piece of bare flesh.

"Quick, Oric, run!"

"Where to, Master Ichtheus?"

"Into the water."

Yelling and swatting, Ichtheus and Oric slithered down a steep bank and into the brook. They lay on their backs in the shallows with only their noses poking above the surface to enable them to breathe. Parzifal, thinking it a glorious game, found himself a deeper spot and wallowed in the water. In so doing he became horribly muddy. The bees hovered, then, as if at some secret command, they regrouped and buzzed back to their hive.

"I am stung in places I never knew I had places," wailed Oric, rubbing at his smarting skin.

"Do not scratch, boy! You must pull out each sting individually." Ichtheus tore leaves from a dock plant. "Rub yourself with these when you are done; they will help to alleviate the burning sensation."

Not keen to blunder on through the gathering darkness, Ichtheus suggested they seek a place to sleep.

"I would like to know where," muttered Oric. "There is naught but dense forest as far as I can see – not that I can see far," he added, peering into the gloom of late evening. "Perhaps we should crawl under the cart and await morning."

"Wolves roam the countryside after dark," warned Ichtheus. "I do not want to endanger our lives. And the dog will attack any creature that approaches." He patted the dog's head, for he had grown fond of the big animal. "I would be sad to see any of us come to harm for we have no weapons to defend ourselves against wild beasts. Let us drive a little further, we are sure to arrive at the edge of the forest soon."

"If you say so, Master Ichtheus." Oric was not convinced and, the further they travelled, the more concerned he became.

Chapter Eleven

Summer Solstice

Oric had almost given up hope of finding a resting place when Braccus bumped into a forester's hut. Overgrown with ivy and ferns, the small building was nigh on invisible in the darkening conditions.

The door creaked as Oric prised it open and the smell of damp belched out. "Pwah," he exclaimed, "the place stinks." He stepped inside and immediately began to scratch. "The place is infested with lice," he cried.

"Better we get chewed by insects than eaten by wolves," retorted Ichtheus. "Just be glad we have discovered a safe place to sleep."

Because they had brought no bedding and had little food left, Oric and Ichtheus were glad when daylight returned. Hungry, itchy and irritable, they battled their way through Scraggswood Forest until they recognised landmarks that led them back to Bayersby Manor.

Despite the difficulties they had encountered along the way, Oric had collected a reasonable amount of new specimens. Keen to deliver the plants into Josh's care before they wilted, Oric dropped Ichtheus and a very hungry Parzifal at the manor gates and drove on to his moorland garden.

Apart from a few sheep that cropped grass outside the garden walls, the place was deserted. Oric plunged his plants into the water butt beside the hut, hoping Josh would soon return and dig them into the ground. Unable to spare any more time, Oric drove back to the manor.

Inside the manor compound, serfs with arms full of foodstuff dashed hither and thither. Caged chickens, waiting to be lifted onto a cart, squawked and two milking cows, tethered to the cart, mooed dismally and stomped their hooves.

Oric filled a nose bag with oats and thrust it under Braccus' nose. Since everyone was clearly in a hurry to leave the manor, it seemed pointless to stable the donkey and put the cart away.

Mother Morghan, the armpits of her baggy dress stained dark with sweat, yelled orders from the kitchen doorway. "Get a move on, you good-for-nothing wastrels. We ain't got all day! The rate you lot are going we will still be here when Mother Olive's demons arrive." She shoved Ichtheus in the back. "For goodness' sake, Apothecary, get out there and sort those lazy toads out."

"Never mind about them!" wailed the manor Bailiff. "What about me? There are plenty of other folk able to organise the transportation of fuel to High Moor. Why does Sir Edred say it has to be me?"

Trapped between the disgruntled pair, Ichtheus suffered a brow-beating from both directions.

Mother Morghan pushed her face forward until her nose was close to the Bailiff's cheek. "If I were you, I would save my breath to cool my gruel," she smirked nastily. "As you see, we ain't getting any help from the apothecary." Turning on her heels, she flounced into the kitchen.

"Ha! 'Tis all very well for Mother Morghan to shout at me," said the Bailiff, fixing Ichtheus with a miserable stare. "My wife says I must return home and pack up our cottage, whilst she deals with the children. Frankly, Master Apothecary, I do not know what I fear most: disobeying Sir Edred's orders or gainsaying my wife." Without waiting for Ichtheus to reply, the Bailiff stormed off to berate anyone else that would listen.

"Oh, my giddy aunt," Ichtheus cried, "someone save me from this mayhem."

Oric entered the kitchen and Mother Morghan immediately set upon him. "Where have you been?" she screeched. "I expected you back here along with Master Ichtheus yesterday afternoon."

"Where we have been is none of your business," Ichtheus shouted to make himself heard above the din. "Just be thankful that we are here now, for someone needs to sort out this chaos. What, pray, is going on?"

Mother Morghan's jowls trembled with indignation. "Have you forgotten 'tis Summer Solstice Eve? Folk are preparing to leave for higher ground."

A young serf tore through the kitchen with a handful of stakes to make flares. Oric grabbed hold of his arm. "Slow down, young fellow, before you impale someone."

"I dare not stop," panted the small boy, darting a nervous glance at the housekeeper. "She says we must head for high ground. She reckons the moor is the only place we will be safe from the soothsayer's demons."

Dian's dishevelled arrival prevented Oric from giving Mother Olive's prophecy any further thought. "What ails you?" he cried.

"Josh is in dire trouble," Dian sobbed.

"Trouble? What kind of trouble? Where is he?"

Dian sobbed harder. "He is lashed to a post behind the stables."

Rather than wait for Dian's explanation, Oric ran to check out Josh's predicament for himself.

Hatless, his hair standing up in sweaty spikes, Josh sweltered in the midday sun. At sight of Oric he hung his head.

Oric applied his dagger to the ropes that bound Josh's hands. "Stand still while I cut you free."

"Nay, Oric, best leave well alone." Josh protested. "Sir Edred ordered that I be trussed up like a banquet fowl. 'Tis my punishment for the wrong I have done. I must remain here without food or water until he chooses to release me."

"Wrong – what wrong have you done?" Oric demanded.

"With all the upset in the district, I advised Mother Morghan that I must return to Kilterton to see how my brothers and sisters were faring," explained Josh. "Then, on second thoughts, I decided it best to wait in your garden until you got back." He glared accusingly at Oric. "But you failed to return."

"I am so sorry, Josh, but we lost our way in the forest. Master Ichtheus and I were obliged to shelter in a woodman's hut overnight."

"Be that as it may," moaned Josh, "I am now in a bigger pickle than I dare to think about. When my punishment is complete, Sir Edred plans to send me back to my parents."

"For Heaven's sake," Oric exclaimed. "What happened?"

"The moon had barely risen above the trees when I heard a noise outside the hut. I went to investigate and found someone hauling out your plants. I grabbed him and gave him a good thrashing." Josh gulped. "Unfortunately the culprit was Master Guwain."

"Master Guwain!" Oric gasped.

"Aye, it was Master Guwain alright. I reckon he overheard me telling Mother Morghan I was going to Kilterton and he thought he would have your garden to himself. It must have been him doing the damage all along."

"What happened next?" Oric asked tightly.

Josh tried to open his blackened eye. "He planted this on me before he roared off to tell Sir Edred how I had beaten him. So here I am tied to this post for my sins."

"Not for much longer, if I have anything to do with it." Oric went in search of Sir Edred and found him in the stables harnessing his destrier, Balthazar. The big man was not in a good mood and he was even less pleased to see Oric. "What do you want, Apothecary? Can you not see how busy I am?"

Oric doffed his cap. "Indeed I can, sir, but I require only a moment of your time."

"Very well, but be quick about it. My wife wishes to repair to higher ground before nightfall and, for the sake of peace, I am going along with her demands."

"I am sorry, sir," said Oric. "I am about to add to your burden."

"Are you, indeed?" Sir Edred frowned, bristling his copper-coloured eyebrows together. The last thing he needed was more trouble, but he respected the young apothecary and he was prepared to hear the lad out.

Oric plunged on, anger lending him courage. "Through no fault of his own, sir, Josh Cole is lashed to a post behind the stables."

Sir Edred's frown deepened. "The young upstart attacked my son. When he has served his penance I plan to thrash him and send him home to his parents."

"Nay, sir, Josh is an honourable fellow. He would never behave in such a disrespectful manner, unless he had good reason. Please allow me to put his side of the story."

Sir Edred listened to Oric's tale without interruption and his heart sank. The young apothecary never lied, which was more than could be said for Guwain. Disgusted with his wayward son, Sir Edred sighed woefully. "You may release the Cole boy, but I warn you, Oric, if he ever lays hands upon my son again, I will deal with him harshly."

The moment Josh was freed he thanked Oric and took off for Kilterton. If his father refused to budge from the inn, Josh planned to shepherd his mother and younger siblings to higher ground.

On his way back to the house, Oric bumped into his friends, Egglebart and Etheldrida. "What brings you two so far from home?" he asked, slapping Egglebart on the back.

"It seems the world is about to end," said Egglebart with a disparaging grin. "If that be the case, we would rather spend our last evening amongst good friends. Besides, Etheldrida seems to think folk could use the cart full of food she has brought."

Hearing the commotion outside, Ichtheus left the kitchen to investigate the noise. "My word, dear lady, I am very pleased to see you," he beamed, salivating at the thought of all the tasty treats that were sure to be on Etheldrida's cart. "We can always rely upon you in the culinary department."

"The soothsayer has a lot to answer for," said Etheldrida. "As we drove through Kilterton, folk were leaving the village in droves. If anything goes wrong whilst their homes are unattended, I would not be in Mother Olive's shoes for all the pies in Christendom." Etheldrida climbed down from her cart, and gave Oric a big hug. "Nor, I might add, is Frida Cole helping the situation by running around like a headless chicken because her husband refuses to come out of the inn." Etheldrida shuddered at the memory. "Frida has decided to go up Rosederry Hill without him and I dare not think how she will cope with her unruly brood by herself."

"Worry not, Josh is on his way home," said Oric. "He is a good lad and will see that his family is properly cared for."

Ichtheus groaned and, resigned to the chaotic state of affairs, he patted Oric's arm. "Come, lad, we had best join the exodus to High Moor for fear our expertise is required."

-oOo-

Sir Ragnald and his party rode into Kilterton, planning to spend a night at the inn. When they saw the crowds that thronged the high street, they changed their minds.

Folk hurled armfuls of timber onto ox-drawn carts, and cottage doors hung open as more villagers poured into the street with tatty bits of furniture. Adults argued, and snot-nosed children bawled. Thunder rumbled in the distance and black clouds closed in, making the already dense atmosphere more stultifying.

In a hurry to leave her cottage, a woman ran full tilt into Sir Ragnald's horse. "What is going on?" he demanded. "Has everyone taken leave of their senses?"

"I neither know nor care," retorted Joffrey. "This mob looks insane and I am for travelling on. I would not want to spend the night here for fear some madman may cut my throat."

The woman straightened her clothes, and stared belligerently at Sir Ragnald."Everyone in the district knows what is going on! If you ain't got no idea, I ain't got time to tell you."

More thunder rumbled, and Sir Ragnald laughed. "If the threat of a mere storm sends these folks into a panic, imagine how they will react when I return with my army. I fancy the Bayersby mob will surrender before they feel the first prick of a sword." Heeling his horse he shouted, "Let us get away before the storm catches up with us!"

Chapter Twelve

Bayersby Evacuated

Guwain followed his parents out of the Bayersby compound, his face blacker than the thunder clouds that gathered overhead. His backside smarted from the whip-lashes he had received from his father and he shuffled about in his saddle, trying to find a comfortable place to sit. Clenching his teeth, he silently fumed over how best to pay back the apothecary's assistant for his defence of the Cole boy.

After the racket of the past two days the deserted compound became eerily silent. No horses or donkeys stomped and whinnied in the stables, and pigs and chickens left behind were locked inside their enclosures with enough food to tide them over for a few days. The wild birds seemed to have flown away and no blade of grass or leaf stirred in the breezeless, humid atmosphere.

Regardless of his mentor's scathing remarks, Oric remained unconvinced that Mother Olive's prophecy was untrue. "I would not care to spend the night at the manor on my own," he said with an involuntary shudder. "Goodness knows what is about to happen." Too late he noticed Dian's pale face and wished he had bitten his tongue.

"How many times must I tell you there will be no demons?" Exasperated, Ichtheus flapped the reins on Braccus' back. "For goodness' sake, Oric, climb aboard beside Dian and let us get going. At this rate we shall never catch up with Sir Edred."

The column of evacuees trailed along the path that led to High Moor. Apart from foodstuff, they had left most of their personal possessions behind to allow maximum room for fuel on their carts. Eight oxen, yoked together in pairs, hauled four dray-loads of freshly-hewn logs.

"Heaven help Mother Olive's demons if all that timber is set alight," Dian whispered, not daring to voice her opinions too loudly for fear of further antagonising Master Ichtheus.

Oric pointed to a bank of bilious-green cloud roiling over the horizon. "Always supposing we are not deluged with rain before the beacons can be lit."

"I am afraid of storms," Dian cried, catching hold of Oric's hand. "Please stay close by me."

Secretly thrilled, Oric squeezed Dian's fingers. "Never fear, I will not allow anything untoward to happen to you."

At the top of a steep incline, Sir Edred called a halt. "Do you suppose this plateau is high enough to ensure our safety, my dear?"

Ignoring her husband's sarcastic tone, Lady Myferny tilted her nose in the air. "It will do very well, thank you, Edred. We shall set up camp right here and stay put until the danger has passed."

Serfs erected beacons, and womenfolk set up makeshift shelters around their carts. The moor was imbued with sinister green light as the monstrous cloud bank built overhead. Suddenly a spiteful wind sprang from nowhere and spiralled dust into people's faces.

Ichtheus climbed down from his cart to help Egglebart and Etheldrida hand out food to all and sundry. "No doubt we are in for a soaking," he grumbled. "Just what we need, exposed as we are to the elements."

Supressing a chortle, Etheldrida passed oatcakes and a pot of honey to Ichtheus. "We may as well enjoy a little supper before we meet our doom."

"I have yet to see Sir Oswold and Lady Malla," said Ichtheus, drizzling honey onto a crisp, golden oatcake. "Did they climb Rosederry Hill with the folk from Kilterton?"

"Not them!" replied Egglebart, stuffing his mouth full of food. "They told us they planned to stay at home." Feeling chilly all of a sudden, Egglebart drew a sleeveless cowhide jerkin over his rough, woollen tunic.

"How I envy them!" Ichtheus mumbled. "I would prefer to have remained at Bayersby Manor, but Lady Myferny insisted that everyone repair to High Moor. As an obedient servant, here I am."

A plump, bald little man drew his smart conveyance to a halt alongside Egglebart and Etheldrida's cart. Tewdric Bascoomb climbed down from the driver's seat, knocked a stake into the ground and tethered his horse to it. He then hastened to help his wife, Helled, and twin daughters, Lunette and Novena, down from the back of his cart.

"Pity the Bascoombs did not see fit to follow Sir Oswold and Lady Malla's example and remain at home," grumbled Egglebart. He liked Tewdric well enough, but he had no time for the butcher's ill-tempered wife. Nor did he trust skinny women, and Helled Bascoomb was reed thin. "No wonder she is always in a foul mood," said Egglebart. "I doubt she ever eats a proper meal."

"Do not be uncharitable, Egglebart," hissed Etheldrida, thrusting more oatcakes into her husband's hands. Nodding to the Bascoombs, she bid them good evening.

"How good the evening turns out remains to be seen," replied Helled peevishly. Darting black, shrew-like eyes around to make sure Sir Edred was not within hearing range she added, "I care little for the landed gentry but, since trouble is brewing, I reckon being with you lot is our safest option." She hauled down a bundle of wolf pelts and threw them under Tewdric's cart for bedding. "Everyone in Kilterton is scurrying hither and thither with no sense of direction, and St Griswald's horrible priest is ranting and raving like a madman." Helled sniffed derisively. "The stupid man cannot be right in the head."

A flash of lightning followed by a mighty crack of thunder stopped Helled's diatribe. She ushered her daughters beneath the cart and crawled in after them.

"Why not join us, Master Ichtheus?" Etheldrida suggested kindly. "There is ample room for us all to shelter beneath our cart."

Egglebart's cart was larger than most and Ichtheus gladly accepted Etheldrida's kind offer. He had not looked forward to cramming under his own cart with Oric, Dian and, no doubt, the dog Parzifal.

Wind ripped across the moor, bringing with it fat drops of rain. Having had no time to erect decent shelters or finish the beacons, the folk of Bayersby followed Helled's example and scrambled under their own carts. An old woman, outlined by jagged lightning, ran from her lookout position on the hilltop. "Prepare to meet thy doom," she screamed. "Mother Olive's demons are coming."

"Ye gods, folk are gullible!" exclaimed Ichtheus. "We will suffer a soaking at the very worst." Perplexed by people's foolhardiness, Ichtheus dragged his cloak more firmly around his shoulders and prepared to sit out the downpour.

Guided by Oric, Dian crawled beneath Ichtheus' cart. Oric followed her and covered her with a waterproof pelt. Just as he was about to snuggle up to protect her from Mother Olive's demons, Parzifal charged in. Shaking like a leaf in a gale, the dog pushed under the pelt and lay down beside Dian. Full of sympathy for the soppy wolfhound, she soothed him and hugged him close.

Oric had forgotten Parzifal's terror of thunder, but he certainly remembered now. The dog lay with his shaggy head on Dian's shoulder and a front leg draped over her chest. Frustrated by another missed opportunity to get close to Dian, Oric slumped to the ground and stared at the underside of the cart.

Chapter Thirteen

Farewell Master Figg

Figg approached Bayersby Manor with caution. Seeing no-one, he placed his hands around his mouth and cooed like a dove. At the pre-arranged signal Figg's Master at Arms sauntered out of a nearby coppice. Big and burly, Maddock wore a long rumpled tunic, belted at the waist. His leggings were creased and his cloth shoes looked all but worn out. The only thing that indicated his warrior status was the pointed, battered helmet he wore on his head.

"Are the men ready?" Figg demanded.

Maddock nodded curtly. He cared little for upstarts but Figg's promised reward for services rendered was too good to forego. The sooner the coming fray was over, the sooner he could retire. "Aye, Master Figg, your mercenaries are ready, but some of them want more money."

"The men will get the rest of their pay when the job is done," snarled Figg. He jerked his thumb at the dense copse behind Maddock. "I trust you are encamped somewhere nearby."

"Aye, we are," Maddock smirked. "What, pray, do you want of us next?"

"Mother Morghan will signal when the coast is clear for you to enter the manor. Pick out all the most valuable items and transport them to St Griswald's crypt." Figg's nervous tic was getting the better of him and he placed his finger on the offending eyelid to try and stop it from jerking. "When you have secured the plunder, ride back to the manor and finish off any of Sir Edred's men still left standing."

Maddock's insolent smirk disappeared. "Oh, aye – and what will you be doing during the fray?" He eyed the wooden box and satchel that Figg carried, wondering what they might contain.

"I shall be engaged in a dangerous mission elsewhere."

Maddock had watched Sir Edred and his entourage leave Bayersby Manor along with cart-loads of timber and several animals. Too tired to fathom what Figg meant about the last of Sir Edred's men still standing, the old warrior returned to the coppice and hunkered down to await Mother Morghan's signal.

Figg scrambled down the hillside below Bayersby Manor until he came upon the hidden cave Ned and Joe had described. He parted the thick curtain of vines that obscured the entrance and stuck his beaky nose inside. The light was low but, as far as he could see, no-one lurked within the cave. Dropping the leather satchel from his shoulder, he lifted the flap and scrabbled inside for a flint and char cloth to light his lantern.

Curious to discover what kind of new skulduggery their employer might be engaged in, Ned and Joe followed Figg from St Griswald's Church to Bayersby Manor. They crept down the hillside and watched him disappear into the cave.

Joe hung back, his peaked little face covered in consternation. "I ain't going in there again. 'Tis too dark and we never brought no lanterns."

"We got this far!" snapped Ned. "I ain't leaving 'til I see what yon villain is up to." He grabbed a handful of ivy and eased it away from the cave's entrance. "You can stop outside 'til I get back if you like."

Even more afraid to stay outside by himself, Joe reluctantly followed his friend into the dark cave.

They tiptoed along and, hugging the shadows, they kept their master's bobbing light in sight. At the final bend in the tunnel Joe dragged at the back of Ned's tunic. "I ain't going no further," he quavered. "If Maser Figg sees us he will likely kill us. We could lie in here 'til our bones turn white and still nobody finds us. "

"Do not fret so," whispered Ned. "Master Figg cannot see us in the shadows." He braved a look around the bend in the wall and then jerked back his head. "Whatever is he doing?"

Joe plucked up his courage and took a sneaky peek. "Eee by gum – it looks like he is disrobing."

Figg stripped off his tunic, and unhitched the waterproof pouches of black powder from the belt he wore around his waist. Setting one pouch aside, he emptied the contents from the remaining six pouches into the wooden box he had brought for the purpose, and tamped down the powdery substance. He climbed the stairs and placed the box directly under the trapdoor that gave access to the Bayersby kitchen. A strip of char cloth hung from a knothole in the base of the box and Figg sprinkled it with black powder. Using the contents of the remaining pouch, he trickled more powder in a line along the narrow ledge that ran beside the stairs. Experiments he had conducted in the past had caused fantastic effects, and he believed a greater quantity of the substance would produce a most spectacular result. Hardly daring to believe how easily his plan was falling into place, Figg blew air out of his mouth in a silent whistle. Mother

Morghan would now be signalling Maddock and his men to remove everything of value from Bayersby Manor. If his ruse failed he would have his army to fall back on.

The hot weather getting the better of her, Mother Morghan entered the Great Hall and damped down the logs on the hearth to a gentle smoulder. She returned to the kitchen and did the same to the inglenook fire. Enjoying the absence of other folk in the manor, she sprawled in her chair and fell asleep.

Joe watched the lantern's light advance back along the tunnel. "Figg is coming too close for comfort! Let us clear off, afore he spots us."

For once, Ned wholeheartedly agreed and the boys hastened back the way they had come.

Unaware that he had been observed, Figg continued to trickle black powder along the tunnel until the last pouch was empty. Satisfied that he had allowed sufficient time to make his escape via the well shaft once he set light to the powder, he retraced his steps to the foot of the stairs, and settled down to await Sir Edred's return to the manor. Everybody would return the morning after Summer Solstice Eve, when no demons had appeared.

Ned and Joe had been correct in everything they had described – the cave, the tunnel – and Figg contemplated the possibility of allowing them to live. Reluctantly he was beginning to think the boys might be more use alive than dead. Delighted with the way events had turned out, Figg allowed himself a small chuckle as he removed a bite to eat from his satchel. Well-fed, he settled down at the foot of the stairs to wait.

It was uncomfortably warm underground and Figg nodded off. He awoke with a jolt when a rat scurried across his feet. Startled, he kicked out. The lantern overturned and fell into the black powder. Oil spilled out and flames streaked up the stairway toward the box under the trapdoor. Unable to catch up, Figg turned and fled toward the well shaft.

Debris propelled by a rush of wind roared down the tunnel and filled the boys' eyes with dust. Ned clapped both hands to his ears. "Gawd help us," he squealed. "What the devil was that?"

"I told you something bad would happen if we followed Master Figg," Joe howled. "The world has come to an end, and here we are stuck underground like rats in a trap."

As if on cue, a column of terrified rodents flowed along the tunnel. Ned swiped at a big male hell-bent upon running up his leg. "Quick, let us get out of here!" he hollered.

Above ground, parts of Bayersby Manor collapsed. The roof tumbled into the damped-down fire in the Great Hall and, in no time at all, the smouldering logs set light to the fallen thatch. Soon the entire building became a blazing inferno.

Believing some supernatural force was at work, Maddock mounted his horse and fled at full gallop. The army of petrified mercenaries needed no command to follow their leader. They all rode as if the devil chased them, until they deemed it safe to stop. In a clearing some distance from the manor they drew to a halt. To a man, they agreed to cut their losses, each keen to seek his fortune in a less dangerous place.

-oOo-

Summer Solstice Eve saw the worst storm in living memory rip across the Bayersby and Kilterton districts. Trees were blown down, crops flattened, and many roofs were damaged. Relieved to still be alive, the folk from Bayersby emerged from their makeshift shelters on High Moor. Not one demon had materialised and the general consensus of opinion was that Mother Olive had caused mass upheaval for no good reason. One and all were out for the old woman's blood.

Helled Bascoomb slapped Tewdric with considerable force. "You stupid little butcher," she shrieked. "You dragged us all this way for nothing!" She chose to forget that it was at her own behest the family had repaired to High Moor; her normally pale face red with rage, she continued to lambast her husband.

In a foul mood, Sir Edred helped Lady Myferny to mount her pony. "When I get my hands on that poxy soothsayer, I shall make her punishment fit the crime," he growled, easing his wife's dainty feet into the stirrups. "If yon Bascoomb woman does not cease her rattle she will suffer a similar fate!"

Tired, irritable, and hungry, the bedraggled column of Bayersby residents retraced their steps across the moor toward home. Nearing the manor, Ichtheus noticed that clouds of smoke belched skyward. Moorland fires were quite common at this time of year but, in this instance, the ground was soggy after the storm. "Surely 'tis too wet for the bracken to ignite," he remarked.

The source of the fire was not burning bracken but Bayersby Manor. Crimson flames licked around what was left of the building, and bright sparks pricked the acrid smoke that billowed up into a clear summer sky.

Sir Edred tore toward his home followed by every able-bodied man and boy, but they were too late to save the house Charred timber and fallen masonry were all that was left of the once grand building.

"Something far more evil than Mother Olive's demons has been at work here," Oric gasped, barely able to believe his eyes.

"Nonsense! A lightning bolt most likely caused the fire," Ichtheus insisted. He did not mention the gaping hole that had once been the Bayersby kitchen, for he dare not imagine what had caused such devastation. *Thank God I took my medical journals to High Moor,* he thought, clutching the precious parchments to his chest.

All that remained of Bayersby Manor were a couple of upright walls and one or two charred roof beams. Only the outbuildings and stables around the perimeter of the compound remained intact.

A sudden blood-chilling scream stopped everyone in their tracks.

"Oh, my giddy aunt! What now?" Ichtheus exclaimed. He placed his precious journals on the cart, covered them with a sack, and hastened to investigate the latest disturbance.

A goggle-eyed kitchen maid pointed to where Mother Morghan lay dead, pinned down by a fallen beam. Caedmon, the cat, sat on her chest gnawing at her nose.

Ichtheus kicked the cat, and covered the housekeeper with his cloak. For the first time in his life he wished the woman could speak, and so throw some light on the horrendous situation.

Returned from Kilterton, Josh Cole ogled the remains of Bayersby Manor. He scratched his head, causing his hair to stand on end. "Thank God we all evacuated; many folk would surely have died had we stayed put. I spent the night on Rosederry Hill with my family and the folk from Kilterton; all we got was a monstrous thunder storm and a thorough drenching. Mother and the bairns returned home this morning, but I came straight back here to see how you all fared." Josh grimaced, his crumpled sun-bronzed face looking like a ripe, dried-up apple. "Maybe Mother Olive's demons missed Kilterton and got to work here instead."

Ichtheus flapped his hands to silence Josh. "For the sake of sanity, keep your thoughts to yourself, lad! Folk are already in a state of shock without you adding to their concern."

The rainstorm had come too late to douse the inferno that consumed Bayersby Manor, and Oric thanked God he had placed the alchemist's key with Master Ichtheus' few valuables in a cavity under the floor of Braccus' stable. Had he left the key in his medicament chest in the kitchen, it would have been incinerated along with everything else.

"Is it wicked to say I am glad Mother Morghan is dead?" Josh's expression showed a mixture of relief and remorse. "She was a tyrant and Bayersby Manor will be a much happier place without her."

"Nay, you are not wicked, Josh, you speak the truth." Oric squeezed his friend's shoulder. "What say we make my hut on the moor comfortable? At least we can offer Master Ichtheus temporary shelter until a new manor is built. Though Lord knows how long that will take."

Chapter Fourteen

Survival

"We should nearly be back to the cave by now," said Ned, feeling his way along the wall in the dark.

Almost at the end of the tunnel a pile of rubble blocked their way.

Joe fell, spreadeagled upon the mound of earth and rocks that had dropped from above. "We will never get out of here," he sobbed, beating his dirt-encrusted fists on the ground.

"Stop blubbering," snapped Ned, trying hard not to panic. "We shall go back along the tunnel and escape via the well shaft."

"But what if we run into Master Figg?" quavered Joe.

"We shall deal with that event if it happens," Ned replied, crawling along as fast as the rough terrain allowed. "For goodness' sake keep up with me, Joe, I do not want to keep stopping because you are lagging behind."

Where Ned deemed the well shaft to be, they ran into another pile of rubble.

"See, I told you! We are buried alive in this horrible tunnel," Joe whimpered.

Ned looked up and drew Joe's attention to a chink of light. "I believe we are closer to the surface than you think." He scrambled up the mound of earth and began picking at the fissure. "Wait!" he cried. "I can hear voices. Someone just said Mother Morghan is dead!"

"The rate we are going we will soon join her," moaned Joe.

"Give over little'un!" Ned fumed. "I never knew anyone lose hope as quickly as you do! Get up here and help me to dig. If we clear a way to the surface we might be able to escape come nightfall."

The boys clawed at the debris until their fingers bled, but they made little headway. Exhausted, Joe sat back on his haunches. "I see no way out of here other than to shout for help."

Joe sucked his ravaged fingers. "A slow death from thirst and starvation will be worse. If we grovel a bit, Sir Edred might give us another chance. Working in the Bayersby kitchen without Mother Morghan hounding us morning, noon and night would be better than most jobs we have had in the past. Come on – on the count of three, shout!"

"Over here!" Ichtheus cried. "Someone is trapped below ground. Round up some help, Oric. We need to lift these roof timbers aside."

The fallen beams were soon removed and, armed with shovels, Oric and Josh began to dig. They had not advanced far when Oric struck something soft. He recoiled in horror when he saw the object he had sliced into was the body of a man. Upon closer inspection he saw that the corpse was Esica Figg. "Did I not say that villain would turn up again?" Oric raged. "I would not be the least surprised if he is the cause of all this destruction."

Josh helped Oric to haul Figg out of the ground, and Ichtheus listened for a heartbeat. He heard none, but he could hear a curious crackling sound. He slid his hand beneath Figg's undershirt and withdrew a crumpled document. More shouts sounded from underground and Ichtheus hastily shoved the parchment into his pouch for safekeeping. Oric and Josh returned to their shovels to dig with renewed vigour.

Ned and Joe blinked in the bright sunlight, greatly relieved to be rescued from their temporary tomb.

"Well, well, well!" Ichtheus eyed the grubby pair with distaste. "What mischief have you two been about, since you escaped from Mother Morghan's clutches?" He indicated the smouldering ruin that had been Sir Edred's manor. "I sincerely hope you had nothing to do with this disaster."

"On my life, Master Ichtheus, we ain't never had nothing to do with this mess." Ned's Adam's apple bobbed up and down the front of his neck as he gulped. "We just followed Master Figg into a cave down the hillside to see what he was up to. Not long after we entered the tunnel there was a terrible noise and the roof caved in. Me and Joe was buried deeper than a pair of corpses; we been trying to dig ourselves out ever since."

Tears made pale tracks in the dirt down Joe's thin cheeks. "Master Figg bullied us into doing his dirty work," he snivelled miserably. "I swear on my mother's grave we ain't got no idea what he was up to." Joe rubbed at his eyes, and wiped his drippy nose on the heel of his thumb. "All I ever wanted was to work for a living fair and square, but no-one ever gives us a chance."

As if picking pouches and petty thievery could be classed as a fair living, thought Ichtheus; nevertheless, his soft heart overruled his head. The lads were only bairns and had probably been turned out of their homes at an early age. "This could be your lucky day," he growled. "Oric and I will plead your case with Sir Edred."

Many hands would to be needed to rebuild Bayersby Manor and, in view of the boys' tender years, Sir Edred gave Ned and Joe another chance. In so doing he earned two hard workers, and Oric gained a pair of lifelong friends.

-oOo-

Grateful that Mother Olive's demons had not materialised, folk cleaned up without complaint. Lady Myferny commandeered Sir Edred's largest stable and set her serfs to work, making it habitable. Against her husband's wishes she had removed some household items to High Moor and their new abode soon looked homely with a few familiar possessions scattered about. She had also taken some of her clothes, and she looked as beautiful as ever with her fair hair secured in a silver snood and a jewelled belt around her slender waist. Hardly proper apparel for working, but she felt the need to boost her morale.

Barns were cleared of dung, and incumbent animals were led out to pasture alongside Sir Edred's ousted warhorses. Serfs barrowed in fresh straw to make sleeping places for everyone, and woodsmen were despatched to the forest. They returned with felled timber to construct new tables, benches and bed frames.

Ichtheus graciously accepted the offer of accommodation in Oric's moorland shack, and chose a corner in which to sleep. Everyone agreed that the situation was tolerable, for the short term at least, and certainly better than sleeping in amongst other serfs in a barn.

Seeking his son, Sir Edred confronted Ichtheus. "Have you seen Guwain? I have not clapped eyes on him since we returned from High Moor."

Ichtheus wondered what mischief the Bayersby heir might be up to, but he kept his thoughts to himself. "No, my lord, I have not seen him since yesterday. Try not to worry, I am sure the young master will turn up when he is hungry."

Sir Edred scowled and slapped a small whip against his thigh. "If you come across him send him directly to me, there are chores aplenty for him to do. Meanwhile I must plan the rebuilding of Bayersby Manor."

-oOo-

Hersica Horzefell had cowered under a table in St Griswald's crypt whilst the storm raged overhead. She had barely managed a wink of sleep and she was not pleased when, at break of day, Bertram, one of Figg's villains, slammed through the crypt's back door.

"Lawks alive!" she shrieked. "You scared me half to death! What in Heaven's name is amiss now?"

Bertram took a few steadying breaths. "Figg is dead, mistress!"

"Dead? What do you mean, dead?"

"Just – what – I – say!" Bertram spoke slowly and loudly as if addressing a simpleton. "Figg is dead! Finished – corpsed – gone to meet his maker."

Hersica eyed the podgy fellow suspiciously. "How do you know he is dead?"

"The pickings in Kilterton were not the best so I left the rest of Figg's men to steal what they could. I figured there might be summat more worthwhile to thieve from the rich folks at Bayersby, so I rode over there." Bertram hawked and spat. "When I arrived the manor was afire with a blaze so fierce I stood no chance of getting anywhere near. I expected to run into Maddock and his men but I never saw hide nor hair of them."

"That is all very well," snapped Hersica. "But how do you know Figg is dead?"

"I waited 'til morning to find out what was going on. What a to-do there was when Sir Edred and his mob returned from the moor and saw the devastation."

On the point of desperation, Hersica yelled, "Yes, yes, I hear you – but *how* did Figg die?"

Bertram shrugged his shoulders. "I dunno, mistress. The apothecary said Figg was dead. All I know is that there ain't nowt left of the manor. Apart from that, I ain't none the wiser."

Hersica pressed her lips together to hide her delight. Bertram's resemblance to her dead son, Zebediah, was uncanny – plenty of brawn but not quite so stupid. Hersica imagined the great things she might achieve with such a fellow at her back.

Chapter Fifteen

Oric's Heritage

On their return journey to Lockton Castle, Sir Ragnald and his party rode via Bayersby for a final reconnoitre. Appalled by the devastation, Sir Ragnald asked a group of fieldworkers what had happened, but no-one seemed to know.

"Just look at the Bayersby serfs," Joffrey guffawed. "Yon silly fools know not what to do next. Not much point coming back here – there ain't nothing left worth fighting over."

A sly expression crossed Sir Ragnald's face. "Do not be so sure, my son. Sir Edred will soon rebuild and, when he least expects trouble, we shall return with our army and seize his brand-new manor. Lord knows we need to find a new income from somewhere." Over the years Sir Ragnald had taken high rents and tithes from the farmers within the Lockton estate. Most of the common people were now so poor they could barely feed themselves let alone give money to the landowner. Many farms stood empty because the tenants had moved elsewhere.

-oOo-

Angry at his father for the thrashing he had delivered, Guwain lay low in a disused stable, making plans to run away from home. Skulking out of sight to avoid work, he watched the Lord of Lockton and his party pause at the compound gates. They viewed the devastation and, after a few heartbeats, they wheeled their horses away and cantered off.

With everyone at the manor engaged in some task or another, Guwain seized his chance. The few belongings he had packed to take to High Moor remained in his saddlebags, and no-one noticed as he led his pony out through the compound gates. Safely outside Bayersby's walls he climbed onto the pony's back and made haste after Sir Ragnald.

Alone on High Moor, Guwain's bravado quickly evaporated. Sucking bogs his father had warned about seemed to be everywhere, and stormwater from the night before had turned small streams into raging torrents. Many narrow tracks made by sheep trailed between the heather and Guwain was unsure which one to follow. The land undulated and, cresting a small rise, he was relieved to see Sir Ragnald and his party not far ahead.

"Good day to you, sir," said Guwain, putting on his most ingratiating smile. "Would it be convenient for me to travel alongside you for a while? I am seeking an adventure and you might be just the man to provide it."

Sir Ragnald looked the richly-dressed popinjay up and down. "Indeed, young sir, you are most welcome to join us," he said, dropping one eyelid in a barely perceptible wink at his son Joffrey. The objectionable heir of Bayersby would make a wonderful bargaining tool against Sir Edred should the need arise.

Joffrey guessed what Sir Ragnald was thinking. "I have missed your company since father and I were last at Bayersby Manor," he lied, giving Guwain a sympathetic smile. "Please accept my sincere condolences over the loss of your magnificent home. Ride alongside me and I will endeavour to cheer you up."

-oOo-

Sitting on a stool outside Oric's hut, Ichtheus struggled with the enormity of what had happened. Worried about his mentor, Oric dragged up a second stool and sat down beside him. "You look a little pale, Master Ichtheus. Are you unwell?"

"Nay, I am well enough – under the circumstances," Ichtheus mumbled. He rubbed his aching knees with gnarled fingers. "Time spent outdoors in the damp weather last night has set off my sciatica and inflamed my joints. The fire burned most of my medicaments and I have no ammoniacum to soothe my pain. Even if I did there is no vinegar with which to mix it." He shrugged unhappily and the pain of his action caused him to wince. "Now I am reliant upon the store of medicaments you keep in your moorland hut."

"You are welcome to everything I have," replied Oric generously. In truth, he would give the shirt off his back if the old man needed it. "Say what you like," Oric added, trying to remain positive, "Mother Olive inadvertently saved many lives. Imagine the carnage that would have occurred had she not frightened everyone away from Bayersby Manor with her prophecy."

"I hear what you say, Oric, but what about the folk in Kilterton? Whilst they were away it seems a band of thieves helped themselves to whatever they fancied. If the villagers had remained at home their possessions may not have disappeared. Few of them can afford the losses they have sustained. There is now real hardship and, mark my words, that kind of situation leads to violence and crime." He fixed Oric with tired eyes. "And – answer me this – what was Figg doing here, and why did Mother Morghan fail to evacuate Bayersby along with everyone else? Perhaps they had a hand in the manor's destruction. If that be the case, something must have gone dreadfully wrong, for I am sure they did not plan to die."

Ichtheus eased his bony buttocks on the stool, and his pouch fell from his knee to the ground. He stared at the old, brown leather bag speculatively. "Apart from the clothes I am wearing, and the small stash of items that remain hidden with your key under the stable floor, this pouch and its contents are all I have left to call my own." He lifted the pouch flap and began to check through the contents. "Good Heavens," he gasped, his white eyebrows climbing his forehead. "What with one thing and another, I forgot all about this."

"What is it?" asked Oric.

"I am not sure. 'Tis something I rescued from Figg's dead body." Ichtheus pulled out the battered sheet of yellowed parchment, and squinted at the writing upon it. "I have not had time to look at it until now."

Barely able to contain his curiosity, Oric shuffled forward on his stool. "Can you decipher the words, Master Ichtheus?"

Ichtheus held the parchment up to catch the last, pink rays of sun. "'Tis penned in Latin, a sure sign the scribe was an educated man." Ichtheus read to himself, stopping every now and again to relate salient points for Oric's benefit. "A foreign monk arrived at Dunburton Manor. According to this parchment, he spoke a strange language; however, he had some grasp of the English tongue. It seems the fellow produced a handful of black powder." Ichtheus' hand flew to his mouth. "When ignited, it had flared up in spectacular fashion."

"Suppose it was the same black powder I found inside the old iron chest at Dunburton?" cried Oric. "What if Figg got to the chest before I did and stole the contents? Maybe he used the powder to destroy Bayersby Manor."

"There are many questions I would like to have asked Master Figg," replied Ichtheus. "'Tis a pity I did not get the opportunity before he died." Coming to the end of the parchment all colour drained from Ichtheus' face. "You will never believe who signed this document."

"Who?" shouted Oric. "Tell me, for Heaven's sake!"

"None other than Deveril of Dunburton. *Instructions on how to mix potassium nitrate, charcoal and sulphur follow.* I suspect these are the ingredients that make up the monk's black powder."

The stool crashed over as Oric leaped to his feet. "If you are correct, imagine what we could do with the substance should anyone ever threaten us again!"

Ichtheus flipped over to the reverse side of the parchment. "Before we charge off to create the makings of mayhem, perhaps I should first read what else is written here."

"Is it also scribed in Latin?"

"Aye, but it looks like a letter and the handwriting is different. *My dearest Oric,*" Ichtheus began.

Oric's eyebrows shot up in surprise. "Surely the writer does not refer to me."

"Allow me to continue, dear boy, and we might find out."

"*In the event of my passing, Deveril, the Dunburton alchemist, has pledged to care for you until you become of age. Since you are now reading this letter I must assume that day has arrived. Trust Deveril, he is a good friend and he has your best interests at heart. He will lead you to a chest, and he will give you a key with which to open it. The double knots engraved upon the chest and the key form part of our family crest. The knots represent strength and fortitude; both of which I fear you will require in abundance if you are to reclaim our family seat."*

"Family seat?" Oric wrung his hands in agitation. "What family seat?"

"For goodness' sake allow me to finish," snapped Ichtheus. "Then you can work yourself into a lather – if you must."

My beloved Oric, your mother and I lived together in peaceful harmony for many moons. Life was good and we became overly complacent. Unfortunately we were unprepared for the sudden, vicious attack from an evil knight and his mercenary army. Our faithful servants were swiftly overwhelmed and, to my eternal shame, there was nothing I could do to save them. You were but a babe in your mother's arms when we escaped with our lives and precious little else. Thus we made the journey to the village of Dunburton where the lord of the manor employed me as scribe and your mother as companion to the lady of the house.

As I write, I am suffering from a severe fever and do not expect to remain on this earth much longer. Lady Isolda, your sweet mother, died from the same malady a few days ago. I pray, Oric, that your young life will be spared.

The chest that Deveril is about to give you contains a modest amount of gold plus a few family heirlooms. The key that unlocks the chest will also open a door to great wealth. I dare not write more for fear this letter falls into evil hands, but Deveril will explain all. My dearest son, you must right the terrible wrong that has been perpetrated upon our noble family.

May God speed and keep you

Your loving father

Askell

"The signature is dated thirteen years past and is witnessed by Deveril," Ichtheus concluded.

"What do you suppose it means?" Oric gasped.

Ichtheus arose from his stool and bowed. "It means that I am at your service, my lord."

Oric jumped two paces backwards. "Do not bow before me, sir." Shocked to the core, he spoke more sharply than he intended. "I am not worthy of such an honour, I am naught but a humble apothecary. I want no part of the aristocracy save to serve them."

"You are upset," said Ichtheus, feeling thoroughly sorry for the lad. "But I believe you are duty-bound to honour your father's last wishes. Deveril cared for you and protected your heritage to the best of his ability; we must now redouble our efforts to unearth the information that he carried to his grave."

"I shall work hard to achieve that aim, Master Ichtheus." Oric rolled up the parchment that would change his life. "But what I choose to do with such enlightenment remains to be seen. Please keep my father's secret between us, for I want everything to carry on as normal until I fathom what to do for the best."

Observing the set of his assistant's jaw, Ichtheus knew not to pursue the topic any further. Not for the time being, anyway.

-oOo-

Another day came and went with still no sign of Guwain. Sir Edred sent out a search party, but the men returned at sunset with no news of the missing boy.

"No doubt he is spending time with one or another of his friends." Unable to offer his wife any better words of comfort, Sir Edred added, "Mark my words – our wayward son will return as soon as he thinks there is no more work to be done. When he does show his face I shall thrash him soundly."

Lady Myferny glared at her husband, her violet eyes flashing in suppressed fury. "I suspect it was your harsh treatment that caused him to run away in the first place. He is our only child, what will we do if he fails to return home?"

Sir Edred's bark of laughter was humourless. "Hah – that is highly unlikely. Our avaricious young son has his eyes firmly fixed upon his inheritance, he will return to Bayersby eventually."

Trying to push her worries aside, Lady Myferny threw herself into designing her new home. Thatchers, carpenters and stonemasons were soon hard at work and the framework of a splendid dwelling rose in place of the old manor house. Servants, unable to help with building work, were kept busy with late summer haymaking.

Mother Morghan's demise brought peace and harmony to the serfs' quarters, and the manor ran more smoothly than it had in years.

The hut on the moor provided sleeping accommodation for Oric, Ichtheus, and Josh, but they spent their days each going about his own business. Josh tended the garden and planted new herbs that Oric gathered from the woods and fields. Ichtheus spent time concocting new medicaments to replace the ones he had lost in the fire. In-between times both apothecaries tended to folks' illnesses and injuries.

Dian ran herself ragged with chores in and around the makeshift Bayersby quarters, sharing a stable at night with other female servants. Oric missed seeing her every day, and he pined for her company.

Medicaments stockpiled, and Oric's small reserve of containers was soon used up.

Ichtheus suggested that a trip to the potter and glassblower in Kilterton was in order and, feeling sorry for the two would-be lovebirds, he suggested that Dian might like to go, too, and visit her family.

Dian liked the idea, and immediately obtained Lady Myferny's permission to take a day off from her chores.

"Since you are going to Kilterton I may as well tag along for the ride," said Josh. "Everything is up to date in the garden so I have some time to spare."

"No, no, Josh, you must stay here. Master Ichtheus is too frail to stop any passing itinerant from stealing our stock of herbs." Desperate to gain some time alone with Dian, Oric could think of no better excuse on the spur of the moment.

Josh was not to be dissuaded. "Ned and Joe will keep an eye on the place until we return." He smiled happily, thinking he had killed two birds with one stone. "The boys would be in serious bother had you not pleaded their case with Sir Edred. They are more than keen to repay you in any way they can."

Chapter Sixteen

Malla Maligned

Angry shouts greeted Oric, Josh and Dian as they drove into Kilterton. Many possessions had disappeared from homes and shops during the villagers' evacuation to Rosederry Hill. Folk were accusing each other of thievery and a public brawl was in full swing.

Oric leaped down from the driver's seat and tossed the reins to Dian. "Tie Braccus up before he bolts. You come with me, Josh; we need to calm this mob before murder is committed." Racing to the forge, he snatched a breastplate and a hammer from the blacksmith's hands and clanged one against the other. "Stop this nonsense at once!" he hollered.

Josh ran along the opposite side of the street. "Why are you doing this?" he cried, grabbing the potter's flying fists to stop him from assaulting the innkeeper. "None of you are to blame for the robberies."

"Josh is right!" bellowed Oric. "I now believe that Esica Figg paid Mother Olive to spread untrue threats, and we all fell for the story. I suspect Figg's cohorts entered the village and helped themselves to whatever they fancied, whilst you were all sitting on top of Rosederry Hill. Figg is no longer a threat because he is dead."

News of Figg's demise passed from one to another of the villagers, and a hush gradually spread the length of the street. Over the years most folk had been duped by Figg's nefarious money-lending tactics and no-one mourned his passing.

"If we all work together," continued Oric, "we might discover what has happened to your possessions."

Shamefaced, the villagers calmed down and apologised to one other, but not Helled Bascoomb. The butcher's wife had lost less than most but she continued to browbeat her husband. Daughters Lunette and Novena, who were the exact opposite to their mother in looks and temperament, pleaded with their parents to stop the upset.

A farmer's wife, passing by with a tribe of youngsters, rolled her eyes sympathetically and shook her head at the beleaguered butcher.

Helled saw the look, and melded her dark eyebrows into a single line across her brow. "You miserable hussy!" she hissed. "I know exactly what you are about!" She seized a handful of the astonished young woman's hair and yanked. "You distract my husband with saucy nods and smiles and your brats sneak into the back of our shop to steal our meat."

The farmer's wife had no choice but to defend herself against Helled's furious onslaught, and the pair clawed and spat like a pair of wild cats.

"Stop, stop!" cried Tewdric, dragging his wife off the young woman. "Surely we can clear up this silly misunderstanding." He smiled pleadingly, "Then the two of you can part friends."

"Friends with her? Not 'til Hell freezes over!" Helled shrieked.

The young woman massaged her throbbing scalp. "Sheesh! Yon harpy needs to curb her temper afore she kills someone." She gathered her frightened brood together. "Come along my lovelies, this ain't no place for civilised folk."

Riding into the village to enquire after his tenants' welfare, Sir Edred observed the fracas and his ruddy face darkened with anger. "It seems you are in a spot of bother again, Master Bascoomb."

Tewdric shrugged apologetically. "I am that, my lord! Mistress Bascoomb is a woman of extraordinarily strong character."

"And you are naught but a cowardly milksop," Helled squinted at her husband. "Had I known what a weakling you were, I would never have wed you in the first place. But most men are of the same ilk if you ask me."

"Hold your tongue, woman!" Sir Edred roared. He beckoned two stalwart villagers to come forward. "Take this objectionable creature away. Lash her to the ducking stool and dunk her in the pond until she falls silent."

Helled had suffered the ducking stool once before, and she fought her captors tooth and claw. She shouted her innocence but her protestations fell on stony ground, for Sir Edred had already ridden away.

"Ye gods, Mistress Bascoomb is a tyrant," said Josh, covering both ears with his hands. "I would rather remain a bachelor for the rest of my life than get saddled with a shrew like her."

The ducking stool, attached to the end of a pivoted pole, hung over a deep, murky pond. Helled kicked and snarled as the men strapped her to the wooden seat. Villagers, eager to witness Mistress Bascoomb's degradation, jostled for good positions at the water's edge.

Tewdric trotted around the perimeter of the pond, wringing his hands. "Oh, dear, oh Lord! My poor Helled;

what am I to do?"

"Tell her to shut her mouth," cackled an ancient crone, "unless she wants to swallow a bellyful of pondweed."

The tiniest of smiles twitched at the corners of Tewdric's mouth. "Aye, turtle dove, you had best do as the old woman suggests. Keep quiet and your ordeal will soon be over."

Going underwater for the third time, Tewdric's turtle dove was finally silenced. Released from the stool, she sat on the pond's foul-smelling bank, shivering and gagging for air.

The blue-eyed Bascoomb twins fiddled with their long blonde braids. They were not impervious to the villagers' sniggers and they wished the earth would open up and swallow them. Faces red with embarrassment, they tried to wring out their mother's saturated clothes.

Helled did not care what the villagers thought – but she was angry that her girls had witnessed the undignified procedure. "Stop fussing, I shall be right as rain in a minute." *One day,* she thought, *I will see yon fancy lord pay for his overbearing ways.*

Visiting the village with a cartload of pies, Egglebart and Etheldrida tried not to laugh at Helled's misfortune. The butcher's wife had a reputation for getting her own back and the couple had no desire to rub her up the wrong way.

"Halloo, Oric," Egglebart boomed. "What brings you to Kilterton on this fine, sunny day?"

"I might ask the same of you, my friend," replied Oric. "I thought you planned to stay at home for a while."

"Aye, we did," said Egglebart, giving his plump wife an affectionate squeeze, "but Etheldrida insisted we bring food for the robbery victims." Egglebart helped Etheldrida down from the cart. "The raiders helped themselves to food as well as other goods. We got word that some poor souls have nothing to feed their families, so here we are."

"Were you not robbed?" Dian asked.

"Nay, my lovely, we were lucky." Etheldrida gave the little maid a hug. "Our smallholding is well off the beaten track and the thieves must have passed us by."

Egglebart patted his round stomach. "All this excitement has given me a thirst, what say we deliver your pies, then we can repair to the inn for a pot of ale?"

"Save me a space, please," said Oric. "I will join you presently."

Lady Myferny had sent a hamper of food for the Cole family, and Josh lifted it off the cart. "I will walk Dian across the road," he said. "Wait for me, Oric, I ain't planning to stay with the parents."

Oric nodded unenthusiastically. "I will be with the potter when you are ready." He left Josh to deliver the hamper to the Coles and wandered down the street toward the potter's cottage. Nothing was the same since Bayersby Manor had burned down, and his life seemed to be jinxed when it came to spending time alone with Dian. Clearly he was not going to have a meaningful conversation with her today.

A little gentlemanly haggling with the potter saw Oric back on the street with a boxful of pots and a bundle of straw. His next port of call was the glassblower's establishment. Glassware was expensive, but Oric had a special use in mind for two or three pretty bottles that caught his eye.

Josh reappeared in time to help Oric pack his purchases in straw and lift them onto the cart. They found a willing urchin and promised to pay him a copper coin if he kept an eye on the goods.

Inside the inn Oric and Josh dodged a beefy serf as he manhandled an oak barrel toward the cellar steps. They claimed the two seats Egglebart had saved for them, and Josh immediately looked around for a serving wench to bring food and drink.

Sir Oswold, Lady Malla, Egglebart and Etheldrida were engaged in lively conversation but Oric remained withdrawn, busy with a multitude of thoughts. Wisps of blue smoke rose from a peat fire on the hearth, and the inn's gloomy atmosphere exactly matched Oric's sombre mood. He wished Master Ichtheus had never found the parchment, but now the wretched thing had come to light he felt duty-bound to do something about it.

"You are uncommon quiet this evening, my young friend," Egglebart stated affably. "Is aught troubling you?"

"I have rather a lot on my mind at present," replied Oric, swallowing a draught of ale.

"Why not share your thoughts with us?" Etheldrida suggested kindly. "Bringing things out into the open can sometimes help."

Oric observed his friends' concerned faces. Etheldrida, plump and jolly, Egglebart solid and reliable; both utterly trustworthy. Sir Oswold, the one-armed knight, and his dainty blue-eyed wife, Malla, were as honest and kind as the day was long. As for Josh, no-one could wish for a better friend. Oric had already shared information about Deveril's double knot key, but he was not yet ready to divulge the staggering news of his inheritance. Besides, protocol dictated that Sir Edred should hear the news first. *Just as soon as I can find the right words to tell him,* thought Oric.

"Are you still fretting about the old key that belonged to the alchemist?" Asked Lady Malla, tucking a strand of white hair into the plait she wore on top of her head.

Oric helped himself to a piping hot trotter from a tray proffered by the inn's serving wench. "Aye, the very same, my lady. I think the key might have belonged to my father," he ventured.

Sir Oswold sighed gustily. "I vaguely recall a crest depicting double knots on a pennant many moons ago, but I am dashed if I can remember exactly when or where." Deep in thought, he scratched his neat beard. "Perhaps your father was a high-ranking servant; as such he would be entrusted with the care of his lord's keys. If that was the case, your father would have been well paid." Pleased with his deductions, Sir Oswold slapped Oric on the back. "There might even be a small stash of gold hidden away somewhere."

If only they knew, thought Oric miserably. *When I tell them the truth about my father and his will, my life will surely change forever.*

Escaped from the squalor of her parents' cottage, Dian slid along the bench beside Oric. "Why the long face?" she asked, digging him playfully in the ribs with her elbow.

Josh leaned across the table to make eye contact with his sister. "Mind your manners, girl! Oric might well be a man of means."

"That I am not," Oric growled. *Surely Josh cannot know about my father's will.*

"That, you are," Josh winked theatrically. "None of my other friends owns a plot of land with a hut built upon it."

Relief washed over Oric and he went back to his pig's trotter with more enthusiasm. He was safe for the time being, but he would have to tell his friend the truth eventually.

Lady Malla held Oric by the arms, her bright eyes sympathetic. "Do not despair, my dear. With all of us on the lookout for your double knots I am sure we shall discover something of interest soon."

"I appreciate your concern, my lady, but now we must head for home. Come Josh, I want to get Dian back to Bayersby before nightfall."

-oOo-

Lady Malla's reputation as a herbalist grew, and Oric occasionally accompanied her as she went about the district administering simple remedies to needy families. During their travels they occasionally came across Father Chrispian. An astute judge of character, Lady Malla recognised the priest for the charlatan he was and, concerned for the parishioners that attended St Griswald's Church, she voiced her opinion to Kilterton's incumbent young priest. Father Franciscus listened to the midwife's complaints and, unable to do anything to help, he promised to mention her concerns next time the bishop paid the priory a visit.

Meanwhile, Father Chrispian continued an unrelenting offensive. He spread stories of witchcraft, persuading people that the midwife was casting spells upon them, and was the cause of all their misfortune. Superstitious in the extreme, local folk believed him and began to shun Lady Malla.

Autumn days shortened and seasonal mists drifted across the countryside. An influx of people arrived to attend Kilterton's annual horse fair and the high street hummed with activity. Glad of the opportunity to make extra money, Oric transported a cart full of new medicaments to the village and set up his stall. Dian accompanied him, bringing a few homemade gewgaws of her own. Eager to meet up with his village friends, Josh also cadged a ride and, once again, Oric missed the opportunity to get Dian to himself.

Jars filled with tinctures to ease maladies of heart, lung, and liver lined the back of Oric's stall. Smaller clay pots containing rubbing ointments and emollients for stiff joints, bruises and toothache stood at the front of the display. Bottles of rosewater, as well Dian's dried flower posies and wreaths made from copper-beech leaves, added a feminine touch to the table.

Tanners Lanaval and Meerig had recently set up in business beside Roxdale Beck, and their reputation for fine leather had spread far and wide. They brought their hides to sell in Kilterton and Uther Tidwall, the bootmaker, was in a hurry to purchase the best leather before it was seized by other buyers. He swiftly picked his way between piles of animal dung on the road to become the tanners' first customer of the day.

Lanaval, the tallest of the pair, raised his hand in greeting. "A very good morning to you, Uther. God has granted us a fine day for the horse fair, has he not?"

The bootmaker nodded. "Aye, and looking at this crowd, I believe we might make a killing today."

Oric overheard Uther's comment and hoped the 'killing' would be confined to the successful selling of merchandise rather than someone's death. He freely admitted that, since Figg's demise, robberies across the district had eased off; nevertheless, Oric remained vigilant and cautious. Stray vagabonds were not above slitting a traveller's throat in a lonely spot and making off with the victim's possessions.

Father Chrispian meandered amongst the stallholders. Buying nothing, he missed no opportunity to blacken Lady Malla's name. Soon it would be unsafe for the woman to go anywhere. Perhaps he needed to tone down his approach. After all, he did not want to antagonise the villagers to such an extent that they took matters into their own hands. Oh dear no. He shuddered with anticipation. The pleasure of burning the witch was to be his and his alone.

Deep in conversation, Frida Cole and Mistress Goodall approached the apothecary's table. "Mark my words," hissed Mistress Goodall, "yon midwife ain't to be trusted." She removed the cap from one of the perfume bottles and snorted deeply. "Some folk say Lady Malla is a witch and I am thinking they might be right." Mistress Goodall squinted one eye and nodded her head. "Moments after she paid me a visit the other day, the milk in my churn turned sour."

Frida Cole folded her arms across her thin chest as if to protect herself from evil. "Aye, Father Chrispian was right to warn us against witchcraft – and he should know – being a clerical gentleman."

Dian dashed out from the behind Oric's stall and shook Frida by the shoulders. "Mother! Pay no attention to Father Chrispian's wicked lies. You should be ashamed of yourself. As for your milk, Mistress Goodall – it turns sour so quickly because you are too lazy to wash out your churn."

"Lies, are they?" Mistress Goodall sneered, liberally splashing rosewater onto her soiled tunic. "After yon so-called midwife administered to my baby, the wee mite pumped his legs up and down and flailed his arms, like he was possessed." Banging the bottle of perfume back onto the table she added, "Yon witch needs stopping before she causes beasts in the fields to drop stillborn young."

Oric glared at the two women, appalled at their wicked gossip. "How can you be so stupid? Lady Malla has shown you nothing but kindness and, if I remember correctly, the lady you so loudly malign treated your families free of charge, last time you called upon her services. No doubt she also told you, Mistress Goodall, to feed your baby properly to stop him from screaming all night with an empty belly." Oric made a dismissive slicing motion with his hand. "You choose to disregard Lady Malla's advice, and then you have the nerve to blame her for your own stupidity and ignorance." Oric hoped the women would take his words to heart and drop the subject, but he did not hold out much hope. He was even more perturbed to see other villagers cross themselves as Lady Malla passed by. Concerned for the midwife's safety,

Oric left Dian in charge of their stall and went in search of Sir Oswold.

The one-armed knight ran his hand over the withers of a sturdy horse. "What do you think of this fine fellow, Oric? My old destrier is ready to be put out to pasture and I need a young beast for ploughing."

"I imagine he will make an excellent plough horse," said Oric, admiring the animal's muscular legs and fetlocks. "However, I am not here to discuss the finer points of horseflesh."

"You look uncommon serious, Oric. If you need assistance, I am your man."

"I am not the one with a problem," replied Oric gently. "Folk are spreading untrue rumours that Lady Malla is a witch. I fear 'tis unsafe for her to venture out alone, until the villagers have been disabused of this dangerous idea."

"Oh, dear Lord!" Sir Oswold was so shocked he paid for the horse without barter. "I will try to keep an eye on Malla but, if she is called out to a birthing, she will pay little attention to what I say. Would you and your friends care to accompany us back to Rookery Cottage for a bite of supper? Malla might listen if you have a word with her."

Sir Oswold hastened away to find his wife, and found her sobbing in a quiet alleyway. He suspected what had caused her distress and his heart sank. "What ails you, sweet lady?"

"The villagers have become hostile," cried Lady Malla. "They are accusing me of witchcraft, and I have no idea why." She dashed a tear from her cheek. "Some of them spat at me, but the greatest hurt was when they dragged away their children as I approached." Swallowing hard, she added, "I would never harm children, I love them."

At a loss for words, Sir Oswold reached for his wife's hand. "I know that and so should everyone else. Come my love, let us return home, I have invited Oric and his friends to supper. Their company will surely cheer you."

Market day drew to a close without further incident, and the stall holders packed up and headed for home. Oric had done well and he had little to pack apart from the bottled rosewater. Times were hard and the villagers had little money to spare for frippery.

Seated around the table inside Rookery Cottage, Oric and his friends discussed the villagers' peculiar behaviour.

"I believe Father Chrispian is causing the villagers' unrest." Oric extracted a promise from Lady Malla that she would take more care when she was out, about her business.

Daylight faded and Oric jumped to his feet. Concerned about getting Dian home safely, he silently berated himself for allowing time to slip by unnoticed. He should have refused Sir Oswold's invitation to supper but, at the time, his major worry had been for Lady Malla. Oric glanced at Josh and his worries diminished. Together they would ward off any person who posed a threat – always supposing it proved necessary.

Chapter Seventeen

Ghosts and Ghouls

Oric deemed the back road safer than the busier Roman Road where thieves were more likely to lie in wait for wealthy travellers. He clicked his tongue for Braccus to trot faster and the cart bucked and tossed along the rutted track. His few unsold pots and jars rattled despite their protective layers of straw, but Oric didn't care. Broken merchandise would be easier to cope with than broken skulls.

"At this rate we shall *soon* be home," said Josh, his tone reproachful. "Always assuming we are not shaken to pieces before we get there."

St Griswald's Church loomed into sight and a cold hand of fear squeezed Oric's stomach. He yanked Braccus to a sudden halt and tried to still his trembling hands.

"What are you about, Oric? We almost fell off the cart," Josh grumbled resentfully. From his perch in the back of the cart he failed to see what had spooked Oric.

Lights bobbed about the churchyard and amongst the uppermost branches of the old yew trees. Out with his mentor many moons ago, Oric had experienced similar strange phenomena but, at the time, Master Ichtheus had pooh-poohed any idea of ghosts or ghouls. Observing the horrible scenario again, Oric was far from sure the old apothecary was right.

Off the cart, Josh peered into the darkness ahead and spotted the lights. "Foof – I do not like the look of those one little bit. What do you suppose they are, Oric?"

"I know not – but that is why I stopped so abruptly," Oric whispered, easing down from the driving seat. "We had best wait a while – 'tis not worth courting trouble."

Braccus tossed his head and shifted uneasily. Distracted by a patch of verdant grass, the donkey dropped his head and began to crop the succulent stalks.

The lights in the trees multiplied, and something floated along the top of the churchyard wall. Blood-chilling howls accompanied by hollow rattling sounds caused Josh's blood to run cold. "Heaven help us!" he croaked. "What in the name of Christendom is that?"

Despite the warm evening, Dian shivered. "Satan's imps are surely at work here," she whispered.

"Hush," soothed Oric, drawing her within the comforting warmth of his cloak. "All will be well. Only when I deem it safe shall we continue our journey."

Dian buried her face in Oric's shoulder and time stood still as he held her close. Had he not been so concerned over the dangerous situation, Oric would have liked the night to last forever.

Before dawn the lights disappeared and the cacophony of rattles and howls ceased. Disinclined to linger a moment longer than necessary Oric, Dian and Josh climbed back onto the cart and made all speed for home.

-oOo-

Bertram clattered down the crypt steps with his arms full of lanterns. "If yon priest fails to fly the coop after last night's performance, I shall eat my boots."

"Aye," Hersica Horzefell wheezed, wiping tears of mirth from her cheeks. "And I will eat my hat!"

Rather than risk discovery by employing local urchins, Hersica had bribed a gang of young vagabonds from further afield to do her dirty work. The boys' latest efforts had far exceeded her expectations.

"The lads looked grotesque, dodging around the churchyard with the lanterns held under their chins," Bertram cackled. "I doubt their mothers would recognise 'em. Once word gets out that ghosts have returned to haunt St Griswald's, no-one will dare to come near the church."

"Aye, 'tis all well and good," grumbled Hersica. "But yon priest is taking longer to get shut of than I anticipated. Maybe we need to increase the menace."

St Griswald's was central to everything Hersica needed and she was keen to move back into the manse. The surrounding woods and countryside provided sufficient food in the form of rabbits and hares, the occasional stoat, birds' eggs in spring and stolen turnips almost year-round. With Bertram's help, a nice living could be made from a robbery every now and again. There was also Figg's stash to fall back on, if only she could get her hands on it. All in all, Hersica foresaw a very pleasant future.

-oOo-

With his bottles and jars safely returned to his hut, Oric left Josh to catch up on lost sleep, and went in search of his mentor. He approached the compound gates and almost collided with Otty as she careered out with Ichtheus clinging to her back. Ned and Joe followed hot on the donkey's heels.

At sight of his assistant, Ichtheus yanked at the reins and Otty halted abruptly. "Where have you been?" howled Ichtheus, clinging to the donkey's neck to save himself from falling. "This wretched beast only has two speeds. Full tilt or dead stop!" He glared at Dian. "And you, miss, had better make haste indoors. Lady Myferny is asking where you are." He returned his attention to Oric. "Not a wink of sleep have I had, worrying over where you all were, and waiting for dawn to break so I could come and seek you." He loosened his grip on Otty's neck, slid to the ground, and tossed the reins over to Ned. "Take this beast back to the stables before I throttle her!"

"We were obliged to spend the night hidden away in the forest," said Oric. "I am surprised we escaped unscathed."

"Escaped… Escaped from what?" Ichtheus snapped. "And why would you hide in the forest? If this is a ruse to avoid my wrath I assure you it will not work."

Relinquishing Braccus and the cart into Joe's hands, Oric told Ichtheus what had occurred.

Ned and Joe exchanged glances, remembering all too well similar tricks they had once played at Figg's behest.

"It was too dark to see properly," Oric explained, "but I swear one of the visions looked like Hersica Horzefell."

Ned cleared his throat. "There is something we should have told you long since," he mumbled, agonising how best to face up to the truth. "We dared not say anything in case you sent us away."

"Why should we send you away?" Ichtheus asked. "You have proved yourselves to be good, trustworthy workers."

"You might change your mind after you hear what I have to say," replied Ned.

Concern made Ichtheus irritable. "For goodness' sake, spit it out, boy."

"If we has to leave the manor because of our honesty, so be it." Joe hung his head, exposing the back of his grubby neck. "At least we will go with a clear conscience."

"Figg used St Griswald's Church as his hideout," Ned explained. "He took on a bunch of rough thieves to rob travellers and he forced me and Joe to pick pouches in Kilterton. Everybody moved into the crypt. Figg was that scared his hideout would be discovered, he told the Horzefells they had to scare strangers away."

Joe tittered nervously. "Aye – it was a clever trick we played, and it worked well. Whenever we heard folk approaching, we rattled dried-up skeletons and jumped about with lighted lanterns held under our chins. You have no idea how scary we looked."

"Oh, I think we do," muttered Oric, feeling more foolish by the minute.

"We soon had the place to ourselves," tittered Joe, "and that was how it stayed, 'til yon daft preacher shifted into the manse."

"Father Chrispian scared the villagers that much they dare not disobey him," continued Ned. "In no time at all, the church was lifting with folk again. Master Figg was that mad, he told us we had to see the priest and his followers off, or else…"

Joe spluttered with sniggers. "So we howled around the churchyard at night and played tricks on the priest during the day. In the end I think he went off his head."

"You little devils!" Ichtheus exclaimed. "I should give you both a good hiding."

"We had no choice," Ned interjected miserably. "Master Figg is… *was* a nasty piece of work and he would have killed us both had we disobeyed his orders."

Ichtheus shot Oric a triumphant look. "See! I told you the goings-on at St Griswald's had nothing to do with anything supernatural. But did you believe me?" he snorted. "No you did not!"

"Aye, me and the rest of the local population," replied Oric huffily. "In view of the exhibition we observed last night, I reckon Hersica Horzefell is at it again."

"Perhaps," said Ichtheus. "Though I doubt yon old biddy poses much of a threat."

Oric ran fingers through his tangle of straw-coloured hair. "Judging by Father Chrispian's recent behaviour, I reckon Joe is right. Apart from spreading terrible rumours about Lady Malla, Father Chrispian is presenting similar traits to a madman I treated recently. The afflicted fellow escaped from his family and caused a good deal of trouble before he was recaptured." Oric shrugged. "I reckon Father Chrispian might do much the same if we do not restrain him."

Chapter Eighteen

A New Housekeeper

September brought cooler evenings, shorter days and crops of oats, wheat and barley ready to harvest. Sir Edred's serfs toiled in the fields from dawn until dusk, and extra men were brought in from Kilterton to help. Womenfolk picked fruit from the orchards, and packed rosy apples in layers of straw. Stored in a dark, dry barn, the fruit remained edible until well after Yuletide. Plums, pears, and quince were gathered and dried; wild cherries and blackberries were made into wine, and honey into mead. Oric and Ichtheus collected roots, herbs and seeds until their volume of medicaments was almost back to normal. Oric grew many new plants in his garden, all of which survived since Guwain had stopped vandalising the plot.

The Bayersby heir remained absent from home, and Lady Myferny visited a makeshift chapel each day to pray for her son's safe return. In a short space of time she lost weight and became pale with worry. "Pray God nothing untoward has befallen Guwain," was her regular plea.

"Of course nothing has happened to the boy," blustered

Sir Edred. "He is a wily little pest and I am convinced he will turn up the moment the new manor house is finished. I wager the lad has spies out, reporting on our progress; meanwhile, he is reclining in the lap of luxury somewhere. Had I an inkling as to where that might be, I would go and fetch him." Sir Edred snorted furiously, "When our son deigns to put in an appearance, I will make sure he shoulders his responsibilities."

"Please do not be too hard on the boy," begged Lady Myferny. "When he does come home I do not want him to run off again." Nearing the end of her childbearing years, Lady Myferny was concerned that Guwain would be their only child.

The shell of a new manor that grew from the ashes of the old was considerably larger. The painstaking job of cutting stone for the walls would take many moons, and so too would the felling and seasoning of timber for cross-beams and supports. Lady Myferny insisted upon separate quarters for the family to enjoy some privacy away from the general hubbub of the manor, and the large room was to occupy a mezzanine floor accessed by a flight of stone stairs from one end of the Great Hall.

To shield the manor's future inhabitants and guests from cooking smells and noise, a large kitchen was erected a short distance from the main house. Less ornate than the manor, the timber kitchen was soon erected. It was into this building that everyone moved. A seamstress was employed to make new clothes for Lady Myferny and Sir Edred, and the items hung from wooden poles bracketed to the walls. Curtains enclosed the family's sleeping area, and feather-filled mattresses on timber-framed beds held the promise of deep comfort.

A long, narrow lean-to tacked onto the kitchen had the serfs all of a twitter. Having their own quarters meant they no longer needed to fight for sleeping spaces wherever they could find them. Each person now had his or her own small area in which to sleep, and the occupants were responsible for collecting straw and leaves to rest upon.

Ichtheus was allotted the opposite end of the kitchen from the family quarters. A pot-bellied brazier for heating medicinal potions stood in one corner of the area, and two sleeping platforms were constructed nearby. Although it was not a perfect arrangement, Ichtheus was happy enough. Once the manor was completed, Sir Edred and Lady Myferny would move in, leaving their quarters in the kitchen for Oric and Ichtheus to use.

Ploughing began, marking the end of summer. Pairs of oxen yoked together dragged wooden blades through the earth, and acres of dark brown stripes replaced the golden stubble of harvested crops.

Scarlet hips hung like jewels from the prickly stems of wild rose bushes, and shiny black brambles glistened on top of tangled thickets. Oric salivated as he imagined the wonderful syrups and wines he would make from the berries.

Gathering berries early one chilly morning, Oric stopped to marvel at a web strung between two posts. The spider's intricate threads reminded him of his own convoluted life. At his present rate of non-progress, he feared he would be dead before he fully understood the content of his father's will.

Returned to the manor, Oric handed his bucketful of berries to a kitchen serf for cleaning. In a hurry to concoct a new medicinal remedy, he fetched the scales and rolled up his sleeves. He weighed a small amount of black-alder bark, placed the substance in a bowl and poured in a cupful of brown vinegar. Standing the bowl on top of the brazier, he stirred until the contents came to a simmer.

"What are you doing?" Dian asked, intrigued by the pungent smell that arose from the dish.

"Etheldrida asked for a potion to save Egglebart's teeth." Oric smiled wryly as he visualised his friend's gappy grin. "But I fear her request has come a little too late." He tapped drips from his spoon and lay it down on the hearth. "At least the mixture might help to preserve Egglebart's few remaining molars."

"Good luck with that," laughed Dian. She gathered up the bowl of dried fruits that Lady Myferny had requested, and disappeared back upstairs.

The apothecaries had put their time to good use gathering supplies during the summer months and now a large new chest held tinctures, rubbing oils and ointments. Ichtheus opened the curtains across his alcove and popped out his head. "Good morning, Oric. You are out and about bright and early." He threw on a deep purple tunic, shoved his feet into a pair of slippers, and shuffled across to the other end of the room. He returned with a pot of ale in one hand and a chunk of bread in the other. "We must make a list," he said, sitting down at the table. "That way we can see at a glance what medications we have used and which ones we need to replace." Opening a ledger, he dipped his quill into a container of iron-gall ink. "Ready to start when you are, lad."

Oric crouched down beside the medicine chest and began to itemise the contents. "Distilled herbs for cleansing the blood; four bottles. Eight jars of lavender oil. Six pots of primrose-salve to heal wounds and sores." He lifted out each potion as he counted. "Ten bottles of Solomon's seal, and nine tinctures of liquorice-root for the relief of coughs and colds. One, two… Stch, stch – what a nuisance! We have almost run out of rubbing balm. I had best make up a new batch. Elderly members of the community are sure to need a good supply to ease their sore joints come winter."

Ichtheus shook his quill and a blob of ink splattered onto the ledger. "Do slow down, Oric! I am having trouble keeping up with you."

Reaching into the bottom of the chest, Oric brandished two small packages. "Last, but not least, are my new remedies for pain relief." He sat back on his haunches, thinking of his visit to Roxbrough Abbey. "The friars taught me that three drams of powdered mugwort mixed with wine cures sciatica. A decoction of mugwort, camomile and agrimony, warmed and applied externally, soothes aching sinews and eases cramp. If these potions are as effective as the friars promise, folk will surely demand that I produce more." He tapped his forehead thoughtfully. "I may raise a tidy sum without overcharging my patients at the next market day in Kilterton."

Ichtheus stood up to ease his back. "You had best powder some mugwort for me, my sciatica is giving me gyp at present." He stuck a bony leg out at right angles, and leered in eager anticipation. "I just happen to have some nice elderflower wine with which to mix your concoction." Wishing he had not been quite so energetic, he sat down again.

Oric wound a cloth around his hand, and carried the hot dish of tooth tincture to the table. He poured the liquid into a jar and set it aside to cool. "I shall deliver Egglebart's potion as soo…"

The arrival of a tall woman stopped the words on Oric's lips.

Startled by the stranger's sudden appearance in the doorway, Ichtheus jumped to his feet. "Can I help you?" he asked, wincing as a stab of searing pain cut through his right buttock.

The woman thrust a bulging bag into Ichtheus' hand. "I sincerely hope so," she snapped. "I am your new housekeeper and I have been instructed to share the apothecary's accommodation. I believe a curtained sleeping cubicle has been reserved for my use." The woman raked Ichtheus from head to toe with her pale eyes. "Kindly put my things away."

Ichtheus' expression was worth bottling and Oric did not know whether to laugh or cry. Like or not, he would be expected to relinquish his comfortable bed to this woman.

Leaning her staff against the wall, the new housekeeper dropped a large bag onto a stool and shrugged off her cloak. "Agnes Foley is my name, but you may address me as Mistress Foley. I have been caring for a sick sister in Roxbrough; now she is well again I am ready to take up my new post." She raked the apothecaries' jumble of pots and jars with narrowed eyes. "You will be relieved to hear that I am charged with the smooth running of this establishment." Mistress Foley pointed to the apothecaries' littered table. "You can begin by clearing up that mess!"

Mistress Foley was the exact opposite to the obese and dirty Mother Morghan. Tall and angular, the new housekeeper's dove grey spotless tunic hung obediently from a pair of bony shoulders. Hair scraped back from a thin, pale face accentuated her beaky nose. Grey hair, grey eyes, grey skin, grey tunic, and grey cloak – never before had Oric encountered such a drab-looking woman. Colourless Agnes Foley might be, but the servants of Bayersby Manor were soon to discover that she possessed a spine of iron.

Curled up beside the brazier, Parzifal wagged his tail. He stood up and wandered over to sniff the newcomer in a friendly fashion.

Mistress Foley snapped away her skirt. "Furthermore, you can get rid of that tatty hound – I do not hold with dogs indoors."

Ichtheus stalked out of the room and slammed the door behind him. At the first opportunity, he planned to approach Lady Myferny to see what could be done about the new and intolerable situation.

Oric gathered up his medicaments from the table and dropped them back into the chest. He rolled up his bedding and hooked his finger into Parzifal's collar. "Come on, old lad – you had best come with me. If anyone needs us," he said, "we shall be in the stables with Braccus and Otty."

Apart from the occasional whinny, the stable block was silent. Oric tossed his bedding down in the corner of Braccus' stall. "Looks like you are to have company for a while," he said, rubbing the donkey's soft nose.

On a whim Oric removed Ichtheus' box from the small cavity dug into the dirt floor. Inside was a bag of gold coins belonging to Ichtheus, a smaller pouch containing Oric's few silver coins, and the key with double knots. He picked the key out and stared at it for a long while. The words Master Deveril had uttered on his deathbed were now quite clear. The danger had manifested in the volatile black powder; the wealth the old man had hinted at was clearly Askell's family seat. *My family seat,* Oric thought with a shudder. He tickled Parzifal's ears. "What am I to do, old lad? I know not who my ancestors were, nor do I know where their property lies. I am secure and happy at Bayersby Manor but now, for the sake of my family honour, I feel obliged to seek the meaning of Askell's will." On a whim he hung the key on its chain around his neck, hoping it might bring him good luck. He returned everything else to the box, and slid it back into the cavity. Sitting on the floor with his back against the stable wall, he wondered what to do next.

Chapter Nineteen

Lady Malla Terrorised

A few souls, more afraid of Father Chrispian than the ghosts that purportedly haunted St Griswald's, continued to attend services in the old church. After one such occasion the priest waited impatiently for his meagre flock to depart. On his own at last, he fetched a sharp axe from the tool shed and followed his parishioners' footsteps to Kilterton. As he walked, he talked to himself. "That ghastly Malla female is an evil witch. 'Tis all her fault my congregation has deserted me. How dare she call me a charlatan when I am spreading naught but the word of God? We shall see how she fares when I send her up in smoke."

Autumn mist drifted across the moors, reducing visibility. Paying scant attention to where he was putting his feet, Father Chrispian tripped over a tussock of grass in front of Rigg Farm, and gashed his face on a stray rock. Picking himself up, he held his head and yowled with pain. The noise he made carried in the still air and the occupants of the farm stared at each other in consternation.

"Dear Lord," the shepherd muttered. "What is causing that racket?"

Norbert's young wife gasped, her hand flying to her mouth. "Perhaps a wolf is after our sheep."

"The beast will take no more of my flock," growled Norbert, shrugging into a sleeveless sheepskin jerkin. Grabbing up a hefty wooden club he added, "Do not expect me back until I have disposed of the vicious creature."

Blubbering and weaving like a drunkard, Father Chrispian continued his journey. About to offer assistance, Norbert caught sight of the axe that dangled from the priest's hand. Convinced something was amiss he followed, keeping a safe distance behind the man. The outskirts of Kilterton loomed out of the mist but Father Chrispian kept going.

A clearing amidst dense woods south of the village was the priest's destination. Deeming the area perfect for his purpose, he had driven a tall stake into the ground. Now he was back to finish the job. He chopped branches from surrounding trees and collected dry twigs for kindling. "The witch will burn," he chanted over and over again. He danced around the completed pyre, his vestments flapping around his bony shanks. A ribbon that held back his black hair came undone and long, greasy locks obscured his face.

Fear momentarily robbed the shepherd of breath. The priest looked Satanic and, convinced some poor woman was about to meet a terrible fate, Norbert broke cover and wielded his club. "I know not who you plan to burn, but I intend to stop you!"

Aided by the strength that insanity provides, Father Chrispian wrenched the club from Norbert's hands and brought it down upon the shepherd's woolly head with sickening force. Norbert's knees buckled, and he pitched face-down onto the ground.

Leaving the shepherd in a crumpled heap, Father Chrispian wandered off to lie in wait beside the highway for Lady Malla to pass by.

-oOo-

Gored by one of his own bulls, Tewdric Bascoomb had developed a painful fistula on his back. Not trusting Helled to do the job properly, Lady Malla visited Rookery Farm on a daily basis to dress Tewdric's wound. She dissuaded Sir Oswold from accompanying her, saying that he had enough work to do around their smallholding without following her back and forth on such a short journey.

Cowslip Cottage, Lady Malla's home, was the last dwelling on the road out of Kilterton. Aware that she regularly rode her donkey along the lonely stretch of road, Father Chrispian lay in wait. Hearing the clop of hooves, he poked his head up between the tall stalks of grass that grew along the edge of the ditch in which he lay.

Lady Malla drew abreast of Father Chrispian and he leaped from his hiding place. He dragged the petrified woman from the donkey's back, seized her in a stranglehold and knicked her neck with his dagger. "Utter a single sound and I shall slice your gizzard," he snarled.

Unable to draw breath, Lady Malla fainted.

Slinging the woman's limp body face-down across her donkey, Father Chrispian led the animal into the woods. He entered his chosen clearing and, slavering like a rabid dog, he dragged Lady Malla onto the pyre he had prepared, and secured her to the stake with lengths of horsehair rope. Still unconscious, white hair awry, she hung from her bonds like a rag-doll.

Intent upon his purpose, Father Chrispian failed to see Lady Malla's donkey trot from the clearing.

Norbert remained on the ground where he had fallen, his skull oozing blood. Father Chrispian lashed the shepherd's wrists and feet together for fear he would regain consciousness and cause trouble. He returned his attention to Lady Malla, reached up and patted her foot. "Scream all you like, witch, there is no-one nearby to hear you."

The lady made no sound and, incensed by her silence, Father Chrispian pricked her ankle with his dagger. Drops of blood oozed from the incision and the priest laughed like a creature possessed. "I am away to the village but I shall soon be back with a few supporters. When I return, we shall hear you squeal."

The morning's exertions gave Father Chrispian an appetite and, hungry as a hunter, he entered Kilterton's inn in search of food. The innkeeper's wife eyed the dishevelled priest, and suggested that he might like to freshen up.

"There is naught wrong with my appearance, woman! All I am lacking is food and something to drink."

"Would you care for a pot of ale until I can bring you something to eat?" she asked.

"Nay, woman, I would not. I do not indulge in such devil's brew." Father Chrispian disliked ale, but he was not averse to imbibing communion wine when no-one was looking. A total hypocrite, he stared pointedly at Eadbald Cole, who was sitting beside the counter with a pot of ale in his hand. "Let us be upstanding whilst I pray for yon sinner's mortal soul."

Several ales already under his belt, Eadbald Cole was vexed to see Father Chrispian. He had been on the receiving end of many a tirade on the evils of drink and he was not prepared to listen to another. "Listen to yon God-bothering priest!" he growled, dragging his wet mouth down his sleeve. "I did not leave a cottage full of snivelling brats and a wife that never stops carping to suffer yet another diatribe from the likes of him." A pronounced squint made it difficult to ascertain which glassy eye the man was using at any one time. Eadbald supported his pot belly with one hand, swivelled around in his seat and turned his back toward Father Chrispian. "Hi landlord!" he slurred. "Fetch me another pot of ale."

"Why should I waste my breath on the likes of you, Eadbald Cole?" Father Chrispian sneered, stuffing a pickled egg into his mouth. "I have far more interesting goals to pursue."

Eadbald winked and nudged another fellow drinker. "That makes a pleasant change! 'Tis not often yon priest misses an opportunity to browbeat us poor sinners."

"Perhaps the cleric is sickening for summat," sniggered Eadbald's crony.

"I never felt better!" Father Chrispian retorted. "After much prayer I have finally received Divine permission to burn a witch." His mouth still full of food, he sprayed the table with bits of egg. "If you wish to see Lady Malla punished for her evil doing, follow me." He dropped a few coppers on the counter in payment for his food and stalked toward the door.

Keen to be rid of the woman they blamed for their misfortunes, several of the inn's patrons followed hot on Father Chrispian's heels. Part way down the street, Mistresses Cole and Goodall joined the procession. "At last something is about to be done," cried Mistress Goodall. "I shall be glad to see our district free of the evil sorceress."

"Aye," Frida Cole piped up. "Only t'other day I heard tell that a cow dropped a three-legged calf. 'Tis time we burned yon black-hearted spell-caster afore she disfigures our unborn bairns."

The potter heard the racket and ran from his shop. "Have you all taken leave of your senses? Lady Malla has shown you nothing but kindness, which is more than can be said for the priest."

The bootmaker, a man of integrity and intelligence, could barely take in what was happening. "Go home at once," he cried, "before you all get into serious trouble!"

Whipped up by righteous frenzy, the villagers ignored Uther's wise words. They had the smell of blood in their nostrils and nothing was going to deter them from their mission. The bootmaker and the potter ran along beside the villagers, trying to persuade them of their folly, but no-one wanted to listen.

-oOo-

Lady Malla, now fully conscious, struggled to break loose from her bonds.

"Squirm all you like, mistress," Father Chrispian cooed. "You will wriggle a good deal more before I am finished with you."

"How can you allow this to happen?" Lady Malla cried out to the villagers. "I have done naught but help you."

A little woman stepped up and faced the crowd. "Aye, the midwife has always been kind to me. I say we should cut her down."

"You would do well to pay attention to what this good woman says," thundered Uther.

Ashamed of their initial enthusiasm, two more women shouted for Lady Malla's release, but the ghoulish majority would have none of it. Outnumbered, the five would-be saviours were overpowered and tied to trees.

His face contorted into a fearsome grimace, Father Chrispian screamed at the top of his voice. "You, madam, are the perpetrator of all that is evil! The sooner we rid the district of your foul presence, the better." Malevolence oozing from his every pore, he fumbled with a tinder box and set light to an oil-soaked torch. "Make your peace with the devil, for now you shall burn." He ran around the pyre, thrusting his torch into the kindling.

-oOo-

Lady Myferny heard that the yellow-flowered sweet flag masked bad smells when scattered on the floor amongst common rushes. Desperate to find something to perfume the atmosphere in the overcrowded kitchen, she asked Oric if he knew the whereabouts of such a plant.

"Aye, my lady, I noticed a goodly crop at the edge of the wetlands south of Kilterton. I plan to deliver a tincture to Egglebart, would you like me to collect some sweet flag whilst I am in the vicinity?"

"That would be wonderful, thank you, Oric… Oh, by the way, I believe Dian would benefit from a day in the fresh air, she is looking a little pale. Why not take her along with you?"

Oric gulped, barely able to believe his good fortune. "Oh, aye, my lady, I am sure that can be arranged. I have some dried herbs for Sir Oswold's wife, too. Dian is very fond of Lady Malla, and she will be pleased to spend a little time at Cowslip Cottage." *Perhaps, whilst we are out,* he thought, *I might find the right moment to share the news of my new status and possible inheritance.*

Oric failed to summon up the courage to talk about anything other than inconsequential topics on the journey, and they arrived at the wetlands just before midmorning. Sweet flag grew in abundance around the edge of a pond, and the cart was soon filled with greenery. In a giddy mood, they continued their journey to Cowslip Cottage.

Depositing Lady Malla's herbs in her storeroom, Oric returned to the yard just as Dian stepped out of the cottage.

"No-one is home," she announced. "I wonder where Sir Oswold and Lady Malla are." The words were barely out of Dian's mouth when a riderless donkey trotted into the yard.

"I think this is Lady Malla's mount," said Oric, grabbing the animal's bridle and tethering him to a post. "Since he is still wearing a saddle, I wonder what has happened to his rider." He helped Dian onto the cart. "Hurry, we had best take a look! Lady Malla might have taken a tumble; though I know not where."

On their way out of the yard Oric and Dian met Sir Oswold coming in with his new horse and plough. "What brings you two here this lovely autumn day? Pray stay for a bite to eat. Lady Malla has gone to Diggitdow Farm to dress a wound for Tewdric but I am expecting her back at any moment." The one-armed knight grinned and added, "She does not remain at Diggitdow a moment longer than necessary."

"I am afraid that your wife may have met with an accident," said Oric, indicating Lady Malla's riderless donkey. "We are on our way to look for her."

"Heaven preserve us," Sir Oswold cried, his grin swiftly disappearing. "You begin the search, Oric, I will unhitch the plough and follow you directly."

Oric set Braccus off at a smart trot. In view of recent threats against the midwife, he worried that she may have suffered something worse than a tumble.

In no time at all Sir Oswold cantered past Oric's cumbersome donkey and cart. Halfway between Rookery

Cottage and Diggitdow Farm he heard distant jeering. Making a snap decision, Sir Oswold branched off the road and entered the woods. Following the sound, he soon came to a clearing.

A woman, tethered to a stake on top of a pyre, sobbed pitifully. Smoke puffed from the base of the pyre and she lifted her head briefly.

At sight of his beloved wife, Sir Oswold charged. He scattered people in all directions and, urging his horse alongside the pyre, he unsheathed his broadsword and slashed through the ties that bound Lady Malla.

"Leave the witch be," babbled Father Chrispian, brandishing a flaming torch. "She must atone for her sins."

Drawn by the noise, Oric and Dian also entered the clearing. In blind fury Oric leaped from the cart and grabbed hold of Father Chrispian. Dian ran to help. "You despicable heathen!" she screamed, pounding the priest with her fists. "You are not fit to tread the same ground as yon poor lady."

"Stop me not, for I do the work of the Lord," shrieked the priest. Held in Oric's iron grip, Father Chrispian's torch came into contact with his cassock and the fabric ignited.

With his precious lady released and seated upon his horse, Sir Oswold struck out with flat side of his broadsword. The almighty *thwack* toppled the priest like a felled oak! "Pick the bones out of that, you evil toad!" roared the one-armed knight. Ramming his sword back into its scabbard, he clasped Lady Malla to his chest and used his heels to back his mount away from the pyre. Not able to see where he was going, the horse stepped upon Father Chrispian's recumbent form.

Almost insensible, Father Chrispian lay battered, singed, and half-strangled upon the ground.

Dian released Uther, the potter, and three women from their bonds, and Oric rounded on the now silent and contrite villagers. "You stupid dolts! Do you not know that burning people is against the law? Thank God Sir Oswold came to Lady Malla's rescue in time, otherwise you all might be facing the death penalty."

"I never thought Lady Malla was a witch," Frida Cole smarmed, in an effort to ingratiate herself with Sir Oswold. She jerked a thumb at her neighbours. "But that lot there was keen to see the poor woman burn."

"Mother!" Dian exclaimed. "You should be ashamed of yourself!" She pushed Frida hard between the shoulder blades. "Get off home before you find yourself in serious trouble!"

"Aye, so she should," Mistress Goodall simpered. "I only came along to see if there was aught I could do to help. 'Tis plain as the nose on my face them foolish folk got it all wrong. What is more, I told Frida Cole she should not come, but would the daft article listen to me? Oh, dear me no, not her!"

Oric's expression spoke volumes. "I suggest that you clear off, Mistress Goodall, before I really lose my temper."

Norbert regained consciousness and struggled to sit up. A trickle of blood ran down his face.

"Ride home with us," suggested Oric, after freeing the shepherd and administering to his wound. "You are not well enough to walk." Norbert smiled his thanks and, feeling like death warmed over, he made himself comfortable on top of the sweet flag in Oric's cart.

Pale and trembling, Lady Malla thanked Oric and Dian. "Without your timely intervention I would be naught but a lump of melted flesh by now."

"Take the poor lady to Etheldrida," Oric advised Sir Oswold. "Your wife is in shock and needs the gentle ministrations of a woman. I have a tincture to deliver to Egglebart, we shall join you there soon."

Lady Malla shuddered at the memory of the priest's vacant eyes and saliva-frothed mouth. "No normal human being would behave in such a manner," she murmured. "I believe Father Chrispian has lost his mind."

Sir Oswold scowled. "The fellow will lose more than his mind if he ever threatens you again, my dear."

-oOo-

The villagers returned to the inn and tongues, loosened by copious quantities of ale, wagged.

"We never should have believed that wicked priest," muttered Aide Kirtle, the village haberdasher.

"What else were we supposed to do?" demanded the blacksmith. "The priest threatened us with hellfire and damnation if we failed to do as he bid." Ashamed, he squinted down at his leather apron, wishing the floor would open up and swallow him.

Eadbald Cole had remained at the inn but he heard about the day's happenings from his wife. "By all accounts," he slurred, his tongue numbed by drink, "Sir Oswold killed yon batty priest with a single thrust of his broadsword, and good riddance to 'im. Perhaps our Frida will stop at home and mind her own business in future."

Uther Tidwall, the cobbler, wholeheartedly agreed. "Just as a matter of interest," he ventured, "did anyone check to see if the priest was dead?"

Chapter Twenty

Into the Woods

Oric, Dian and Norbert followed Sir Oswold and Lady Malla to Rookery Farm. In the yard, Sir Oswold dismounted and helped his wife down from the horse's back. Dian ran to find Etheldrida.

"Oh dear Lord," cried Etheldrida, hastening to Lady Malla's aid. "Whatever has befallen you? Come inside, my dear."

A cheerful fire snapped and crackled in the grate and supper lay on the table. Perfume from a jar of late, russet-coloured roses mingled with the smell of spit-roast pigeons and freshly-baked bread.

Lady Malla sank into a chair beside the hearth. "I cannot tell you how dreadful this day has been," she whispered, gratefully accepting a soothing herbal drink from Etheldrida. A tear or two sparkled on her eyelashes. "I truly thought I was about to die."

"Hush now, you are safe with us." Etheldrida eased Lady Malla out of her her filthy kirtle and was appalled to see plum-coloured bruises all over her arms, back and shoulders.

A blood-encrusted cut showed on her pale neck and another on one ankle.

"Quickly, Dian," Etheldrida, pointed to a blackened kettle suspended on a hook above the fire. "Fill a bowl with warm water and fetch it here." She turned her attention back to Lady Malla and chaffed her cold hands. "There, there, my dove. We shall soon have you cleaned up."

Washed and wrapped in one of Etheldrida's enormous nightshirts, Lady Malla looked and felt better.

The door of the cottage opened and Sir Oswold peeked inside. "How are you, my dear?" he asked anxiously, crossing the room and dropping to his knees beside his wife.

"Recovering nicely, thanks to the splendid ministrations of Etheldrida and Dian." Lady Malla chuckled when she saw that her husband was still dressed in his muddy work clothes. "Dearest Oswold, my saviour but not quite my knight in shining armour."

"I cannot imagine what those foolish villagers were thinking, allowing such a thing to happen," said Sir Oswold. "I shall be having words with them when next I visit Kilterton."

Safe with her friends, Lady Malla was ready to forgive. "We must not blame the simple country-folk, Oswold. Many of them were too afraid of the priest to disobey his orders."

The warmth of Egglebart and Etheldrida's hospitality enveloped everyone. Etheldrida added smoked herrings and more bread to the roast pigeons and the seven friends shared a hearty supper washed down with pots of mulled ale.

Greatly restored, Lady Malla yawned and tapped her husband's arm. "We must take our leave, Oswold. I am quite worn out and longing for my bed. I will return your nightshift tomorrow, Etheldrida," she added, nodding gratefully.

They said their farewells under the stars and, leading his horse with Lady Malla seated comfortably upon the animal's broad back, Sir Oswold walked the short distance back to Cowslip Cottage.

Dian watched them go, dreading the longer journey to Bayersby Manor. "I am afraid to travel so late in the day," she whispered to Oric. "What if Father Chrispian lives? I would not like to stumble upon him in the dark."

"Etheldrida will not mind if we stay overnight," replied Oric, giving Dian a quick hug. Suddenly overcome by shyness, he dropped his hands to his sides. "We shall return home at first light."

Etheldrida made up a straw pallet inside the cottage for Dian, and draped a pile of wolf pelts over Norbert's arm. "You and Oric can sleep in the stable. You will be as snug as a pair of bugs in a cowpat."

A smile played around Etheldrida's generous mouth as she watched Oric and Dian bid each other goodnight. They made a handsome couple and she hoped their friendship would blossom into a more serious relationship.

"Look," murmured Oric, pointing at a fingernail sliver of moon in the dark sky.

"It looks like a new moon," replied Dian, shivering. "Lord help us, I dare not imagine what new disasters might occur before we see the next one."

-oOo-

Had the power-packed blow from Sir Oswold's broadsword landed a hand-span lower, Father Chrispian would have lost his head. As it was, the flat side of the blade slammed the top of his skull, nicked off a tuft of hair, and knocked him senseless. The priest lay beside the pyre in the clearing until fierce heat from the flames dragged him back to consciousness. He lurched to his feet and stared into the fire. It took several moments for his mind to clear, and when it did, his fury knew no bounds. He dusted himself off and shambled into the woods with no idea of where he was going, or what to do next.

-oOo-

Bertram grew too big for his boots and, after suffering years of Esica Figg's dominance, Hersica was not inclined to skivvy for another master. With this idea in mind, she unearthed Figg's plunder from graves in St Griswald's Churchyard, and lashed it to a two-wheeled cart. Pockets in her shift bulged with smaller items including jewellery she had stolen from Helled Bascoomb. In Father Chrispian's absence, Hersica also helped herself to some of his stash. Blowing air through her toothless gums, she picked up the shafts and heaved the cart into motion.

Hersica had barely travelled two furlongs when a strange noise issued from some nearby bushes. "What funny business is this?" she quavered. "Is someone playing the fool?"

A woman crawled out onto the track and struggled to her feet. Torn clothing clung to her thin frame, and the hem of her kirtle was caught up with burrs. Bits of twig and straw protruded from her bird's nest hair. "Oh dear Lord, am I glad to see you, Hersica!" the woman cried. "I dare not return to my little house in Scraggswood Forest for fear the folk of Kilterton come after me. I have been running in fear for my life ever since Figg died."

"Lawks-a-mercy!" exclaimed Hersica. "That is never you – is it – Mother Olive?"

"Yes, I am afraid it is – somewhat the worse for wear."

That is the understatement of the century, thought Hersica, *but maybe I can turn this woman's miserable state to my advantage.* "I am sorry to see you so badly used," she said, her voice dripping with fake sympathy. "How would you feel about joining forces with me? We would make a formidable pair, if we worked together." Mother Olive was well known for her ability to use her feet and fists when backed into a corner.

Mother Olive jumped at the chance of salvation. She did not care much for Hersica Horzefell, but right now it was a case of any port in a storm. She had no money, no change of clothes, no food, and certainly no better offers.

Final destination unknown, the two women set off for Dunburton. Hersica believed the derelict village would serve them well, until they decided what to do with the rest of their lives.

Hungry, tired and thirsty, Father Chrispian blundered through the woods. Ahead two old crones crossed the pathway and he wondered if they were hallucinations.

Unaware that they being observed, Hersica screeched with laughter. "Figg would turn in his grave if he could see us now."

"Aye," chimed in Mother Olive, "a pox on all men and masters. From now on I intend to carve my own destiny."

Such audacity, thought Father Chrispian. *Who does the doxy think she is, maligning all men and masters?* He quickened his step. *The first witch escaped her punishment – these two will not!*

Hersica and Olive failed to recognise the man that loomed out of the dusk. Singed clothes flapped around his thin body, a pair of glazed eyes stared from sunken sockets, and he carried a large axe. A tremor of fear ran through Hersica. *The man looks deranged,* she thought. Lowering the cart's shafts to the ground, she sank to her knees and crawled behind. "Get down Olive, if we remain silent the man might walk by."

Father Chrispian did not walk by. Coming abreast of the cart, he bent down to get a better look at his victims. One of the faces that peered back at him resembled the apparition he had encountered, night after night, in St Griswald's Churchyard. "Ha, ha – now I have you!" he giggled gleefully, a trickle of saliva dribbling from his bottom lip. He seized a handful of Hersica's hair and yanked her to her feet. "Come with me, you horrible witch. Your time is up."

Terrified, Hersica pulled free of his grasp, leaving behind a handful of hair. "How would you like to be wealthy?" her voice trembled and she pointed to the cart. "You can have all of that if you let us get off about our business."

All Father Chrispian could see was the ghastly face that had haunted him since he couldn't remember when. "Prepare to meet thy doom," he burbled, swinging the axe around his head. "I shall fasten you to a stake and there you shall stay until I find kindling enough to set you alight. Only then shall I be free of you. Free, do you hear? Free, free, freeeeee."

Now Hersica realised who she was dealing with. Petrified, she shed her heavy cloak. How she wished she could dump her shift, too. Wealth meant little to her now that her life was at stake. *Stake? What am I thinking?* The word seared her brain. *The priest is going to lash me to a stake and set me alight.* Hersica tried to hobble away but the heavy gold coins and jewellery she had stashed in her shift pockets banged against her shins, preventing her from moving faster than a snail's pace.

Mother Olive looked on, her eyes round with horror. *I must get away! Maybe if I wait until yon madman is busy with Hersica…*

Father Chrispian played cat and mouse. Babbling and keening, he darted along beside Hersica, jabbing her with his axe handle. Every now and again he let rip with a cackle of crazy laughter.

Reaching the river, Hersica had nowhere else to go. On trembling legs she sidled across to the edge of an overhanging bank. Way below, dark water frothed and churned.

The priest reached out claw-like hands. As he made contact with Hersica's arm, the bank gave way.

Hersica clawed at thin air. She flailed down twice the height of a man, and Father Chrispian followed her. The pair hit the water with an explosive splash. Had Hersica not been wearing her plunder-filled shift, she might have floundered to the opposite bank. As it was, she sank into the deep water like a stone.

Mother Olive waited a long time before she plucked up the courage to creep to the bank and peep over the edge. There was no sign of Hersica or the priest.

Humming softly, she walked back along the track until she came across Hersica's discarded cloak. She threw the garment onto the cart, picked up the shafts and set the heavy load into motion.

Chapter Twenty-One

A Long, Cold Ride

Replete on fresh-laid eggs from Etheldrida's chickens, Oric and Dian, accompanied by a fully restored Norbert, set off on the journey back to Bayersby Manor. Braccus, his belly full of Egglebart's best hay, maintained a swift trot along Kilterton High Street. Early risers waved as the three friends passed by but, disgusted by her mother's disgraceful behaviour the day before, Dian resolutely turned her head the other way as she passed her parents' rundown cottage.

Leaving the village behind, they soon came to the ford at Roxdale Beck. Meerig and Lanaval's tannery was going full tilt and the stench of urine and dung, used in the tanning process, fouled the air.

Dian drew her shawl across her nose and mouth. "How that pair live with that dreadful stink is beyond me."

"I suppose they are used to it," Oric replied, urging Braccus across the beck.

Norbert insisted that he was well enough to walk the rest of the way to Rigg Farm and so spared Oric and Dian the detour that would take them past St Griswald's Church. They bid the shepherd farewell and, leaving behind a trail of muddy water on the track, they carried on toward High Moor.

Oric sneaked a sideways glance at Dian and his heart swelled with happiness. For the moment, he could not care less about his father's legacy. *Am I not the luckiest boy in the world?* he thought. *I have a few silver coins stashed away in a chest, my own plot of land, a position as junior apothecary, and the best friends any mortal could wish for.*

By the time Bayersby Manor came into sight, Oric had talked himself out of pursuing his noble destiny.

-oOo-

Obsessed with keeping things tidy, the new housekeeper made Oric and Ichtheus' lives miserable. Whenever they lit their brazier to heat potions, she complained about the smell. Several times a day she insisted they clear away their equipment and scrub off any trace of spilled medicaments. Her tongue was sharper than a newly-honed knife and the servants soon learned to keep out of her way.

"The way Mistress Foley glides around trying to catch folk doing something wrong gives me the creeps," Oric grumbled. "In the beginning, the keys she carried jangled as she walked, giving some warning of her approach; now she holds them close to her skirt to deaden the sound. She is downright sneaky!"

The housekeeper had as little regard for the apothecaries as they had for her. Having spent several moons with her sister in Roxbrough, she did not take kindly to sharing accommodation with Ichtheus. "That medical nincompoop drives me to distraction with his slovenly ways," she told Lady Myferny, "and his assistant is worse. They strew their jars of evil-smelling substances all over the kitchen, and the old man snores like a pig. I am getting so little sleep I can barely function."

Thoroughly disgruntled with the housekeeper, Ichtheus also complained.

Lady Myferny listened patiently to both parties but she was less than sympathetic with Ichtheus. "Tosh, we are all adults, are we not? Surely you can come to some amicable arrangement between yourselves. Good housekeepers are as scarce as hen's teeth, I do not wish to lose Mistress Foley."

Eventually a compromise was reached. Mistress Foley moved out of the kitchen and into a one-room dwelling in the compound. She continued to rule the house with a rod of iron and was omnipresent in the kitchen during the day. Parzifal, relegated to the stables on a permanent basis, never set foot in the kitchen.

Winter weather brought the growing season to an end and Josh, well rounded with extra clothes, heaped manure-rich straw onto Oric's garden beds. The mixture would fertilise perennial herbs and protect their shallow root systems from frost. In between caring for the garden, Josh journeyed to the woods and, with Sir Edred's permission, he chopped logs to feed the brazier.

To escape the housekeeper's carping tongue, Oric spent a good deal of time in his hut.

He produced many new medicaments and administered to sick folk around the district. His reputation as a healer grew. Poor folk who could not afford to pay money for treatments made up the shortfall with an egg or two, a piece of fruit in season and occasionally a freshly caught fish. Oric was often out of pocket, but to see sick people made well was reward enough.

Parzifal abandoned the chilly Bayersby stable and claimed a corner of Oric and Josh's hut. The boys made simple suppers, which they ate by the light of an oil lantern. Rather than walk home in the cold and dark, Oric often stayed overnight.

Oric and Josh had enjoyed just such a supper when someone tapped on the door. Awakened from a deep sleep, Parzifal growled. Josh grabbed an axe, and Oric drew his dagger. With many a rogue still on the loose, it paid to be cautious.

They need not have worried, for the visitor was Master Ichtheus. Oric put away his knife and pulled up a spare stool. "Sit by the brazier and warm yourself, Master Ichtheus, you look frozen to the bone."

Glancing around the interior of the hut, Ichtheus nodded his approval. *No wonder Oric prefers to spend his time here rather than in the Bayersby kitchen,* he thought. The building might be small, but every nook and cranny had been put to good use. Two rough-hewn benches stood against the walls; at the back of the hut stood a trestle table littered with the tools of Oric's trade. The hard-packed dirt floor was strewn with clean, dry bracken.

"Judging by the troubled look on your face, this is not a social call," said Oric, handing Ichtheus a pot of mulled blackberry wine.

Ichtheus nodded and cupped his hands around the warm vessel. "It transpires that Mistress Foley was housekeeper at Lockton Castle before she left to care for her ailing sister. Apparently she fell afoul of Sir Ragnald and his men, but that was not Mistress Foley's only reason for leaving the castle. She confessed that several of Sir Ragnald's men suddenly dropped dead. Sir Edred thinks the deaths may have been caused by a fever and he believes there might be an epidemic." Ichtheus rubbed at worry lines on his forehead. "Several moons have elapsed since Mistress Foley left Lockton Castle and any epidemic would have burned out by now, but I have failed to convince Sir Edred." Ichtheus looked crestfallen. "He commands you to leave for Lockton Castle at first light. Braccus and the cart await outside to transport whatever medications and equipment you deem necessary. I will borrow Otty whilst you are gone – if I may."

-oOo-

Oric gobbled down his breakfast and hastened outside into a bitterly cold dawn. He had almost filled the cart with supplies when Ned appeared, leading a young gelding. Joe sat astride the animal's back clutching a large hamper. "Sir Edred says you can borrow this beast for the sake of speed. His name is Jester." Ned rolled his eyes. "The horse is well named – be prepared for an antic or two." He detached Braccus from the cart's shafts and backed Jester in. "In view of Otty's aversion to carts, Master Ichtheus will be heartfelt glad to have Braccus back."

"Dian has packed enough food to keep us going for the journey," said Joe, lifting the hamper onto the cart.

"What do you mean – to keep *us* going?" Oric demanded. "Surely you are not coming with me."

"We are indeed!" Ned hooked his thumbs into the belt of his new grey tunic and strutted up and down. "Sir Edred has ordered me and Joe to look after you. By all accounts it is a four-day ride to Lockton Castle; more if the weather conditions are not good. Our lord and master thinks you might need help when you get there."

"How very considerate of him," said Oric with a hint of sarcasm. "Nevertheless, I shall be glad of your company."

Dian appeared with three flagons of ale in a handcart.

"Good Lord! I trust you are not planning to join us!" On any other trip Oric would have welcomed Dian, but this time he deemed the journey and the destination too dangerous.

"I would like to come with you," Dian replied. "But Lady Myferny forbids it. She says it is not seemly for a young maid to travel unchaperoned with three young men."

Oric blushed scarlet with anger. "Good Heavens, what does my lady take me for? Surely she must know I have only your best interests at heart!"

Ned winked knowingly at Joe. "I reckon Oric has more than a passing fancy for the lass," he whispered. "Otherwise he would not get into such a state."

"Aye, and she him," tittered Joe, noticing Dian's rosy flush while adding the flagons to the cart.

Dian caught hold of Oric's arm. "Please take extra care. I would not trust Sir Ragnald, or his son, for all the apples in an orchard."

"You worry overmuch," soothed Oric, patting Dian's hand. "Ned and Joe will take good care of me." He grinned mischievously. "In view of their questionable past, I am sure they can smell trouble, long before anything untoward happens." Oric wanted to kiss Dian on the cheek but, with Ned and Joe watching, he would never hear the end of it. Instead he squeezed Dian's hand, and moved away to the cart. He raised his boot level with the mounting board but, before he found his footing, the horse jerked three paces forward. Oric lost his balance and smacked face-first into the cart. Hastening to grasp the horse's bridle, Oric received a sharp nip on the backside. "Jester by name and Jester by nature," roared Oric. "Seems I need to keep a close eye on you, my lad."

Mounted sideways upon Braccus, Dian smothered her giggles and set off back to Bayersby Manor.

Parzifal followed the cart. To avoid being sent back to

Bayersby, he crept through long grass that grew alongside the track.

Entering a dense forest, fallen trees blocked the way and the boys were often forced to seek a roundabout route. At midday they stopped to eat, and water Jester. Oric rested back against the bole of a tree, wondering what the next few days would bring. In the distance, a dog yapped.

"Shush!" Oric silenced Ned and Joe's chatter. "That sounds like Parzifal! Judging by the tone of his bark, he is in trouble."

Not far from the rough track, Oric came upon the dog. Seeking a drink, Parzifal had floundered into a bog. All four legs were entrenched in mud, and he was sinking fast.

"Keep still, boy!" Oric cried, trying not to panic. "If you wriggle, you will soon be completely submerged."

Ned and Joe arrived on the scene, panting from their sprint.

"Oh, my!" Ned gasped. "How are we going to get him out of there?"

"Talk to him, Ned, keep him calm until I get back. Joe, you run and fetch a rope from the cart." Oric gathered up several fallen branches, lugged them to the edge of the bog, and crisscrossed them across the glutinous surface. "Pray God these will support my weight."

Joe returned with the rope and Oric tied one end around his wrist. "Hold this," he said, thrusting the other end into Ned's hands. "We will use the rope to haul Parzifal out."

The branches spread Oric's weight and he squirmed his way across the surface of the bog. Parzifal saw him coming and made odd grunting sounds. Reaching the dog, Oric looped the rope around his chest and front legs. Then he plunged his arms into the mire and tied another loop under the dog's belly and hind legs. Knotting the rope securely, he gave Ned and Joe the go-ahead to begin pulling.

Parzifal felt the strain on his makeshift harness and struggled.

"Steady, boy, steady," soothed Oric, holding the dog's head above the slime.

Ned and Joe kept up the strain until Parzifal gained purchase on firm ground and scrabbled out of the bog.

"Quick, throw back the rope," Oric yelled. "I am sinking."

The rope snaked through the air, but fell short of Oric's grasp. "Try again," he cried in panic.

The raft of branches sank further and the bog claimed Oric's lower torso. Soon the sucking mire would consume his entire body.

Several attempts later, Oric caught the end of the rope and wound it under his armpits. Knotting it around his chest he yelled, "For the love of God, pull me out of here!"

Submerged in thick mud, Oric's weight doubled. Ned and Joe strained but lacked the strength to drag Oric clear.

"Fetch Jester!" Oric screamed.

When Joe reappeared with the horse, Oric had sunk to his armpits. "Tie the rope to Jester's harness. Urge him to walk forward." *Pray God the stupid animal does not choose this moment to misbehave,* thought Oric.

Jester behaved impeccably. He took the strain and never faltered. It was a painstaking project, but at last Oric lay trembling on the bank. "Oh dear Lord," he cried. "I truly thought my time was up."

Delighted to be reunited with his human friend, Parzifal jumped all over Oric.

"Get off me, you stupid mutt," Oric cried. "You stink!"

"Hark at the pot calling the kettle black," said Ned, overwhelmed with relief. "You ain't smelling like no bunch of flowers neither, my friend."

Oric staggered to his feet, and went to pat Jester. The horse laid his ears back, swung his head around and nipped Oric's bottom again.

Oric jumped aside, rubbing his backside. The horse was a puzzle, make no mistake. He ignored Ned and Joe's raucous laughter, and inspected the sky. "Darkness will soon be upon us," he said. "We must seek a place to rest for the night."

Not far away the boys came upon a small lake and set up camp. Oric stripped off his filthy clothes, and dragged Parzifal into the lake's cold shallows. Having scrubbed the dog clean, he struck out into deeper water. Blue with cold, he swam back to shore, and rinsed his soiled garments. He wrung them out as best he could, and rubbed himself dry with a piece of rough sack.

Using the last dregs of daylight, Ned and Joe searched for wood to make a fire. As darkness fell they toasted chunks of bread over the embers, drank a flagon of ale, and ate apples and cheese from Lady Myferny's hamper. Before lying down to sleep, Oric loaded more branches onto the fire, and rigged up a frame of saplings and twine. He hung his wet clothes close to the flames, hoping the garments might dry before morning. Exhausted by their adventures, the boys rolled themselves in blankets and curled up beside the fire to sleep.

A multitude of stars pricked the blue-black heavens and moonlight sparkled on frosty grass. In the distance a lone wolf howled. Ned threw another branch on the fire. Joe shivered and drew closer to the flames.

Naked, apart from his cover, Oric shivered with cold. "Here, Parzifal," he called, lifting a corner of the blanket. Parzifal crept in and Oric hugged him close, enjoying the warmth that emanated from the dog's whiskery body. "Stupid mutt – you have no idea how close we came to death this afternoon." Lulled by the hiss and slap of small waves on the lake's shoreline, boy and dog fell asleep.

-oOo-

The fire died down and the boys awoke at dawn, cold and sore. Oric was gratified to find that his clothes were only a little damp and, frozen to the bone, he hastily put them on.

Ned made up the fire, toasted more pieces of bread, and handed round chunks of salt beef. Their breakfast over, Joe doused the hot embers with water from the lake.

"I hope that spindle-shank housekeeper gave us the right directions," muttered Joe. "The sooner we get to Lockton Castle, the happier I shall be."

Equally miserable, Oric squinted at the map Mistress Foley had scribbled. "According to these instructions, we face another two nights sleeping rough before we reach our destination."

Rain fell during the afternoon of the third day and the boys donned waterproof cloaks. Woodland tracks turned into quagmires but they soldiered on, digging out the cart each time it became bogged. As the miserable day wore on the countryside gradually changed. Giant fir trees replaced oak, ash and beech, and pine needles carpeted the forest floor. Instead of gentle rolling hills, jagged mountains reared up in the distance.

On the afternoon of the fourth day they came upon a vast lake. A village straggled along the eastern shoreline but many cottages lay derelict. The few dwellings that housed families were in a dreadful state of repair. One or two ragged folk scurried along the street, heads down against the downpour. Apart from one woman, everyone ignored the newcomers.

"Good day to you, mistress," said Oric. "What is the name of this place?"

"Skelgutt," the woman replied, sniffing up a dewdrop that hung from the end of her nose, "but folk hereabouts call the village Hell's Gate."

Shocked by the woman's aura of despair, Oric questioned her further. "Why would that be mistress?" And where are the missing inhabitants?"

"Sir Ragnald and his brat have bled us dry. Those of us still here are barely able to feed ourselves." She shrugged miserably. "We only stay 'cos we ain't got nowhere else to go."

Oric wished he could help the villagers but he did not have the wherewithal. "We are seeking Lockton Castle, are you able to give us directions?"

The woman pointed to a mountain at the far end of the lake. "Rather you than me," she said. "I wish you luck if you plan to visit that evil place."

Chapter Twenty-Two

Lockton Castle

Lockton Castle could be accessed by two tracks. The first, narrow and steep, climbed up the southern side of the mountain; the second, wide enough for an ox-drawn cart, wound back and forth across the northern gradient, making for an easier climb. With the horse and cart in mind, Oric chose the latter path.

Leading Jester by his bridle, Oric dodged potholes and overgrown trees. "Whoever is responsible for maintenance hereabouts needs taking to task," he complained, fending off yet another low-hanging, water-sodden branch. Parzifal's wiry coat stuck to his sides and he appeared thinner than usual.

They gained altitude and the rain turned to sleet. Wet, cold and miserable, Oric, Ned, and Joe rounded the final tree-clad bend and emerged onto a wide grassy plateau.

From the high vantage point, Lockton Castle commanded an extensive view of Lake Coughcat and the valley below. Formidable mountains to the rear of the castle protected indwellers from would-be intruders. The outer castellated walls were encircled by a deep moat filled with stagnant water and pondweed. A few spindly rushes grew at the base of the castle walls.

"Whoever built this place certainly understood self-defense," said Oric, pulling a face at the smell drifting up from the moat. "What a pity everything is in such a state of disrepair." He held his nose. "'Tis easy to tell where the effluent from the garderobe flows. You'd think somebody could muck out the moat once in a while."

The castle consisted of two double-storey stone buildings set at right angles to one another, and a square, three-storey castellated tower joined the dwellings together in the center. At ground level a gatehouse and stout portcullis gave access to a large, walled bailey.

Peering through the gate's crisscrossed ironwork, Oric spotted a well, a small church, and several more shabby buildings. Maintenance was clearly not one of Sir Ragnald's priorities.

Nothing stirred within the bailey and Oric's heartbeat sounded loud in his ears. "Let us see if we can attract some attention," he said, sounding more confident than he felt. He drew a ram's horn from his pouch and blew three sharp blasts.

Startled by the noise, Jester reared, his front hooves missing Oric's head by a whisker. He soothed the horse's velvet neck. "Easy, old lad, I did not mean to frighten you."

Above the gatehouse was the outline of a battered stone shield. "What do you reckon to that?" Oric asked, pointing to what remained of the chipped insignia.

"I doubt the weather is to blame for all that wear, though it probably does get wild up here." Ned brushed ineffectually at clarts of mud that stuck to his leggings. "I reckon someone has hacked at the stonework with an axe."

Wind howled around the battlements and Joe shivered, more from fear than cold. "Why would anyone do such a pointless thing?"

Nobody came to the gate, and Oric blew his horn again.

Curious to see who had arrived, Guwain pushed aside the shutters in his turret room and stuck his head out of the window slit. "Holy jumping toads," he spluttered, striking his skull on the surrounding stonework in his haste to withdraw from the embrasure. Leaping down from his vantage point, he overturned a table that held the game of chess he had been playing with Joffrey.

Returning from the garderobe in the other turret, Joffrey had not heard the horn. He viewed the spilled chessmen, and imagined Guwain had ended a game he could not win. Tired of the Bayersby heir's tantrums, Joffrey's temper snapped. "What ails you now?" he snarled.

Guwain paced the room, wringing his hands. "Oric is outside with a couple of youths! Do you suppose he has discovered my whereabouts?"

"Calm down," hissed Joffrey. He sidled up to the embrasure and took a peek outside. "I doubt Oric knows you are here. Some other business has brought him to Lockton, for sure; nevertheless, you had best lie low until our visitors depart."

Guwain enjoyed life in Lockton Castle as a pig enjoys clover, but he failed to grasp that the clover had almost run out. Feeling like the man his father never allowed him to be, Guwain had joined the Lockton army, drilling alongside Sir Ragnald's soldiers with gusto. In his dreams he led a column of men into battle, but his dreams never portrayed the bloody brutality of war. Nor did Guwain realise the men he trained with may well cause the downfall of Bayersby Manor.

Thoroughly enjoying the irony of the situation, Joffrey played along with Guwain's delusions.

-oOo-

Sleet turned into snow, and wind moaned around Lockton Castle's battlements. Oric pulled his cloak more tightly around his neck and, with Parzifal close on his heels, he strode up to the portcullis. "Halloo – is anyone there?" he shouted.

A fellow with a black moustache approached the inside of the portcullis and peered out. "What d'you want?"

"I wish to see Sir Ragnald."

The bewhiskered fellow scrutinised the three boys and the dog, thinking them of little account. "I doubt Sir Ragnald *wishes* to see you!"

"My good man," said Oric, glaring at the weasel-faced gatekeeper, "I have journeyed for several days, I am soaked to my skin, and I am running short of patience. Kindly inform Sir Ragnald that the Bayersby Apothecary awaits an audience."

Surprised by the youth's authoritative tone, the gatekeeper raised his dark eyebrows. "I cannot promise Sir Ragnald will see you," he grumbled. "But I will tell him that you are here."

Oric paced up and down, water from his hat dripping down his neck. "Hang it all! How long are we to be kept waiting in this accursed blizzard?"

At last the portcullis squeaked open, and Oric's party was allowed into Lockton Castle's outer bailey.

"Sir Ragnald will see you now," the gatekeeper announced, "but he says to leave all your weapons in the gatehouse."

"Weapons? We have no weapons!" Oric retorted. "We are here to offer medical assistance. Rumour has it that Lockton is beset by a fever epidemic."

The gatekeeper's shifty expression changed to one of fear. "Aye, there have been deaths aplenty, but none of them from any epidemic." Refusing to enter into further conversation, he waved Oric's party into the castle's inner bailey.

Two stable-boys came forward. One youth made a thorough search of the cart; the other reached out to unhitch Jester.

Over the last day or so Oric had taken note of Jester's slightly mad look just before he misbehaved. The horse had that look now. "Er... I would approach the animal with caution if..."

Oric's warning came too late.

The second youth tried to unhitch Jester's harness and the horse squashed him against the stable wall.

"Get 'im off me," the boy gabbled, his eyes almost popping from his head with the horse's weight pressed across his chest.

Parzifal made matters worse by growling and nipping at the stable-boy's ankles.

Oric grabbed Jester's bridle and yanked him away from the wall. The youth wriggled free and hastily backed away. He held up his hands, flashing resentful glances at Oric. "I ain't going near that black devil again. You can deal with 'im yourself and, whilst you are about it, get a grip of yon 'orrible dog."

The gatekeeper sniggered and introduced himself as Rory. Satisfied the visitors carried nothing more dangerous than a small dagger and an axe for chopping wood, he ordered the first serf to look after Oric's horse. The lad unhitched Jester from the cart, and coaxed him into the stables.

Rory pointed to a flight of steps that gave access to an arched timber door on the second floor of the square tower. "Sir Ragnald awaits you in the Great Hall. When you are ready to leave, I shall be waiting in the gatehouse to let you out."

Holding tight to Parzifal's collar, Oric climbed the stairs at the side of the tower. Ned and Joe followed, wondering what kind of hornets' nest they were entering into.

Two wooden chests, a battered suit of armour, and a carved table were the only pieces of furniture within the gloomy entrance hall. Ancient leather shields scraped free of insignia hung on the grubby, lime-washed walls. Several doors gave access to other rooms, but only one door stood ajar. Masculine laughter issued from within and Oric surmised that the noise came from the Great Hall. Quashing his forebodings, he stepped boldly into the room with Ned, Joe and Parzifal close on his heels.

Rush sconces illuminated the vast room. Furniture was minimal, but of excellent quality. One or two tapestries depicting hunting scenes and mythical beasts hung against the dirty walls; cleaner squares of stonework indicated there had once been many more wall hangings. Sturdy timber columns supported blackened overhead beams and, on closer inspection, Oric saw that sections of carving had suffered the same harsh treatment as the shield over the gatehouse. Logs cut from apple trees belched smoke from a central hearth but the pleasant smell of fruit failed to mask the rancid odour of masculine sweat.

Parzifal, in his element, immediately began snuffling amongst the floorcovering for morsels of discarded food.

Playing for time, Sir Ragnald speared a chunk of meat from his platter and popped it into his mouth. "To what do I owe this dubious honour?" he regarded Oric quizzically from his chair on a dais. *Perhaps the Lord of Bayersby has learned of his son's whereabouts,* he thought. *Maybe he has sent the youths to spy upon us.*

"I understand that your people have been plagued by an epidemic," Oric stated, staring boldly at the Lord of the Castle. "I am come to offer my professional advice and assistance."

Sir Ragnald relaxed slightly. "How did you hear of this 'so-called' epidemic?"

"From your ex-housekeeper," Oric answered tersely. "She claims that your men are dropping like flies."

"Ah, the redoubtable Mistress Foley!" Sir Ragnald smoothed his moustache with a thumb and forefinger. "She left here many a long moon past and I was glad to see the back of her. She drove me near insane with her overzealous attention to cleanliness."

Despite Lockton Castle's unsavoury conditions, Sir Ragnald and his men appeared to be in robust health. "Perhaps Mistress Foley exaggerated the severity of the epidemic," Oric added lamely.

"There is no epidemic, never was! The cook's rotten meat was to blame for the deaths." Sir Ragnald waved his hand dismissively. "There will be no repeat occurrences, I can assure you. Return from whence you came, Master Apothecary, we have no need of your skills here."

In truth Sir Ragnald had unearthed a plot to poison his food, and he had ordered his cook to feed the culprits a portion of their own medicine. Having disposed of his traitorous henchmen, he served the cook a drink laced with deadly hemlock.

"We would appreciate a meal and an overnight stay," said Oric, thinking that was the least Sir Ragnald could do. "To negotiate our way back down the mountain in the dead of night would be foolhardy."

Sir Ragnald clicked his fingers at a passing serf. "Bed these fellows down in the stables." In a quiet aside he added, "See they do not stray from their quarters, and make sure they leave at first light."

More of Sir Ragnald's men wandered into the Great Hall and clustered around the fire to warm themselves. Bannulf, the Master at Arms, separated from his fellow mercenaries and climbed onto the dais. "Who are the three young bucks I passed on the stairs?"

"Fellows from Bayersby!" replied Sir Ragnald. "For the sake of all our futures, keep Guwain out of sight, otherwise we shall be obliged to dispose of our young guests." He smiled sardonically. "I would rather Sir Edred did not send a party to search for his missing employees, for that would spoil the element of surprise."

Bannulf stomped up the tower stairs to Guwain's third-floor quarters, rapped sharply on the door and entered the room without waiting for a response.

Of all Sir Ragnald's men, Bannulf was the one Guwain liked least. The fellow was well past his first flush of youth; nevertheless, he remained full of himself. Tall, blond and arrogant, the warrior was clearly of Saxon origin. Even his voice was guttural, and he clearly thought he was some kind of god.

"Sir Ragnald requests that you remain in hiding until after the apothecary and his party leave tomorrow morning."

Guwain pulled a pet-lip. "Oh, pish! I was looking forward to a game of dice with the squires in the Great Hall this evening. Now I am confined to my room whilst yon poxy apothecary enjoys a night of jollifications. Is there no justice?"

"I doubt the apothecary will spend a comfortable night. He is confined to the stables with his two cronies and their animals."

Bannulf was short with the Bayersby heir, for the boy possessed the same unpleasant characteristics as Sir Ragnald and his son Joffrey. Their type swaggered through life, killing and plundering with little thought for their victims. Fed up to the teeth with bloodshed, Bannulf longed to find a plot of land, raise a few cattle and grow his own vegetables. Many of Sir Ragnald's older mercenaries had felt the same.

Chapter Twenty-Three

Oric Explores the Castle

Jester snickered as Oric, Ned, and Joe entered the Lockton stables. The cart, with its load intact, stood in an empty stall. Joe fell upon it gleefully, dragging out Lady Myferny's food hamper. He passed around the last few salted herrings and chunks of cheese, urging Oric and Ned to make the most of their supper. "Sir Ragnald is a mean beggar. Fancy him giving us nowt to eat."

"Aye, and I bet he gives us nowt for our return journey to Bayersby," groaned Ned. "I can see us suffering a long, hungry ride."

Stripping off their damp outer garments, the boys made beds out of fresh straw and settled down for the night. Ned and Joe fell asleep immediately. Parzifal, with his back pressed along the length of Oric's legs, yawned, placed his head on his paws, and closed his eyes.

Oric lay with his arms crossed behind his head, unwelcome thoughts whirling around his brain. *Had Sir Ragnald told the truth? Were the inmates of Lockton Castle accidentally poisoned by rotten meat? If that be the case, what is the gatekeeper so afraid of?*

The flickering lantern illuminated sticky cobwebs, and the earthen floor, hard-packed with horse droppings, smelled stale. *It seems Sir Ragnald cares as little for his outbuildings as he does for his castle.* Frustrated with his sleepless state, Oric fondled the dog's silky ears. "Y'know what, old lad? We just might take a sneaky look at Lockton Castle whilst everyone is abed."

Always game for an adventure, the dog was on his feet in a flash. Oric dragged on his damp top clothes, and stepped outside. The sleet from earlier in the day had ceased and frost had hardened the snow, making it crunch as Oric walked.

Keeping within the shadow of the castle's outer walls, Oric crept around the bailey. With Parzifal close on his heels, he dashed across the wide strip of ground to the main dwelling. For as long as it took to tiptoe up the steps to the entrance in the central tower, boy and dog were visible. The bailey remained quieter than a graveyard and Oric blessed the cold weather for keeping everyone indoors. He eased open the iron-studded door that gave access to the main part of the castle, and stepped inside. Barely daring to breathe, Oric stood with his back against the door. Candles held in iron wall-sconces flickered, giving scant light. He recognised the entrance to the Great Hall and was relieved that no sound came from within. A wide corridor led away from the square entrance area, and Oric tiptoed past several closed doors. Parzifal's long claws rattled on the timber floor, sounding loud in the silence of the night.

At the end of the corridor a flight of stairs spiralled downward. Holding tightly to Parzifal's collar, Oric descended. At ground level he peeped around a pillar that supported the stone steps. Several oil lamps illuminated a long room, and smoke from a brazier drifted across the forms of fifty or so men at rest. Ripe farts, coupled with loud snores, reverberated around the room. Judging by the smell, Oric surmised that the food at the castle was not all it might be. The length of one wall was hung with an impressive arsenal of weapons. Oric gasped. Sir Ragnald's lack of care clearly did not extend to his arms department.

Cattle brought in from the fields for winter lowed softly at the far end of the vast area, and the pungent odour of animal dung, unwashed bodies, and spilled ale was overwhelming. Parzifal growled and Oric grabbed the dog's muzzle. *Please God, do not let him bark now.*

Returned to the entrance hall, Oric cracked open an ornately-carved door directly opposite to the Great Hall. The room appeared to be uninhabited. Oric stepped inside and quietly shut the door. He felt around in the dark and stumbled upon a timber-framed bed. Further investigation unearthed a feather mattress, a bolster, and a fur coverlet. Oric's eyes gradually adjusted to the gloom and he was able to make out four chairs, a table, and a large chest. Items of female apparel hung from a pole affixed to the wall. Trailing his fingers through the garments, Oric inhaled the faint smell of lavender. Dust that clung to the soft fabrics tickled his nose, and he fought the desire to sneeze.

He believed the room to be a woman's bower – but where was the occupant?

Ashes on the hearth felt colder to the touch than a marble slab, and there was no sign of fresh kindling or any other fuel. A small wire cage on the window ledge bore skeletal evidence of a neglected bird. Despite Mistress Foley's redoubtable reputation, the room had not been cleaned for a very long time. In the poor light Oric stumbled over a child's cradle, trapping one of Parzifal's paws under the wooden rockers. The dog's sharp yelp of pain echoed loudly in the stillness of the night, and Oric's heart almost stopped with fright. He waited for his heartbeats to return to normal and, when no-one came to investigate the noise, he crept from the room and closed the door.

Access to the turret's third floor was gained by another spiral stairway hewn from stone. Hanging on to Parzifal's collar once again, Oric began the ascent. Partway up the stairs the dog began to drag on his collar, his claws scrabbling as he tried to escape. Oric yanked him back. "For goodness' sake," he hissed. "What ails you?"

A door at the top of the stairs stood ajar. Inside the room a single oil lamp shone across a sleeping form, and Oric immediately understood Parzifal's discomfort.

The individual spreadeagled on the bed was none other than the heir of Bayersby.

Guwain had inflicted pain upon Parzifal many times and the dog clearly had no desire to renew the association, and who would blame him? Oric was not keen to renew his acquaintance with the objectionable youth either. The unlocked door and opulent, albeit untidy room suggested that Guwain was no prisoner. Not wanting a noisy confrontation, Oric resisted the urge to strangle the little toad for the distress he had caused his parents. Instead he crept back downstairs with Parzifal in the lead. He would report Guwain's whereabouts to Sir Edred and it would be up to the boy's father to make the next move.

On the bottom step, Parzifal rumbled with growls again. Out of the dark an arm encircled Oric's neck and a hand covered his mouth. "Promise to remain silent and I will release you," the perpetrator whispered hoarsely, his hot breath fanning against Oric's cheek. Parzifal gargled like a mad dog, his teeth bared, his eyes glazed. "And for the love of all that is holy, keep a grip on your dog before he takes a chunk out of me."

Oric nodded, and the pressure on his mouth and neck eased.

"Follow me," said the voice.

A fire on the hearth in the castle's basement kitchen smouldered, keeping the room smokily warm. Benches set alongside the walls held the bodies of sleeping serfs.

Oric's captor pushed open the door of a lean-to room and ushered boy and dog inside. In the lantern light, Oric recognised Bannulf, Sir Ragnald's leading henchman.

"This is my domain," said Bannulf, pointing to the only chair. "Sit down – I need to talk to you."

Keeping tight hold of Parzifal, Oric did as he was told.

"Too many folk have died over the years and I am heartfelt sick of bloodshed," Bannulf confessed. "Sir Ragnald has sacked every manor in the district; any owner that put up a fight has been slain along with his family and retainers." Bannulf snorted derisively. "All Sir Ragnald wanted from the other manors were valuables. He was not interested in property, and he burned most of the buildings to discourage the return of the inhabitants. Lockton escaped such a fate because it is the finest castle hereabouts and Sir Ragnald wanted it for himself. He rode here with his men, deposed the rightful lord and moved in. He has been in residence ever since." Bannulf hawked and spat into the brazier. "Over the years, our noble lord has squandered Lockton's considerable funds. He is not keen on work and, because of gross mismanagement, he has allowed the castle and the entire estate to deteriorate. Now the coffers are all but empty, he is on the warpath again. I was a half-starved youngster when I became a mercenary soldier. Many lords have employed me in my time but, of all the masters I have served, Sir Ragnald is the most brutal."

The brazier flared and Oric's gaze fell upon a wooden chest against the wall. Double knots, similar to the ones engraved upon Deveril's key, were carved into the lid. Oric licked his suddenly dry lips. "Er… What actually happened to Lockton's original owner?"

Bannulf's face twisted with self-loathing at the memory. "Most of the servants were killed, but I helped the incumbent lord and his family to escape. They left with a few personal possessions and a babe-in-arms."

"That old chest by the wall…" Oric struggled to contain his excitement. "Have you any idea who it belongs to?"

"No idea – it was here when I arrived."

Oric feigned nonchalance. "Does it contain anything of interest?"

"Not unless you call logs for the brazier interesting. Sir Ragnald sold everything of value long since. But never mind that piece of old junk, I have more important things to discuss."

The warrior's scarred face was careworn. His fair beard, liberally speckled with grey whiskers, was divided in the middle and each half tied with crisscrossed twine. His accent was guttural, and Oric suspected the man to be of Saxon descent.

"Before I meet my maker I wish to redress the balance." Bannulf's slate-blue eyes were troubled. "And that is why I am warning you that Sir Ragnald plans to sack Bayersby Manor."

"What?" Oric leaped from his seat. "We will see about that!" Startled by Oric's sudden movement, Parzifal began to bark.

A sleep-befuddled cook appeared in the doorway of the lean-to. "Wass th' matter?"

Before other kitchen serfs came to investigate, Bannulf

seized Oric's ear and gave it a vicious twist. "This foolish fellow was trying to steal food. Go back to sleep, there is naught to worry about." Bannulf faked an amused guffaw. "Since it is food this fellow seeks, I will make sure he gets his just desserts."

Safely returned to the stables, Bannulf apologised to Oric. "Sorry if I caused you pain, but I dare not risk an overzealous serf alerting Sir Ragnald."

The warrior's rumbling voice awoke Ned and Joe. They stared at Oric in alarm. "What is he doing in here?" Ned demanded.

"Shush! No need to worry, Bannulf is here to help us."

Joe jumped up, pulling bits of straw from his dishevelled hair. "Why should we be in need of help?" he challenged warily. "We are leaving in the morning."

Oric silenced the boys again. "Bannulf has some disturbing news."

The warrior sat down heavily on a pile of straw and drew a hand across his eyes. "Master Guwain is here. Sir Ragnald and Joffrey brought him here when they returned from the Bayersby joust."

"'Od's blood! Did they kidnap him?" Ned demanded.

"No, he came of his own free will," replied Bannulf. "The boy ran away from home because he wanted to punish his father for unfair treatment. The young fool thinks he is a welcome guest here, but my master plans to use the boy as a hostage. Sir Ragnald imagines the Lord of Bayersby will surrender his manor in exchange for his son's life."

"What if Sir Edred resists?" Oric demanded.

"Guwain is the only heir. Under the circumstances, Sir Edred is unlikely to put up a fight." Bannulf was matter-of-fact. "The boy will die if his father fails to comply. Despite his straitened circumstances, Sir Ragnald maintains a passable army and he will seize Bayersby Manor by force if necessary."

"Hah! How little your bloodthirsty lord knows of Sir Edred," Oric exclaimed. "He is unlikely to give up his son or his manor easily."

"Sir Ragnald convinces himself of all manner of things," Bannulf sneered. "However, he is unaware that a few of his men, including me, want an end to the killing. If we all back Sir Edred, I believe we might topple Sir Ragnald."

"When does Ragnald plan to make this bid for Bayersby?" The title 'Sir' no longer came easily to Oric's tongue.

"He will leave Lockton before the next full moon. By my reckoning, that is fourteen or so days away. That gives you ample time to return to Bayersby and warn Sir Edred." Bannulf became businesslike. "I recommend that you leave straightaway." He tipped his head at Ned and Joe. "You pair had best remain here, for you will impede Oric's progress. His horse is well rested and he will ride faster by himself."

"Huh! I ain't keen on that idea," mumbled Ned. "Is Sir Ragnald not going to wonder why we are still here when Oric is missing?"

"I have given that some thought as well," Bannulf reassured. "A barn on the road below the castle will provide you with a place to hide. I will bring food and water to you when I can. Once Sir Ragnald departs with his army, you pair can clear off. Now, Oric, let us find a saddle for your horse."

Making the most of stygian conditions, Rory emptied his bladder against the castle wall. With his back to the bailey, he did not see Jester and the boys follow Bannulf to a side gate.

"Will Guwain be safe for the time being?" Oric demanded.

Bannulf's reply was low and gruff. "Sir Ragnald is unlikely to kill his bargaining tool – not immediately, anyway."

To be rid of Guwain would be heaven indeed, but Oric did not wish to see the boy dead. He grasped Bannulf's shoulder. "Please take care of Guwain, for Lady Myferny's sake at least."

Rory failed to recognise Bannulf, nor did he hear his gruff reply, but the apothecary's lighter tone of voice carried clearly on the cold night air. The gatekeeper sat on his bed, thinking over what he should do. In his ale-befuddled state, he decided he would likely get a thrashing if he disturbed Sir Ragnald at such a late hour. Morning would be soon enough to report that the apothecary knew of the Bayersby heir's whereabouts.

Chapter Twenty-Four

Homeward Bound

Dawn light woke Rory, and the sickening realisation of what he had failed to do came rushing back the moment he opened his eyes. He tottered to the gatehouse door and wrenched it open. Workers were going about their daily business in the bailey, and Rory called to a young lad with a barrow full of manure from the stables. "Hey, you! Have you seen the apothecary and his party?"

The boy let go of the barrow handles and eased his back. "No, I ain't. They never showed up for breakfast this morning and they ain't in the stables, neither."

Rory's eyelids were gummed with sleep, and a shaft of bright sunlight hammered pain through his skull. His stomach churned from overmuch ale and trepidation. If he survived the morning, he swore never to drink again. He made a cursory but unsuccessful search of the outbuildings and, bracing his shoulders, he tottered across the courtyard to seek out Sir Ragnald in the Great Hall.

Sprawled in a chair upon his dais, Sir Ragnald speared a chunk of bread with his dagger. "Pay attention!" he bellowed, spraying the men seated at the trestle table below with bits of partially masticated food. "In a few days we shall march upon Bayersby Manor. The skirmish will be over almost before it begins; however, you will continue to drill until the last moment, for I ain't paying any man to idle away his time at my expense."

The warriors in the Great Hall looked at each other. They had received no pay for some time but, having come this far with Sir Ragnald, they were not about to forego the spoils that Bayersby Manor would provide.

Nerves all of a-jangle, Rory grabbed a goblet from a passing serf and climbed onto the dais. He proffered the drink to his lord and master. "Here you are, sir, a fine drop for a grand gentleman."

Sir Ragnald grabbed the vessel and quaffed the mead in one, long swallow. Drops of liquor joined bits of food that decorated the front of his stained jerkin.

Rory shuffled from foot to foot, making no move to leave the dais. He rotated his bony hands, one over the other, and bowed repeatedly.

"Is something bothering you, man?" Sir Ragnald's lip curled up in a faint snarl of disgust. Thin and weedy, the fellow looked revolting. His droopy black moustache was clogged with grease, patches of crusty scalp showed through his thinning hair, and his bloodshot eyes dripped moisture. "If you have something to say, spit it out and be gone – the very sight of you makes me want to puke!"

"I, er… I have something to say." Rory wafted his hands about, making his situation worse by the heartbeat.

"For pity's sake, tell me, man!" Sir Ragnald roared.

Chatter died down as everyone in the Great Hall awaited Rory's next utterance with undisguised relish.

"Er… The apothecary knows Master Guwain is here, sir."

"What!" Sir Ragnald's face turned puce, and veins stood out in his temples. He catapulted to his feet, sending his chair crashing off the dais. "When did you come by this piece of information?"

Nervous perspiration beaded Rory's forehead. "Late, sir! Very late – I dare not disturb you."

"Disturb me?" Snatching up his dagger, Sir Ragnald nicked a piece of skin from Rory's neck. "You addlepated numbskull – where is the apothecary now?"

Rory pressed his fingers to the wound, trying to staunch the flow of blood. "I know not where he is, sir. I have looked everywhere and I cannot find him, or his two cohorts. They cannot have escaped, though. I would have heard the portcullis." Rory smiled and twisted his head to one side, hoping to placate Sir Ragnald. "They will be somewhere within the castle confines for sure."

Incandescent with rage, Sir Ragnald shook Rory until the gatekeeper thought his neck might snap. "What about the side gate? Did it not occur to you that they might depart that way? Argh! They are probably halfway back to Bayersby by now. Get after them. They must not be allowed to reach their destination. When you catch up with them, kill them. Bring back their severed heads and I might, just might, spare your worthless life."

A leather-faced Scot stood beside the dais, enjoying Rory's discomfiture.

"Take that smirk off your face, Hamish," Sir Ragnald added tiredly. "You had best go with the gatekeeper to make sure he accomplishes the task. If he fails, complete the deed for him and add his addlepated skull to the pile. On no account must Oric and his cohorts be allowed to return to Bayersby Manor with news of Guwain's whereabouts."

-oOo-

Ned and Joe escaped to the barn below Lockton Castle.

"This is a fine kettle of fish," grumbled Joe. "I am famished and there is nowt to eat, save animal feed." His eyes watered from the cold wind, and his nose dripped unpleasant mucus.

"Never worry, little'un," replied Ned. "Bannulf will bring us food as soon as he can. Do me a favour and wipe yer nose."

The vista from the barn was breathtaking. Snow dusted the distant mountains, and a river in the valley below linked a string of silver-blue lakes like gems on a gossamer thread. The wild beauty of the area was lost on the boys, for they could think of nothing other than their rumbling bellies.

Dark clouds blotted out the sun and fat snowflakes floated from the darkened sky. Wind whistled between the barn's planks, and Joe blew hot breath onto his chapped knuckles. "How long do you suppose we will be stuck in here?" he asked.

"Not more than a few days, I hope," Ned smiled.

The arrival of two horsemen outside the barn wiped the smile from Ned's face. "Quick! Lie low," he hissed. "Looks like we have visitors, and neither one of them is Bannulf."

"Och, 'tis a fine mess ye have landed me in this time, ye daft wee beggar," grumbled the larger of the two men, pulling a thick plaid around his shoulders to ward off the cold.

"Do not lay the blame at my doorstep," Rory yelled, bringing his horse to a stop alongside the other rider. "If you had kept a better watch on the apothecary he would not have gone snooping about, and he would not have found Master Guwain."

"Ho'd yer tongue and ride, ye wee runt. The sooner you collect the heads of the apothecary and his friends and present them to his high and mightiness at the castle, the sooner I will get oot o' this foul weather." Engulfed by a fit of fine Scottish temper, Hamish kicked Rory's horse. The animal took off down the track, bouncing Rory about like a sack of turnips. Hamish heeled his mount and followed. Within a few heartbeats, both men were swallowed up in the blizzard.

Ned hauled Joe out of his nest in the hay. "I do not care what Bannulf said, we must find Oric. If we fail to warn him, he will lose his head."

-oOo-

Descended from the mountain, Oric kicked Jester's muscular flanks. Glad to be given his head, the big horse broke into a steady canter. Parzifal loped alongside and they lumbered across the countryside until they came to the shores of a lake. Entering a forest, Oric slowed his pace to avoid an accident with low branches or tangled roots.

Snow was beginning to build up on the ground and, his mind busy with many unanswered questions, Oric strayed from the track. Surrounded by massive pine trees, he quickly lost his sense of direction. He whistled to cheer himself along but his lips soon became too cold to produce any sound. Parzifal struggled to keep up, his legs buckling under the weight of snow that adhered to his whiskery coat. Oric dismounted, and pulled lumps of ice from under the dog's belly. "Come on, old lad, you need to ride along with me." He lifted Parzifal onto the saddle, and climbed up behind the dog. As if he sensed the urgency of the occasion, Jester did not turn a hair. *So much for dumb animals,* thought Oric.

As Oric entered a clearing, a large black crow took fright. The ungainly bird flapped close to Jester's head and the horse reared. Oric lost his seat and crashed headfirst onto a toppled tree trunk. Parzifal swiftly followed but landed more easily on all four feet. He licked Oric's face, but he received no response.

Chapter Twenty-Five

Headhunt

Bannulf led his horse through the open portcullis and, in the general hub-bub of morning chores, no-one noticed him leave. He collected a donkey from a shelter outside the gates, and hastened down the track toward the barn where the boys were hiding.

"E-eh!" Joe squeaked, as Bannulf wrenched open the barn door. "You nearly frightened me to death."

Both boys looked like waifs and strays, for they had donned sacks to keep out the cold, and tied them around the waist with twine.

"Did you see Rory and Hamish pass this way?" Bannulf demanded. "I was worried they might have discovered you."

"Aye, we saw them, they stopped outside the barn to talk," answered Ned. "Thank God they did not come in 'cos, by all accounts, our heads would no longer be attached to our bodies if they had."

Bannulf's voice throbbed with anger. "There is no time to lose. We must find Oric before those two barbarians get to him."

"We were just about to leave," said Ned. "But Oric has a head start on us, and Sir Ragnald's henchmen are already hot on his heels. I know not how we will catch up."

"You must to do the best you can." Bannulf smiled tightly and indicated the donkey he had brought. "I dare not take a horse from the stables for fear of drawing attention to myself. There is a new fellow on duty in the gatehouse and he has the eyes of a hawk." Bannulf passed the donkey's reins into Ned's hands. "This little fellow was tethered in a shelter outside the castle walls. No work will be done in this weather; I doubt anyone will miss him. When they find him gone they will surmise he broke loose from his tether and wandered away." Bannulf handed Ned a cloth pouch with a drawstring top. "It ain't much, but I grabbed as much food as I could without raising suspicion. Ration yourselves and the contents of this bag should last three or four days." A sack of hay roped to the donkey would provide feed for the animal. Eyeing the boys, Bannulf rubbed his cheek doubtfully. "The short cut I have in mind is dangerously steep. Do you think you can handle it?"

"Aye," said Ned, "I am sure we can." He grabbed a handful of the donkey's mane and vaulted onto the animal's back. "Jump up behind me, Joe, and hang on tight."

They crossed the slope in the lea of an overhanging ledge below Lockton Manor. Not game to let Joe know how afraid he felt, Ned guided the donkey along behind Bannulf's big warhorse. At the edge of a precipice, Bannulf pointed to a narrow track hacked out of the mountainside. "If we make it to the bottom without mishap, we can ride around the narrow end of Lake Coughcat. Going that way, you stand a chance of reaching Oric before Rory and Hamish get to him."

A vertical rock wall soared upwards on the right side

of the narrow pathway and a steep slope to the left dropped away to the valley far below.

The surefooted donkey managed the steep, twisty descent until he struck a slick of ice. His back legs slid forward, and he landed heavily on his rump. Joe catapulted over the donkey's tail and off the edge of the precipice. The donkey picked himself up, no damage done. Ned, his heart in his mouth, dismounted and peered out into the white abyss.

Hooked on a sturdy shrub, Joe gazed up at Ned. "I am a goner this time," he mumbled, his terrified eyes the size of chicken's eggs. "I will never be able to climb out of here. You had best leave me to my fate and save Oric."

"I ain't doing no such thing," Ned replied stoutly. "I will think of a way to get you out."

Well ahead of the donkey, Bannulf failed to witness the accident. Ned dare not shout for help as they were directly below the castle. Instead, he lay down on the ground and extended his hand to Joe, but his arm was too short to reach.

"Hang on, Joe, I have an idea." Ned removed the sack, his jerkin and tunic and tied them all together. *Pray God they will be long enough,* he thought. Dithering about in his undershirt, he made a loop out of one sleeve. He lay belly-down in the snow and, bit by bit, he paid out his makeshift rope. The sleeve came within Joe's grasp and Ned sent up a silent prayer of thanks. "Put your arm through the loop and hang on," he hissed. "I will haul you up."

Joe, his teeth chattering like a skeleton in a gale, did as he was bid. Considerably heavier than his friend, Ned hauled the less weighty Joe upwards until they were able to grasp hands.

Back on the track, Joe fell into Ned's arms and sobbed. Ned gently chucked him on the chin and pushed him away. "Holy jumping frogs, boy, we have no time for this nonsense,

I am frozen to the bone. For pity's sake, help me to unknot my garments so that I can get dressed again."

Shaking with cold and fright, the boys moved on down the steep pathway. Ned led the donkey, for neither boy felt like remounting. Rounding a steep corner, they came upon Bannulf, who was waiting for them.

"Where the devil have you been?" the old warrior growled. "I thought you had been discovered and taken back to the castle. I have been sitting here considering what best to do."

Joe told Bannulf how he had almost plunged to his death. "Had Ned not rescued me, I would not be here to tell the tale."

"Exercise more care in future," Bannulf warned. "From here on the track gets steeper."

Ned's face became paler than the falling snow. "Huh! Some track. I feel more like a fool on a tightrope."

Step by tortuous step, Bannulf, Ned, and Joe made their way down the mountainside. When they reached the valley bottom, Joe fell to his knees. "Praise the Lord," he exclaimed. "I never want to face anything like that again!"

The trio came upon the lake and skirted around the expanse of slate-grey water. Ice was crystallising along the water's edge and, if freezing conditions continued, it would only be a matter of time before the entire surface iced over.

Bannulf pointed to a rock face where huge icicles had formed. "A spring that feeds the river is situated behind the castle, and it normally races down the mountainside to join the southern end of the lake. Icy conditions have slowed the cascade, so we should be able to cross the watercourse with ease."

"I ain't wading into no freezing water," said Ned firmly. "Come on little'un, let me give you a leg-up. We will ride the donkey across." The ford's icy water lapped around the donkey's belly and he let out a strident bray, but he stoically followed Bannulf's horse.

"The village folk from Skelgut once ice-skated on this lake, but none of them have the energy or the inclination these days," remarked Bannulf sadly. "Thanks to Sir Ragnald's mismanagement of the estate, the poor beggars that still live here are half-starved."

A track of hoofprints inside Firbrook Forest indicated that only one horseman had passed by. "That is a good sign," said Bannulf. "Looks like Rory and Hamish have not yet caught up with Oric. The fools probably think they can take their time since they are two against one."

Apart from the occasional creak of snow-laden branches, the woods remained eerily quiet. Bannulf became more concerned by the heartbeat. "We need to make haste or we shall lose sight of Oric's tracks."

Snow continued to fall, and Bannulf almost missed the place where Oric had veered off the pathway. "Why would the lad turn off at this point? There are no other hoof prints so Rory and Hamish have not yet caught up with him." Bannulf tipped back his leather helmet and scratched his head. "I think we should part company here. You two follow Oric. I will obliterate your tracks and act as decoy."

"Will you be safe on your own?" Ned asked.

Bannulf nodded and winked. "Oh, aye, I have a ruse that will stop Sir Ragnald's toadies dead in their tracks."

Ned and Joe wished Bannulf godspeed and, keen to find Oric, they plunged off the pathway and were soon swallowed up in a white wilderness.

-oOo-

"What if these hoofprints ain't Jester's," Joe questioned. "We could be following a stranger."

"Who else other than Oric and his pursuers would be out in weather like this?" replied Ned. "Sit tight, we have no choice but to keep going."

"Hey – look over there." Joe pointed to a lone horse. "Ain't that Jester?"

A shiver of dread spiralled through Ned. "Aye, 'tis him alright, but where is Oric?"

"We need to be careful," whispered Joe. "If this is an ambush, we could be within a heartbeat of losing our heads."

A dog yapped, and a scruffy head appeared over the top of a fallen tree trunk.

"Look, 'tis Parzifal," cried Ned. He ran forward and vaulted over a fallen tree. Oric lay unconscious and Ned almost landed on top of him. The dog, refusing to leave his beloved human's side, yapped intermittently and wagged his tail.

Joe stared at Oric's pasty face in horror. "He must have come a-right cropper, look at the gash on his forehead."

Hushing the dog, Ned patted Oric's cheek. "Wake up! Wake up! Oric! You will freeze to death if you stay on the ground."

Ned's familiar voice finally got through to Oric, and his eyelids flickered open. He sat upright and blood dripped down from his forehead, staining the snow red. He tested his limbs tentatively. "I might be losing blood but I have no broken bones, thank God!"

"Did Jester throw you?" asked Joe.

"I think a bird startled him and he shied. I must have fallen off and banged my head."

"Most nags would have bolted. 'Tis a miracle he stayed with you," said Ned.

Oric fondled the horse's soft muzzle. "Sir Edred reckons Jester is fit only for transporting apothecaries. But I am beginning to think he is a very intelligent fellow."

"Never mind yon daft horse," snapped Ned. "Look at your head."

Oric explored his wound carefully with his fingers. "You must sew it up, Ned. Look in my pouch and you will find a bone needle, some horse-hair thread, and a small pot of salve." He managed a feeble grin. "This is the first time I have needed them for myself."

"I ain't never done nothing like this before," Ned groaned. "I ain't sure I can do it."

"You have no choice, my friend, for I cannot sew myself up!" replied Oric. "Come on, now, I will talk you through."

The needle was thin, and Ned drew it in and out of Oric's flesh without too much difficulty. It was a painful business, and the patient looked deathly pale at the end of the procedure. Joe spread the wound with salve of primrose and then bound Oric's head with his neck cloth. "Now, my friend – are you fit to ride?"

Wrapped in his thick cloak, warmth seeped back into Oric's body and a tinge of pink returned to his cheeks. "What are you two doing here?" he asked, suddenly recalling that Ned and Joe should still be hiding in the barn at Lockton Castle.

"It seems Sir Ragnald wants our heads," said Ned. "He sent a couple of his men to kill you and we had to warn you."

"We had best make haste," Oric exclaimed. "We do not want Ragnald's men catching up with us."

Ned managed a wobbly grin. "Bannulf has a plan. If you feel up to it, we should retrace our steps. He might be glad of our help."

More exhausted by the heartbeat, Oric tried to sound positive. "Bannulf is capable of looking after himself. We must ride back to Bayersby Manor to warn Sir Edred of Ragnald's imminent arrival."

Formidable shadows loomed at every turn, but the boys soon rejoined the regular track. Several fresh hoofprints indented the snow, and Oric scrutinised the track ahead. "Looks as if the enemy has passed this way. From here on, we must exercise great caution."

Chapter Twenty-Six

Bannulf's Revenge

Rory heeled his horse's ribs in a vain effort to keep up with Hamish. "Slow down," he hollered. "This knock-kneed nag will travel no faster."

"If ye no can stay wi' me, I will do the deed on m'own," Hamish bellowed back. "And we both know what Sir Ragnald will think about that."

"Shut yer face, y'great lump of Scottish brawn. I am going as fast as I can." Still suffering from his night of excess, Rory winced as his mount bounced him about on the saddle.

In his haste to move forward, Hamish failed to see a leather thong stretched between two trees at throat level. He slammed into it and crashed to the ground.

Unable to stop his horse in time, Rory charged into the same trap.

The impact shook the trees and a mountain of snow slid from grossly overloaded branches, engulfing the hapless pair below.

Startled by the unexpected turn of events, Rory and Hamish's horses kept going and, down the track, came to the bush in which Bannulf hid. Bannulf caught the animals and tethered them to a tree. Keeping low to the ground, he crept nearer to Hamish and Rory to hear what they were saying.

"What the devil happened?" Rory rasped, clawing his way out of the snowy mound.

Pain gripped Hamish from ankle to knee. "Ye stupid Sassenach! Do ye no ken? We ran into a booby trap." He swivelled his head around wildly. "Brace yersel' – any minute now we could be set upon and robbed."

Rory wallowed about in the snow. "Whoever is out there," he hollered, "clear off and leave us alone, we have nowt worth taking."

Hamish wanted to clout Rory, but he was in too much pain. "Help me to m'feet, ye stupid wee man."

Bending to take a closer look, Rory saw that a jagged shard of bone poked through the skin just below the big Scot's knee. "Why should I help you? I have a mind to leave you to the robbers."

"Can ye no see I have broke m'leg?" Hamish howled. "For pity's sake stop yer blather and find our mounts. I canna walk in this condition."

Rory dug in his heels. "I ain't crashing about them woods for fear of who I might run into. Besides, there ain't no point looking for our stupid horses, they will be long gone by now." He glanced furtively at the trees. "Why do you suppose the robbers have not yet shown themselves?"

"I neither know nor care," growled Hamish, his face grey with pain, "but ken well, wi'out m'horse ye will need t'carry me."

Rory was appalled. "Go back to Lockton? Not likely! Since we failed to do Sir Ragnald's bidding, 'tis *our* heads that will likely end up on a platter."

"If I was in your boots, I'd reconsider my decision," replied Hamish.

"Well you ain't in my boots, and I ain't going back." Without further comment, Rory stomped off along the track in the opposite direction to Lockton Castle.

Hamish groaned. A night outdoors in freezing temperatures would surely kill him; somehow he had to get Rory back. "Sir Ragnald will draw up a warrant to have ye hanged, drawn and quartered if ye fail to return," he yelled.

Before he reached the bush in which Bannulf hid, Rory faltered and looked back.

Hamish made descriptive slicing motions with his hands, driving home his point.

Rory turned green and felt faint.

"On the other hand," Hamish wheedled, "we could tell Sir Ragnald that we did the job."

"Oh, very clever," Rory replied disdainfully, "and I suppose you just happen to have a pair of look-alike heads in your pouch."

"We could say that wolves scared off our horses, and took the dead boys before we could bring back their severed heads," Hamish connived. "If we stick to our story, I reckon the worst we will suffer is a flogging."

Rory considered his options and decided the Scot was probably right. He lifted Hamish onto his back and, bent almost double, he shambled off in the direction from whence they had come.

Bannulf chuckled. Rory would tell Sir Ragnald that Oric and his two friends were dead. Sir Ragnald would become complacent, and the boys could travel back to Bayersby without jumping at every shadow.

Oric, Ned, and Joe plodded through the silent forest until, without warning, Oric reined Jester to a halt. "Quick, get off the pathway! Someone is coming."

The trio had barely gained shelter behind a large holly

bush when a rider, leading a pair of horses, ambled into sight.

Oric let go his breath in a gust of relief. "Thank God! 'Tis Bannulf. I would recognise that mane of golden hair anywhere."

The big warrior hauled his mount to a stop and saluted the boys. "I have acquired a couple of extra nags for Ned and Joe to ride, instead of the donkey."

"Those horses look exactly like Hamish and Rory's mounts," Ned challenged.

Bannulf adopted a ludicrously innocent expression. "Is it my fault the foolish pair decided to walk back to Lockton Castle? They allowed their animals to wander – it seemed a shame not to make use of them." He sniggered gleefully. "Truth to be told, only Rory is on foot; Hamish broke his leg and Rory is carrying him. They will be lucky to reach Lockton Castle before dark."

"How did you best both men?" exclaimed Oric.

"Oh, I have my ways." Bannulf's blue eyes twinkled with quiet satisfaction. "Now I must bid you farewell and ride back to Lockton."

"Should you return?" asked Oric. "You have been gone all day – Sir Ragnald's suspicions might be aroused. I would not like to see anything untoward happen to you."

"There will be no questions asked. I am often away from the castle for lengthy periods of time." Bannulf opened his saddlebags and hauled out a brace of rabbits and a pair of large turnips. "Helped myself to a poacher's catch, and I stole the vegetables from a farmer's winter store; the food will sustain you during the long journey ahead. Ned, remove the hay from the donkey's back to feed your horses. I plan to slaughter a stag, so I will take the donkey to carry my prey."

With the bundle of hay secured to the rump of Joe's horse, Bannulf wheeled his stallion around, raised a closed fist in farewell, and disappeared into the woods.

Jester plodded along, and Parzifal dozed on the saddle in front of Oric. Soothed by the horse's steady gait, Oric drifted into a dreamlike world.

Wooden chests carved with ornate knots flew through the air. Fancy padlocks hung from every tree. Ahead, a huge oak door barred the pathway, but Jester pushed through the obstacle as if it was a cloud of mist. On the other side of the hallucinatory door, light from a multitude of golden nuggets seared Oric's eyes. A parchment floated before his face and he threw out his hands to catch it, but it burst into flames. Someone's voice echoed in his ears – *Go forth and right the terrible wrong that has been perpetrated upon our great family* – but Oric had no idea to whom the voice belonged. His head throbbed with pain and, feeling unbearably hot, he threw off his cloak.

"What on earth is wrong with Oric? He is weaving from side to side like a drunkard." Joe dismounted and retrieved the discarded garment.

"I fear his head wound is making him delirious," called Ned, moving his horse forward to stop Oric falling from his saddle.

Believing Ned to be an enemy, Oric heeled Jester into a canter. The horse stumbled into a snowdrift, tossing his passengers to the ground. Parzifal picked himself up, but Oric lay deathly still.

"Has he broke his neck?" Joe wailed.

Ned leaped from his horse and placed a hand on Oric's face. "His neck ain't broke, but he is burning up. We must find shelter until his fever breaks."

Jester laid back his ears, but he made no attempt to misbehave as the boys hefted Oric up onto his saddle. "I will ride with Oric and stop him from falling," said Ned. "Look after Parzifal and lead my horse, Joe."

Time dragged slowly by, and Ned's arms ached with the

strain of holding Oric upright. On the point of desperation, he spotted a woodsman's cottage. Light glimmered between gaps in the planks, and a curl of smoke rose from a hole in the roof.

"I hope we can shelter here for the night," said Joe.

"Approach with caution," Ned warned. "We know not who lives within, be prepared to run if you feel threatened."

Joe hooked his fingers in Parzifal's collar, and knocked on the cottage door.

A hand with a club thrust out followed by a bearded face. "What d'ya want?"

"We are travellers seeking rest." Joe remained on the balls of his feet ready to run if the man brought his club too close. "A member of our party is sick."

The man backed off. "Sick? What d'ya mean – sick?"

"Our friend has nothing infectious," Joe hastily reassured the man. "He is running a fever as a result of a wound he received."

Ned coaxed Jester closer to the hut. "We have food to share if you will take us in."

The man's belly rumbled, for he had supped naught but weak broth and boiled beets for days. "Bart's my name," he said. "There is a lean-to at the back of the cottage, tether your horses in there. If the dog is friendly you can come inside, and welcome."

A rush light inside the single-room dwelling illuminated two benches and a rough-hewn table. Fresh bracken for bedding lay piled beside the hut's back wall and Ned and Joe dragged a bundle of ferns close to the fire for Oric to lie on.

"One thing I do not lack is fuel," grinned Bart, throwing logs onto the central fire.

Warmth seeped into Oric's bones and he opened his eyes. "Where am I?"

"In a woodsman's cottage," replied Ned. "You are burning up, I suspect your wound has festered."

"I have a decoction of endive juice in my pouch," said Oric. "The medicament will help to diminish my fever."

Ned tipped the contents of the pouch onto the floor, and singled out the small bottle Oric indicated. He removed the stopper and held the medicament to Oric's lips. Sitting up caused pain to sear through Oric's head, and he prayed the remedy would work swiftly.

Joe skinned and jointed the rabbits and added them, along with chopped turnips, to Bart's broth. Whilst the meat and vegetables cooked they chatted about inconsequential things. Despite the woodsman's many questions, the boys chose not to mention the true reason for their journey.

"You two had better bed down before you fall down," laughed Bart. "You look half dead. I will build up the fire to keep us warm."

Oric's fever diminished overnight, and he nibbled a piece of cold rabbit from the stew pot for breakfast. Wiping his greasy fingers on his breeches, he shook Bart's hand, and thanked him for his hospitality. "I am sorry we must rush away, but we have a long journey ahead."

"Where are you headed?" asked the woodsman.

"North," Oric lied. "We are visiting family at Wrackford." The fewer people that knew of their destination, the better chance they stood of saving their necks and Sir Edred's manor.

Bart spooned leftover stew into a pot. "You have a long journey ahead, and bad weather to boot," he said, handing the pot over to Oric. "I wish you godspeed."

Not far from the woodsman's hut, the snowfall ceased. A watery sun broke from behind the clouds and lifted everyone's spirits. A large cave at the foot of the Farnrock Mountains provided shelter for the second night. Someone had used the cave in the past, and a plentiful supply of fuel lay scattered on the ground. The boys fed hay to their horses, rabbit skin and bones to Parzifal, and made a fire to heat their leftover stew. Supper over, they bedded down close to their animals.

Good weather continued throughout the following day, and they continued their journey without mishap. At the end of the third day they stopped briefly to eat the last of their raw turnip. With no shelter in sight, they decided to ride on through the night.

-oOo-

After bidding the boys farewell in the forest, Bannulf stalked his stag. Day was almost done when he finally managed to corner the beast. He hurled his sharp axe, embedding it in the animal's skull. It was a clean kill, and he strapped the stag's body, still warm, to the donkey's back. Feeling pleased with himself, he returned to Lockton Castle.

Running short of good food, the cook welcomed Bannulf with open arms. They carried the stag inside, and sharpened knives with which to butcher the carcass. "You ain't seen Rory and Hamish have you?" asked the cook. "Sir Ragnald wants proof that the fellows from Bayersby are dead and he is giving us all a hard time."

"I ain't seen that feckless pair since they went off after the apothecary and his boys this morning." Bannulf shrugged out of his damp sheepskin jacket and hung it near the fire to dry. He smiled to himself and left the cook to his preparations. Filling a platter with pickled herrings, he joined the gatehouse keeper to await Rory and Hamish's return.

-oOo-

Rory staggered the last few steps toward Lockton Castle and

dumped Hamish in the snow beside the closed portcullis. Straightening his aching back, he pulled the bell rope.

Bannulf cranked up the gate, but he offered Rory no help to drag Hamish into the compound. "What happened to you? Your friend looks half dead."

"That great sack of Scottish turnips ain't no friend of mine," Rory wheezed. "He wants to think himself lucky I carried him home."

"Well, fancy that!" Bannulf suppressed a bubble of mirth. "I would swear you both were mounted upon fine horses when you left here this morning. Sir Ragnald is not well pleased at your absence, he wants to know if you have caught the apothecary and his cronies."

Rory screwed up his weasel face. "Oh, aye, we caught up with Oric and his cronies all right, and we killed all three." Scared the truth might cost him his life, he trotted out the lie that he and Hamish had concocted. "Before we could cut off the lads' heads, a pack of wolves carried their bodies off. Our horses took fright and ran away." Rory dug Hamish with his toe. "This fool fell and broke his leg, but I managed to drag him home."

Past caring whether he lived or died, Hamish kept his mouth shut.

Entertained by Rory's creative untruths, Bannulf played along with his tale. "A pack of wolves, you say?"

"Are you calling me a liar?" Rory shouted. "Wolves is what I said, and wolves is what I meant." In no mood to discuss the matter further, he added, "Give me a hand to get this Scottish lump off his back and onto his bed. He will likely need some medical attention afore he's much older."

They deposited Hamish in the men's quarters and, in no hurry to confront Sir Ragnald, Rory shambled off to fetch the barber-surgeon to administer to the invalid.

Chapter Twenty-Seven

Out in the Cold

An overwhelming sense of relief overtook Oric, Ned, and Joe when dense woodland gave way to the old Roman Road. Following the overgrown track from Lockton Castle had been hazardous and, riding with barely a stop, the boys and their horses were exhausted. The final challenge of High Moor lay ahead.

Fingers of dawn poked through the night sky as the boys passed through Kilterton. Loose, powdery snow banked up against cottage doorsteps, and roof holes chuffed out smoke as families stirred their fires ready to heat gruel for breakfast. Snow fell more thickly, and Oric doubted that anyone would venture abroad on such a wintery day.

All too soon, High Moor loomed out of the snow. Feeling decidedly unwell, Oric pulled his hood more tightly around his head, and hunkered down in his saddle.

Jester ploughed into a driving blizzard until his chest was plastered white with snow and his eyelashes coated with ice. Ned and Joe stuck close behind Oric, hoping he would not lose his way.

The moorland offered no shelter and wind, cold enough to strip the flesh from their bones, howled across the desolate landscape. A warning given by Ichtheus many moons past rang loud in Oric's memory: *Only fools and madmen cross High Moor in bad weather.* In his weakened state, Oric became delirious again. He lost consciousness and fell from his horse, taking Parzifal with him. Once again Ned hauled his friend back into the saddle and climbed up behind to support Oric's dead weight.

Jester proved invaluable not only for his strength, but also for his sense of direction. He seemed to know where he was going and, with no better ideas, Ned allowed him his head. When Bayersby Manor finally came into sight, Ned sent up a silent prayer of thanks.

With the smell of familiar territory in his nostrils, Parzifal leaped down from Joe's horse. He ran up and down outside the compound gates, barking hysterically.

Busy in the kitchen, Ichtheus dropped his pestle and mortar, and went to investigate the noise. Peering out into the whirling snowstorm, he was astonished to see the boys.

"What are you doing back so soon?" he called out. "Have you cured the sick folk at Lockton Castle already?"

"We will answer all your questions soon, but first we must attend to Oric."

Ichtheus ran up to Jester in time to break Oric's fall as he slid to the ground.

Parzifal crept into the kitchen and headed for the inglenook fireplace.

Mistress Foley swiped at the dog with a broom. "Get outside, you filthy brute!" she shrilled.

Ichtheus tore the broom from the housekeeper's hand and hurled it across the room. "Never mind about the dog, woman! Can you not see we have a sick boy, here? Fetch coverings, Oric is near frozen to death."

Ned and Joe carried Oric to the fireside. "Please help him, Master Ichtheus," sobbed Joe. "I fear he is sick unto dying."

Refusing to leave his beloved friend's side, Parzifal lay down and placed his shaggy head on Oric's feet.

"Come on little'un," said Ned, pulling Joe away from Oric's side. "Master Ichtheus will look after him now. We need to get into some dry clothes before we become sick, an' all." He nodded to Ichtheus, "We will be back soon."

Word of Oric's return spread throughout Bayersby. Dian heard the news and raced into the kitchen to investigate. She saw Oric stretched out on the flagstones beside the fire, and realised something was dreadfully wrong. "Oh, dear Lord!" she gasped, chafing his cold hands. "Whatever has befallen you?"

A tiny smile quirked the corners of Oric's mouth. "What is your name, sweet maid? You are very pretty."

Dian stared wildly at Ichtheus. "Why does he not recognise me?"

"Because he is not quite himself," Ichtheus smiled gently, drawing Dian away. If Oric had succumbed to the epidemic, Ichtheus did not want anyone else catching it. "Run along, my dear. There is naught you can do for him at present. I will dose him with medication when I ascertain what the problem is."

Dian retreated into the background, but she refused to leave the kitchen. She planned to stay put until Oric got better.

Ignoring Mistress Foley's surly presence, Ned and Joe returned to Oric's bedside. They had donned rough woollen breeches and shirts, and both looked a good deal warmer. "How is he?" they chimed in unison.

"Too early to tell," Ichtheus replied quietly. "Can you explain what form the Lockton epidemic took so I can better treat Oric's affliction?"

"There is no epidemic at Lockton – never was," exclaimed Ned. "The deaths were brought about by rotten food." Concern for Oric's welfare put all thoughts of Guwain and Sir Ragnald out of Ned's mind.

Puzzled, Ichtheus peered more closely at his prone assistant. "He seems to be presenting all the symptoms of a severe fever. Did he eat bad food?"

"No, no – Oric ain't afflicted by no epidemic. He fell from his horse." Ned grimaced. "He gashed his forehead, and I stitched him up as best I could."

Ichtheus pushed Oric's hair out of the way, and inspected the wound. Impressed by the row of neat stitches, he congratulated Ned. "You did a good job, lad, thanks to you the scar will be minimal, but I fear the wound has become infected. That is probably why Oric is not himself."

Informed of Oric's problem, Ichtheus fetched a decoction of burnet from his medicament chest and gently cleansed Oric's wound. He applied dried marigold flowers mixed with hog's-grease, turpentine and rosin to the patient's chest, reassuring Ned and Joe that the mixture would strengthen Oric's heart. "We must keep him warm and quiet, and someone must stay beside him until he recovers."

Everyone took a turn at watching over Oric and, a day and a half after returning to Bayersby Manor, his fever broke. The fog that had clouded his mind lifted and everything he had experienced at Lockton Castle returned with a clarity he had not experienced for days. In a panic, he pushed himself up on his elbows. "Have Ned and Joe already explained what is about to happen?"

Aghast, the two youngsters eyeballed each other. "I am so sorry, Oric," said Ned, hanging his head in shame. "Your poor state of health put everything else out of our minds."

Joe looked equally contrite. "We left your cart behind an' all, Master Ichtheus."

Ichtheus rolled his eyes. "The cart is of little consequence – but I am eager to hear what is going on."

Dian held a goblet containing marigold petals and broth to Oric's lips. "Will your story not wait until you have drunk your medicine? Master Ichtheus says it will help to fight inflammation from within."

"Nay," Oric pushed the potion away. "I must speak now, for there is no time to lose. Master Guwain is at Lockton Castle and he is in mortal danger!"

"What in Heaven's name is he doing there?" Ichtheus exclaimed. "Is the wretched boy not aware that his parents are near demented with worry?"

"No, he is not," croaked Oric. He took a sip from the goblet Dian held to his lips. "Nor do I think he cares. According to Bannulf, Guwain ran away to pay Sir Edred back for punishments he deemed unfair."

"Why did you not bring the boy home?" Ichtheus demanded.

"Because we were not supposed to know he is there. When Ragnald heard that I had accidentally discovered Guwain's whereabouts, he ordered his men to kill us. 'Tis only thanks to Bannulf we managed to escape."

"Who is Bannulf?" Ichtheus asked, aghast at how close the boys had come to losing their lives.

"He is one of Ragnald's warriors. He says he is heartsick of the bloodlust and violence. He says he wants to redress the balance before he meets his maker."

Ichtheus snorted. "How does he propose to do that?"

"By secretly helping us in any way he can. Several of his fellow mercenaries feel much the same. According to Bannulf, a few men openly crossed Sir Ragnald and they are the ones who lost their lives."

"Are you sure we can trust this Bannulf?" Ichtheus asked, unwinding the linen strip that bound Oric's head. "You will be glad to hear that your forehead is healing nicely, we should be able to remove the stitches in a day or two."

Oric shook his head impatiently, not caring overmuch about his wound. "Bannulf informed me that Ragnald plans to use Guwain as a bargaining tool. He wants Bayersby Manor for himself, and he believes Sir Edred will surrender without a fight in exchange for his son's life. If Sir Edred refuses to give in to Ragnald's demands, Guwain will die. Trouble is – the stupid boy believes he is a guest at Lockton Castle, because he went there of his own free will. He is prancing about in Joffrey's best clothes, leading the life of a lord. Why would he want to come home?"

Chapter Twenty-Eight

Moment of Truth

The rebuilding of Bayersby Manor was progressing well, and the Great Hall was almost finished. Not quite back to full strength, Oric wandered into the vast new room in search of Sir Edred.

Lady Myferny rose swiftly from her seat and offered her arm. "It is so good to see you, Oric." The young apothecary looked pale and tired, but at least he was now up and about. She had visited him in the kitchen whilst he was unconscious, and had worried for his life. "How are you feeling?"

"All credit to Master Ichtheus' ministrations, I am almost back to normal, my lady." *Which is more than can be said for this poor woman*, thought Oric.

Lady Myferny's rose-pink gown added little colour to her pinched face, and her usual array of jewels was missing from her neck and wrists. Concern for her son had brought about a terrible depression, and she could barely drag herself out of bed some days.

Looking to discuss the current predicament, Sir Edred came straight to the point. "I understand you have brought us good news, Oric."

"Aye, some good news, in that Master Guwain is alive and well, but there is bad news, too." Oric explained all that had happened during his visit to Lockton Castle, including Sir Ragnald's threat to Bayersby.

Sir Edred's face flushed purple with rage. "The insufferable nerve of the man! If his prowess on the jousting field is anything to go by, we have little to worry about."

"I wish I could agree with you, sir," replied Oric, "but Sir Ragnald maintains a sizeable army and he has many well-honed weapons. I believe he poses a threat to us all. He is also holding Master Guwain hostage and plans to use him as a bargaining tool."

"Whaaaat! That piece of filth competes in my tournament, sups at my table, and then has the audacity to imprison my son! I shall ride to Lockton Castle immediately and rescue Guwain."

"I doubt your son wants to be rescued, my lord – he joined Ragnald and his party willingly." Oric clenched his teeth and grimaced. "Sad to say, Master Guwain is enjoying his new life at Lockton Castle. He has no inkling that Ragnald is planning to make a bid for Bayersby Manor."

Lady Myferny laid a hand on her husband's sleeve. "Please, Edred, pay attention to Oric. He has visited Lockton Castle, he understands what we are up against."

The enormity of what lay ahead caused Oric's head to spin. "Ragnald believes that Ned, Joe and I were murdered before we were able to warn you of his intended attack upon Bayersby Manor. With that idea in mind, I believe he will wait until the weather improves before he makes his move. Ragnald's complacency might just give us time to muster our men, and discuss battle strategy."

"The fool can dither about to his heart's content!" Sir Edred roared. "I am done with waiting. I plan to rescue my son before that maniac finishes him off."

"Please, I beg you to think again, sir," Oric tried to sound convincing. "Master Guwain will remain safe as long as Ragnald believes you will surrender Bayersby Manor in exchange for your son's life."

"Safe! How can my son's safety be assured as long as he remains in the clutches of that Lockton Castle maniac?"

"Because," Oric promised, "one of Ragnald's men will see that Master Guwain comes to no harm."

"Who is this man?" Sir Edred frowned. "I cannot imagine that one of Sir Ragnald's toadies gives a tinker's cuss for any kith or kin of mine."

"Bannulf is his name, my lord," Oric pressed home his point. "He says he has seen enough bloodshed to last him a lifetime, and he longs to live in peace. Several of his fellow warriors feel the same. They have no interest in fighting any further battles for Ragnald or, indeed, anyone else."

"Tell me more," Sir Edred demanded, his interest aroused.

"My idea is to hide in the woods on either side of the valley below Bayersby Manor. Ragnald will not expect us to lie in wait and, with luck, we will be able to round up his men before they have a chance to draw their swords. Thus we stand a chance of lessening the damage to both armies."

"I am not so sure," Sir Edred snarled. "The Lord of Lockton is unlikely to concede defeat; I foresee much loss of life".

"We may give him little choice," said Ichtheus, nodding his head knowingly. "Whilst Oric was away, I experimented with a recipe that belonged to Master Deveril. I believe my concoction will sway the odds in our favour."

Oric's sharp intake of breath momentarily silenced Ichtheus. "Did we not decide that Deveril's substance was too dangerous to play around with?" he accused.

"Aye, we did, but properly used I believe the powder could save our lives," Ichtheus shrugged his bony shoulders and spread his hands. "I have made a considerable amount of the substance, so we may as well put it to good use."

Ichtheus explained exactly how Deveril's black powder worked and, fascinated with the apothecary's idea, Sir Edred gave his permission to go ahead with ambush preparations. If Master Ichtheus' powder worked, hand-to-hand fighting might be cut to a minimum; if the ploy failed, there would be a full-on battle. Either way, Sir Edred planned to win.

Malgwyn, one of Bayersby's ancient warriors, was brought out of retirement and reinstated as Master at Arms. "A fine time to be cavorting about outdoors," he grumbled. "I swear 'tis cold enough to freeze a man's backside to his saddle."

The old warrior's complaint about the weather fell on deaf ears. Obeying Sir Edred's orders, he travelled around the district and rounded up forty or so serfs, fieldworkers and villeins. The men, carrying an odd assortment of weapons, reported to the Bayersby compound where Malgwyn drilled them mercilessly.

Leaving his Master at Arms in charge of the men at Bayersby Manor, Sir Edred decided to confer with Sir Oswold and Egglebart. Always keen to visit her siblings, Dian begged leave to accompany him to Kilterton.

Swathed in a brown woollen shawl, Dian thrust her feet into a pair of stout boots. Having obtained Lady Myferny's permission, she loaded a cart with provisions for the Cole family, and fetched Otty from her stable.

Oric's mouth fell open as he watched Dian back the donkey between the cart's shafts.

"How did you get Otty to do that?" he demanded. "I have tried and better tried, all to no avail."

"Aaah! That would be telling," Dian giggled, and steadfastly refused to give Oric any information.

Oric tied Jester to the cart, and climbed onto the driver's bench beside Dian. "Allow me to drive. I want to talk to you."

"You sound cross, I trust I have done nothing to offend you," Dian smiled timorously, dimples indenting her rosy cheeks.

"Of course not!" Oric blurted, silently cursing himself for his abrupt manner. Though they were friends, he often felt tongue-tied in Dian's presence – especially when he had something important to say.

"Giddy-up!" Oric clicked his tongue, and Otty plodded along the moorland track toward Kilterton. Winter sun radiated precious little warmth through a thin veil of cloud, and scribbles of heather poked stark and black out of the snowbound landscape.

"I reckon more bad weather is brewing," said Oric, by way of opening a conversation. *Dear Lord, what am I rambling on about – get to the point man.* "Er… Remember how I told you about Master Deveril's key?" he began. "And how you pledged to help me find the wealth he talked about – even though it might be dangerous?"

Dian slid her hand along the seat and squeezed Oric's fingers. "I remember, and my promise still stands."

Encouraged by the warm physical contact, Oric soldiered on. "After the destruction of Bayersby Manor, Master Ichtheus found a parchment on Esica Figg's body. I have since learned that the parchment was stolen from the old chest I found at Dunburton."

"Well, I never!" gasped Dian. "There was I thinking that chest was just a piece of old rubbish."

Oric kept a tight grip on Dian's hand, and shuffled around to face her. Otty plodded on without guidance. "The writing on the parchment is, Latin, which Master Ichtheus translated for me. One side of the page portrays ingredients for making black powder, on the other side is a will."

"Oooh, that sounds exciting!" cried Dian, her hazel eyes shining with expectation.

"I am not so sure about that!" blurted Oric. "The will was written by my father."

A few heartbeats passed whilst Dian grappled with Oric's statement. She had never heard of a peasant able to write, let alone write a will in Latin.

"It seems I have inherited property, but my father failed to explain what it is, or where it is. He also wrote that the key given to me by Master Deveril would open a box. I now believe that box was the one I found at Dunburton Manor after the fire. According to the will, Master Deveril was supposed to explain everything when I became of age, but he died before he was able to tell me anything. By the time I found the box, it was empty apart from a thin layer of black power." Oric gazed at Dian in desperation. "Now I am supposed to put right some dastardly deed that has been done to my family." A crimson flush suffused Oric's face and he gulped. "I think Lockton Castle might be my ancestral home."

Dian snatched her hand away from Oric's grasp. "Heavens above! Whatever gives you that idea?"

"Because I saw a similar box when I visited the castle recently to investigate an epidemic. The box, hidden away in the kitchen, carried the same double knot insignia that I now believe to be part of my family crest. All other evidence of identification has been obliterated throughout the castle." Oric stared at Dian, his face a mask of puzzlement. "Why would anyone ruin so many fine carvings – unless that person had something to hide?"

Dian's world came crashing down around her. *Oric – landed gentry*, she thought. *Why would he bother with a common servant girl like me?*

Eager to tell all, Oric failed to notice Dian's stricken expression. "The Dunburton alchemist concocted a quantity of deadly black powder, and he used the back of my father's will to list the ingredients. He stored bags of the stuff alongside the parchment and a few family heirlooms in the box. Dunburton Manor is sacked, and along comes Esica Figg. He steals the chest and helps himself to the contents. Master Ichtheus now believes that Figg used Deveril's black powder to destroy old Bayersby Manor. Can you imagine what might happen if such a powerful substance fell into the wrong hands again? The entire district could be held to ransom. However, Deveril's powder would make a marvellous weapon for our cause." Oric reached for Dian's hand again, but she moved aside before he could catch hold of her. Puzzled and hurt, he added, "I beg you to keep this information to yourself until I decide what best to do."

Dian bobbed her head as she did when addressing Sir Edred. "I am sure you know what you are doing, sir."

Dian's deference was not lost on Oric, and he stared at her aghast. "Why are you calling me 'sir' and bobbing your head like a servant to her master?"

"Because that is what I am," Dian bobbed her head again. "You are landed gentry and I must obey the laws of society."

"Society be damned!" Oric jumped to his feet and almost fell off the cart. Otty stopped and looked back, wondering what her driver was about. Oric's voice became thick with distress. "I will not have you curtsy to me! We are friends."

"Nay, sir, we are no longer friends. I will serve you to my dying day, but a faithful retainer is all I can be."

"Dian, please – it makes no difference what we are. I hold you in high regard, and I need our friendship to continue."

Dian swallowed a lump that threatened to block her throat. "Society will never accept me as a suitable companion for you, and I have no intention of causing you embarrassment. Our friendship must cease now."

Dumbfounded, Oric stared at the girl he loved more than life. Because of a single sheet of parchment, his dream of sharing the rest of his life with her was over.

Chapter Twenty-Nine

Sir Edred's Men

Ichtheus completed his daily chores, saddled Braccus and followed Oric and Dian to Kilterton. He arrived at the inn just in time for the midday meal. Serfs stirred cauldrons of food over a huge fire in Kilterton Inn's kitchen, and their heat-reddened faces poured with sweat. Smoke from the fireplace billowed into the room, causing everyone's eyes to stream. "Where is my feckless husband?" yelled the landlady, coughing fit to turn herself inside out.

A mountainous man, who looked like an unmade bed, shambled into the kitchen. "Did you call me, my duck?"

"Did I not ask you to clear the smoke-hole of dross and snow first thing this morning?" shrieked the equally large lady. "For the sake of our lungs, husband, climb onto the roof and deal with the job immediately."

Moments later, lumps of snow and bits of twig dropped into the fire. The innkeeper's round face appeared in the cleared smoke-hole above. "Will that suffice, my duck?" he hollered. "Can I get back to my customers in the ale room now?"

-oOo-

Word of Sir Ragnald's evil intentions had spread around the district, and countrymen loyal to the Lord of Bayersby crowded into the Kilterton Inn. Sir Edred, Sir Oswold and Egglebart welcomed them, and soon only standing room remained.

Warming his backside before the inn's log fire, Sir Edred called the meeting to order. Battle strategy was discussed during the consumption of much venison stew and copious quantities of ale. Oric suggested that the tanners, Lanaval and Meerig, be pressed into service as war wizards again. The brothers had plastered themselves with woad and cow dung, cursed and cavorted, cast spells, and put the fear of death into Figg's army. Oric imagined that a repeat performance would have a similar effect on Ragnald's men. Meerig and Lanaval were more than happy to oblige, and went home to their tannery on the banks of Roxdale beck to organise their war paint.

Pleased with the outcome, Sir Edred retired to the inn's best guest room and was soon snoring in deep sleep. Less comfortable quarters were allotted to his entourage in a communal loft.

Taking pity on Oric and Ichtheus, Uther invited the apothecaries to share his modest premises across the street from the inn. "I reckon this lot will carouse all night," he said, jerking his thumb at revellers still thronging the inn's ale room. "At least you will enjoy a bit of peace at my place."

Oric and Ichtheus gratefully accepted the cobbler's invitation, but Oric begged leave to remain at the inn for a while longer.

The pungent odour of leather pervaded Ichtheus' nostrils as he entered the cobbler's shop but, unlike many other premises along Kilterton's high street, it was a clean smell. Uther cleared partly-constructed boots from two workbenches in the shop, and fetched sheepskins and blankets. "You should be snug enough in here," he said. Dragging off his thick top clothes, he rammed a sleeping bonnet onto his head and retired to his small, private quarters at the back of the shop.

With a heavy heart, Oric went in search of Dian. He found her helping the landlady in the kitchen. "I have come to escort you to your parents' cottage," he said.

Dian bobbed a curtsey. "Thank you, sir, but there is no need to trouble yourself. My brother Josh is here, he will see me home."

In the act of lifting a boxful of empty ale pots into a bucket for washing, Josh made eye contact with Oric. "Women!" he mouthed, shrugging his shoulders. *What the devil ails that pair? They seemed so friendly a few days ago.*

Oric gave Josh a nod and left the inn. Clearly Dian had kept his new status secret as she promised, and Oric was grateful to her for that at least. Outside in the quiet street, he stared at the dark sky, but his tears blurred the few stars that peeped through the clouds.

-oOo-

"Open our shop at once!" Helled Bascoomb shrieked at her husband. "We have meat to sell, why should we forgo a day's trading to answer the Lord of Bayersby's call? We owe him nowt. Let the pompous ass fight his own battles," she shrilled. Helled bore Sir Edred nothing but ill, for her last confrontation with him had earned her a session on the ducking stool in the village pond.

Lunette and Novena stared round-eyed at their parents. Placid, like their father, the two little girls hated confrontation. Cowering beside Tewdric's cart, they held hands and hoped this latest spat would come to an end before their mother got into trouble again.

"Listen to me, my turtle dove," begged Tewdric. "If we do not stand together, Sir Ragnald will claim Bayersby and Kilterton for himself." He gave his wife a placating smile. "You would not like the district to be taken over by a nasty stranger, would you?"

The flat of Helled's hand made contact with Tewdric's bald pate. "I do not give a pig's trotter for Sir Edred!" She came nose-to-nose with her rotund husband. "In fact I shall be glad to see the back of his High and Mightiness. Now give me the keys to our shop."

Tewdric clapped a hand over Helled's mouth. "For God's sake hold your tongue, woman, your words are traitorous. Carry on in that vein and our daughters will soon become orphans."

"You join in Sir Edred's battle!" cried Helled, snatching the keys from Tewdric's hand. "I shall open the shop. You two come with me," she demanded of the unhappy twins. Tossing her dark hair, she stomped across the dirty snow that covered the ground in front of the shop, and unlocked the door. "Girls, fetch sweeping brushes! Clear away this filth before folk tramp it indoors."

Feeling utterly miserable, Tewdric stood in the street agonising over what to do next. Lunette and Novena, plain as pikestaffs, were the apples of his eye and he hated to see them upset but, to protect them, he needed to join Sir Edred's forces and keep the district safe from invaders. His parental instincts overtook his fear of Helled's disapproval and he strode across the street to the inn.

Disturbed by the noise outside, Ichtheus watched the fracas between the Bascoombs from the cobbler's doorway.

Uther dragged at Ichtheus' sleeve. "Come inside before that hellcat sees you," he begged. The last thing Uther wanted was a confrontation with the butcher's wife. "If Mistress Bascoomb pursues her current line of attack, she will end up in the stocks at the very least, and serve her right."

Trying to shut out the day, Oric burrowed deeper into his sheepskin and hauled a rough blanket over his head.

"What ails the lad?" Uther whispered, his brown face crumpled in consternation. "He ain't been acting right since he got here."

"No idea," shrugged Ichtheus, giving the blanket-covered lump on Uther's workbench a prod with his finger "Are you feeling unwell, lad?"

Oric's freckled face emerged from his cocoon of bedding. "I feel perfectly well, thank you, Master Ichtheus." A deep sigh belied his words, and he rubbed his puffy eyes. "Just give me time to wake up."

The morning wore on and the village square filled with people. Ichtheus welcomed Lady Malla, Sir Oswold's wife, with open arms. Her assistance was invaluable in troubled times, and she seemed quite back to normal after her horrendous run-in with Father Chrispian. No-one made mention of the incident, and Ichtheus hoped the priest had left the district for good. Mother Olive had also disappeared. An angry crowd of villagers, out for her blood after the Summer Solstice fiasco, had failed to find hide nor hair of her. *Just as well the pair have vanished,* thought Ichtheus. *If they remained in Kilterton, the irate villagers would demand retribution.*

The next person to arrive in the village square was Egglebart's raven-haired wife, Etheldrida, followed by Dian. The little maid seemed to have shrunk, and her head hung forward until her chin touched her chest. She had spent the night with her parents and siblings, and had been tongue lashed by her father, Eadbald Cole. Dian had no money to give him for liquor and he was in a terrible mood. Dian worried about the children, but drew comfort from the knowledge that her mother would give a good account of herself if Eadbald raised his fist to anyone. Eadbald would not volunteer to fight with real men, and his cowardice added to Dian's feelings of inferiority.

Ichtheus drew Uther's attention to the young woman. "The lass seems more miserable than Oric. Do you suppose they have had a falling out?"

A confirmed bachelor, Uther was unable to offer any words of wisdom.

Another day and night passed in frenetic preparation for battle. Weapons were honed, leather shields were buffed with tannin, and men were separated into groups. Each group had its own leader, plus strict instructions.

Oric did everything that was asked of him, but his mind was not on the job. Dian filled his every thought, and he agonised over how to win back the warm friendship they had enjoyed such a short time ago.

Snatching a moment alone with his assistant, Ichtheus broached the subject of Oric's depression. "Am I right in thinking Dian may have something to do with your unhappy state of mind?"

"I am puzzled," Oric admitted, not wanting to tell his mentor just how miserable he felt. Shivering with cold, he pulled the hood of his short cape over his head.

"Tell me what ails you," Ichtheus encouraged kindly. "I might be able to help."

Oric had agonised over his problem and, having come to no useful conclusion, he decided to share his concern. He led his mentor to a quiet corner of the square, and invited him to sit on a mounting block.

"I found a chest in the servants' quarters at Lockton Castle, which bore a double knot symbol upon its lid. Strangely enough, all other insignias around the castle have been obliterated, and I think Lockton Castle may be my ancestral home." Oric kicked at a pile of dirty snow. "I told Dian what I had seen at the castle, and explained about my father's will. Now she believes I am a member of the aristocracy, and she thinks herself too lowly to continue our friendship." A wave of crimson embarrassment suffused Oric's face. "What she fails to understand is that I want more than friendship. I love her and I planned to ask for her hand in marriage when we became of age. My heritage means nothing to me and I would gladly give up everything to make her happy."

"Nay, lad," Ichtheus sucked in a deep breath to give himself time to think. "You cannot just 'give up' being a lord. The position is your birthright and, for the sake of your family name, you must bear the title with pride."

"Please, Master Ichtheus, I beg you to keep news of my heritage to yourself, and Dian has pledged to do the same. I need time to get used to the idea before I tell anyone else."

"Your secret is safe with me, lad, but you will have to inform Sir Edred sooner rather than later. In the meantime, we had best get on with the job in hand."

A group of bowmen dragged straw targets into the square, and began to practise with their bows and arrows. The noise they made put a stop to any further conversation, and Ichtheus shuffled his backside off the mounting block. "Cheer up, lad," he said, shaking bits of straw from his cloak. "I am sure true love will prevail."

Deep in conversation, Egglebart and Sir Oswold walked

amongst the ranks of Kilterton volunteers. "When we join with Malgwyn's men from Bayersby, I reckon we can muster almost seventy fighters," estimated Sir Oswold.

"Aye, but I am told Sir Ragnald has more than eighty men, all well trained in the art of modern warfare," replied Egglebart. "Surely too many to defeat easily, unless a miracle occurs."

"Do not lose hope, my good fellow," replied Sir Oswold. "A miracle might be forthcoming. Oric has inside information that a quarter of Sir Ragnald's older warriors will turn against him."

Standing nearby, Oric overheard Sir Oswold's remarks. He had trusted Bannulf's word, but now that he was away from Lockton Castle, doubts weaselled into his mind. *Suppose Bannulf has lied? What if he is acting on Sir Ragnald's orders? Maybe Guwain will die.*

Not caring much whether he lived or died, Oric followed Ichtheus into the inn.

"I have decided to ride back to Lockton Castle," he announced. "I plan to rescue Guwain and bring him back to Bayersby."

"Are you insane?" Ichtheus cried. "I absolutely forbid you to go back to Lockton. If Sir Ragnald catches you, he will show you no mercy."

Grinning lopsidedly, Oric replied, "Then I must make sure he fails to find me."

"Make sure who fails to find you?" Joe asked, catching the tail end of Oric's remark.

Ned was mopping up gravy with a chunk of rye bread and, not wanting to miss out on anything, he jumped to his feet. "Aye, come on Oric, tell us what is going on."

"Manage to get any sleep last night, lads?" Oric asked in a bid to change the subject. He hunkered down beside the hearth to warm his cold hands.

Ned gave his friend an old-fashioned look. "Do not play us for fools, Oric. I know when you are up to something." He jabbed Oric in the chest with the heel of his dagger. "And say what you like – you ain't going nowhere without us."

"Aye, Ned is right," Joe piped up. "Wherever you go, we go."

"No-one is going on this jaunt but me." Oric made a poor job of hiding his anxiety. "It is too dangerous. Besides, in this instance, I can manage better by myself."

Ned wiped his greasy dagger on the seat of his woollen breeches, and replaced it in the leather holder attached to his belt. "Do as you please," he said. "We will follow you anyway."

"Oish!" Oric exclaimed. "What am I to do with you?"

Joe winked. "Give in and tell us what is afoot."

Seeing he had little choice, Oric outlined his plan. "At this stage I have no reason to doubt Bannulf, but I feel the need to watch out for Master Guwain. It would be terrible for Sir Edred and Lady Myferny to lose their only child."

"Just tell us how we can help," offered Ned.

"Be aware," Oric warned, "we will all lose our heads if Sir Ragnald catches us."

Parzifal strained at a leather strap tied around his neck, desperate to follow his beloved Oric. "No, old lad, you cannot accompany the boys this time," said Ichtheus, hanging on to Parzifal's collar. "Stealth is paramount, and I fear you would be more of a hindrance than a help."

His heart heavy with sadness, Ichtheus left Kilterton for Bayersby. As he rode away from the village, he wondered if he would ever see the boys alive again. Whatever the outcome, Ichtheus was sure that nothing would ever be quite the same again.

Chapter Thirty

Battle Preparations

Rory told lies with a sincerity that had Sir Ragnald and Joffrey eating out of his hand. They roared with laughter at the manner of Oric and his friends' demise, but Sir Ragnald was not amused over the loss of two perfectly good horses. In the fullness of time, he would make Hamish and Rory pay for their carelessness.

Joffrey guffawed as he visualised the overweight Hamish clinging to Rory's puny frame all the way back to Lockton Castle. That the Scot would likely never walk properly again was of little account, as far as Joffrey was concerned. "Your long walk might teach you pair to tether your horses more carefully in future," he chided. "Clear off about your business and leave father and me in peace."

The fire burned low and Joffrey reached for more logs, but there were none. "I do not relish the idea of the four-day ride to Bayersby in a blizzard," he grumbled, chafing his cold hands. "Now that Oric and his cronies are silenced, can we not wait until the weather improves?"

Sir Ragnald shifted uncomfortably in his chair. "The

local peasants have no food left to give us, and I am heartily sick of eating turnip stew with the occasional addition of a rabbit. Had Bannulf not killed the stag, we would have dined on yet another meat-free dinner. We are out of money and down on supplies, and we need to make a move soon."

"I have been thinking about the demise of Oric and his cronies," mused Joffrey, narrowing his tawny, cat-like eyes. "Perhaps we should catch a few wolves, starve them, and let them lose on work-shy peasants in a makeshift arena. We could charge like-minded people a handsome sum to watch the fun." He grinned wickedly. "Such an occasion might rival the Romans' long-ago ritual of feeding Christians to lions."

An unpleasant tightness gripped Sir Ragnald's stomach. He had trained his boy to be hard, but this look-alike son displayed inhumane streaks of cruelty that could well turn in the wrong direction one day.

"Do you think Sir Edred will surrender easily?" Joffrey asked, wriggling his toes before the fire's dwindling embers.

"With a knife at his son's throat, I expect opposition from that quarter to be minimal," replied Sir Ragnald, testing his dagger on the ball of his thumb. "Once the Lord of Bayersby is dead, the manor will be ours for the taking." *Not to mention the delectable Lady Myferny,* he thought.

The Bayersby heir lay daydreaming in his turret room, blissfully unaware that he was Sir Ragnald's prisoner. Allowed to pursue pleasure rather than the strict academic regime Sir Edred had insisted upon, Guwain was in his element. Weather permitting, he hunted weasels with dogs, shot birds and other wildlife with a bow and arrows, and practised the skills of swordsmanship with Sir Ragnald's men. Wenches were missing from Lockton Castle but he intended to take up that issue with Joffrey in the very near future. Maybe they could go down to Skelgut and have some fun. Ignorant of the threat to his family inheritance, he made up his mind not to return to Bayersby Manor until after Sir Edred died.

-oOo-

A wintery sun broke through the clouds as Oric, Ned, and Joe emerged from the woods below Lockton Castle. Oric estimated the time to be around mid-afternoon and, deeming it unwise to proceed further until nightfall, he called a halt.

"Snatch this opportunity to get some sleep," he advised. "God knows when we will next get the chance to rest."

"What are your plans when we get up to the Castle?" Ned asked, hooking a nosebag of oats over his horse's neck. "Surely we dare not approach the main portcullis, not even after dark."

"I have a small grappling iron with a rope" replied Oric. "When everyone is abed, I shall scale the wall behind the kitchen block. Once inside the castle, I shall seek out Master Guwain."

Nothing that Ned and Joe said would change Oric's mind. Defeated, they wrapped their blankets around themselves, and rolled under an evergreen shrub to sleep.

Oric lay on his back, staring at the sky. Cold seeped through his blanket, to match the cold that encompassed his heart. Dian's change of demeanour had cut him to the quick; without her, his life no longer held any meaning. He intended to save Guwain, but he no longer cared if he died in the process.

The evening sky turned bronze and rays of setting sun stained the snow-covered countryside red. Nature's beauty was lost on the boys as they ate a small supper before leading their horses up the frozen track to Lockton Castle. At the halfway point they reached the old barn, secured their horses within, and waited for darkness to fall.

-oOo-

The wind moaned eerily around the castle's battlements, but no other sounds came from within the bailey. "I might as well scale the wall now," Oric whispered. "When I reach the top, I will throw down the grappling iron; collect it and go back to the barn. Remain hidden alongside the horses until I return with Master Guwain."

"How will you get down the inside of the wall without the rope?" Joe asked. "Yon wall must be nigh on a hundred foot high – you will likely break an ankle if you jump."

"Nay, 'tis no more than forty foot – if that," said Oric, putting on a show of bravado. "If I remember rightly, the kitchen roof is not far below the battlements and the thatch will break my fall. From there it will be an easy slide to the ground."

"That is all well and good," grumbled Ned, "but I doubt you can rescue Guwain without causing a fearful ruckus."

"Aye, and then you will end up dead!" Joe blubbered.

Oric shrugged out of his cumbersome cloak. "You worry overmuch! Bannulf will help me when the time comes."

The frozen moat proved less smelly, and easy to cross. At Oric's first throw, the grappling hook clunked onto the inside of a castellation. He waited for a heartbeat or two to make sure the noise had not attracted any unwanted attention. Hearing none, he tested the strap and began a slow, hand-over-hand ascent. Icy wind at the top of the wall cut through his tunic, and his teeth chattered. Cold or apprehension? Oric was unsure which. He looked down into what seemed like an abyss to see Ned and Joe's upturned faces illuminated by thin moonlight. He freed the grappling hook and tossed it down. Giving his friends a final wave, he jumped from the wall onto the kitchen roof. The tough thatch held, and he was soon standing on the ground inside the bailey. He remained in the shelter of the kitchen's overhanging eves until he was sure no guards were on duty.

Moving like a black spectre, Oric eased his way up the stairs that led to the main entrance, halfway up the central tower. Despite his careful ascent, he stumbled on the uneven risers; a clever ruse to trip and slow the passage of unwary raiders in a hurry to gain access to the inner castle. Oric wondered how many poor wretches had felt the heat of boiling oil, poured upon them from above as they struggled to regain their balance.

The latch clicked into action at Oric's first twist, and the massive oak door creaked open. An inexplicable instinct drew him back to the woman's bower. Once inside, he stood with his back pressed against the door, breathing deeply to slow his racing pulse.

Moonlight picked out cobwebs and dust lay thick on every surface. The little skeleton remained in its cage where Oric had last seen it, and he surmised that no-one had entered the room since his first, brief visit. He fished in his pouch for his tinderbox and a candle.

Bit by bit, Oric explored the room. He lifted a tapestry here, a box lid there, but nothing remarkable came to light. Coming to the alcove that held a feather mattress, he crawled onto the bed. *Perhaps my mother slept here,* he thought, pushing down a sudden flush of emotion.

A draught blew his candle out and Oric grabbed the bed drapes to keep his balance. An ancient tapestry broke adrift from its hanger and fell on top of him. Almost suffocated by a welter of dust, Oric lay still. Had someone entered the room? Hardly daring to breathe, he waited a while and then peeped out from under the tapestry. No shadow stirred. With shaking hands, Oric felt for the tinder box, and relit his candle.

The patch of wall where the tapestry had hung moments before glowed pale in the candlelight. A small door with a keyhole drew Oric's attention, and he fingered the key that dangled from a chain around his neck. Words his former mentor had uttered moments before his death pounded inside Oric's head: *This key unlocks the secret to great wealth. You must promise to keep it safe. If it falls into wrong hands, untold disasters could occur.*

Oric lifted the chain over his head, and pushed the key into the door lock. He twisted, there was a slight click, and the small door swung open. With trembling hands, Oric reached into the cavity and drew out two sheets of parchment. Disappointment bit deep when, once again, he realised that the writing was in Latin. Feeling inside the cavity again, he withdrew a small, well-worn leather box. Inside the box he found a gold ring set with a red stone.

Stuffing everything back inside the cavity for safekeeping, Oric rehung the tapestry and blew out the candle. The chance of someone discovering the door, let alone opening it without the aid of a key, was small. There would be time enough to delve further into the mystery once the battle against Ragnald was won.

Back in the moment, Oric set out to find the Bayersby heir. He climbed the spiral stairway to Guwain's turret room, and peeped inside. But the room was empty. *It would be foolhardy to begin a search on my own,* he thought. *I will seek out Bannulf and get him to help.*

A gaggle of serfs slept in the kitchen, and Oric tiptoed

past. Bannulf snored in his chair beside the fire, and Oric shook his shoulder gently.

"Wass th' matter?" Bannulf snorted, spluttered, and opened his eyes with a start. "Ye gods! What are you doing here, Oric? If anyone sees you, your life will not be worth a handful of chaff." He grabbed a voluminous cloak from a peg on the wall and thrust it over Oric. "Pull the hood over your head. At least it will provide you with some cover until I can get you out of here."

"I am here to rescue Guwain and I will not leave without him," rasped Oric.

Bannulf put a finger to his lips, and ushered Oric out of the kitchen. Outside in the bailey, he pushed the youth roughly against the wall. "Guwain is incarcerated in the dungeons and Sir Ragnald is in possession of the only key. If you are caught, Sir Ragnald will see you tortured until you beg for mercy and tell all. Unless you wish to cause the death of many people, including me, I suggest you obey my instructions. First up, remain hidden in the shadows until I return."

Oric might not care if he lived or died because of Dian's change of heart, but he certainly did not want to suffer an ignominious death at the hands of Sir Ragnald and his son Joffrey. Nor did he want to cause any other person's demise. *If I must lose my life,* he thought, *I want my death to be honourable, doing something useful.* Oric trusted Bannulf to a point; nevertheless, he had no intention of telling the big warrior anything he did not need to know.

Bannulf reappeared and Oric meekly followed him around the bailey walls, until they came upon the small gate they had used last time they escaped from the castle.

Outside the walls and across the moat, Oric relaxed slightly. "What happened to Rory and Hamish?" he whispered, his curiosity getting the better of him.

A ghost of a smile flickered beneath Bannulf's flowing moustache. "Hamish is confined to his bed with a badly broken leg, and Rory concocted a pack of lies as to how the accident happened. He said they were unable to return your severed heads to Lockton Castle because you and your friends were killed and dragged away by wolves. Rory is now so afraid that you might reappear, he drinks himself insensible every night." Bannulf grinned and jangled a bunch of keys. "That is how I managed to get hold of these to open the gate."

Down the hill, Oric opened the barn door and called softly. "Ned, Joe, are you in there?"

From behind a pile of hay came a hoarse whisper, "Aye, we are still here. Did you find Bannulf?"

Bannulf's deep voice answered Ned's question. "Sir Ragnald is planning to leave for Bayersby at first light. You three must ride like the wind and warn Sir Edred. At least that will give him some time to prepare for battle. Now be off with you, and godspeed."

Almost at the bottom of the track, Oric reined Jester to a halt. "I am going back to hide in the barn," he stated. "When Sir Ragnald and his men pass by, I will follow at a safe distance to make sure that no harm befalls Guwain."

"Why put yourself in unnecessary danger?" Ned asked. "If yon spoilt brat gets into trouble, so be it. His life ain't worth you losing yours."

Oric leaned forward to gentle Jester's velvet neck. "I appreciate your concern, Ned, but I intend to see this thing through to the end."

Aware that begging would fall on deaf ears, Ned grasped Oric's hand and squeezed it hard. "You know I ain't happy about leaving you, but we have no choice if we are to get back to Bayersby in time to warn Sir Edred."

Convinced that Oric had signed his own death warrant, Joe flung his arms around his friend's neck. "Other than Ned, you be the best friend I ever had. Be sure to take good care of yourself."

Overwhelmed by Joe's show of affection, Oric hugged the small boy to his chest for a brief moment. "Aye, lad," he said gruffly, "and the same goes for you. Now, be off with you."

Back in the barn with Jester, Oric settled down to wait. He lay on the ground under his blanket and counted the icicles that hung down from the roof. Unwelcome thoughts chased around his mind, and he wondered if Bannulf was guilty of treachery. But Oric could think of no reason why the big warrior would go back on his word. Hunger eventually drove him out of his warm nest and, unsure how long his meagre food supply would need to last, he rationed himself to a small meal. Meanwhile, Jester licked up strands of hay that littered the barn floor. Eventually Oric drifted off to sleep.

The distant rattle of Lockton's portcullis snapped Oric into wakefulness. Rubbing sleep from his eyes, he peeped through a crack in the barn door. In the early morning light Sir Ragnald's men rode two-by-two past the barn and down the track, away from Lockton Castle. Stable boys followed the main cavalcade with spare mounts and pack horses in tow. Despite Ragnald's straitened circumstances, the black knight was clearly well prepared for battle.

Bannulf brought up the rear of the convoy, leading Guwain along on a pony. As they drew closer to the barn, Oric saw that Guwain was lashed to his saddle.

When Sir Ragnald's column of men had disappeared down the hillside, Oric led Jester from the barn. Keeping at a safe distance, he followed along behind the enemy.

Chapter Thirty-One

Bloodshed

Guwain struggled to free himself from the bonds that tied his hands and feet to the saddle. "How dare Sir Ragnald treat me thus? My father will have him thrashed when he learns of my predicament."

Heartily sick of the Bayersby heir's complaints, Bannulf lost his patience. "Shut your face! If you behave yourself, your ordeal will be over soon enough." The boy was a cowardly brat, but Bannulf had pledged to look out for him and that was exactly what he intended to do.

Gaining no satisfactory answer from Bannulf, Guwain turned on Joffrey. "I thought you were supposed to be my friend," he whined. "Where are you taking me?"

"That is for me to know and for you to ponder over," Joffrey replied smugly. "Thinking about your future, always supposing you have one, will help to while away your journey."

-oOo-

Ned and Joe rode as if the devil chased them, stopping occasionally to rest their mounts and allow them to graze wherever the snow had melted. Having no food left, the boys went hungry, but quenched their thirst from icy streams. Eventually they broke free of woodland and joined the old Roman Road. They chose not to stop in Kilterton but headed full tilt for Bayersby.

Down in the valley, winter snow was beginning to melt. Water raged across the road at the Roxdale Beck ford and Ned and Joe crossed their feet atop their saddles to keep dry.

People ran hither and thither on the northern side of the ford. "Ye gods!" exclaimed Ned. "Must be fifty or more folk milling about."

Joe recognised one or two familiar faces from Bayersby and Kilterton. "I wonder what they are up to?"

"I reckon they are preparing to do battle with Sir Ragnald." Ned shifted in the saddle to ease his frozen bones. "Seems to me they picked a mighty funny spot. Surely the manor would be a better place to engage with the enemy. At least folks would have some cover behind the compound walls."

Ichtheus spotted the boys from his hidden position in the woods, and raked the near distance for sight of his assistant. "Where is Oric?" he demanded, approaching Ned and Joe at a trot. "Is he alright?"

"Aye, Master Apothecary, he was fine last time I saw him." Ned dismounted and grimaced as pain from his stiff legs surged through his body as far as his skull. "He stayed behind to keep an eye on Master Guwain."

"He did what?" Ichtheus' horrified expression spoke volumes.

Joe jumped down from his wet horse, and grasped the old man's forearm. "Try not to worry, sir. Oric promised he would not get into any unnecessary danger."

"Huh! I am more concerned about *necessary* danger," Ichtheus huffed. "That boy puts everyone's safety before his own."

"There is no time to lose," said Ned, handing the two exhausted horses into the care of a squire. "Bannulf warned us that Sir Ragnald will soon be on the move."

"Let them come," said Ichtheus. "Our ambush is almost ready."

On the northern side of Roxdale Beck lay a flat area of ground. The land sloped down on either side of the track, forming a shallow valley. Woods covered the hillsides, giving cover to the men who lay in wait for Sir Ragnald's army.

With Uther's help, Ichtheus placed twenty-four bags of black powder three paces apart along both sides of the track, linking each one with a continuous line of loose black powder. Serfs cut bundles of dead bracken, which they used to camouflage the trails and bags. Satisfied with their work, the cobbler and the apothecary joined Sir Edred, Egglebart, and Sir Oswold in the woods.

The three elderly warriors had only past battles to go by, and the introduction of Ichtheus' newfangled powder was a cause for great concern. That Ichtheus had sworn them to secrecy further added to their anxiety.

"I pray to God your ruse works, Ichtheus," grumbled Egglebart, twirling his lengthy carrot-coloured moustache between his fingers. "I cannot say I have much faith in your peculiar concoction."

"Aye," agreed Sir Edred, "and I sincerely hope that Oric is right about this Bannulf fellow. If he and his men fail to support us, we could find ourselves in serious trouble."

-oOo-

Nearing Kilterton, Bannulf and his few supporters lagged behind Sir Ragnald's soldiers. When it was safe to do so, Oric broke cover and rode alongside the old warrior.

"'Ods blood! What the devil are you doing here?" Bannulf demanded. "I thought you had ridden ahead with Ned and Joe. For pity's sake, keep your head down; if anyone recognises you, your goose will be well and truly cooked."

Oric's rumble of laughter was low. "I doubt anyone will notice me, they are all too busy facing forward, anticipating what is to come." Feeling slightly guilty, he added, "Forgive me, Bannulf. I am here because I did not completely trust you. For my own peace of mind, I have ridden in your wake ever since you left Lockton Castle."

"I might have known you would have a hand in this treachery," hissed Guwain. Red with fury, he glared at Oric as if the young apothecary had grown an extra head. "You are naught but a filthy traitor and I will see you hanged before this day is done."

"Cease your rattle," snapped Oric. "Your foolhardy actions may well cause the downfall of Bayersby Manor and all who live there. If we live through the forthcoming debacle, your father can deal with you as he sees fit."

Oric reached over and unhitched Guwain's leading-rein from Bannulf's saddle. "If you wish to see the light of another dawn, my friend, I suggest that you and your men maintain a goodly distance between yourselves and Sir Ragnald's mercenaries." Oric gave Guwain's leading-rein a tug. "I will take care of this fellow."

Nodding his thanks, Bannulf reined back his horse and signalled his twelve followers to do the same.

In a hurry to get to Bayersby Manor, Sir Ragnald failed to notice that Kilterton was suspiciously quiet. He left the deserted village behind and, at the head of his army, he crossed the Roxdale Beck ford and rode straight into Ichtheus' trap.

The Lockton men were strung out between the bags of black powder when tanners Meerig and Lanaval crept out of the woods. Plastered from head to foot in animal dung and blue woad, they brandished flares and screamed imaginary spells.

The terrifying sight stopped Sir Ragnald dead in his tracks. Unable to rein in their horses quickly, the mercenaries behind collided with their leader and each other.

Under cover of the noisy melee, Ichtheus and Uther crept from the woods and dropped lighted tapers into the powder on either side of the track. Meerig and Lanaval did the same at their end. Their task accomplished, the four men raced for cover in the woods.

At each end of the ambush, two lines of white fire snapped and crackled along both sides the track. The first four bags of black powder erupted together, sending sheets of flame and clods of earth into the air. The fire ignited the bundles of dead bracken, which set light to the next set of tightly-packed powder bags.

"Scatter, scatter, or we shall lose every man!" howled Sir Ragnald, swivelling wildly from side to side in his saddle. "What in the name of Christendom is causing this evil?" At the head of his column, Sir Ragnald had avoided the worst of the eruptions, but his men were trapped within a raging inferno.

Petrified horses bucked and shied, tossing their riders to the ground. Foot soldiers' skulls cracked under the onslaught of flailing hooves, and men without protective armour became human torches as their hair and clothing caught light. They ran screaming into the ford to douse the flames.

Ichtheus' black powder continued to explode until the

countryside disappeared in a pall of smoke. Bracken on each side of the track burned with flames higher than the men's heads, and a terrible smell of scorched flesh permeated the air. In blind panic, Sir Ragnald's soldiers fought each other in an effort to escape the devil's cauldron of smoke and heat. The clash of their weapons carried as far as Kilterton to the south and Bayersby Manor to the north.

When the inferno died down, men still able to stand crossed themselves. Weapons at the ready, they darted terrified glances around the area for fear more fire-breathing spectres would appear.

Unhorsed, Sir Ragnald's breastplate and chain mail saved him from the flames. In a state of shock, he dragged himself up from the soot-encrusted ground. Soldiers at the back of his column had missed the worst of the damage and, seeing their leader had escaped death, they drew their swords and marched forward.

Mounted upon his war horse, Balthazar, Sir Edred gave the signal for the Bayersby and Kilterton men to charge out of the woods. Peasants and villeins brandished digging tools, three-pronged forks, scythes, and any other item they thought would do damage. One or two old soldiers carried pikes and quarterstaffs. Having only one arm, Sir Oswold abandoned his shield in favour of a long sword. Egglebart, carrying his old halberd, led a dozen or so archers. At his command, the bowmen formed a line, drew their arrows and awaited the order to let fly.

Sir Ragnald grabbed a riderless horse. With escape in mind, he mounted and heeled the animal forward.

Sir Edred was waiting for him. The Lord of Bayersby's teeth gleamed white in a snarl of pleasure. "Prepare to die, you bastard."

Sir Ragnald slashed his sword from side to side.

The blade sliced into Sir Edred's arm, but he hardly felt the pain. In blind fury, he swung his mace and smashed it through Sir Ragnald's armoured helmet. The sharp spikes pierced his skull, and he dropped his sword. Reaching up with both hands, he tried to pull the mace from his head. A waterfall of blood spurted from the wound and poured into Sir Ragnald's eyes. Pitching from his horse, the fake Lord of Lockton was dead before his body hit the ground.

Joffrey clung to his mount. "Father is down," he screamed at the few Lockton men still upright. "Obey my orders from now on."

A horn-blast echoed along the valley, and arrows flew through the air. More Lockton mercenaries fell to the ground. Miraculously unscathed, Joffrey swiftly weighed up the odds. Cutting his losses, he fled for the woods with a pitiful few of his father's men.

When the smoke cleared, Oric surveyed the damage. Saddened by the carnage, he rolled up his sleeves and administered to the few casualties that still clung to life. Ichtheus joined his assistant and they worked quietly together. Men who lived were transported to Bayersby Manor where Mistress Malla, Etheldrida, and Dian cared for them.

A gang of Bayersby fieldworkers buried Sir Ragnald and his dead mercenaries at the foot of High Moor. The ground, still frozen, made digging hard, and the villeins complained bitterly. Inundated with questions from all and sundry, Ichtheus chose not to share his knowledge of Deveril's black powder. Folk failed to understand what had caused the mayhem, and the area was evermore referred to as Sorcerer's Gully.

-oOo-

Alone in the Bayersby kitchen, Oric and Ichtheus discussed the appalling injuries inflicted by the black powder, understanding, at last, the true meaning of Deveril's warning.

Deeply disturbed, Ichtheus remarked on the mayhem he had caused. "I doubt I shall ever concoct any more of the dreadful substance. My job as an apothecary is to save life, not end it."

Oric patted his mentor's thin hand. "Nay, Master Ichtheus, do not browbeat yourself overmuch. Many of our friends and neighbours might now be dead, had you not organised the ambush. We might also be under the thumb of Sir Ragnald."

Furious at Guwain's perfidy, Sir Edred decreed that his son would return to Roxbrough Abbey. "The monks will mete out the discipline you are clearly in need of," he roared. "However, for the sake of your mother, you may remain at home until after Yuletide."

Each time Guwain complained, Sir Edred added another moon cycle to his son's incarceration. Silenced at last, Guwain considered his forthcoming exile. No girls, no gambling, no exotic food, and constant prayer coupled with lessons made him feel as if he had been given a life sentence.

People quickly pushed the skirmish with Sir Ragnald to the back of their minds, and life in Kilterton returned to normal. Helled Bascoomb was kept busy selling salt beef and had no time to nag her husband. Therefore she avoided Sir Edred's threat to encase her head in a scold's bridle. Tewdric enjoyed a respite from his wife's vicious tongue and felt happier than he had in a long while. Meerig and Lanaval returned to their tannery on the banks of Roxdale Beck, but they visited the village regularly to sell their wares. Delighted with the quality of the tanners' products, Uther often purchased whole hides. Stooped over his workbench, he tapped away in his shop, making footwear for whosoever could afford to pay the price. Father Chrispian failed to return to St Griswald's and his browbeaten parishioners neither knew nor cared what had happened to him.

Few of Sir Ragnald's wounded mercenaries survived. Those that did were incarcerated in one of Bayersby Manor's stout outbuildings, until Sir Edred felt inclined to mete out appropriate punishment.

Swearing allegiance to Sir Edred, Bannulf and his faithful followers were accepted into the Bayersby fold. They worked hard, rarely grumbled and soon became popular with everyone – especially Sir Ragnald's two squires, Erik and Arnald, who had escaped serious injury in the ambush.

Keen to inspect the purportedly magnificent property he had won, Sir Edred invited his entire household to join him in Yuletide celebrations at Lockton Castle.

Josh declined Oric's invitation, saying he felt duty-bound to spend some time with his family in Kilterton before the spring planting season began. "The cramped conditions in my parents' cottage will make me appreciate your hut and herb garden all the more," he grinned.

To Oric's delight, Dian was required to attend Lady Myferny, which meant she would travel to Lockton Castle with the rest of the Bayersby servants. Given time, Oric hoped the little maid might allow him to rekindle their friendship.

Mistress Foley packed up Bayersby Manor with military precision. The sun shone and, in holiday mood, folk travelled through the crisp winter countryside toward their Yuletide destination.

Cock-a-hoop over Sir Ragnald's defeat, Ned and Joe capered about like a pair of court jesters. Little did they realise that life was about to take a giant leap in a very different direction.

Chapter Thirty-Two

A New Beginning

Upon close inspection, Lockton Castle proved a great disappointment. Over the years, badly maintained battlements had shed chunks of stone, and a moat, little more than a weed-choked ditch, reeked of human excrement dropped from a garderobe in one of the turrets above. The Bayersby folk gagged and held their noses against the stink.

Sir Edred scrutinised the castle's ragged stonework, wondering which family crest had once graced the archway above the main entrance. He shook his head, disgusted by the general lack of maintenance. "We will have our work cut out if we decide to restore this place to its former grandeur," he grumbled. "The first, most pressing task will be to clear out that moat."

Lady Myferny could see beyond the current disorder. "Take heart, my lord! With a few improvements, the castle will make a delightful summer residence." Grabbing her husband's hand, she dragged him to the gateway and tugged on the bell rope.

Disturbed from his drunken stupor, Rory shambled

out of the gatehouse and peered blearily through the closed portcullis grill. Unfamiliar faces stared back at him. "Clear orf!" he slurred. "Sir Ragnald ain't 'ere, and we ain't doing no entertaining today."

"How dare you speak to me thus!" Sir Edred roared. "Open the gate at once."

Bannulf brought his horse alongside and dismounted. "Allow me to deal with this fellow, my lord." Barely able to contain his delight at the turn of events, Bannulf yelled for Rory to present himself once more.

Recognising a familiar voice, Rory returned at a gallop. Bannulf whispered a few quiet words in his ear, and the portcullis rolled up within a few heartbeats.

Sir Edred's party explored the interior of the castle. Regrouping in the Great Hall, they all agreed that much hard work would need to be done to make Yuletide a comfortable and happy affair.

"This establishment has gone to wrack and ruin since I was last here!" snapped Mistress Foley. "At least in my day it was kept clean." Her angular features took on a familiar, sour expression and she yelled, "Oriiiiic! Fetch a broom!"

"No, no, Oric is not the person that should be fetching the broom," huffed Ichtheus. "I suggest that you…"

Oric silenced Ichtheus with a barely perceptible shake of his head. Before he announced his new status in life, he needed to know what was written on the parchment he had found in the unknown woman's quarters. With that idea in mind, he found a brush and entered the sad room. Daylight slanted through the narrow window slits, highlighting dusty surfaces. A lacework of cobwebs hung from every wall-mounted candle sconce. The curtains he had pulled across the sleeping alcove on his last visit to the room remained closed. He pulled them apart, climbed onto the bed, and unhitched the tapestry that hid the small door in the wall. For the second time, he inserted his double knot key into the lock. The two pages of parchment and the box containing the ring remained just as he had left them. He placed the items in his pouch, planning to ask Ichtheus for a translation at the first available opportunity.

Mistress Foley gave no quarter and every person able to hold a broom or a cloth was given a task. Several work-filled days passed before Oric had a chance to corner his mentor.

The old man dozed by the fire, but his eyes flew open at Oric's gentle tap.

"I have another two parchments for you to translate, Master Ichtheus." Oric thrust the sheets into his mentor's hand. "I hope they might throw more light onto my predicament."

Ichtheus rubbed his tired eyes and focussed on the rows of writing. The more he read, the more astonished he became. "Was there anything else with these parchments?" he asked.

"Aye, there was," replied Oric, producing the box containing the gold ring with the red stone. In daylight, Oric saw that the stone was held in place by entwined, golden knots.

Creaking down onto one knee, Ichtheus removed the ring from its box and slid the jewel onto the middle finger of Oric's right hand. He kissed the ring and looked up at his young assistant with ill disguised reverence. "The parchments state that you, Lord Lockton, belong to one of the noblest families in the land. I am honoured to offer myself as your humble servant."

In silent misery, Oric stared at the top of his mentor's head. Confirmation of this unwanted, elevated position meant the end of life as he knew it and, like as not, the death knell to any future romantic entanglement with Dian. *She spurned me when she thought me landed gentry. Now that I appear to be a lord in my own right, will she ever speak to me again apart from 'yes sir – no sir'?* Needing time to consider his options, Oric put the ring back in its box, and handed it to Master Ichtheus for safekeeping. The enormity of his position grew and Oric suddenly felt sick. *How on earth can I explain this awful situation to Sir Edred?* The last thing Oric wanted was to cause the Lord of Bayersby embarrassment, and he swore Ichtheus to secrecy whilst he agonised over how to announce his news.

-oOo-

A substantial fire snapped and crackled on the central hearth in Lockton Castle's Great Hall. Wreaths of copper birch hung from the rafters, bringing a warm, homely touch that had been missing from the castle for years. Visitors from Bayersby and Kilterton laughed and chattered happily as they awaited the arrival of the celebratory Yuletide dinner Sir Edred had promised.

Having defeated Sir Ragnald, Sir Edred claimed his spoils of war and settled comfortably into the castle as the rightful lord. He sat, ruddy-faced and beaming, at the top table with his dagger ready to demolish whatever the cooks served.

Oric crept about the castle like a waif and stray until Ichtheus put his foot down. "The longer you allow this situation to continue, Oric, the more difficult it will become to impart the truth. I insist that Sir Edred be informed before he is made to look a complete fool." Without further ado, he took Sir Edred to one side, and handed him Oric's family parchments and the ring.

Ever the gentleman, Sir Edred took everything in his stride, but his ruddy face flushed deeper crimson as he recalled the many times he had punished Oric for pranks perpetrated by Guwain.

Re-entering the Great Hall, he walked to the table where Oric sat with his friends. Taking the young apothecary by the hand, Sir Edred guided him up onto the dais. Thereupon the mighty Lord of Bayersby dropped to one knee, slipped the ruby ring onto Oric's middle finger, and brushed it with his lips.

A sucking gasp whooshed around the Great Hall and a babble of voices started up as people asked each other what was going on. "Has Sir Edred taken leave of his senses?" Ned gasped. "What is he thinking – kissing Oric's hand like that?"

Sir Edred rose to his feet and, in the hush that followed, he addressed the household along with all his invited guests. "Dear friends," he began, beaming at Oric. "A few short years ago, this young man came to Bayersby Manor as a homeless waif. I took him in and, under Master Ichtheus' tutelage, he learned an apothecary's trade. In that capacity Oric has more than proved his worth. I, for one, shall miss him sorely."

Guwain choked on a chicken bone. "What are you doing?" he yelled, his eyes bulging as he tried to dislodge the obstruction. "The deference you are affording that upstart is nauseating." Guwain spat the offending bone onto the floor, and continued his diatribe. "I realise Yuletide is the time for playacting, but you have taken this farce far enough." He banged both fists down on the tabletop, making Lady Myferny jump. Pointing his finger at Oric, he screamed, "Get that yokel out of my sight, and let the jollifications begin."

Sir Edred looked as if he might combust. "Be silent, you stupid boy! You are not fit to lick this nobleman's boot, let alone kiss his hand." With a flourish, he produced Oric's family pedigree and translated the Latin script for everyone to hear.

A queue of people formed to pay homage to Oric, and Mistress Foley was at the front of the column. "First time I clapped eyes on you," she said, "I knew something was vaguely familiar, but I failed to make the connection. Now I see that you are the image of your dear mother."

"You knew my mother!" Oric gasped, grasping the woman's thin shoulders and shaking her. "How well did you know her?"

"Ah, 'tis a long story, my lord," Mistress Foley admitted. "As a young woman I was employed by your parents. Your father was a much-loved and peaceable nobleman, until Lockton Castle fell into Sir Ragnald's hands. Your parents were forced to flee, taking you with them. I remained here because I had nowhere else to go." Mistress Foley hung her head. "As long as I kept the castle running smoothly, Sir Ragnald left me to it. Eventually I employed a few male serfs, for no women would stay here. I tried to keep the place spotless apart, that is, from your mother's bower." Mistress Foley shrugged dismissively. "Sir Ragnald had no lady of his own so I saw little point in making extra work for myself. For years I turned a blind eye to his uncouth behaviour – until he began poisoning his men." She stared straight at Bannulf. "He thought they were plotting to kill him, and he was right, was he not? In mortal fear of losing my own life, I left and went to stay with my sister. Eventually I ended up at Bayersby Manor."

Oric's knees gave way, and he sat down with a plop. It was all too much to take in.

A wrinkled old man was the next person to climb the steps up to the dais. He doffed his cap, exposing his almost bald head, and bowed. "Mi name is Archie, and I 'ave served at Lockton Castle all mi life," he wheezed. "I knew yer grandfather, and yer parents." He beamed, showing two stumps of teeth in his otherwise toothless mouth. "Eeeh, the true Lockton family were grand folk to work for. Whilst they were at the castle, no-one went 'ungry and everybody was 'appy." The old fellow brushed tears from his rheumy eyes. "It was a sad day when Lord Askell and Lady Isolda were forced to flee. After that, everything in the district went wrong. Sir Ragnald gambled and drank away yer father's fortune. He pillaged every 'amlet within range of Lockton and left a trail of death and destruction wherever he went. People 'ated him, but those of us left alive were too weak or afraid to stop him. The land belonging to the estate went to wrack and ruin, and the peasants were forced to grow stuff to feed Sir Ragnald and his men. In the event, many farmworkers and their families near starved to death. Many of 'em cleared off. Then I 'eard that Sir Ragnald was after Bayersby Manor."

"Hah! That was the biggest mistake of his life!" roared Sir Edred. He beamed at Oric. "It may take a while, but I am convinced this young man will achieve great things."

One after another, people climbed onto the dais to pay homage to Oric, until he became hotly embarrassed. "Please stop," he begged. "I neither want nor deserve this reverence. Whatever my inheritance may be, I am still Oric, the simple boy that you all befriended. I will do my utmost to make sure everyone is taken care of, but please, return to the celebrations and allow me to sup with my friends."

Before Oric stepped down from the dais, Guwain followed his father's example and dropped to one knee. Speaking loudly for everyone to hear, he said, "I pay homage to your noble birth." Raising hate-filled eyes, he dropped his voice to a whisper, "Never fear, Oric, Lord of Lockton, I will see you discredited if it takes 'til my dying day."

-oOo-

Festivities came to an end, and enough food was packed to see the Bayersby and Kilterton folk home. Copious quantities of leftovers were set aside to feed the inhabitants of Lockton Castle until fresh supplies could be sent. Oric requested seeds and rootstock to start up a new growing program come spring, and Sir Edred promised to send two cows, a bull, a couple of pigs, two sheep in lamb, a ram, and some chickens. He assured Oric that repayment could be made in kind once Lockton Castle lands were productive again.

Oric stood beside the open portcullis to bid everyone farewell. Egglebart and Etheldrida hugged him, Sir Oswold shook his hand and Lady Malla planted a kiss on his cheek. Mistress Foley declined Oric's offer of employment as housekeeper, saying she was now too old to take on such a large, ramshackle establishment. She reiterated that she was more than happy to return to Bayersby Manor.

Dian curtsied, but avoided the kiss Oric tried to peck on her cheek. Looking into her warm hazel eyes, Oric made a silent promise. *One day, however long it takes, this beautiful young woman will be mistress of Lockton Castle.*

Ichtheus was last to leave. "Well, well, well!" he smiled and bent his bony frame in a deep bow. "Who would have thought it, eh, lad? Lord of Lockton Castle!"

"Nay, Master Ichtheus! I'll not have you bow before me." With tears in his eyes, Oric wrapped his arms around the old man and hugged him tight.

Ichtheus returned Oric's embrace, then pushed him away. "Oh, my giddy aunt, this will never do! You will have me sniffling like a street urchin at this rate. And, speaking of urchins, where are Ned and Joe?"

"Here we are," cried Joe, jumping about like a flea on

a hot log. "We are staying at the Castle with Lord Lockton, ain't we, Ned?"

"That we are," Ned replied with a wry smile. "I doubt Oric… er, Lord Lockton, can manage without us."

"I shall miss you sorely, my boy," Ichtheus' blue eyes looked unnaturally bright as he shook his finger at Oric. "Mind you take care of yourself, lad, and remember everything I taught you."

"I intend to continue learning," Oric assured his mentor. "With hundreds of acres to my name, who knows what I might achieve in the future?"

Turning his attention to Ned and Joe, Ichtheus patted the youngsters warmly. "You both turned out better than I expected," he chuckled. "'Tis amazing what kindness and a little gentle discipline can achieve. No more picking pockets, I trust."

"Lord, no!" grinned Ned. "Oric has appointed us keepers of the castle. Positions of great importance, I might add. We ain't never going back to a life of crime, are we, little'un?"

Joe puffed out his thin chest like a small pouter pigeon. "No, we ain't – and God help anyone who attempts to ill-use our Lord Lockton."

Mounted upon Braccus, Ichtheus said his final farewell. "You ain't seen the back of me, lad. I will return from time to time. Lockton Castle will provide a welcome escape from the redoubtable Mistress Foley." The old man waved his hand and trundled off after Sir Edred and Lady Myferny.

Oric watched until he could no longer see his mentor, and felt more wretched than he had ever been in his life. Head down, he turned to re-enter the bailey and was almost knocked over by a shaggy dog that bounded out of the long grass beside the moat. Spiked with dead leaves and bits of twigs, Parzifal jumped up and down, trying to lick Oric's face. A note was attached to his collar.

No point dragging the hound back to Bayersby against his will! He is more yours than mine and will likely pine to death without you.

I am at your service should you ever require my assistance.

I wish you well,

Edred

Lord of Bayersby.

Tongue lolling, Parzifal looked up at his young master with unadulterated adoration. Feeling better, Oric took hold of the dog's collar and together they entered Lockton Castle's inner bailey.

Rory emerged from the gatehouse, and all but curtsied. "Will I close the gate now, your worshipfulness?" he asked.

Oric clenched his teeth against the screeching, clanking sounds as Rory wound down the portcullis. *First thing tomorrow morning,* he thought, *I shall deal with Rory, take a look at Hamish's leg, and fix this wretched gate.*

If you enjoyed Oric's adventure, I would absolutely love it if you could let the world know. There are two easy ways to do this.

Firstly, if you bought this from an online bookstore, please leave an honest review for this title on the online bookstore you bought it from, it really helps other people find it.

Secondly, if you have a Goodreads account, please review it or add it to a book list, so other people can discover and enjoy it too.